Songs of No Provenance

Also by Lydi Conklin

Rainbow Rainbow

Songs of No
Provenance

LYDI CONKLIN

Chatto & Windus
LONDON

1 3 5 7 9 10 8 6 4 2

Chatto & Windus, an imprint of Vintage, is part of the
Penguin Random House group of companies

Vintage, Penguin Random House UK, One Embassy Gardens,
8 Viaduct Gardens, London SW11 7BW

penguin.co.uk/vintage
global.penguinrandomhouse.com

First published in Great Britain by Chatto & Windus in 2025
First published in the United States of America by Catapult in 2025

Copyright © Lydi Conklin 2025

The moral right of the author has been asserted

Book design by Laura Berry

Printed and bound in Great Britain by Clays Ltd, Elcograf S.p.A.

The authorised representative in the EEA is Penguin Random House Ireland,
Morrison Chambers, 32 Nassau Street, Dublin D02 YH68

A CIP catalogue record for this book is available from the British Library

ISBN 9781784745653

Penguin Random House is committed to a sustainable future
for our business, our readers and our planet. This book is made
from Forest Stewardship Council® certified paper.

For MC

Songs of No Provenance

Stag of No Provenance

1

JOAN SCRAMBLED TO DUMP THE PUSHCART OF HER POS-
sessions into a Coney Island trash can on the beach off the
boardwalk way down from her building so her landlord
wouldn't see. Night fell in rumpled black over the Atlantic,
her phone buzzing angrily at her hip. She should've been gone
already, across any bridge, through any tunnel—whichever
chute from the city was swiftest—but if she left her life intact,
she might be tempted to return.

Salt water slid underfoot, the call of children in her ears. She
nestled the Martin on some newspapers in the sand, free of its
case—she couldn't help treating it delicately even now—while
she stuffed her tortoiseshell picks and boots and half-used bottles of walnut oil and her camel-hair coat and mustard-colored
suitcase and toy lobster into the can on top of cotton candy
cones and french fry boats. Next came the old CDs of the four
other singer-songwriters in the Gonewriters' Collective. And
on top of that, her wire recorder, used for experiments and
one-offs, which had required its own brutal, dedicated trip

from the apartment, that beast. Then the ribbon mic and the cassette 4-track that built her signature sound—the precious machines she could barely afford and that she'd serviced for years—crashed through garbage to the base of the can. This nothing trash can, where she'd discarded the ends of so many hot dogs shared with Paige and Maya and Nick Blade, cigarette butts, the crumpled flyers of one another's shows. Two hours ago, Joan had fled the venue, Paige's face crumpling in confusion as Joan dodged her, the crowd already roaring for the next act. Arms trembling, Joan reached for her Martin. Her fingers met its neck. She'd crush it against the seawall, and then she'd be gone.

The prewar Martin was a parlor guitar, svelter and nimbler than the muddy dreadnoughts rampant among folksingers and dabblers, hailing from the age of field recordings and songs of unknown origin: tight, punchy, cutting through the mix. The short scale of the neck made the strings more accommodating to Joan's athletic fingers. Perfect for her own compact body, distinctive and elegant. And its sound was focused, pure, so unlike plodding, woofy dreadnoughts. Other musicians thought Joan ridiculous for hating dreadnoughts, but she wouldn't waste her talent on some brutish clanger designed to drown out resonator-backed banjos. Not that she could bear to think of her career anymore.

The Martin was Joan's second guitar, her main squeeze for the last twenty years, since after college when she'd retired the pudding-yellow acoustic she'd bought for nothing at a yard sale at fourteen. The Martin had cost all her meager savings, plus the last two installments of her undergraduate student loan, plus a hundred dollars she'd made on a blow job, a bad-faith transaction with an acquaintance and the only time she'd taken money for sex, and only because she needed that Martin before it sold to some SoHo trust-funder who'd hook it to the wall and let it die. She'd walked by it for a month, pausing to gaze through the window at its dark mahogany frame, sleek and almost skeletal, the opalescence of its fretboard, the marks on the pickguard that told her it had been loved before, it had been played hard, it held history. She grieved over the spectrum of hacks and douchebags who'd one day abuse it with power ballads or gift it to an indifferent nephew who'd abandon it under laundry while playing video games nearby. The day she bought the Martin was the best day of Joan's life. She'd rescued it from the rest of the world, carrying it home like it weighed nothing, bundled in sweaters because she couldn't afford a case.

She hovered the Martin above the seawall, her skinny arms steadying under its heft. She could play a whole concert standing up without a strap—savoring the pain and masochistic bending it required, foot on the monitor to relieve pressure—so suspending the Martin for its last moments was nothing. The sea nudged the wall in looping rolls, ingesting and regurgitating unwanted bits of Brooklyn: the severed head of a toy cheetah, empty spectacle frames cocked curiously toward the light, cartons rinsed of their creamy Russian salads, all the waste fresh and sharp-cornered, never submerged long enough to burnish smooth or blanch. Children laughed at her, but children laughed at Joan on normal days, the way she followed her nose down the beach with curious intensity from the cement slab of her apartment building, with its pastel umbrellas and bikes packed into bathtub-sized balconies, all the way to Brighton Beach and back every night she didn't have a show, which was most nights lately, which would be every night now.

She raised the Martin so high that the tendons in her arms locked. Her phone zapped her: a text from Maya Banerjee, one of the Gonewriters, the group of scrappy musicians who'd supported her for twenty years. Joan lowered the Martin. Steady. Steady. *Why the fuck, Joan?* said Maya's text.

Joan's organs hardened to a knot. So Maya knew. Paige must have told her. In a heartbeat all the Gonewriters would hate her. The core of her community, destroyed by disgust. They were her life. Without them, even just without Paige, there was nothing.

Joan couldn't bear to release her grip on the guitar and respond. She had to escape. Phones had been raised tonight, so many glossy rectangles, watching. Videos recorded in Love und Romance, the punk bar she'd played two hours ago. She wasn't punk but indie-folk rock-whatever, though once you grafted genres, they hemorrhaged meaning. And now all those phones held Joan's image in the fog of the club, a slim, dark shard between bouncing orange circles of light, stepping to the edge of the stage. Hair swollen into a triangle above her shoulders, that sliver of air between her front teeth that it had never occurred to her parents to correct. Though she was forty-three, Joan was as skinny as a teenager, which a man had told her once before she peed on him. Lines fountaining from her eyes and gray hair fluttering at her temples, flesh pale in the club gels, as she reached her arms down off the stage, into the crowd. If Joan didn't respond to Maya's text, or anyone's, maybe her life could remain the same: meager gigs, Paige's twenty-one-year-long friendship, one-night stands, boiled vegetables in her dank apartment, the ocean loud and invisible beyond its walls. She reached into the memory as though she could seize herself by the shirt, pull herself back, rewind reality. *Step back, Joan, from the edge of that stage. Pick up the Martin. Play your next song. Don't be a maniac.*

2

ENTERING LOVE UND ROMANCE THAT TUESDAY FOR AN
early show—a dog slot, but her first non-dive in months—Joan
had bounced along, the Martin's case bashing the old bruise
on her thigh all the way down Delancey, Manhattan vivid in
the buttery pink light. Earlier that week her date opening for
an aging eighties diva had been canceled and "Lakeshore" had
been pulled from an underfunded film out of Bellingham, but
these were minor disappointments. Tonight she had a show at a
small but decent venue. And tomorrow she'd record a verse on
Paige's second album with Black Tree, her first in three years
since *Pink Haven*, which had been her debut hit with the label. Paige worried the album wouldn't live up to anticipation,
but the label was funneling in as many resources as the first
time around. Joan had spent weeks hiding out in Coney Island,
composing a guest verse to "Pretty Little Lion." She'd sent a
demo to Paige last week and awaited revisions for tomorrow.
Paige was famous now—indie famous, at least—but still struggled with writing, and Joan had drawn out the song's themes

and built depth. Paige would appreciate what Joan had seen in her work and what she'd added, would love her for it. She'd contribute history too. Those who knew Joan respected her. But mostly, she couldn't wait to be tucked up in the studio together, heads bent in concentration, obsessing over the dynamics and layering of each track. Paige had a mini tour right after recording, but before that they had this time, working, close and thrilled, through the night.

Joan had dressed for the show, which she never did, in her soft Norwegian sweater and dark jeans, had applied deodorant. Lesbians, who formed the healthiest portion of her fan base, filed in, decked out in hoodies and mullets. In back, hipster men in neon sweatshirts and granny glasses balanced whiskies on the bar, smirking behind their bangs like everyone else was attending an inferior event. They thought they'd discovered Joan. And she let them have her, to a point. She never fucked fans. She drew few boundaries in her life, but that was one. It would've been too easy anyway. No fun at all. After the concert, before her high wore off, she'd find some random in a nearby bar, blow him until his logic shrank, and then piss.

Joan adjusted the mic, smoothed the rug over the wires, and heaved the Martin to center stage. By now, a hundred people filled the small room. Though it was only four, in the windowless bar it felt like midnight. Below her, as close as the garbage cans allowed, collected her superfans: women who looked like they'd already lived at least a couple of lives. Paige had coined the term as a joke a decade ago, when Joan barely had regular fans yet. But by now, she had a dedicated handful of obsessives. They shared a haunted stare, like they'd missed out on life, women who'd raised ungrateful kids with selfish husbands, scraping dust off moldings and browsing online, in their darkest hours, for vacations to Bulgaria, houses on the shore, bodies that could stop a car, young guys, women, both at once. They stood in somber witness to Joan's freedom.

She had a minute until the show started, so she shoved her way to the bar, setting her gaze on the back wall to forestall chitchat. She pushed past a line of people on stools. The last stool held a patron with petite shoulders and tumbling black curls, standing out in relief against the blur of strangers. Joan tapped the patron's hip.

Paige turned, offering a thin smile. "Oh. Hi."

Paige was six years Joan's junior, part French and part Lebanese, with a face as slim and foxy as Joan's but with tighter skin and fuller lips, teeth someone had invested in, and the dark dash of a mole below one eye.

"I was going to find you after," Paige said.

Joan embraced her. She didn't even like being touched in sex, but she hugged Paige whenever they met, burying her hand in Paige's dark curls and grounding herself in her friend's heat, her pine odor. Paige was warm in Joan's arms, and the comfort of a familiar body slowed her blood like she'd dropped underwater.

When they released, Paige's expression was stricken in the red haze.

"Are you okay?" Joan asked.

"Of course." Paige's focus twitched toward the stage. "I thought we could have a drink after your show, and talk."

"That would be great." Joan hopped onto the stool beside Paige, squishing the air from the cushion, and set her elbows on the sticky bar. "I'll defer my next victim."

Paige pursed her lips. "It doesn't have to take long."

"I'm kidding. I'd rather see you, obviously." She sparkled beside Paige. The last time Paige had attended one of Joan's gigs was a thousand years ago. Joan had assured the Gonewriters she didn't need their support. She'd fallen off from Maya and Christopher a while ago, anyway, and saw Nick Blade only rarely. But this camaraderie was nice, actually. Joan and Paige could kick-start their week recording.

"Don't you have to go up now?" Paige crossed her wrists.

"They can wait. I haven't seen you all week." Joan leaned in close to Paige, absorbing the comfort of her best friend's long nose, the curls framing her forehead, and the bony frame of her face. "What have you been doing? You look pale."

"Just prepping." Paige's lips clicked together and vanished.

"You didn't leave it till the last minute, did you?" Sure, Paige had techniques left to master: needed to fine-tune her breath support, needed smoother thumb alternations and to sink her patterns into her bones before she chased speed. But mostly, her lyrics wanted depth. If you loved rabbits and rainstorms, Paige was golden. And thousands did. But depth would raise her from the twee and secure her spot in the canon. Joan's verse would push her over the edge. "Did you fix the bridge of 'Bluster Days'? And tweak the hook on 'Marchhound'?"

"Yes, yes. I did everything you said." Paige bobbed her delicate chin. She was luminous in the club lights, her most flattering environment. A true star. "You were right about it all, obviously."

"And you polished 'Stop Where the Rain Falls'?"

Paige fiddled with a puddle on the bar. "A hundred years ago. It's all approved."

But she was acting sheepish. She'd neglected some area of preparation. "Have you rested your voice?"

"Yeah." Paige lit up, wiping her fingers on her pants. "That's why I haven't called. I got that awful tea."

Warmth spread through Joan like the tea itself. "It works. I swear."

Paige offered that endearing scowl that collapsed her jaw. "It tastes like soil."

"You'll be amazing." Joan tried to grin but couldn't bend her lips into the correct angle. But everything was okay. Joan would be on Black Tree, too, if only for a verse. Paige had asked her for the contribution, needed Joan's words to fill out the album. She took Paige's hands. They blazed so hot she dropped them. "I can't wait for tomorrow."

"Right." Paige looked down.

The house music cut out with a brutal zip. Beyond Paige, the sound guy gestured to Joan.

"Oh," Paige said. "You have to go up."

"What time should I be there?" They hadn't even had a chance to talk logistics. Joan had been so deep in songwriting this whole week, jazzed out of a minor block by this show and the verse, staying up until two or three, noodling and revising, springing awake at six with words bursting out of her. But they had to work the details out. In a few hours, they'd be side by side in the dim, quiet room where every syllable popped, recording the verse. Joan would stay and help with the other songs too. Paige treasured her critiques. The studio Black Tree normally used was nearby, on the Lower East Side, part of a cluster. Joan had rented one in the same complex to record her last couple of albums. The door to the building was dingy yellow with red trim, as thickly painted as frosting applied with a knife.

"We'll talk after." Paige's cheekbones were delicate in profile. "What are you playing tonight? You must be excited. This really is a decent place."

Joan wished she couldn't hear that strain. "Did you get my demo, though? Do you like the verse?" Sending the material in advance had been a silly formality. But Paige was jittering on her stool, picking at her skin, glancing around like how she got sometimes, a fawn at the tree line.

"I got it, yeah." Paige gazed to some point way far down the room.

"Joan," shouted the sound guy, over a row of *Pitchfork* bros. "You ready?"

Joan raised one finger. When his expression didn't relax, she jabbed the beery air.

"Go, go." Paige turned, exposing the corner of her jaw, the bone stretching her skin.

"You think I care about some random sound guy?" Joan wanted to swallow her words as soon as they were out.

Paige's lips shrank into her mouth. "Let's talk after. Go enjoy your show, okay?" Her eyes were big and shiny. Crazily, they were breakup eyes. What was this?

"What is going on?" Blood beat through Joan, bumping into her ears. "Just tell me already. You're freaking me out."

Paige pulled a string of liquid off the puddle on the bar. It was whisky, or soft drink, unwilling to release her. "It's cool. Let's talk after."

A moth in Joan's throat, fluttering for its life. "Just tell me."

"Are you sure?"

"Yes." The room was deafening, even with the music off. "Or I'll never concentrate."

Paige stretched her neck, peering around as if a lesbian could save her. "I just think tomorrow's not going to work."

Joan sighed. "That's all?" She stood from the stool. The crowd pressed toward the stage. "You're in the studio all week, right? It doesn't have to be the first day." It stung that Paige didn't want to enter the studio together so Joan could suss out the new Black Tree label reps and engineers for her, protect her from their peacocking. But it made a certain sense. Joan had done a couple of financed albums years ago with a label down in Athens. The oversize headphones, the control room glittering with buttons like a spaceship—silly as it was, the toys had made Joan feel professional. For Paige's first album, Joan had gone in with her. But if this time Paige wanted the excitement for herself, that was sad but understandable. "You've earned this. You should enjoy it however's best for you."

Paige let a curl flap back over her forehead. "Thanks. Yeah."

"Joan?" The sound guy was two rows of heads away. The fans watched Joan. All those hungry eyes in darkness. Their desire a fine heat coating her.

"You really have to go up," Paige said.

"So we'll figure out afterward which day works best? Can we just say Thursday?" A shaft of aqua light sliced Paige's cheeks. The presets for the show had switched on. "Just say Thursday so I can relax and play."

"God, Joan," Paige growled. "You always do this."

Joan stepped back. "What?"

"Sorry." Paige reached out like she'd touch Joan, but her arm wilted, hand flopping down. "It's just you always push me on shit like this. Like bullying, almost." The words were so high and quiet that Joan could almost believe they weren't real.

"What are you talking about?" Paige had never spoken this way before.

Paige stuck a hand in her curls, dragging tendrils over her face. "I don't know. It's not your fault, exactly." Her voice shook, the words bouncing out. "Our dynamic got started so early."

Joan's mind jangled. She couldn't feel her way through it to what Paige meant. "But things were great early."

"Look—never mind." Paige's face dipped into the light: blue, then pale, then blue again. "We don't have to get into this. It's beside the point. Go up. We'll talk after."

Joan snatched Paige's wrist. She didn't intend to grab it so hard, and she released it immediately, but Paige sat back, the hollows around her eyes caving. Joan's palm stung. She rubbed it down her jeans. "What is this? Do you not want me to record with you or something? Because I'm pushy?"

"No, no. That's not why. And look—it's not my decision." The words rushed out with relief. "You have to know that."

Joan had said the worst thing without believing it could be true. "Wait, seriously?" Her brain swelled, thoughts spiraling until they made no sense. "They didn't like my verse?"

"It's not that. It was really cool." Paige's hands scraped the air like she'd find purchase there.

"Forget it," Joan said. "You don't have to fake it." She tried to tame her voice, but it squeaked.

"It's stupid shit." Paige waved her hand like she could push the conversation out into the crowd. "Black Tree doesn't think you're 'positioned right' or whatever."

"What does that even mean?" She knew exactly what it meant. It meant Paige had overtaken her. Not just for the last album, not just for the last couple of years with her corporate alternative radio plays and college tours and songs in indie films, but to the point where Joan was unworthy to sing with her for twenty-five seconds. But there were ups and downs with any career, always. And Joan had cachet. An arty label like Black Tree could surely appreciate that, if anyone could. Now Paige wouldn't need her anymore for anything, would drift out on the current of fame into some golden land Joan would never visit.

"It's stupid corporate bullshit. They're Black Tree, but they're still the big guys. I'm sorry. It sucks for me too. I really thought I could do this for you."

Joan's scalp tightened. She stepped back, the crowd shrinking to make room. "What?"

Panic flared across Paige's face. "I mean I wish we could do this together. The whole Black Tree thing."

"No. You said you want to 'do this for me.' What did you mean by that?"

Paige blocked her mouth with slender fingers. Her dark eyes went wild. "Nothing. Joan—totally nothing."

The sound guy's beefy palm shelled Joan's arm. She didn't turn. Fuck that guy for thinking he could touch her. Blood thumped through her arm, her neck. "It was charity. That's all this was? You were helping me out?"

"I know you don't need it, but"—she was whining now—"I thought it would've been cool for your career? Am I saying the wrong thing?" Her pale hands were in her hair, swimming through the curls.

"Wow. Okay." Joan writhed in the itchy container of her skin. "You think I'm that pathetic."

"No way." Paige slashed her arms through the air. "Joan. Never."

"Even when we're in a room surrounded by my fans, you think that?" Her voice cracked as it pushed out.

"Just play. We'll talk after."

A howl cut through Joan's lips, but it was inaudible in the deafening crowd. Unless, of course, that blaring thrum was the blood in her head. Fans turned, opened-mouthed. Joan spun around. She couldn't look at Paige a minute longer.

The sound guy blurred as she spun, and then she was cantering through the crowd, pushing people away as they gasped and teetered and nearly fell, her glass wheeling out of her fist and exploding on the floor. The stage lit up ahead, red and blue and purple, each cone overlapping at the edges into new shades. This colorful tent of light dedicated to her. How could Paige act like Joan needed charity when all these people were here for her? She vaulted onto the stage and grabbed the Martin. It settled perfectly in her arms, like always, light and easy. She pushed her lips to the mic's wire dome, damp with the lyrics of performers past. "I'm Joan Vole."

The crowd released a tattered cry. Joan's pussy flamed, the sensation redoubled because the fans had no idea how she melted at their attention, their focus on her, their cheers, all reducing her to soggy heat. Those stupid executives were wrong about her career. This was perfect. This was intense. The lights scalded her cheeks, and her feet trembled on the boards. All these admirers under her, submitting in the shadows. Like hanging above some man and pissing on him. Sour shame mixed with a rising steam of pleasure. The whole room watched.

She slammed out the opening chord of "Rooster, Too," her voice pushing up, biting, words stretchy. "Guys with their hands on other guys' hands, guys with their hands on dicks." Her subgenre, which included only her, had been nicknamed Mad Stories, meaning both angry and crazy, a realist subset of anti-folk, for her quick, raw voice and vivid narratives hissed over skeletal chords. She couldn't understand musicians who complained about performing the same songs over and over. She never tired of the thrill. See? She was a professional. Her guitar was acoustic, but she played hard, and the pickup carried, her sound stripped down but feral. She calmed as she played. Performing was what she was made to do, and no stupid label could tell her otherwise.

Joan spoke-sang so close to the mic she could've swallowed it, scraping like she could bite and fuck at once, voice thickening as it gathered heat above the quick strum of her chords. "Straps on backs and straps on thighs, sticky spots cross the floor. Brothers, my brothers, I want your straps. Strap us together as one." She siphoned the energy of the lesbians under her, who awaited the Easter eggs that proved Joan was one of them: this fearsome brat, this mascot. She didn't even need "Lakeshore," that hot, bright monument to woman-on-woman love, to make the set good. She was killing it, could've floated into the sky on her own hectic energy and the rich voice of the Martin. The usual gallon of water she drank before the show to gear her up and turn her on pressed on her organs, an elastic promise. She scanned the crowd. If Paige was still out there, she had to be in awe of Joan crushing it, all these fans drawn in. And there she was, black curls bobbing toward the front of the pit, embedded among dancing lesbians. Her expression was all wrong. She bit her bottom lip, her face taut, like she was willing Joan not to humiliate herself—no, actually, she looked mortified. Like Paige was Joan's cool teenage daughter embarrassed by Mommy. Joan squeezed the neck of the Martin and rattled out the last of the lyrics, swift and brutal.

Black Tree was wrong. Joan's fans would do anything for her. Not even Paige had fans this dedicated. Joan set down the Martin and dashed to the edge of the stage.

At her feet were the superfans. All that hair, waves of damage from years of styling. See? These people loved her.

She dipped her arms into their mass, hands dangling in moist heat. Like a fish, a superfan caught hold and, pulling on Joan's arm, climbed up from below. And then they stood, facing each other across the stage.

The superfan's shoulders were set back, her expression proud above her vaguely medieval tie-up blouse. She wiped her palms down her shapeless brown skirt and raised her worn-out face. She was about fifty, with sagging cheeks, a stubborn slash of mouth, and a proud cant to her chin. She reeked of tequila. "Joan Vole," she said. "Oh god."

Every muscle in Joan tensed. Despite attempts, fans had rarely joined her onstage. She'd barely spoken to one in years, had managed to float through their numbers with her focus fixed on the beyond. This fan was taller than Joan, which felt impossible; Joan had towered for years above so many sunken heads.

The fans below drew closer, and the atmosphere solidified. The whole room went quiet; even the bartender stood still. No door opening or closing. The silence electrified Joan. Everyone watched her, expecting to be shocked, hungry for it. She could feed them whatever.

Her hand strayed to the crotch of her jeans. The attention in the room locked in. She grazed her flesh through the flimsy denim. Her heat pulsed through the room.

The superfan probably played Joan's records at home, all eleven, in rotation. She probably googled Joan's name, ferreting out rare photos, copying concert dates posted to Joan's janky website. She probably sang when "Lakeshore" came on the radio—a rare treat but not impossible, even now—wiggling in her car, her teen son turning to the window and groaning.

The superfan watched Joan openly, swaying, like she was too drunk to hold still. Her eyes were swimmy. Her gaze tingled Joan's folds. The superfan inched closer. Joan inched closer. She prickled under the focus of the fans watching her float toward the torso of this stranger. Joan was two feet from the superfan now. A humid smell rose off her complicated blouse.

"You good?" the superfan slurred, stumbling so her back was to the audience, like she forgot anyone else was out there. "Your eyes are haywire, baby."

Of course Joan was good—she was great; she was amazing. She was onstage with fans watching. She was loved, famous in her own right, in the dark and temporary community of this room tonight. And not only that, she was free. She threw her arms around the superfan, pushing hard against her, too close, but that was good; it was right. Like weren't they here, together, in the insane intimacy of performance? Joan latched her crotch to the superfan's thigh. The superfan emitted a squeak. Joan's chin settled on the superfan's shoulder, so she faced the audience with the superfan's back. She pushed the button of her jeans through its hole, unzipped. Her crotch was blocked by the superfan, but the zip was so loud that the whole room must've heard. A hot, alcoholic breeze blew at her groin.

She pulled down her pants and underwear. The murky club air surrounded her vulva. She pressed it against the fan. The pressure was immediate, flattening. She rubbed up and down so the superfan could feel she was wet, could see what a sicko she was.

"Joan." The superfan sighed. "Wait."

Joan let her pussy lift off the corduroy, only grazing the superfan's skirt now. Pleasure coursed through her. The superfan's head loomed close: matronly, teeth locked.

Joan couldn't stand looking at her. She shifted her gaze toward the whole of the audience. Yes. Those fans below—the devoted lesbians, the hipsters. Peaceful and blurry in the dark, as though seen through amber glass. The superfan's body was a banister on a balcony, queasily high. Her lips brushed the superfan's leg. Joan dragged herself down the length of the thigh, letting the pressure build slowly so her lubrication caught up. Her mind flared white, the muscle of her brain releasing.

And there, cutting through stale hops, was a familiar odor, usually lost under a mist of piss—her own scent, rising, so hormonal, so animal, that there was no way the room couldn't smell it.

"Stop," the superfan whispered, the word broken. She lifted

a fist and landed it on Joan's sternum, so lightly it was almost loving.

Joan inched back, missing the pressure. The superfan's mouth rounded, her nose glowing with broken capillaries. "Why would you do that?" she murmured. A tongue of stain up the superfan's skirt, high contrast on the corduroy. *Look at me, horny as fuck and singing to you. Look at this long, dark mark and judge.*

But fuck that. Joan was up here. She was herself. She was amazing. She lunged back toward the superfan and hugged her close, hooking her chin over the fan's shoulder. The superfan relaxed in her arms. Joan let heat bleed through her. She was perfect; this was perfect. Her life was perfect. She relaxed. Her muscles loosened and let go.

A jagged, white-heat arousal like lightning. Her crotch was hot and wet, and then it was splashing, emitting piss. She couldn't stop herself once she'd started, and she couldn't un-hand the soft shoulders that supported her, so she let the warm water run through her and out, that rush, heat of nerves waking up, the pee streaming from Joan and onto the fan, connecting them under the colored gels, absorbing into the superfan's thigh and rinsing out evidence of Joan's lust. She flared with a pleasure so intense it ached. She was half aware, at the limits of her vision, of the glint of phone screens raised. She squeezed harder, working out the last golden cramp.

She'd never peed on a woman, and she didn't feel that drunk power she felt with men. The feeling was new, sexual only in the base mechanics of friction and pressure. The audience was the overriding sensation, a shame so thick and sudden it was good.

Joan clawed out of her fog. The superfan clarified before

her, expression twisted. "Okay," the fan whispered, breath heavy pumps on Joan. "Enough."

Joan zipped her pants and staggered back, groin seizing. The superfan slipped down into the crowd.

Joan spun around and grabbed her Martin. She ripped out the quarter-inch, the live wire buzzing. The crowd grew louder, talking and shifting away from the stage. She jumped down and dodged fans, pushing through the crowd, slapping away any hand that tried to touch her. The blood in her head pounded. She had to get out. Not just out of the bar but out of New York. Not even Paige respected her anymore; Joan was nothing to Black Tree, and now, look what she'd done. The fan would have her arrested. A mob of witnesses, everywhere. People who, minutes ago, had loved her.

The next act took the stage. The crowd cheered. When Joan was almost to the door, Paige hurried up beside her.

"Joan?" Paige said, that tang of Ohio in the consonants. "What's going on?"

Joan couldn't look at her. Paige loved Joan so much that she couldn't even be angry for what Joan had just done. She watched Joan, even now, with steadiness. Joan's muscles locked at that open face. She pushed past Paige and out into the churn of Delancey.

3

THE SAND DARKENED TO NAVY, CONEY ISLAND LIGHTS
blurring the border of the sea. Joan couldn't bear to pop the
bubble of the Martin's body, much less shove all that rich, dark
wood under half-eaten pizza and sausage. The waves beat in
her eardrums. The dross of her life blew over the sand. Of
course word had spread about what she'd done, was spreading
still, the exchange of information swift and invisible. Maya's
text confirmed it. And if Paige couldn't keep quiet about Love
und Romance, the fans wouldn't either. Any second, videos
from the evening would mushroom onto the internet. Joan had
to get out. She tucked the Martin under her arm and raced up
the beach.

Breath ripping through her, feet pounding and sinking
in the sand, vomit rose into her throat. She'd humped a fan
like the family dog before his collar was grabbed, dinner
guests laughing in discomfort, grateful when the beast was
consigned to another room. Her pussy chafed like her underwear was burlap. All those phone screens raised—there

was footage. The watching wasn't over, would continue on to infinity. She turned her phone off before she could read its messages.

She threw herself and the Martin into her battered, candy-apple-red sedan. She flinched away from the guitar so close in this tiny, humid container. She kept her elbows to herself. A note of acid rose onto her tongue at the smell of her soiled pants in such a small space. She usually changed directly after an encounter; she had a whole system. But she didn't have time now. She'd drop the guitar with Paige, get it out of her sight. Paige used to mock Joan as much as anyone for hating dread-noughts, used to love the same dull-ass common guitar as all the world, even anti-folk musicians and dark storytellers, but she'd come around to parlors eventually.

Joan drove up Ocean Parkway, swerving around jams, and took Ditmas to Flatbush. She floored the accelerator at every pause in traffic, squished the brakes when she hit a new backup, inevitably, seconds later. A man glared at her from across two lanes, underbite and gold chain as tight as a dog collar. He was replaced by a woman shaking the pink ball of her fist. Joan drove as recklessly as Paige, which made her wrists twitch, like Paige was here in the car, hogging the wheel, stomping the pedals. She double-parked at Paige's building, tossed the Martin against the door. Her hand burned as she released it, straining not to snatch the neck back the second the hot wood left her palm. She punched the doorbell and hesitated, stepping backward, keeping the Martin in sight all the way to her car, that proud body leaning with perfect posture against the weathered skin of the brownstone. Then she was gone.

*

After the mess of bridges and ramps at the border of the city, the highway led west, deep into unknown stretches of New York—how was this all her state: these dark, sad towns, these lumpen mountains? Her hands trembled on the wheel so hard she had to slide them around for purchase. Whenever a car came up behind, she shot forward, certain the cops had caught her at last, breath beating in her throat. She raced around cars so close the flanks of her Corolla trembled, swerved onto the shoulder to circumvent bottlenecks. If she stopped, she'd check her phone, and then she'd release every squirming thread: Paige calling her a charity case, the superfan, the police, lawyers, social media blowing up, evidence of her whole life being taken away even as she took it from herself.

She'd slid a note under her landlord's door saying she was gone, that she'd broken her lease, that she'd forfeit her security deposit and the last days of June and she hoped he'd understand. He wouldn't—he considered them close because they fucked occasionally, an unspoken supplement to her rent—but the apartment cost practically nothing, the last affordable unit in the five boroughs, and firebombing the relationship was the only way to ensure she'd never return.

Joan's tongue was so dry it was inert in her mouth, an alien object. She passed countless dark fields, anonymous crops stretching into the distance. What did musicians do who were put out to pasture? Taught, she guessed. They were all trapped in schools someplace, mournfully lecturing.

She couldn't shake Paige's face, confounded at the bar exit, giving nothing—almost innocent. She pressed the pedal, and the Corolla spat forward. She couldn't stop driving even as her gas dwindled. She peed in a yogurt container she kept on the floor for the purpose, tossed the piss out the window without even slowing down. The drops stuck like pale gems to the glass, but that was good. That was great. Her car was hungry too. With her whole body she longed for the days of her childhood before she'd known what people would think of her peeing, though she'd always known enough to do it in private. She'd peed in the sandbox and under the swings, down from the top of a tube slide, once on a friend's cat. The release jolted her every time, coloring in different parts of her brain. The cat had coiled and hissed but hadn't fled or scratched, which had mesmerized her. Pure, curious joy had spread through Joan, relief, confusion as to why everyone wasn't pissing their pants all the time. She held the steering wheel like it was all that fastened her to earth.

Twenty miles after the gas light illuminated, she pulled over, giving in even as her breath stoppered to do it, at a gas station in a bleak little town called Swiftwater. Somehow, in her haze, she'd crossed into Pennsylvania. This was the Pennsylvania night around her, the asphalt of Pennsylvania holding up her car. Before she braked beside the pump, her phone was in her hand, igniting before she felt the cool depression of the power key. Her screen flashed and twitched as the phone revived, a complaint of beeps and manic unscrolling, and there it all was: the tapestry of consequence. Missed calls from Paige and Maya and Christopher and Nick Blade, every member of the Gonewriters. Seven calls from her landlord. He must've read her note by now, cursing her in Russian, poring over her laptop while raking fingernails across his psoriasis. And the texts. She couldn't bear to read even the previews, but she could tell from a few words they were angry, disgusted, the kindest ones only shocked. From Paige, at the top, the screen blinking with fresh ellipses as she continued to reach out: *Joan, what are you . . . Fucking answer . . . I just can't . . .* Angry or sad or sickened, it all meant the same. How would Joan function? Who would she talk to? Her only family. She was still pressing on the brake pedal with all her strength, so hard her foot prickled with pins and needles. She slid the shifter into park.

And these were her friends. Imagine what her fans were saying, strangers on Twitter. Videos of Joan pissing on a fan, shot from every angle and in every hue of gel light. Joan had always considered the superfans her secret weapon: this army ready to battle for her. They brimmed with anger and mischief, all that energy that was normally spent for the good of Joan, but didn't have to be. If she stroked them against their fur, they'd wheel around and nip.

"You getting anything?" asked an attendant, blue work shirt sagging around a naked shoulder, the bare skin shiny and clean despite his neck smudged with grease. "Or just gonna hang out all night?"

"Yeah, one sec," Joan said.

She twinged under his scowl, rolled up her window. A musician a little more famous than Joan, Alfred Honey, had been canceled last year for punching his wife. No one had been surprised. Alfred was a rangy, girl-faced fighter, bouncing as he ranted to strangers in bars. He had a signature gesture: finger guns cocked and leaned against his temples, aimed out. He was high-cheekboned with pretty eyelashes and a hefty chin, but his complexion was bad. Distorted by venue presets, he turned monstrous. His girl had posted the guilty picture in wan fluorescence, her hair dirty, cheek caving under the bruise. An uproar on Twitter had followed, with fan accounts deleted and threads screenshotting Alfred's worst tweets: descriptions of fucking the corpses of celebrities, lists of fans who'd blown him in green rooms, graphic critiques of his own dick. Sometimes, among friends, he slid it out of his pants, flaccid, and held it like a comfort toy. Joan had been young when she'd met him, and his behavior had thrilled her. Here was this feral world, boundaries dissolved. Even if she never told anyone about her peeing, at least she belonged in a world with people like Alfred.

Alfred hadn't seemed the type to live by the fickle tides of social media, but after the takedown, he vanished. He'd slipped too far, had hurt someone who loved him. Occasional reports surfaced of him slinking around an even deeper subculture, populated by marginal musicians who traded shows in empty warehouses, who shared fentanyl, whose work knifed the ear. But he'd fallen from a tier of fame two clicks above Joan. Joan's world was too underground already for anyone in it to be canceled, a safer place to act out than Alfred's world. Until Paige had risen, none of what the Gonewriters'had done mattered to anyone, and that was the fun of it. Maya could write songs so dense and unlistenable that her fan base shrank to ten, winding her braid into a tower on her head before shows, blasting notes from neon melodicas. Christopher, in all his green-eyed beauty, could pretend he hadn't gone to Harvard, splashing whisky on a tiny stage, condescending to his fans like they were fools. And Paige was the teen, the pet, this novelty kid tagging along to smoky shows and the afterparties of feral adults. So what if Joan was the wildest of their set? She was beloved for it.

But maybe Joan would be okay—she was a woman after all, and pee was sterile, basically water. Male musicians had done worse for years. Joan had only been frisky, had gone a step too far. But even as she clung to these thoughts, the oil seep of dread leaked in from the back of her skull. Footsteps approached from somewhere behind her, and she whipped around, bracing herself for the attendant. But nothing.

The gas station pad reflected the neon lights in crisp detail, though it hadn't rained where she'd come from. Her phone was down to 3 percent, having exhausted itself with its news, and its charger lay at the bottom of a beach trash can. Wriggling on the sweaty seat, she activated her maps app, pinching the screen until she opened up the space from here to Coney Island, miles and miles traveled already. The distance relieved her. She'd find a town that no one would ever guess and memorize the directions. Somewhere as far away as she could reach tonight. She was a genius with directions from her years of touring, didn't believe in GPS anyway; it was cheating.

As she widened the digital map, Chicago entered the field. Imagine if she returned to where her parents lived. She hadn't spoken to them more than a few times in the twenty-two years of her career, hadn't seen them once, though she'd toured through Chicago countless times, had even had a love there once, early on. A music program for college students had invited her to teach out there last summer, but of course she'd refused. She had many such invitations and always turned them down because she couldn't picture herself in a classroom. Maybe it was her modest indie fame that made her approachable to teacher types. Some people called her lyrics "literary." But a program like that was probably her best shot—she'd never been offered any other type of work. Someplace to hide out for a few weeks and get paid, housing provided, where she could build resources to find a truly hidden spot or wait out the media storm and let people forget. Give her time to settle into a new nowhere, find some simpleminded job far from any art. She hated the idea of classroom teaching—it reminded her of her father, who'd been a poorly paid charter schoolteacher in Ravenswood—but surely the teaching at such programs was a formality, the camp an excuse for teens to escape their families and drink. She wouldn't have to do much but stand around and make sure the kids didn't die.

A car honked, and she froze. If she moved at all, she'd take off with no destination. A pickup truck ripped around and passed her, middle finger stuck to the window, gummy against the glass. She curled her spine until she disappeared, hunched there on the car floor, for ages.

She filled the car with gas and returned to her phone. The program in Chicago was last year, and there were a few in Brooklyn, which, obviously, no. Earlier that summer there'd been an invitation to a weeklong gig in Florida. She expanded the map to include the South. Florida would've been nice—as far as she could get in a certain direction, teeming with alligators and iguanas and abandoned jungle snakes, dinosaur plants with their great frayed leaves convincing her she was in a foreign land—but when she looked it up, the program had ended weeks ago. But there, Virginia, yes. That camp that had hassled her every year for the past three. She might've even emailed them last week, but she couldn't remember. She fielded so much bullshit, couldn't absorb what emails she'd sent when she bothered to reply at all. She'd been vetted last year to teach by Virginia and one other program in Cleveland, which she couldn't find a record of now. She'd lined up those backups when her career started to dip—the first warning signs had panicked her—had weathered the application and background check, but ultimately withdrew because of what she'd worried it meant to teach. The Gonewriters venerated mentoring—the pure and free exchange of insider knowledge and skill from veteran to novice artist—but scorned formalized teaching, even Maya, who'd once suffered scurvy from lack of nutrition and whose apartment was rattled five times an hour by the D train, but who, even still, even with immigrant parents beaming their hopes at her, refused to abandon making a living through art, the natural rhythms of creation decimated by 6:00 a.m. wakeups and hours festering in classrooms, donning silly robes for graduations, burning off mystery with each tap of chalk against the symbol of a treble clef.

Joan had a recent email from that camp, she was sure. And there it was, not too far down, though not as recent as she'd hoped. Her phone ticked to 2 percent. Yes, an email from months ago, when applications went live. But then, look—another last week. They'd had a last-minute cancellation. Would she join them? From a woman with the pleasingly old-fashioned name of Georgina Lillian Morehouse. Joan had shot back a lazy "I'll think about it," to which she'd received an enthused and detailed reply, dense with logistics, and then Joan had dropped the thread. The camp started June 22. That was tomorrow. Faculty was supposed to be there today by four, hours ago, and Joan was nowhere close. Other details, listed below: this was a writing camp, and her role was teaching songwriting. Her heart skidded. But why else would they want her? They seemed intent on the teaching, like they wanted more than her name. She pushed through to other details. The program was housed on the campus of some crappy college in rural central Virginia, attracting wealthy, intelligent high schoolers from New York and the South. Only forty students total for five faculty members, so each student would expect extensive instructor attention—unfortunate. The camp, acknowledging this practice was old-fashioned, did not abide the use of cell phones or the internet. Vaguely familiar from the interview—Joan wouldn't have clocked the detail; she hated social media, hardly used her phone. All devices were confiscated upon arrival. The kids would "free their minds to write" without "modern-day distractions" in order to "reclaim their attention spans."

The term was six weeks, the pay six thousand dollars, enough to start a new life. When she arrived she'd claim she'd responded, but they hadn't received her reply because they had no internet once on campus. There was no way they'd found someone else in the last three days, and if she showed up, surely they couldn't refuse her. And no internet. She'd last longer there, no matter how fast she went viral.

The only problem was the teaching. Her father had suffered the woes of teaching all her life, his skimpy salary less than her mother made as a cocktail waitress. Joan's dinners with him, while her mother worked late nights at the upscale place downtown, were spent absorbing frustration over his students' hormonal energy and inability to grasp remedial math. She'd had to attend his school, though it was worse than the public schools, for the convenience of commuting, and when she passed his classroom, she could barely look at him, spindly before rows of puffy students, his bony shoulders hunched in a button-down. He'd been scrawnier than the high schoolers, and they'd chatted through his lectures. She'd promised herself she'd never follow his path. Her parents had been nasty about her music, her "stupid choices" that would leave her broke and homeless. She'd fallen out of touch with them as her life diverged onto a path that repelled them.

But she could give the least of herself possible to teaching. How hard could it be? Standing before a room, entertaining. She did it all the time. A couple of hours a day in exchange for protection.

Her phone dipped to 1 percent. The gas pump played a melody, tinny and jaunty and ear-itching. She jotted down directions, then threw her phone out the window. The glossy rectangle turned through the dark air, screen still lit. She held her breath like it could set the gas station aflame.

4

JOAN'S CAR CLOCK WAS BROKEN, SO SHE HAD NO IDEA what time it was as she closed in on campus, blood pulsing through her limbs. She'd managed without her phone, mostly, had only lost her way once. She pushed through the tangled forests of the last miles, vines climbing powerlines, the air chewier as the road drew her south.

She was deep in Virginia now. The reggaeton and hollow pop crackling through the car stereo as she fled New York had been gradually replaced by cheesy country, twangy male voices sneering about bars and girls. Arms limp, sour breath filling the cab, she pushed the '94 Corolla faster than ever, faster even than Paige would dare, until the engine shrieked in protest. She was exhausted, could've nodded off, but terror rattled her awake at each breath.

At least she'd found a land free of internet. She'd skirt discovery at the camp for longer than anywhere else. Even if she only had a few hours of peace left in the larger world, in Virginia she might have days, weeks.

She ripped off her sweater, drenched in sticky adrenaline. Her ex-boyfriend of years ago, the "Lakeshore" guy, had brought it back to her from Bergen, Norway, a candy-colored town clustered on a spike of coast so far north. He'd said Bergen was the quietest town he'd ever visited, no music in any shop or restaurant, crowds encased in creamy peace. The sweater, crumpled now on the passenger seat, was oversize, for men, like he knew she liked, creamy wool run through with fibers of all the colors of the rainbow. The gift must've hogged half his suitcase, his nose twitching under his wire-frame glasses as he ferried her soft treasure across Scandinavia.

Maybe one day she could reach a place like Norway: quiet, craggy, clean, organized, rich. A foreign place, far from anyone she'd known, where contemporary music was on hold—she'd never met a musician from Norway, hadn't toured there once. The land of black metal—the least musical music—but no kind of music that crossed her path. A place exactly the opposite of where she'd come from, where she could sit in silence and forget the ambition that had driven her for decades.

But a cruiser could be behind her in seconds, flashing blue into the dim cab of her car. Assault. Indecent exposure. Whatever she'd done had to be somehow worse for having occurred onstage. She squeezed the steering wheel, drove fast, faster.

Humidity rolled in through the window. Five miles before arrival, she scanned through radio stations and there, fuzzy and indistinct, the first strums of her favorite folk song. Was it really playing? She turned up the volume through the white noise blurring the song, but as the car shot down the highway, the sound cleared, and yes, it was "Tomorrow, Yesterday." She must've stumbled on the late-night show of some old-timey DJ. The song felt like an omen, but she didn't know of what. Its narrative detailed a friendship between two women. Joan tried to soften her spine against the car seat, tried to absorb every word like she'd never heard it before, tried to unwind the coils of her brain. Her favorite songs were those whose authorship was lost to time, American traditionals or kids' songs, songs that had been reinvented by so many artists that no pure version remained, but whose core emotion rang vivid through the years. Though scarce, Joan loved this type of song best, could appreciate the magic of songwriting most clearly with no author attached. Many songs of no provenance had actually been stolen—right here in Appalachia—white people appropriating troves of music from uncredited Black creators, selling records without attribution or compensation, though she suspected and hoped this practice didn't apply to any of her personal favorites.

The singer of "Tomorrow, Yesterday" had a neutral voice— ideal for such songs, so the lyrics and melody passed cleanly through the vessel. The song opened when the singer and the you were little: "You had my favorite kind of face, just like my momma's own, young and old and wise and bright, I needed you 'fore long." Little-kid Paige was easy to picture, skinny under all that hair, irrepressibly exuberant in her regimented household, which had been as quiet and lonely as Joan's. Joan wished they'd been children together, breaking free of their parents' worlds and living like street cats. They could've roamed Chicago or Zanesville, finding adventure on every city block, in every weed-choked lot. They could've made each other okay.

The friends in the song advanced into separate adulthoods, each alone and magically jobless, committed only to wandering in nature, one in the mountains, one by the sea: "I see your face in tidal waves, on beaches white with snow. No one else could understand, just why I had to go." The highway blurred by as the friends finally reunited on the you's deathbed: "Won't say which tree I grew for you, my garden never rests. Choke-cherry, oak, linden, ash, you'll simply have to guess." Joan's bladder twinged with old longing.

What stilled her nervous system was how easy the friend-ship of the song was, even with years apart, miles of distance, death. The friends of the song had ridden the right track all the way through. The only parallel between the song and her and Paige was constancy: the automatic, unquestioned familial nature of the friendships. Paige alert in the house lights. Joan pushed the accelerator and shot past a parade of eighteen-wheelers.

The singer petered into silence like she hoped she'd never emerge from it. Joan would not make music anymore. Even the idea of touching a guitar made her ill. The highway skated under her, unrolling its endless offer of concrete. She was al-most at the camp. And then, maybe, one day, she'd travel to the Arctic Circle: a music-free wasteland where she could meditate as reindeer clopped by, where she could deliver brown cheese to a hag.

She entered campus, passing through the pretty brick guard station—there was a red light but no one to vet her—new wet leaves draping toward her car, the intricate structures of wildflowers illuminated by her headlights, deer as still as decorations. She navigated speed troughs so deep and sudden they threatened to hobble her Corolla and made her way up a hill past brick buildings that must've stood for centuries. She passed mansions on Faculty Row, a forest puffy with kudzu. The sky sagged with rain.

Georgina Morehouse's email sign-off had listed an address in Randolph Hall. Joan would leave a note and then sleep in her car for the handful of hours till morning.

She parked on a circle of asphalt and pushed open her door,

scraping greasy curls off her forehead. Humidity stung her skin. The clear, black air revealed how badly it stank in her car from her pungent salad. Before she left she'd used the last of her food, dicing garlic and sprinkling it over lettuce and seeds. Her paring knife rested on the counter back in her apartment, on a plastic cutting board she'd found on the street, cloudy with slice marks. The remains of the garlic bulb waited by the burner, three nested cloves, the papery husks of their mates on the floor and in the trash, one scrap clinging so tightly to the rim of the sink that her nail couldn't pry it loose.

She climbed the grassy hill, her body working in separate parts, like an old toy, squinting at nameplates on all the wrong buildings: Mason, Morgan, Bacon, Blair, McClurg. Dead white men morphed into stern brick homes of knowledge. At Randolph, she was relieved to find the door unlocked. She'd scrawl a note somewhere in Georgina's office that she was the Joan she'd been corresponding with, that she was here, ready to teach. Yes, she was late, but she'd claim she'd sent several emails confirming her arrival. She'd declare her passion for the job. If a video had already been posted, if Georgina had somehow seen it, even without internet, well, she couldn't hide anywhere if she couldn't hide here.

She steadied herself in the cool hallway. All she had to do was appear normal in a single note. Then she could rest and be less frazzled tomorrow. Georgina's office, nudged into a corner of the building, leaked a strip of light into the hall. She must've left it on. Joan pushed the door open.

Linoleum floors, a set of modular tables, abandoned for summer. One corner of the classroom was cozily arranged: two ancient school desks with attached molded plastic chairs were pulled together at an intimate angle, their feet resting on a carpet whose pattern had been beaten into a warm-toned muddle of fibers. An antique lamp projected a pool of yellow light like honey.

An old woman was crumpled at one of the desks, her soft body wedged into the molded plastic chair, fist tight around an earthenware mug that steamed her chin as she pored over a slab of paperwork. The odor of eggs lingered, a warm, body smell.

The woman jumped as Joan entered, snatching a clump of blouse over her heart. "Good lord," she cried.

Joan stepped further into the room, pulling her shirt down so the wrinkles flattened. Georgina's face constricted. Joan probably looked like she'd walked to Virginia between wolves.

"May I help you?" Georgina had a conical gray head, neck fringed with grape-sized beads, ears studded with discs, cheeks wrinkled and soft, like crushed satin.

Joan slackened. How was she here, in this calm office? This woman had the aspect of an affectionate, hands-off mentor, someone who'd pop into the classroom to lovingly pat Joan's head. Perfect—too perfect. Joan's mouth dried.

Georgina's smile soured. Was that recognition crossing her face? Was she squinting to recognize Joan's gapped teeth, her frizzy hair, as the head of a now-viral figure? Joan's muscles hardened into strips of stone. But no. This woman had been tucked in this unwired room since before everything.

"Miss?" Georgina said. "This is a private office. Are you lost?" She patted her pockets as though preparing to call security.

"It's Joan." Joan pushed back her hair, bushy from the club and all the driving. She broadcast the queasy smell of skin. "I'm here to teach songwriting." The words flopped out. Even worse than getting canceled was giving up. "We spoke last summer. And then a few days ago."

Georgina frowned. "Oh, right. Joan Vole." Joan quivered at

her complete name, as though it would summon the authorities. Even though it had been her name for twenty-one years, it sometimes still sounded fake. "We reached out, yes. But we never heard back." She drew her hands up into her lap.

"I did write back," Joan said, so emphatically that she almost convinced herself. "I said I'd love to teach this summer."

"When did you write?" Georgina squinted in the low light.

"A few times." Joan reached into her pocket for her phone, as though she could prove it. But her phone was shattered in a gas station in Swiftwater, Pennsylvania. "Two days ago, and yesterday. And this morning."

"Could it have gone to spam?" Georgina pronounced the word as though she was uncertain of its meaning.

"Yes." Joan tried not to let excitement flood in. She stepped closer. "Yes, yes, it could've been spam. My email is often spam."

"I'm sorry I missed it." Georgina touched her collar. "And I'm sorry you startled me. Normally the guard checks in visitors and offers fair warning. Especially at this hour."

"He wasn't there." But maybe he had been, and she'd blown through? She hadn't peered in his window, hadn't even slowed down.

Georgina slid her laptop toward her. Joan hadn't seen it, concealed among the papers. It sent prickles down her spine. What was Georgina doing with a laptop? Had Joan misread the literature? Internet-free had seemed too good to be true.

Georgina clicked around, her wrinkled face illuminated by the damning white dialogue box of an email server. No. No. But of course—how would the administration function without internet? She was so dumb.

"I don't see your email," Georgina said.

Joan jittered on the tiles. Georgina hadn't invited her to sit down. It must have been Joan's odor: car, sweat, sleeplessness, residual piss, the smoke and BO of the club. Best to stay back.

Georgina's eyes were shiny with a surprising sheen of regret. "I'm sorry, Joan. We aren't ready for you. We'd love to consider you next summer, though."

What was that clockwork behind her face, the machine of her brain working? "No," Joan said, too quickly. "No, I just—look. I'd love to teach now, actually. I'm here, and I'm ready. Just a few days ago you wanted me. Did you find someone else?"

"We did not."

"See, then? Here I am." She squared her feet.

"We've gone ahead and absorbed your students into comics."

Your students. An opening. "But they signed up for songwriting, right? So songwriting is what they want. And don't you want to give them what they want?"

Georgina lifted a paper as though it held an answer. "Some already dropped out. There are only three left."

"But the classes are always small." The intimate course sizes had been touted in the materials. Thankfully Joan had read them so recently because that wasn't the type of crap she tended to recall.

"I suppose it's not out of the question. Though this is highly irregular." Georgina pressed on the last words as though "highly irregular" was both alarming and kind of delightful. Mischief flashed behind her eyeglasses. "But we don't have your paperwork."

"I did all that last year. Remember? But then I had to tour." The lie stuck in Joan's teeth. If only it were true and her career woes had just been a dip, that she'd toured all last summer, risen on the momentum to a height where Black Tree would've begged her to sing on Paige's record.

"Not the background check too?" Georgina asked, skeptical.

"I did." Joan had been anxious until the check came back clear. She'd done plenty that should disqualify her from teaching children, though nothing would emerge on an official record. Now maybe it would. Though she'd never wanted to teach, if she couldn't, she'd feel cheated.

Georgina stared at Joan, lips pursed. "I won't regret this?"

Joan's muscles loosened enough to reveal how rigid they'd been, wound up for hours. "No."

Georgina sighed. She thumbed through papers. "Fill these out so I can get you processed before your first class this morning."

"Today?" Out the window, the sky was still dark. So Georgina wasn't still up; she was already up.

"Just a mini class, for intros."

Joan shifted in the doorway, hesitant to accept the packet. Maybe she should get back in the car, find somewhere dank and music-free and more thoroughly hidden. Like a slaughterhouse in Nebraska.

"Then orientation. You must still have your Lesson Cycle on your laptop."

"Yes." Even if she'd ever written such a document, her laptop was in Brooklyn. She'd scrubbed the data before she left. All her landlord would find was corporate blue wallpaper, a generic icon for an empty hard drive.

There, by Georgina's desk—she hadn't noticed it before—was a transparent tub, filled with a jumble of phones, faces pressed to the plastic, blank screens waiting to be stroked.

"Some parents hang on to them," Georgina said. "But most kids don't want to wait when the ban lifts on the last day."

So many hopes and secrets encased in that bin. The kids couldn't look her up, but their parents could, and call in. Georgina could the moment Joan walked out.

Georgina dug out a keycard and sketched a map to the dorm. She apologized that there weren't linens, but Joan had a sleeping bag for tour. "This is quite the surprise, I must say," Georgina said. "But I have a good feeling about you. I did last year too. We were impressed with your little niche career out there in New York. Very 'artful.'"

Joan's shoulder jerked up. She dedicated all her muscles to holding it down. "Oh."

"Get some sleep before class." Georgina closed the door to the office.

Joan crossed the dark quad, under hanging vines and over squishy nighttime grass, birds chirping the day's first hesitant conversations, her chest pulsing with matching lobes of dread and relief.

5

JOAN REBOARDED HER CAR, HUMID SEAT CURLING AROUND her like a friend, the damp odor welcoming, like how it always felt reentering the Corolla after the endless journeys of tour. She drove down the hill to the parking lot overlooking the exurb monstrosity that must've been the dorm: two stories of new construction, bound in gray plastic siding and pocked with bubbled skylights. She grabbed her bag and got out. Hoofbeats sounded in the distance. She had, at least, a little time. Even if just this morning. If only the feral dog of her heart could obey.

She hurried down the stairs cut into the hillside and hovered her keycard until the door unlatched. Bags pounding her thighs in the cold, dry climate of the dorm, she shot past the kitchen and common area, barely registering its mauve corporate stiffness, and down the hallway with three doors. Two were closed.

She shut herself into the empty room and crashed her bags to the floor so hard the walls shook. The minute the door was locked, calm whisked through her. A plain, pine desk, a dresser and twin bed, blue carpeting, the plastic breast of an overhead fixture. The minimum equipment required for a life. The perfect stage set, as though, at forty-three, she'd returned to college. She unpacked her clothes into the particleboard drawers, which rattled as she yanked them open. Why bother folding when she'd have to snatch them back out in a few hours? She dropped her musty sleeping bag onto the mattress manufactured to repel fluid, admiring the design, not that she'd require it here. No. Fuck other people; fuck all of it. All she cared about was hiding.

No time was passing; outside was still velvet black. She set her toothbrush by the door in case she needed to leave in a hurry. How early had Georgina woken? Her fingers vibrated, antsy for a job. Now that her next step was taken care of, she couldn't hold still. A thread of water rushed through the wall, the flow dissonant against its pipe. In Brooklyn she would've paced to Manhattan Beach and back. But the sooner she met people, the quicker she'd arouse their curiosity.

She waited, listening. The dorm was dead, no footfalls from above. She crept from her room. At the end of the hall, starlight glazed the common room carpet. She opened the sliding back door beside the couch. Humidity tumbled in, like a bear rolling over her spine. She stepped into the soupy night. A picnic table crouched on a concrete slab. Sand and glitter were glued to the boards, and when she pressed the spongy wood, her fingers left dents. If only the cicadas would quiet, maybe Joan could make out the woodwinds of night birds, the clap of bat wings, the beat of snuffling groundhogs.

She had to pee so bad, that delicious pressure against her organs, her swollen bladder jolting with burps of pleasure at each step. She shouldn't pee outside. But it was dark; no one was here. And she could never resist post-road trip; the long-held piss was the sweetest.

There had been moments in New York when she'd tried to meet her sexual habits in a healthier place. She'd googled "golden shower enthusiasts," "urolagnia," reminding herself there were thousands of people like her—but their desires didn't map onto hers. She'd even been to a meetup once, and it did nothing for her. Middle-aged women in goth accoutrements chirping about mattress protectors and tunnel plugs and piss gag hoods, showing off at-home catheters, urine drainage bags, bejeweled decanters, hole stretchers, all that silly black-and-yellow rubber, glancing sidelong at Joan: Who was this grouchy creature with no knowledge of proper watersports? Her own preoccupation was at once innocent and so much darker, pervading her whole life, not even always sexual, exactly. She'd tried to explain how she peed to transcendent songs, and they'd squinted at her, open-mouthed. The club had screened a video of a woman forced to hold a quart of piss by her master. The sequence had turned Joan on: that swollen, tortured body, squirming. But the live people had been earnest, even dweeby, and the meeting had taken the fun out for days.

She walked onto the lawn, magnetized to the dark fringe of trees at the border. She squatted there, the night holding her nakedness, and let the hot water rush out of her, so forceful it pushed against her folds and shuddered her. To be outside, in nature, in the dark, fireflies winking green, bound in the tension of pleasure, was unreal. She was a coyote, free to piss wherever he liked. She lingered as long as the urine left her, jumping as she caught illumination in the window of the bedroom that must be next to hers. She hadn't seen the light from the hall. Could someone see her? With bumbling fingers she fixed her pants and hurried over.

The person behind the window sat at a canted desk, bent

over a sky-blue pencil. Joan stood close to the glass—in the dark, she'd be invisible. The person's yellow hair was cut ear-length, her torso loose and soft in a cotton T-shirt, belly and breasts swaying as her elbow fanned out to draw. She checked the number on the end of her pencil, switched it for another from a line of cut-glass jars bristling with pencils sharpened to uniform length. Joan stepped closer. The room was identical to hers but populated by dozens more items. A rubber dog with a noble muzzle stood watch over a computer wired with a hard drive, mouse, tablet, and digital stylus, cords collared with ribbon, tamed and leashed like no cords she'd ever seen, shiny like they'd been oiled. The dresser hosted stacked pads of art board lined up beside brushes in tubes, a row of ink bottles in every richness of black, chromatically arranged. So much careful preparation for the production of art. Joan winced, but she couldn't walk away.

The girl sank into her pencil, moving with lithe energy that exhausted Joan. Her wrist sprang around like it was morning. She touched her forehead with a square of crisply folded hand-kerchief. When her arms lifted off the board, her page appeared: a grid of perfectly uniform panels outlined with inked borders. Joan inched as close as she could before her nose struck glass. In the first panel was a figure composed of stacked cubes, even his pupils and his knees square, speaking a block of text with such mathematical kerning it might've been typed.

The girl looked up. Joan jumped back, but the girl only stared out blindly into the night. She was young—her skin perfect and elastic and alive. Head on, she was a boy—jaw strong, eyes deep-set, hair cresting in a cowlick like a heartthrob. What a handsome, sturdy person. Her boy side was royal, like the young man in one of Joan's favorite songs without origin:

a lost king happy in a peasant's life, scything wheat even after learning his lineage. She wouldn't have been surprised to feel stubble, antsy on her cheek.

The girl murmured. Joan leaned closer, straining to read her lips. The girl's eyes drifted, focus falling apart. The kind of expression made when no one was watching.

The girl pounced on the page, striking at the block man. Her private expression—like the diffuse concentration before orgasm—the way she squeezed the pencil until her hand blazed white, overwhelmed Joan, but she couldn't turn away. The girl relaxed as the blue marks accrued. She seemed like she could go all night, transported into the world of that blue pencil the way Joan hadn't been transported by any work in forever. Joan ripped herself away, stepping back until the scene was illegible.

The horizon. Morning, at last: a bar of magenta behind blue hills. Joan could sleep for a couple of hours before filling out Georgina's packet. She hadn't even closed the sliding glass door, sealing in the dry, circulated air, when a presence shifted in the living room: a rustle of cloth, the waft of artificial raspberries.

"Oh," said a woman's voice, startled.

Joan glided the door shut. Before she turned around, she smoothed her linen shorts until they were flat and dry on her thighs.

Cozied on the armchair was a curvy woman in her early thirties, wings of dark hair set into waves. She wore a nightgown that hugged her hips and breasts but billowed over her stomach, as though she'd trained the fabric to showcase only points of bodily pride. She looked like Joan's mother whenever she got dressed for a court date or a coworker's wedding, trying to appear older than she was in Goodwill business casual, face young and frightened under a glaze of makeup. The woman clutched the stem of a wine glass of orange juice. Beside her sweated a plate of chopped breakfast sausage. "Oh, hi. I'm Meredith."

Joan headed to the hallway. "Good night." The woman's chin tilted toward Joan, expectant. But Joan had lost the impulse to explain herself years ago. Had never had it. In seconds, she could rest.

The woman set down the juice and offered her hand to shake. The readout on the microwave blinked red. Joan only had a few hours left before facing the students.

"I should get some rest."

"What's your name?"

Joan hesitated. But there was no point withholding. The woman would learn soon enough. "Joan."

"Oh, Joan!" Meredith sat forward, smoothing her nightgown. "You're that musician."

Joan's limbs iced into place. "What do you mean?"

Meredith's eyes rolled toward the ceiling. "I've heard about you somewhere."

"No." The word mushroomed out. Joan's hand lifted like she could block Meredith's mouth.

Meredith tapped her lip. "You were going to teach here last year. That's right."

Air sank out of Joan in a long, easy blast. Okay. Okay. "And now I will teach here this year. That's the whole story." Was this how people kept "professional boundaries"? The Gonewriters went broke on each other's merch, hosted drunk critiques in sticky corners of bars where they ripped each other's songs to shreds. They roughhoused in green rooms when there were green rooms, fucked each other's exes, each other's currents, each other. Boundaries were a joke.

"I'm sorry you caught me off guard. It's just Georgina didn't mention you."

"I'm a last-minute hire." Joan wouldn't spend the last hours before her life was destroyed explaining herself to this woman.

"Right." Meredith tapped her lip. "We've had such bad luck with songwriters."

Ice licked down Joan's spine. Was the behavior of songwriters especially scrutinized? Were they kicked out of camp for tepid acts like smoking weed or fucking other teachers?

"Usually they drop out before they even get here. But I remember now. You actually gave notice. Sometimes we start and they're just not here. They get another gig and bounce." She noodled a piece of sausage until her fingers shone. "I'm always telling Georgina not to bother. It's so hard to get the kids enthused about songwriting anyway." That was good. The kids wouldn't mind if Joan was checked out. Meredith helped herself to a sip of juice. "Sit a minute, Joan. I'd like to know you."

"Not a great time."

"Oh." Meredith's lip trembled. "But just for a minute? We're a small community, so it's good when we know each other." Her face was open, like she wanted to get to know all of Joan right now, at five in the morning.

Joan was pulled down onto the couch by the force of Meredith's will. The couch was composed of the same substance as the mattress: dense, unforgiving. Meredith settled into the armchair, thrusting her hips to tenderize the cushion, a kick of self-conscious sexiness. The effort exhausted Joan. She was ready to burrow into her sleeping bag. Even if her pupils bounced all over the lightening room, at least she'd be alone. But she had to find out what this woman knew. "Are you into music?" If she was, let the familiarity be shallow. After all, how many musicians was Joan up to the minute on? Zero, and she was one herself.

"I hate to admit this, but I'm pretty singularly focused on writing." Meredith broke into a grin. "Did you know my memoir is coming out this fall? I can't believe it's finally happened for me."

Cicadas scraped outside, riding their inhuman scale. The arts. The struggle. Here it was, returned to her. "But you're a teacher mainly, right?"

Meredith wrinkled her brow. "I'm a writer."

Joan held onto her own arm. "Right."

"Here." Meredith offered the plate of sausage. Joan didn't move. Meredith jiggled the plate, so Joan lifted one segment, flesh hot on her fingertips.

Silence gelled between them, even the cicadas quiet. Joan nipped the sausage. Spicy fat bubbled over her tongue. She hard-swallowed a gag. Meredith slouched against the backrest, pulled out her phone. Its chocolate shine made Joan queasy. With one hand, Meredith noodled on it.

"What are you doing?" Joan whispered.

Meredith bounced her phone. "God. I didn't even realize. I'm sorry. That's rude."

So it wasn't just some old lady with limited knowledge of email functionality who had access to the internet. By the time Joan awoke, Meredith would know what she'd done. And—worse—that drawing girl. Joan was crushed that such a virtuous, hardworking individual would bear witness to her worst moment.

"Are you all right?" Meredith asked. "You look scared." Her arm reached across the distance between them. Joan shrank back.

"Who lives in the other room?" Joan blurted.

"Sparrow." Meredith glanced at the hall as though the girl might emerge at the raising of her name. "Did you meet her? She's lovely."

"No." Joan dropped the sausage behind the chair.

Meredith's cheeks beamed red. "You'll adore her. She was a kid here. She's still a kid—she's, I don't know, twenty-three?" Meredith sat straighter. "I trust she'd consider me something of a mentor. I'm always pushing her to advocate for herself. She's a bit off, but—you know. A cutie. Quiet. Her name used to be Eliza. She's a lesbian, too, but not actually."

Joan had eaten some pussy, sure, but nothing like everyone thought. Sometimes straight women solicited her after shows, boyfriends hanging back—girls who considered themselves voluptuous and free. Girls who'd been struck with the idea for the first time, watching Joan play, that other girls could be sexy as fuck. They explained it was her ranginess, her flat chest and skeletal shoulders, her structured jaw and cheekbones, her bad teeth; it was "Lakeshore." That quietly fierce, poetic story-song of lesbian love. The straight girls thought their straightness icing, like whatever grainy, gummy cake they were underneath, any lesbian would be starved for the buttercream of their heterosexuality.

"Ugh," Meredith cried, slapping her thigh. A pink print rose on her flesh. "I already slipped because she's not a 'she.' She's a nonbinary. You say 'they' or her name for pronouns."

Nick Blade's person, Lamar, used they pronouns. Joan had envied how the simple shift, the swap of syllables that changed their name, had made them plainly cozier in the world.

"I guess you probably think I'm some hick from Montana," Meredith said.

"I didn't know you were from Montana." Why did it smell

like the club in here still, all yeast and smoke? The odor must've caught up in her nostrils.

"You didn't look us up?"

Joan wedged her hands under the cushion. Was that standard practice? Stalking your colleagues before you met them? A tremble ran through her bones.

"Don't worry. She's—they're—single-minded about her work."

Good thing Sparrow wasn't in the room to hear this introduction. But maybe if they had been, Meredith would've done better. People messed up Lamar's pronouns more when they were absent, as though without their presence, the effort wasn't worthwhile.

"Anyway," Meredith said, "Sparrow doesn't socialize much. I admire her for that."

So Sparrow was an obsessive too: starving, abdicating pleasure, torturing themself. Joan stabbed with longing to hunch down in their ordered room and run herself ragged on some borrowed guitar. She should stay away. But there was something peaceful about how Sparrow worked. Even if there wasn't a way forward in art for Joan, maybe someone else had found one.

"Don't worry," Meredith chirped. "Even if she's working, I'm sure she'll spend time with you. They love you."

"What?" That darling face—did Joan know it? Was that why she'd felt a milky peace at seeing it?

Meredith sat back, brightening. "She's your biggest fan."

"No," Joan said, too fast, automatic. She couldn't abide a fan here. She was divorcing herself from all that. This empty, humid place was free of news, fleshy coils of social media, every note of her music.

"Oh yeah," Meredith said, her voice thickening. "She was all, like, gushing last year when we thought you were coming."

So Sparrow had swayed in darkness watching her. Had they been there in LA when Joan dipped her tit in a cold white Russian? Or in Saint Paul, with her old band, when her bassist let her pull out his dick for a laugh? Or the time in Detroit when a fan leaped onstage and knocked Joan down in desire, and she stood up with a broken rib and kept playing? "I don't want that."

Meredith hiccupped a laugh, halfway between amusement and confusion. "I'm sorry I'm ignorant of your music myself. I would've already indulged in study if I'd known you were coming."

"Don't," Joan said, too quickly.

"Certainly I will, Joan. You're my colleague now. We're a community." She waved her arms to encompass them both.

"You really don't have to."

"But really, Joan." Her face was pinched, genuine. "I'd like to."

"No," Joan said, the word rushing out with force.

Meredith sat back. "Oh." She squinted at Joan, confused. "All right then."

6

ALL THROUGH THE MID TO LATE NINETIES, IF MARY-ANNE wasn't practicing or playing a show or working a shift at the restaurant, if she wasn't caught up in the fervor of writing—which she would have been always if she could have willed the process—she set out into the city to absorb. Even if a show was bad, some boy grinding a saw with a violin bow, moaning about his mom's tapioca, it didn't matter. She sat in the back of the house and let her mind whir: she would animate that bridge, she would stretch her vowels, she would growl that refrain, that verse could be elegant if freed from the boy's treacly voice. That song would be moving with a longer beat on "stay," a creepier key, more surprising picking. She mentally reworked the songs of fellow performers, dissecting and reorganizing melodies, tweaking lyrics, and on the best nights, the bright, clear lozenge of a new song lodged on the wall of her throat and she choked in joy.

This night was 1997, February. The streets of Red Hook were empty, the pavement icy black. SUVs patrolled with tinted windows, lingering at curbs. Mary-Anne had ventured to the waterfront, to an area where no one walked at night, to All Time Elodie's, home of the sole authentic open mic in Brooklyn. She was a hound for any scrap of inspiration, though nothing matched sharing songs with Maya and Christopher and Nick Blade, who'd invited her into their collective months ago, a crazy turn of her life she still couldn't believe was real.

Tonight the smorgasbord on offer contained no shred of talent. Mary-Anne ensconced herself at her favorite table, sticky and rickety, way in back, featuring a singed, blood-red candle, tucked behind the blue and white strips of silk hanging from the ceiling, vibrating in the invisible wind of the bar. The streamers were meant to somehow invoke France but only impeded the view of stage. Mary-Anne hunched in an oversized bomber jacket while a girl with a tambourine rattled and wailed about CD-ROMs and a band of floppy-haired boys sang in such croaking tones there was no way they'd fucked anything but their hands. All this interspersed with the usual lineup of girls with guitars who'd never sung for anyone but their bedroom mirror, opening their mouths too wide, flinging their hair back self-consciously, like actors playing musicians. These girls hadn't yet learned that singing at home and singing onstage were separate skills entirely, and there was no guarantee if you could manage one you could manage the other. Mary-Anne had the opposite problem, could never get wet enough at home to crush a song, never knew she had gold until she unleashed before a crowd.

She should've gone home hours ago. Nights like these revealed she was wasting her youth in a bar that smelled of bad bread and contained no window to the outside, making zero money from music, building no fan base, barely even improving. She might as well have never left Chicago. This sad night at All Time Elodie's, no one was even worth pissing on. But she kept delaying the freezing rain and SUVs, the eighteen-minute walk to the subway through which she'd growl and scramble her hair into a wild mess and act like too much trouble to rape, then the endless wait in the humid underground, the journey in a wobbling subway car all the way to Gold Street—and even then, all that awaited was her apartment on the airshaft, so small you had to mount the bed as you entered the bedroom and keep your knees in the hall while you shat.

She'd have one more beer while editing her newest lyrics, then a cigarette in the smoking area. On her way out she'd say hey to Nick Blade, who'd entered across the room with his Black lesbian girlfriend Marla in the leather jacket Mary-Anne coveted, the one with the buckle at the throat.

The beer had been watered down, though she couldn't complain when it was only three dollars, and she was about to cross it off her to-do list and bounce without the cigarette when a girl entered from the street, no coat, alone this late at night, black curls blustering in her face. She was a shard of a person—too young to be in a bar—and she stormed through the silk streamers, chattering to everyone but never pausing long enough for a response. Was she going to sing? She bore no instrument. But now she was all the way across the room, winter still clinging to her, chatting with the blond wisp with the fancy Gretsch, a rich-looking girl whose guitar was way better than her set had deserved—Mary-Anne's pet peeve. The new girl talked with big hands bouncing, and now she was taking the Gretsch—Mary-Anne shuddered; she could almost make out the fingerprints appearing on the cobalt body even from here—and then she was lurching toward stage, banging the jumbo into the ass of every musical douche in Brooklyn.

It wasn't the girl's turn. It was no one's turn. The music had been suspended for a much-deserved break that no one wanted stolen. That was the thing about music. When you wanted it, you were greedy for it—everyone here had traveled for it through the dark winter city—but when you'd been promised a chat with a friend or a bathroom trip, you hated the best band of the evening with a passion sturdy and abiding.

"Hey, hey," the girl called as she jumped onstage, before she got close enough for the mic to catch her, as though the audience would vanish any second. The next act, a Siberian girl with braids, clutched her banjo and tittered to her friends.

The kid grasped the mic stand and heaved herself upright. She was so young. That was obvious in the stage lights, with her full length revealed: she was too skinny and flexible to be an adult, her cheeks beaming pink, up there clutching the mic with her fist. Everyone thought Mary-Anne was underage because she was scrawny with big hair and crooked teeth, but she was twenty-two. This girl was genuinely a teenager, wearing a T-shirt with a blocky cross and *Zanesville Fellowship* printed in friendly font. Under the hot lights the dirt shone in her curls—her hair was greasy, like she hadn't washed it in weeks, and there was crap in it—a dead leaf, dirt, maybe even the soft finger of a cigarette butt. This kid was sleeping on the street. "I'm Paige Serratt." She stuck out her bird chest, as if anyone had heard that name in their life.

She didn't bother to tune the unfamiliar Gretsch, just set her foot on the stool to brace the instrument on her knee and strummed through its flatness. She watched her hands while she played, nodding when she fumbled a chord. Her hair was in the way—she let it dangle in loose clumps over the Gretsch, tangling with the strings, blocking her view. She opened her mouth to sing.

"Joanie, my love. You meet me up high. You hand me your

dove. You fly up my willow to think of you." Her voice was squeaky, like an alien baby. Mary-Anne stifled a laugh into the back of her hand. She'd never heard such a voice, wouldn't have thought anyone would have the courage to use it.

The first lyrics were the only ones that made sense. The song trailed off into looping verses about moles and firelight and raindrops made of crystal. The kid fumbled, restarted, and, once, burped. Her fingerstyle was rudimentary, and she cycled between D and G like she'd learned to play in the fifteen minutes before she stepped into the club. But somehow, despite all that, the small crowd at All Time Elodie's watched with rapt attention, every subpar folksinger and the croaking boys and the one or two randoms who were only audience; even the girl whose Gretsch the kid took couldn't look away from the stage. And it wasn't because the girl was attractive, which she was, in an undeveloped lamb way, because you couldn't even see her face while she played. The funny thing was, it wasn't because she was any good either.

When she finished, the crowd frothed into as much passion as they could clap together for their size, jumping and whooping. "More, more," cried the tambourine girl.

The kid laughed. She leaned in way too close to the mic and screamed, "That's all I have!" And they cheered louder.

She hopped off the stage, accepting hugs from every shy lurker, congratulations, free drinks. Her curls knocked over a pint glass. She set her hands on the ribs of men, leaning up to talk to them so close it was like she'd kiss them, but she was too alarming to be jailbait.

A guy had arrived who might qualify for Mary-Anne's evening: slumped, older, with Buddy Holly glasses and the striped T-shirt of a child. He had a nice belly that Mary-Anne would've enjoyed splashing in hot piss, too bland a face to react with violence. She usually peed on faces because of the various sites for reaction: a nose could snuffle, eyes could weep or shut as if forever, a mouth could scream or spit or drink its fill. There were ears to flood, hair to soak, wrinkles to smooth with the pressure of her stream. She could judge a man by how his face reacted when she pissed on it, and she took the mental snapshot as a souvenir: aroused, excited, disturbed. Normally the kind of man she hunted—rough-hewn, available to be picked up in a New York bar by some scrappy girl—was not the kind of man who'd be altogether surprised Mary-Anne was a freak. The dick was her second favorite site. She liked seeing if it shrank or grew, and she liked the retribution for all the damage the organ had caused to walls and trees and monuments and innocent, gape-mouthed urinals. She'd wait till the crowd thinned, and then she'd approach the man with the belly.

Nick Blade came over to say hi and bye, Marla gripping his arm. "You look tired, Mary-Anne," he said, true care shining off his baby face. His overgrown scruff somehow worked, sequestered as it was to the peak of his chin, maybe thanks to his angled eyebrows and sweet black eyes. Nick Blade didn't like practicing, struggled to get enough in, fucked around with songs and figured them out onstage. His technique was sloppy and all his songs raw, partly because of his absorption in Marla. He often bemoaned his lack of time to Mary-Anne, expressing jealousy of her free schedule. That he indulged the luxury of a serious relationship when he had so much work he wanted and needed to do on his craft baffled Mary-Anne. Marla tugged on his color-block hoodie. She was awkward around musicians, like she'd rather be hiding somewhere quiet, her expression squinching into a dozen masks, stretching her jacket down low over her hips, pinching her braids, and scanning the room, urging Nick Blade toward the door.

Mary-Anne was so grateful for even a glimpse of the familiar cat face of Nick Blade, still couldn't believe she'd found the Gonewriters and had an actual collective behind her, even if she was too stubborn to request their material support.

The celebration died. The kid returned the Gretsch, the Siberian girl phoned in her set, and then the next act took the stage, a quiet older man named Kwame Evan Rose whom Mary-Anne had heard play many times, who was relentless in his pursuit of music, though he couldn't sing in tune. But his songs had a pleasant dissonance, and Mary-Anne settled down in her seat under the velvet of his voice. The kid headed to the back of the bar. She probably needed the bathroom after all those free drinks. Mary-Anne took a slug of watery beer.

The froth was still fizzing between her teeth when the girl crashed down next to her. "Hey-o," she sang. She was drunk. Her breath gave it away: sour and fruity. "What's that?" She pointed to Mary-Anne's pile of notebooks, which she dragged around everywhere: one for classical study and music theory, another for drafting lyrics, a third for journaling about process, which kept her on track. The notebooks looked like shit: fat and stuffed with rainbows of ticket stubs and scraps of paper she scrawled on when she didn't have the notebooks handy. The covers were marred with smudged ink, brown webs of spilled beer, even, for some reason, blood.

"Just my private crap."

"You playing?"

"Not tonight."

"That's bullshit," the girl squeaked, thumping the table with both hands. "'Not tonight.' What? So you play other nights."

"Yup," said Mary-Anne. If she was short with the girl, maybe she'd scram.

"Why not tonight then? That's bullshit for me."

"'Gathering mode.'" Mary-Anne hated the term, but the Gonewriters used it freely. Christopher, mainly, as an excuse to never work and fuck a bunch of girls. She was glad he wasn't here because he would've gunned it for this kid. How many times had she pulled him off teenagers? "How old are you?"

The girl snatched Mary-Anne's beer and downed it hungrily, like she craved the calories, not the buzz. Her wrist shook. She set down the glass and leaned in toward Mary-Anne.

"You were lying up there, weren't you?" Mary-Anne said, sitting back. "You totally have more than one song."

"I can't stick around this place." The kid scratched her neck and looked at the crowd. She left red marks across her throat, the skin flaking off.

"Why not?"

"Dunno."

That empty look, her knee twitching. All Time Elodie's didn't serve food, not even chips. The bar of self-denial. So this was the girl's schtick. She sang for her supper all over town. All she needed was one song to win dinner every night. She was so young to be on the streets, had been taken care of only recently: her skin clear, her haircut expensive, like a purebred puppy with dust in her fur.

"Who's Joanie?" Mary-Anne asked.

"No one," said the girl. "Actually, you." She gulped more beer, pulling the golden liquid into her throat.

"I'm Mary-Anne." She loved her name for how Midwestern and girly it was, for how poorly it suited her. She loved when nurses and baristas called her name and then wrinkled their nose at who they got, peering beyond her for some cow-faced kid with pigtails.

The girl shook her curls so hard she stirred up stale layers of air. "Not anymore." She stretched her lips painfully wide, even white teeth on display.

"Okay," Joan said. That was fine. Ever since she'd left Chicago, she'd been a different person. So, probably, it was time. And it felt right, somehow, getting her name from this random kid who didn't know her and never would, who was barely a person yet, who'd tossed it off without a thought. The kid clasped Joan's arm with her spindly hand.

*

No restaurants were open in Red Hook that late, at least not around the venue, so Joan walked the kid back to the subway. They descended into the wet heat of the station together, waited on the same platform while rats skittered over the tracks. Joan prided herself on doing everything alone; the more dangerous, the more alone. But it was nice, sort of, having the kid along. She was bouncy and chatty, discussing her Christian father and Muslim mother back in rural Ohio, her days in high school going to bed before sunset, studying the Bible, being good. "Isn't that insane? I was so cheesy. And now I'm here." She looked around like she still couldn't believe it, and then, horror of horrors, sat down on the subway station bench without checking it first. She even touched it with her naked palm.

"Why'd you leave?" Joan asked, scanning the platform. Soon the crew from All Time Elodie's would find their way here, but, for now, they were alone.

"I'm fine," the kid said, squaring her shoulders. "I wanted to come to New York City."

"There's always a reason." Joan's parents had been okay, if remote, but she couldn't be herself living with them back in their rundown apartment in Chicago, couldn't write songs until New York.

The starburst of an approaching train. Hopefully this kid didn't have to travel too many stops with her. Joan was sick of talking.

The kid kicked a pile of french fries, which oozed into mealy mush. The smell of starch bloomed up. "I guess, well, they found me. And they're super, like, religious."

"Found you?"

The girl buried her hand up to the wrist in her hair. "In bed with someone?" She squinted.

"That's so normal." Joan's dad had caught her in the act so many times that he entered her room with a hand over his eyes. He still refused to knock.

The kid bent toward the ground, mumbling at the glob of fries.

"What did you say?"

"A girl?" The word a question, as though Joan had been there, as though she could support this claim.

"Ah." Joan had suspected she was a lesbian in high school, had hoped that might account for her perversity. She'd slept with a boxy lacrosse girl named Bethany, trying for months to convince herself queerness was the answer, but glimmers only sparked when Bethany went down on her while she had to pee. That minor electricity, that hope of some legible brand of alienation, were all that got her through high school. "That's cool."

"Yeah?" the girl asked, looking up through lashes.

"Here's the train." Joan stepped back off the painted safety strip.

*

The girl rode the subway all the way to Vinegar Hill. When they deboarded at York, she followed Joan down Jay Street. "Where's your place?" Joan asked.

The girl laughed, husky and too loud. And she wasn't even drunk anymore. Joan longed to be alone the way she longed to be alone at the end of every night. But fine. She'd feed the girl, and then maybe she'd leave.

She wished she could afford a fancy dinner, if only for the drama of the girl ripping into a steak or a shiny roast chicken, but she was broke herself. So she bought them dollar slices. "You can eat upstairs," she said, pausing outside her building. "But I sleep alone."

"Whatever." The kid couldn't look away from the pizza as it bobbled in Joan's hands, every passing person threatening to knock the slices off their scalloped plates.

"It's a walk-up," Joan said. This news scared some people off. The girl appeared athletic enough, but it was worth a try.

"So long as I don't have to walk down."

Of course the girl wasn't walking down. Even Joan wouldn't send a child into the street in the middle of the night, though the last thing she wanted was this bouncing energy in her tiny apartment. Up they went.

Joan didn't bring men back to her apartment if she could help it, because she needed the freedom to abandon an encounter at will. The Gonewriters never visited because she didn't invite them. She needed to be alone, taming her Martin all day, killing herself to master every fret and string, studying the classical shit at night because she was inferior for having no education and because she loved everything about guitars, no matter how prissy—everything about parlors, at least. So it had been months since anyone but her had entered the place. She hadn't washed her sheets in ages, and why bother making the bed if you couldn't even stand in the bedroom to admire it? The toilet bowl sported a ring of mold. The vegetables in the fridge were still edible, but slimy and limp. When you lived in a fifth-floor walk-up, it was easier to keep trash than lug it down. So, probably, it stank, though Joan was beyond noticing.

The girl bounced into the apartment. "You have this whole place to yourself? Wait, you don't have roommates?"

"I can't tolerate roommates." Joan pressed hard on the words.

"This place is freaking awesome." The girl flounced down on the blocks of foam Joan had set up for a couch. When her ass hit the cushion, two rats emerged and dragged their bellies toward the kitchen. Joan didn't even flinch. Their beefy bodies were always underfoot, losing custody of fleas, chewing out the crotches of her underwear. They didn't even bother to scurry anymore.

"Are those your pets?" the kid asked.

"Have you ever been to New York?"

"Vole," said the kid.

"They're mice." Because if the girl was going to sleep here, she might as well be able to relax.

"No," the kid said. "Your name."

"I'm going to sleep." Joan left the pizza with the kid, mounted her bed, and drew her door closed.

7

JOAN SLEPT FOR A COUPLE OF HOURS BEFORE CONVULSING
into semiconsciousness. She blinked into the overexposed sunshine and reached for her phone. Her hand scraped the bedside
table, fished around in the drawer. And what was all this green
outside, too much green, unreal and toxic, saturating ground
and sky with its wild oil, blaring into her room?

Joan's top half swung to the floor. But her phone wasn't
on the rug. It hadn't slipped under her bed. It wasn't in the
clammy pockets of yesterday's shorts or at the bottom of the
sleeping bag or on the windowsill in the bath of green.

As her palms smoothed every surface, searching, last night
seeped back. Her phone smashed into the rainbow on the gas
station's concrete pad. Rubbing herself down the superfan's
thigh. She slumped all the way to the floor, her front pressed
into the institutional carpet. How had she made it all the way
to Virginia in her mania? She was groggy and sore, worse off
than if she hadn't slept at all. Now she'd sealed off yesterday,
solidifying the events into permanence, like maybe while she

was still living inside that hideous day she could've still somehow stopped the destruction of her life.

The police could show up at any moment. The internet was a ghastly haze all around. Videos of Love und Romance squatted on YouTube, evil boxes spring-loaded between clips of dogs on skateboards and teens brushing lavender dust over eyelids. Reposts on Facebook and Instagram, emailed shares. Joan's old friends and colleagues texting each other, driving up the view count as they watched on repeat, straining for details of her genitals in the murky light, zooming in on stills of her pupils— was she high? But everyone knew Joan acted crazy while of sound mind.

She pulled on the barley linen shorts and wheat linen tunic she'd wear all summer, oversized and high-necked, like a boy's uniform. She stood in the center of the room, jittering. She'd already run. That was good, free, productive, but what next?

Sparrow. She had to meet them. Right now. Not because she wanted to, not because she was intrigued, but because Sparrow, out of anyone, was the most likely to have sniffed out Joan's trespasses. Joan could suss out what they knew, discover what information was floating around: how many videos, how many views. Her cheek twitched.

She knocked on Sparrow's door while fixing her gaze on Meredith's, willing her not to emerge and deem Joan a narcissist impatient for the slobbering of a fan.

Sparrow answered the door rumpled and bleary, face puffed from sleep, tabs of blond hair stuck out every which way. They clutched a pink stone, glinting with chips of mica. The way they held themself, legs apart, shoulders back, their whole manner, was so boy. "Joan Vole?" Joan could never help seeing her name in the rounded orange, sixties-style lettering printed on her albums and website. It was more a brand than a name at this point, tiny a brand as it was.

"Yes," Joan said, voice tight. Let them say right away what they knew; get it over with.

"Whoa, crazy." Sparrow bounced on their toes, skin beaming a pink light. "What are you doing here? Joan Vole! What the heck?" Their laugh spiked. They grabbed their mouth. "Wait, this is insane."

"Let me in," Joan said.

Sparrow pinched their T-shirt, unsticking it from their breasts, the stone still clamped in their fist. Joan slipped past them into the room. She steadied her feet on the ground so she'd appear stable, not like she'd slept for two hours after a brutal night. "Close the door."

Sparrow did. They wore pajamas: a pigeon-gray athletic T-shirt and sweatpants that drooped over their feet. Sorrow lurked in all fandoms. It was tragic to affix hope and power to a star who could never be known. A person must be empty to fill themselves with someone like Joan. Joan had believed in her music, had understood songwriting as the sole worthy pursuit of her life. But in the green sunshine of this morning, the idea of this guileless person using her music for nourishment made Joan wish she'd never made any. "I hear you're a fan of my work."

Sparrow's cheeks pinkened as they gazed at Joan, savoring her like a meal. "Yes." They gritted their teeth. "Seriously, I've been a fan since I was a teenager. Or like, even before." Were they that much younger? "God, this is weird. Why are you here? Are you teaching with us or something?"

"Yes." That she still had a job, several hours after Love und Romance, was itself a miracle.

Sparrow smoothed their T-shirt down their belly. "I heard

you might, last year. God. I'm sorry I'm so weird. I'm kinda, like, freaking." They glanced around like they might find a tray of cheese and chocolate to offer. Champagne. But there were only art supplies, each set nestled in its own polished containment: an olive dish of red crayons, a T-square with a ruler lying neatly on it and a protractor on top of that, a cookie jar of folded rags. They swung their tawny head toward the stacks of drawing boards, the colorful volumes of graphic novels supporting a banker's lamp, the pens inserted in the holes of a toy hunk of Swiss cheese. "I'm dying with you in my mess." They hopped around like they might lift off. "I'm obsessed with your stuff. That's weird to say. Is that bad? Is that weird? Like, I've loved you since *Bone Road*." *Bone Road* was Joan's first album, a run of fifty copies. She'd accrued no fans with *Bone Road*. No one hardly listened to it anymore. Sparrow bounced, rolling their eyes. "I mean, I came to it late, obviously. I was probably like five when it came out." Joan shuddered. "I love 'Bag Head.' And 'Fruit Fly.' I still have 'Fruit Fly' on my daily mix."

Joan vibrated to think of this dear, dedicated person listening to those ragged tracks, which rang like way too much these days whenever she chanced a listen. One lyric in "Fruit Fly" particularly made her cringe, an image of sunlight falling over road head on the BQE. She tingled to picture this little boy creature listening to that depraved scene. She wanted to prod Sparrow, ask what tours they'd seen, which their favorite tracks were. But caring about that stuff was what had fucked her. "I'm glad to be teaching with you." If they were so happy to see Joan, that meant they didn't know what Joan had done. If they were really a fan, and the news of Love und Romance was out there, they'd know. "You seem dedicated."

A burst of laughter. Sparrow hid their face with a soft paw. "It's overkill, I'm aware. I don't need half this junk."

"No," Joan said. "It's nice." The lie popped out. She couldn't linger too long on Sparrow's supplies, that pile of pages, inky at the edges.

"It's just summer is my best work time." The animation of their voice relaxed through Joan like a chemical. They gazed out the window, into the blinding green. "My brain's still unfurling from real teaching." They sank a hand into their blond waves. "I'll think of a project once I chill a second."

"Great." Joan tried to sound upbeat, tried not to imagine Sparrow crashing into the reality that art was an ego-feeding scam.

Sparrow slid over a stack of pages, flipped through. Each sheet boasted ten equal panels, perfectly aligned. Some were blank, and some featured block men speaking perfect block text. "This is what I did last summer, when I last had any time." They lifted a page crawling with blue pencil notes, figures crossed off, arrows to enlarge ears and swap background buildings and bushes. A tug in Joan that they'd feel comfortable sharing such raw work with someone they'd just met. They were plain and relaxed, no glimmer of shame.

When they pushed the stack back, a transparent leaf of paper slid out: a sketch of children, egg-headed and wonky with eyes like stars and pigtails fountaining out of their scalps, mouths sharp with fangs. It was drawn by a different hand: in the smooth, rubbery style of old-time cartoons. A figure rose from the children's midst, with a calm, dewy countenance: a mother with a beard and monumental tits, nipples like fish eyes watching in opposite directions, arms spread high, as though shielding her progeny from rain.

"What's that one?" Joan asked. "That's wild." She couldn't turn away from the fleshy family, quivering on the page, so alive.

"I was just playing." They tucked it under the other pages. "Oh my god. Joan Vole. I can't believe you're here." Their gaze was glassy and intense, knifing between Joan's legs.

"Right." Joan backed up toward the door. When she reached the threshold, Sparrow was still watching her.

*

Back in her room, Joan picked at her wrist. Had she been a freak? She had to be subtler, had to play normal. But more importantly, she had to stick close to Sparrow, had to be there, ready to act, the moment Sparrow found evidence of Love und Romance. Having a plan, small as it was, loosened her limbs.

And now to teach. At least this first meeting was only twenty minutes. She could do anything for twenty minutes. Part of her almost wished she had to teach for eight, nine hours. She was used to days structured and defined by music: writing in the morning, practice all afternoon, study and bureaucracy in the evening. Seventeen, nineteen hours of music a day, filling her brain to the brim.

She headed into campus, late already, picking her way up the steps embedded in the hillside, tensing for sirens. Above the lot, the campus was merry and collegiate, inviting feelings of privilege and good fortune with its grassy quads and pink brick, opposite in every way to the gray institutional commuter college she'd attended in Chicago. The grass was clipped golf-course short, shrubs controlled into cubes. Live oaks and dog-woods swayed at the fringes, an occasional whinny floating down from the pasture on the hill.

The landscape was arranged like a tender village to appease parents up from Atlanta and Baton Rouge. Her life for the last two decades was the opposite: grimy apartments reeking of urine, the rides of Coney Island towering in their 1960s wooden disrepair, bars serving pickled eggs, risers caved in and patched with electrical tape. Dark, close, festered rooms. Stage sets so bleak that a killer song, a really rousing, fierce song, scraped across the filth like the bright edge of a blade. And then, mornings after a show, waking in her bed with an alien dick lolling on her thigh.

The students, scampering late to class, were in high school, scrawny and knock-kneed with outsized glasses and frayed braids. Maybe this was a function of the kind of kid who decided, at fourteen, to march into the countryside and write. Rich kids, for one—Joan's parents never could've afforded camp—but also unimaginative. At their age Joan had made her own fun: slinking across the South Side of Chicago, sniffing out men who couldn't tell how young she was or didn't care or liked it. She hadn't peed on anyone yet, hadn't yet dreamed the possibility that a man might accept her cherished pursuit—but she did kneel on hospitality carpets in video game stores and suck dick, let guys poke fingers into her. She hated to be the grouch who intoned "live first," but what would kids like these write about? Prepared dinners and worksheets, beds crowded with plush unicorns? Had any of them peed into a sewer grate on the Magnificent Mile? Had any of them squeezed their arms until they went white, their strength fueled by years of fear that they were twisted, sick with a terminal illness of endless release? No, considering the way they clasped hands and dragged each other over cultivated grass. Not the way their voices issued, high-pitched and earnest, like birds. Not the way they held notebooks against undeveloped chests. They were beautiful in their ignorance.

She hadn't spoken to a teenager in any real way since Paige was one, had no idea how. But she just had to power through twenty minutes today, then two hours each weekday after that. The internet had a short shelf life. If she made it through camp, maybe there was some chance the world would've forgotten her by then. She could return to a skimpy version of regular life, go back to waitressing. The six thousand dollars would travel far, maybe even to the top of Norway.

Joan's classroom was a rec hall below the cafeteria, padded with seafoam cinderblocks and the frizzy carpet and slouching beanbags of a teen's basement hideaway. Odors of aluminum and ham oozed from above. An upright piano crouched in one corner—perhaps the reason for the room assignment—a sway-backed ping-pong table in another.

On the floor were three teenagers, already watching her from the moment she entered. Joan froze like a horse asked to cross the ice. Despite Georgina's warning, every time she'd envisioned teaching this class, she'd pictured a mob, rendered by their numbers into an anonymous mass. Her father had never learned the names of his students, referred to them by their attitude problems and blemishes, though she could tell when he liked someone if he gave them a particularly colorful name, like Widow's Peak Rage Monster or Orange Sneakers Spitball. With three, they were people. She teetered in the doorway, waiting for them to welcome her, for someone to recognize here was a star.

One of the girls had achieved adult-level dents under each eye. Her hair was cinder red, short and thick, a pixie cut, the kind of hair that probably grew so fast it had to be chopped back into submission, with a white stain on the bangs, like she'd aged inside one dot. She wore a slip handsewn with colored patches, like a goth farm girl. Another kid had a black forelock hiding a dark-skinned, genderless face, elbow balanced on strong knee, forearm dangling, a kid easy in the world. The remaining girl was the palest, blondest person Joan had ever encountered, with a blank pancake face and a rib cage braced for impact. Her hair was cotton tufts, drifting wherever it chose. She kicked around like she couldn't control her legs.

Joan inched into the room as the kids regarded her. She'd pictured being met with a burst of energy—surely someone would recognize her from the good days, at least vaguely—but they were silent in a way her audiences never were. Good audiences were loud with enthusiasm, bad ones loud with inattention. Imagine a whole bar greeting her with the bovine stares of these kids. Joan wriggled, the teens studying her every move. Eighteen minutes remained.

"Are you the teacher?" asked the pale one. She had a square jaw and a surprisingly husky voice. Her expression was that of a severe baby.

"Yes," Joan said.

The kids watched hungrily, eerily still, ready to suck out her substance. Normally the physical details of her audience were hidden in murky crowds amid the clink of tumblers and flavors of smoke. Now there were three pairs of eyes on her, intent in the fluorescence.

"Uh, okay," said the pale one, her hair unsettling itself into tangles as she moved. "So are you gonna, like, do anything?"

Joan peered over their heads. They fidgeted, arms pulling across the beanbags, spines flapping against the wall. She sat at the piano, her back to the keys. "I don't have any plans."

"You don't?" asked the redhead, voice cut with hurt. Her eyes were an intelligent, muddy brown that had seen too much.

"Why do we need a plan?" Joan stared at the kids. They stared back. This class would be like a meeting of the Gonewriters, all parties equal. She'd sit back, and discussion would froth up. But no one said a word. Minutes passed. Were they going to watch her for a thousand years? What was this, a prank? The kids whispered, urgent murmurings behind shelled palms.

"Do you know each other or something?" Joan finally asked.

"Duh, yeah," said the colorless girl, eagerly glancing between her classmates. "We met in the dorms or whatever."

"Oh." So they all lived in their private zone where they'd whisper about Joan after, debate the intrigue of their rockstar teacher.

The clock clacked overhead. A new minute had arrived. Endless new minutes in this endless life.

"So what are we even supposed to do today?" asked the redhead. "Icebreakers or something?"

"If you like." Introductions could kill time.

"Okay," said the pale girl, drawing out the word. "Where are you from?"

Joan hadn't planned to reveal anything about herself. But she supposed she could offer the minimum. "I'm from Brooklyn." A lie. "I'll teach you songwriting." Another lie. She was hit again with the insanity of teaching music when she only wanted to flee as far from it as possible.

"Wow, *amazing*," the girl intoned, shaking her cloud of white hair so it rattled into place.

This kid's flat tone scraped Joan's ears. But the attitude was fine. It was better.

"I'm Lula," said the pale girl, from under her dry white bob. She wore a tucked-in shirt, structured, with epaulets, sandals, and thick athletic socks. Her posture was rigid, like someone had scared her into it. "I'm from Durham. I'm fourteen. Um, I don't know what I'm supposed to say. I enjoy eating fish."

"Have you been here before?" asked the redhead, who,

despite her handmade outfit, spoke with the confidence of middle age. "I don't remember you. What instruments do you play?"

"No. And none."

"Do you sing?" the redhead asked, cocking her head.

"No."

The students weren't even looking at Joan. Couldn't they see she was cool? Surely they considered their schoolteachers old and dull. And here Joan was, young enough, fierce, hot. How would she ever get through this? "Why did you select this class?" she managed.

The pale girl set her lips. "My first choice was fiction. But for some dumbass reason they canceled it."

"They canceled it because they believe in us," said the kid with the dark forelock. As soon as he moved, there was no question he was male. He had an ease only a boy could claim, the clear skin and set-back shoulders of a rich kid. Even his shirt was expensive, glossy, like hotel sheets. "Everyone was an idiot signing up for fiction all the time, so they were like, you know what? If you can't appreciate poetry and playwriting and all the genres you need more than a gram of brain to process, fuck that. You don't deserve fiction. Like songwriting." He looked up at Joan. "Super complex."

"Oh sure," said the pale girl, rolling her eyes.

Was Joan supposed to stop them from swearing? Maybe, but she wouldn't. "Okay, Lulu."

"Lula," Lula said. "It's feminine."

"So is Lulu," said the girl with the white spot in her red hair, like death had touched her with one finger. Her slip was trimmed with sepia rickrack. "What? You think Lulu is a boy's name?"

"Whatever," Lula said.

"Because I've never heard of a boy named Lulu," said the white-spot girl.

"Now that you mention it," Lula said, "it's kind of a hot name for a dude."

Joan raised her voice. "Lula. Why did you list it second?"

"What?" Lula's mouth hung open. Her eyes were beady and blank. Joan wanted to slap some color into the girl, but her hand would spring back like the girl was made of marshmallow. Lula was one of those nerds who'd turned mean from years of abuse. "Oh, like songwriting, you mean?" Lula said, as though the first half of their conversation had taken place years ago. "I didn't. I listed poetry."

She fluttered her eyelids. But Joan wasn't hurt. She would've put songwriting tenth on a list, one hundredth. "Why third?"

"I can sing a few songs okay. 'Kumbaya,' I guess, 'cause we're at camp. It goes, 'Kumbaya my lord, kumbaya. Oh lord, kumbaya.' So sick."

Lula was classically tone deaf. "That is a pleasing rendition." Joan sounded like a malfunctioning robot. How would she manage six weeks of this?

"Victor Mar Ruiz," said the long-haired boy, sitting forward with a fluid confidence Joan longed for in some lizard part of her. How did he learn to move like that? His shirt sparkled with buttons that were translucent and fine as gems, but he wore it like it was nothing. "I'm from Florida. I'm fourteen too. I come here every year because I want to be a rockstar. Or, like, however close to rockstar is a practicable goal." Joan winced. "All year I'm in private lessons and a band with my friends at school." He bared his teeth at Lula, more threat than sign of solidarity. Joan appreciated his ferocity, this tiny, pretty carnivore, a stoat or wolverine. A flare of shame ignited the back of her skull. She couldn't bear it if this pretty, fey boy had witnessed her darkest moment. He was the kind of kid up to the minute on every cultural drama. "I play tuba and harmonica." He slapped his knee. "I'm working hard at my craft. I love Dream Gum." He grinned at Joan like she'd applaud his alternative taste. "I could listen to *Ode to Queen Magnet* for one hundred years." Obsessive, lazy taste bugged Joan, though it was the root of her "Lakeshore" royalties. She was more charmed when people's interests ranged widely and adventurously. The way she'd found Paige crouched over death metal one night, warming herself to Fruit Bat Sandwich. "My songwriting influences are the people I meet in life. Like, their bodies and faces."

Joan vowed to go to any length to prevent Victor from writing about bodies and faces. "That's a poor idea."

"What?" said Victor, eyes red-rimmed, like he'd never once been told no.

"I mean, sorry," Joan said. "That sounds like a fertile field." For what? "For artistic. Expression?" The words bumped out.

The kids stared. "Are you okay?" Lula asked, mouth ajar.

"Of course." Joan smoothed her shorts. The linen was stiff against her body. She'd have to acclimate to this new uniform: neutral Joan. Class must be almost over by now.

"I'm Agnes," said the girl with short red hair, clutching a drumstick so firmly the wood creaked. "Thirteen. Class baby." She pronounced the phrase as though it contained extreme irony, although, even with the dark circles under her eyes and the faux-goth slip and the dot of old hair, she could've passed for eleven. "My mom wants me to 'explore the fun side of music.' I live in Battery Park City."

Joan hated hearing the name of a New York neighborhood, though certainly Agnes's was a different New York. Some carpeted, multiroom apartment overlooking the Hudson, an undocumented nanny, a little New York dog.

Agnes cheersed her drumstick.

"Let me guess," said Lula. "You play drums."

"Nope," said Agnes, pulling up the strap of her slip where it had fallen off her shoulder. "Trained on classical guitar since I was five."

Joan touched the soft dent at the base of her neck. She'd longed to play guitar when she was even smaller than that. She'd seen one on TV, in the arms of a new wave hero. He'd clutched it to his groin, sharp nose pointed at the crowd, strumming with stiff wrists as though the guitar was a dangerous pet. She'd never seen a person engage with any object so fiercely, like he was at war with it. How did that jangly, fierce sound issue from a box of wood? But her father had said no. She'd had to wait until that cheapo at the garage sale at fourteen—her world for fifteen dollars—and never benefited from a lesson. She pressed her fingers harder until she couldn't breathe.

"Cool," said Victor, in a tempered voice.

"Except now I quit forever." The room went still. Agnes jerked a phone out of her pocket. "Want to see?"

Joan's hands iced into claws. She wanted to snatch the phone, explode it on the floor. Why was she so stupid? Of course no one could keep kids from their phones. "Phones aren't allowed." Her voice was brittle.

"It's an antique," Agnes said. "So it is allowed, actually. Pre-Wi-Fi generation." She jiggled the device, the hem of her slip swinging around her ankles. "Just a bunch of shit I transferred from my real phone."

"Doy," said Lula. "We've all got old ones for camp."

Joan flinched from the screen's glare, glinting with all it could know if only its insides were tweaked.

Agnes jumped onto the corpse of a beanbag, raising the phone above her head with two hands. Closer to the fluorescent ceiling tubes, her hair lit flame red. A cascade of notes burst out: Villa-Lobos's Étude No. 7. Famously difficult—the selection of a gunner. But Agnes—and it *was* Agnes, on that tiny screen, bird face perched over her instrument, hair longer then, a scarlet waterfall—played with a gentle touch, a slow confidence, the way a much older musician would. Patiently letting the beauty unspool. Joan floated on the intricacies of the notes. And then, Agnes's tremolo: fluid, quicker, impressive, but restrained. Perfect evenness of attack. Picking up speed, fast now, really fast, but dead accurate, the clear phrasing of multiple voices. She sounded like two guitars; a guitar and a harp. The tinny audio of the phone ran under the piece like a bad current, that tangy ring and compression, the harsh transients, the echo of the room and the limits of the recording, but none of those imperfections mattered. Joan held her throat, her face hardening into a familiar mask of false cheer.

"Whoa," said Victor, gaping at Agnes.

There was genius in the room. Joan wanted to drop down under the tiles and disappear.

"Yeah." Agnes's lips whitened, pressing into a line. The spot on her hair bobbed. In the video, it had been allowed to grow out into a white streak, a pale ribbon twisting as she played.

"Wait, this is real, though," said Victor. "You're the real deal." He looked at Joan, but she wouldn't give the kid the satisfaction. "Were you on TV and stuff?"

Joan's muscles clenched.

"A few times, I guess," Agnes said. "But that's just circus." She bit her lip, glancing at Joan. "And now I don't play anymore, like, ever, so it doesn't matter. Dropped out of music school, canceled everything."

"That's dope, though," said Lula, raising her voice over the playing. "TV? Holy Christ."

"Play it in real life," Victor said. "Georgina has a guitar. At least she did last year."

Joan snatched the phone from Agnes's fist and hit stop. All the golden notes free fell into silence. Such violent silence after the velvet rise and fall of the song. Agnes was stony, but her fingers trembled, curling up without her phone. Joan had longed for that level of intensity, would've delighted in a childhood indentured to an instrument: the indulgence of six, eight, ten hours of daily practice, calluses shocking on plump paws, custody of a multi-thousand-dollar junior guitar. The pressure of competitions and recitals, a mother leaning over her, stickers on instrument cases. A family who cared, organization and purpose and the life-shaping goal of music. She could've handled herself with a structure like that, taken control over her pissing; she could be a better artist now.

"Let's move on," Joan said, handing Agnes back her phone. Agnes lowered herself from the beanbag, slip drooping from her clavicle, rickrack peeling off and dangling. She sat on her phone like she'd crush the juice out. "Who even are you?" she asked.

Finally, someone had asked. "Joan Vole." She spoke the name with weight.

"Pleased to meet you, Mrs. Vole," said Victor. He offered his hand as though they were at a business function.

"Joan Vole," Lula said. "Yeah, right. That's not your real name."

"It is," Joan said, because it had been for nearly as long as any other.

The kids regarded her as though the name meant nothing. Lula checked the high basement window as though she longed to clamor through it. Sunlight caught on her white cheeks.

Shame prickled Joan's neck. Meredith being ignorant, or

any adult, was nothing like these kids watching her, as though all her traction, her biggest venues, her radio play, her tours looping through the same colleges in the same quirky towns— Ann Arbor, Lawrence, Ithaca, Omaha, Salt Lake—meant nothing. Her spit stuck to the walls of her mouth, gummy and impossible to breathe through. "Stop looking at me," she snapped. They leaned away. But the clock. Relief swept her. "Class is over."

*

Joan crossed the quad, calm blanketing her. She'd barely thought of Love und Romance all through class. And being anonymous was nice, in a way. Soon even Paige would forget the Martin had ever belonged to anyone else. Joan liked the idea of her old guitar up on levels of stages she'd never achieve: playing for a thousand people, ten thousand, alongside the Lucky Badgers, or better. Bands bigger than Joan ever could've hoped for: Crowd Sorcerers and Rover's My Man and Dream Gum. Abigail Westerly. The Cat Spins. Maybe even Buddy Storm, who'd plugged Paige in an interview in *Rolling Stone*, accomplishing what Joan had tried for years to do for Paige in his single line of mixed metaphors: *Paige Serratt is a bug-eyed field mouse who sidles up to poison you with her unconscionable alien squeak.* His private letter was smarmier: *You're a sexy girl. But when you open your mouth, I don't even care.* Soon, Paige wouldn't long to play with any particular band, no matter how great, but would be the main act, up there with the Martin. Maybe certain fans would figure out whose guitar it was—it stood to reason Paige would absorb Joan's fans the way she always had, the way Joan had never had wide enough appeal to absorb Paige's—and maybe those ex-fans would see the Martin and remember Joan: not her last, shameful public act, but some old concert, the snappy brutalisms she growled between songs, the way, when she finished a set, she vanished while the last note still rang. Maybe they'd wonder where she was, and they'd never guess: up in Norway, working in a gift shop not even wired with a sound system. Organizing leather reindeer, commemorative shards of lava, potato alcohol, troll statues, herring paste. Silence collecting over fjords, between the crags of the most jagged mountains of her life. Crisp, delicious silence.

8

THAT AFTERNOON, HEADING TO ORIENTATION, A SPIDER of dread clutched Joan. All her life she'd deemed office jobs death. She couldn't picture how she'd dress for one—in what, a blouse?—or sit naturally, keeping her twisted thoughts out of her mouth. She'd been a waitress through college and for her first ten years in New York, scraped by on music after that, her finances floated by gig work here and there—catering and filling in on nights of heavy service at old restaurants. Orientation would be the closest she'd come to a straight job.

Before the meeting, the teachers circulated in the second-floor classroom, with its drop ceiling and modular table and none of the old-time Southern charm of its proud brick facade. Joan had never been to a meeting in her life, but she recognized its smell: chalk, stale coffee, the sweetness of rot.

Sparrow was nowhere. Joan stayed on her side of the room, across from where Meredith clamped the two male teachers in bear hugs. This was the largest crowd she'd been in since New York, and she kept her spine to the wall.

"I can't believe it's been a year," said a bald guy named Willie, with a chaotic beard and long eyelashes. Meredith watched him through half-lowered lids as he rolled up his sleeves, revealing a tattoo of a faceless girl with braids. Meredith shook out her hair, crisp and aggressively sculpted.

"This old room," cried the other guy, shag of cinnamon red hair bouncing. He marveled at the greasy white paint and ground beef carpet as though admiring the ornamentation of a palace. He recounted legends of a ghost who lived in the ventilation system, warring bands of groundhogs, a derecho that had knocked out power one summer, forcing teens to pick two cans each of food from a grab bag for dinner: lima beans and beets, peaches and water chestnuts, canned bread and soda.

The redhead was as skinny as Joan, but longer and narrower, like a worm that fed off the human brain. He marched up to her with a stiff, charming walk, floppy hair bouncing. "I've been too shy to say hi." He had the steady gaze of someone who'd never been shy in his life. Gay guys normally weren't fans. "I'm honored to teach with you, actually."

She steadied her feet. He could say what he needed about her work—if she didn't let him, all summer she'd have to suffer his hope for an opening. She hated that "actually" fans tacked on—"I actually really like your music"—as though they were so cool and rare to know her.

He crossed his wrists over his stomach, cheating his shoulders in. His nose was the long bulb of a marsupial. "Sparrow was obsessed with you."

"If you'll excuse me." She stepped around him, but he shifted into her path.

Sparrow entered in a shirt with darts, clearly for a woman, yellow hair side-parted over the bubble of their forehead. Their focus skidded to Joan, softening as though at a puppy. Joan looked away, cheeks flaming. She fixated on the gaunt cheeks of the floppy-haired guy.

He pulled back his lips. "Fuck, and yesterday."

The room whitened. Joan should've stayed in the dorm. "No," she said, the word hissing out before she could stop it, like a password. Like an option on an automated service call.

His eyebrows hitched up. "What? I meant you must be exhausted."

How was that his reaction to what she'd done? Joan's brain looped like reality had shifted.

He squinted in concern. "I mean, you drove straight from New York in one night. I heard you got here at four in the morning."

The relief was painful, like fingers unfreezing too fast. But then, filling the opening the relief had carved, despair. For the rest of her life she'd clench her jaw like this at every interaction, waiting to see if her conversation partner knew.

Georgina slid into the room as though conveyed, eyes fizzing. She took her seat like a queen. She didn't have the gait of someone who'd just watched one of her faculty members piss on a fan. Joan's limbs loosened, jiggling like restless snakes at her side. Everyone dropped into chairs around the conference table. Sparrow sat opposite Joan, notebook and pens aligned, arms settled on the table, leaning forward. They opened their notebook to a sketch of a man-faced heron. They glanced at Joan.

"Joan," Georgina said. "I called, but I couldn't reach you."

Joan sat up straighter, trying to remember how her father took charge of his classroom in the morning, before the day had worn him down. "I don't have a phone."

"You'll have to remedy that." She made a mark on her paper and then thrust up her child-sized arms. "Everyone, welcome to a fresh summer at Merry Writers."

Sparrow clapped. Their pudgy face had a low-key appeal, like the middle school kid contemporaries don't find cute, but years later, flipping through old yearbooks, everyone wonders why not. Joan's pulse settled watching them.

"Introductions," said Georgina.

"And say your pronouns," Meredith said, setting back her shoulders and winking at Sparrow.

"Right," said Georgina. "And mention your favored pedagogical tidbit. Mine is always ask questions to which you know not the answer."

Joan imagined her father ordered to limit his questions in basic arithmetic to noncommutative algebraic geometry, the only realm of math he'd ever admitted was beyond his capability. What a humane, cheerful burst Georgina would've been in Joan's dark-walled childhood apartment.

Meredith introduced herself, then the redhead, who was called Chester and lived in L.A. "My students write a 'play in a day.' One mythical beast. One laborer. One uncommon veg. And it has to make me cry."

Willie introduced himself into the table, pulling on his tattoo and rocking, bald head catching the green of the fluorescent panels. "I'm from West Virginia. I live in West Virginia." He looked up with clenched teeth, stretching his tattoo girl like taffy. "Poetry."

"I'm Sparrow. They/them." Meredith nodded deeply, like she'd gifted Sparrow the pronouns. "The pedagogy for my students is the same as for myself: make whatever comics feel urgent. Whether it's cramped, fussy drawings of the hospital where they were born or a comedy of unemployed owls."

A song bloomed in Joan: Sparrow scampering between the uneven drawings of teenagers, indicating a crooked cat ear here, a missing alligator tooth there, kids waving brushes in excitement—yes, Sparrow was right; yes, that tooth was all that comic needed, the perfect pointiness between deadly sharp and satirically rounded, that wash of cloudy ink, that dimple.

My owl needs a bigger head, this donkey's back is turning red. Joan pushed her nails into her arm until the shard of song evaporated. Her flesh popped open, and the urge to write dissolved.

"Joan?" Georgina asked. "You went white."

She eased her nails from her flesh and turned her arm to hide the blood.

"I live in Brooklyn," said Sparrow. They watched Joan, serious and careful, though they couldn't have seen the cuts from where they sat. "I graduated two years ago. Now I teach at a public high school."

A room of teenagers demanding a day's attention. There was no way Sparrow had time for their own art.

"Gorgeous, thank you." Georgina pointed her pen at Sparrow. "If you're taking notes, can you type them up after?"

Sparrow grimaced, then nodded a dozen times.

"Joan." Georgina turned the disc in her ear by one revolution.

"Songwriting. I live in Brooklyn."

Willie lit up. "You a singer?"

Joan's shoulders sank. This camp was some other reality, where her years of work had dissolved. "My pedagogical technique is teaching."

"Could you be more specific?" Georgina asked.

"I wasn't finished." She had been.

Georgina raised both hands with a game smile.

"Teaching songs without origin." The words fell out. Yes. That was what she'd do. If she were planning to teach anything, she'd teach songs that were lovely and affecting but dragged no cult of personality. Songs that transcended the fallibility of individuals.

"Interesting," Georgina said. "What does that mean, exactly?"

"Songs without authors," Joan said, "that have absorbed into culture."

"That's so cool," Sparrow said, leaning across the table. "I never heard of anyone teaching that."

"Authorship is fairly central here," Georgina said carefully. "But also, haven't those songs been around for ages? That doesn't really seem like something you can create anew?"

"We can," Joan said, emphatically. Insisting made her want to all the more. Music itself wasn't bad, after all, only the jealous poison it soaked up.

Georgina struck a stack of papers against the table to even it. "Well, I'll admit I'm curious."

"Pronouns," whispered Meredith.

Joan's skin contracted. There'd been a rumor, started in the nineties, though circulating still, that Joan had a penis—"a tiny cock," in the words of the fan who claimed to have spotted it while watching Joan urinate outside a club. "She."

Georgina reviewed what to do in case of Fire, Derecho, Mandated Reporter Occurrence, Conflict Between Students, Incidence of Disturbing Work, Intruder with Intent. "Joan, you'll need a phone for emergency communication, as well as for our online student system. By tomorrow would be ideal." She asked Sparrow to schedule meetings with the teachers and to help with photocopying in the office. Sparrow's brow knit. "Lesson Cycles are due tomorrow. There's a computer cluster in the basement of McClurg. Naturally, it's forbidden to students."

Joan squeezed her cuts until they filled with blood. Somewhere in this green landscape crouched a roomful of computers.

A few steps, a few clicks, and she'd draw up the new limitations of her life. Blood snaked down her arm.

The team broke, gathering the notebooks and computers and the sweaters they'd had on hand for the air conditioner. Before Joan could move toward Sparrow, they shot out the door.

"Joan," Willie whispered, blanching above his sloppy beard, even his naked scalp going white. "You're injured."

Joan touched the commas of blood on her arm. Her neck flushed with dark heat. "It's nothing."

His scalp bobbed, pure ivory, as smooth and even-toned as sculpture. He watched her, picking at his tattoo. With a man she wouldn't fear getting close. She was a machine at boundaries with men.

"Hey," he said. "You're a musician." He spoke as though bearing news that she'd won an award. He had deep eyes, shiny but complex, eyes that passed off confusion for emotional genius. Joan swelled with affection.

"Yes." She couldn't help chirping. Finally someone knew who she was, the good part. He'd never have regarded her with eyes like those if he'd seen the video.

"Sweet," he said. "Did you ever put out an album?"

Joan snorted, but his shiny eyes held steady. He wasn't kidding. "Yes." Her voice was tired. "I have put out an album." She had eleven albums.

"Did you ever meet Axl Rose?"

Dry air itched her nostrils. "I did not meet Axl Rose, no."

"Did you meet Jerry Garcia? You know, from the Grateful Dead?" He raised those pretty lashes. His lips were chubby for a man. They'd feel soft against her tongue.

"You have a nice face," Joan breathed, low enough that no one else could hear.

"What?" He stepped back. "But you fuck girls."

A dime of piss soaked her underwear. That word, in his mouth. "I really don't."

"Come on, Willie," Meredith said, walking over to touch his sleeve. "I'll make us nachos."

*

The group wandered across the headache-green quad in a close pack, shoulder to shoulder, as though they didn't have weeks ahead together. Sparrow kept to the outskirts, lip caught under their teeth, mumbling. Their hand, when it wandered up to palm the back of their neck, was firm, striped with ink, a hand that could hold Joan steady.

"You haven't hammered out the last day of your Lesson Cycle?" Chester asked Willie, scraping back his red shag. "That's risky behavior."

Willie jammed his hands in his pockets, tattoo girl twitching. "Yeah, but all my other days are solid."

"We work up to the last day," Chester said. His fingers had left greasy troughs in his hair. "The last day is where the strands of the course weave together and form a tapestry." His shag bounced around his skull, springing back into its natural shape. "You don't have any day if you don't have the last day."

"It's okay," Meredith said, voice soft. "You'll wrap up tonight. And then the fun can start." She lifted her arms over her head and waved them around like a middle-aged mom drumming up enthusiasm. "Maybe we can take one of our welcome walks all over campus." She set a hand cautiously on Willie's spine.

"Fuck," Willie said, but his shoulders loosened under her touch.

"I finished mine," Sparrow said. "But I've got other stuff."

"Their comics," Meredith told the others, nodding somberly. "They want to focus."

Joan couldn't see a foot in front of her while she was figuring out a song, stumbling down to the bodega for cheese on an English muffin, whacking into pedestrians, mumbling harmonies. Sparrow didn't have the look. No hard jaw, no hunted skittishness, like any second they'd lunge after the tail of inspiration.

"Sparrow always says they're gonna work all summer," Chester said. "But then they hang anyway if you harass them enough."

Sparrow flashed a set of even teeth.

"That's true," Meredith said. "She can't say no, so she just doesn't sleep." Sparrow tensed at the pronoun. Joan tried to make eye contact, but they looked away. "I'm always knocking on her door at two in the morning telling her to cut it out and get some rest."

"Whatever," Sparrow said.

"I'm sure your Lesson Cycle is perfect anyway," Willie said, rubbing his bald head with one hand and his beard with the other. "It's no fair. You're a 'professional teacher.'"

"Why does it matter?" Joan said. "It's just some red-tape paperwork, right? When it comes down to it, you just go to class and say whatever."

Meredith crinkled her nose. "Actually, we work hard on our Lesson Cycles."

The other teachers watched the grass as it passed under them, toxic and bright.

"Even if you feel that way," Joan said, "surely no one will bother to look at our plans."

The whole group stared at her. "Who?" Chester said. "Georgina?" He laughed. "Are you joking?"

"Not very carefully, surely," Joan said. "She has other obligations."

"Oh, she's very busy," Chester said. The depth of his voice and his serious, slender face promised he knew everything that had ever happened at this camp. "She doesn't sleep. You see how she runs this place alone. But the students are her priority. She wouldn't care if we all died so long as sturdy replacements sprouted the next morning."

So Georgina was the only admin. No young employees, rooting through the internet.

"That's not true," Sparrow said. They turned to Joan. "Don't listen to these jerks."

"Joan." Chester cleared his throat as the group crossed through the open field between the classroom buildings and the dorm. "We'd be honored if you'd take a welcome walk with us tomorrow evening. We like to check out the horses. We didn't know if you want to be social."

"I don't," Joan said.

He flinched like she'd hit him. "Right." He turned to Sparrow. "Will you? Or too much work?"

They gritted their teeth. "I have a lot, but, I mean, okay."

Joan clenched. She'd been certain Sparrow would pick their art over socializing. As the group scattered to their different paces, Joan hustled to catch Sparrow. When she finally managed to draw up alongside them, she was so relieved that she had nothing prepared to say. She fell in line beside them. They beamed at Joan, then pointed their gaze down into the grass. The two of them walked along like that, shoulder to shoulder, up and down the jade swells of campus. They were exactly the same height, all parts aligned: hip to hip, neck to neck, ear to ear. But their weights were so different, the swing of their bodies. Sparrow's golden solidity was calming, like they could

anchor Joan to earth, and as they walked, Joan's pace went syrupy with leisure.

They took several synced footsteps without a word. They
could go on like this forever, in simple, fresh silence, march-
ing past the dorm and into the field and then the woods and
the real dense woods as vines subsumed them, leaves brushing
their temples and stuffing their nostrils, kudzu wrapping their
ankles as they penetrated the dense emerald unknown.

"Hey," said Sparrow, voice shaky. "Joan." They spoke the
name like they were still getting used to it. "You don't model,
do you?"

Joan laughed. If people thought her hot it was only the way
a coyote in the grass was hot.

"I mean—sorry." Sparrow pawed their face, muffling a giggle. "Not like that. I mean you could. You so could!" Their face
lit red. They patted their cheeks like they could scrape the color
off. "But I meant, like, artist modeling. Like for drawing."

"No." Joan would not participate in the production of art.

Sparrow held her gaze, then dropped it. "That's okay. It
sorta sucks to hold still."

Look at that innocent face, so clear, so wakeful. Joan needed
to draw them closer, couldn't let them escape to their work.
"Hey, I'm sorry no one gets your pronouns."

Sparrow shrugged, rubber shoulders bouncing. "They're
acclimating." Their voice was plain, like they really didn't
mind. "Like, I don't know. My parents still get it wrong, but
they threw a whole party when I came out. With the purple
cake and everything." They snorted. "It was dumb."

"Whoa." Paige kicked out for fucking a girl and now, just
a few years later, a gender cake. "I have a thing with pronouns
too." The words popped out.

Sparrow ran their gaze up and down Joan, so fast Joan

nearly missed it. "Really?" The word so clear and hopeful Joan could've hugged them.

"Actually, a pronoun sort of changed the course of my career." She walked taller. That was true. See? They actually had quite a bit in common.

"You mean like how Meredith found some rumor on Reddit that you have a dick?"

Joan's legs stiffened. Meredith had looked her up. Sparrow grinned. So they found the rumor cool. Stars flamed in Joan's core.

"There's this whole complicated story." Joan filled her lungs. "I fell in love with this person."

Sparrow's walk loosened into an easy saunter. They watched Joan like they were memorizing every word. "What was her name?"

The "Lakeshore" boy's homely, dear face still got Joan, popping into her head, a zap in the stomach. "It was two decades ago. I wrote a song about him. My best song."

Sparrow's focus sharpened under their cowlick. "Him?"

Joan's head went heavy. "Yes."

"Like a trans dude?"

Joan twisted like she could escape the sunshine. "No."

"But that's a gay song. All my gay friends love it." Sparrow laughed. "My friend, like, fucked to it at a stoplight party, I'm pretty sure."

Joan could never get over "gay." No matter who appropriated it for what, it was always like a kid in the hall accusing, *kid, you gay*, which had happened to Joan often enough after Bethany. She hadn't cared back then, had almost been proud, like at least there was something the boys at school could call her without gagging in her face. Imagine if, instead of licking Bethany's pussy, she'd peed on a dude? At root, most guys could understand a good pussy licking. "It was gay." Community Village rose into view. "It is." "Lakeshore" was off leading its own life without her, starting rumors, shifting identities. "I wrote it the way it happened, but when I finished, I had to twist its heart. So I changed the pronouns. And it worked." They padded over a strip of dead grass, its green having leaked out.

"That's cool." Sparrow's expression clouded in thought. "But that was a long time ago, right?"

"It feels like someone else's life."

"I get it." They slanted their gaze at Joan as they bounced over the hills. "I dated a cis dude, like a thousand years ago. Unfortunate consequence of comphet, right?"

"Actually, no."

Sparrow turned to Joan. Their boy's face, so striking it stopped her lungs. Some people were so perfect it was hard to believe they just walked around on dirty grass in the world. "You're straight?" They said the word like it was a joke.

"Yeah." She'd never said so to any fan. But she could say anything to Sparrow.

"Oh." Sparrow blinked. "Whoa."

Joan had to be careful, had to get this right. She'd never spoken truthfully about the song. "I didn't set out for the song to be gay. It was more complex than that. I'm not sure what happened—my process blurs because I can't eat or sleep or even really leave the house when I'm writing. And then one day I wake up and it's done."

Sparrow swung their arms wide as they walked. "Totally. Sometimes I look at old comics and I'm like, did a man draw this? An old, weird man with shaky hands?"

"Exactly, exactly." Joan's breath was fast in her mouth. "I'm feeling my way around a song, trying to figure out how to make it true to itself. And that's the route I found for this one."

"Huh," said Sparrow, their voice easy and wondering. They'd reached the door of Community Village. The teachers were on their heels, would catch them any minute. "It's cool talking to you." They kicked the grass, then looked up, the steadiness of their gaze a shock. "I still can't believe you're here."

"I'm here," Joan said.

And then the teachers were upon them, scurrying up to chat.

9

THAT EVENING, GEORGINA ASKED TO MEET PRIVATELY.
Joan's limbs fused like steel, crossing the quad. She rushed over the field as fast as she could, the open air itching her. Once Georgina let her into the cozy office, her body relaxed, lamplight welcoming her into its amber gel. Joan hadn't even landed in the facing chair, hadn't even inhaled that old-lady smell of skin and rose or compressed the embroidered cushions before Georgina launched in with the reserve of a long-suffering mother.

"Joan, I must ask, is there a reason you haven't filled out the paperwork?" How were Georgina's teeth so white in such old age? What life had she led to preserve them so perfectly? It was depressing to consider.

"No." Joan held her gaze. She'd slipped by untracked until now, didn't make enough to file taxes. She feared opening that door lest a lifetime of untended bureaucracy slap her down with its dry, fluttering weight. Lest someone deem her entire life illegal.

Georgina lowered her head. "You got the phone, though, right?"

"No."

"Joan. I need to be able to communicate with my faculty, even about small matters. And you should be logging daily notes about the students on the system. Don't you need a phone to get around? I mean, even personally?"

"No."

Georgina sipped from her chunky mug. A soft chuckle. "You have a fierce spirit. We'll work well together."

A prickle spread across Joan's scalp. Her spirit had so rarely been admired, at least not respectfully.

"You probably think I traded my life for this camp." Georgina let both hands flop into her lap. "And you're right." Her bulk gathered inside her blouse. She was proud of this empire of coddled children. "But I considered myself something of an artist, too, at one time." She knuckled a framed photograph. A young blond with a necktie wound around her head gloated over a cornucopia of manuscripts. If it weren't for the typewriter and the haziness of the print, Joan would've guessed it was Georgina's daughter. "Corny, I'm sure. It reminds me I was young, too, once, with my own ideas."

"You help kids so they can accomplish what you didn't?" Joan would die if she had to stare all day at herself at twenty-two, hugging the Martin, innocent to all that lay ahead. But there wasn't a trace of bitterness in Georgina's smile. Either one.

"Whether they do or not is their business. They leave here with the skills to write and to appreciate literature, no matter the field they ultimately select. Now. To the matter at hand." She leaned out of reach of the lamplight.

Chubby packets loomed between them. Each teacher's hope for the summer. Crammed with what? Silly little prompts? Clever asides already mapped out, assuring the teachers' jokes were cold in their graves by week one? Musings on "craft"? Which, if you had to think about craft that hard, you weren't cut out to be a writer anyway. Joan couldn't imagine applying the clumsy weapon of craft to one of her songs, poking its flanks until the magic puffed out in farts.

Georgina cocked her head at Joan's stillness. "Where's your Lesson Cycle?"

"I don't have it."

The aperture of Georgina's mouth shrank to a dark coin. "Joan. I'm firm with the teachers on this point."

Joan shifted on her seat. She wanted to be out in the world, running around. In her life she never had to sit down and listen to anyone. She shouldn't have even attended this ridiculous meeting. "I have a different approach."

"The Lesson Cycle isn't approach dependent. Look." Georgina set her elbows on the table. "Sparrow, for instance, plans their lessons around the interests of each particular class." Georgina beamed. Sparrow was her perfect student. "Last year, everyone was making comics about food—talking cheeseburgers, a melancholy slice of cake, dancing lentils." Georgina bounced her fingers across the table like the lentils' feet.

"But I have a branching strategy. So if I try one unit"—was "unit" the right word?—"and that unit is unsuccessful, I'll branch to a radically different pedagogy."

Georgina squinted at Joan. "If that's how you prefer to teach and it's worked for you, I can't see why not. But the strategy you've outlined calls for an even more elaborate Lesson Cycle than I'd normally require."

That molasses guilt again, crawling up Joan's arms from her fingertips.

"How did today go?"

What could she report? Agnes jumping on a beanbag and blaring a video, which was probably forbidden, no matter how ancient the device? Lula challenging Joan's every word? Certainly the meeting could've been worse, but there was nothing Joan could see her way to bragging about. "We introduced ourselves."

"Okay." Georgina closed her eyes. A woman in her eighties running a camp for teens. She should be covered by a quilt in a mountain cabin, feet soaking in brine. "Class starts in earnest tomorrow. Walk me through your day."

Joan had resolved not to think about teaching until she was in the classroom. Even if she could never be an artist again, still, she had pride. She'd never noodle for hours over lesson plans. "Why?"

"Well, Joan, because I'm your supervisor and I'm asking you."

Joan had liked, as a kid, when her mother snapped at her, maybe because she was so rarely around long enough to bother. Kindness sat worse. "We'll do names again."

"Reinforce introductions. Okay." She ticked a finger. "And then?"

She'd be lucky if they got through that much. Then she'd sit around on the piano bench. The kids could talk if they wanted. But she wasn't going to push them if they didn't engage. "That's all I have planned."

Georgina laughed as though Joan was kidding. "You're a trip, Joan. Seriously. What next?"

Joan hated to obey, but there was a fierce quality to this woman that she liked, strung like wire under her skin. She could lie—whatever. "I'll walk through a song of no provenance. For background."

Georgina sat forward in relief, as though she'd expected Joan's first day to be sex games and an amphetamine grab bag. "Lovely—examples they can use as inspiration for their own work. Perhaps you'll autopsy a song to demonstrate structures they can build on?"

Joan's students would not write their own personal songs. No way could she bear a young person's fame hunger. "Probably not."

"Joan. Can I ask, what is your larger aim?"

Joan longed to spit back some nasty remark. This lady had hired her. Couldn't she trust Joan enough to teach her own class even one single time? "It's not that they won't be writing." She spoke as vehemently as if this class would actually occur. "In fact, I'm stripping down the work to writing alone. To separate it from all the sticky shit."

"And what, may I ask, is 'sticky shit'?"

"Ego." The word cramped through her.

A smile forced up the hunks of meat of Georgina's cheeks. "They're fourteen, Joan. They're only ego."

There was no way Joan knew more about teens than this woman. But still. "I want to do it this way." Why was she fighting for a plan she wouldn't execute? She might as well tell Georgina the kids would write personal songs, happily, forever, piles of paper teetering, intimate lyrics humming out of the guileless holes in their heads.

Georgina worked the delicate flesh at her temples, spinning it under her fingers until it wrinkled. "I'm willing to give your approach a chance. It's a creative proposal, and I respect that. Make a plan and send it in for my approval."

Joan twitched on the rigid chair. "I guess."

Georgina snorted. Her eyes sparkled, taking Joan in like a caged bobcat.

*

Joan stayed up late preparing her Lesson Cycle. Once Georgina was off her back, she could do whatever she wanted with class time, lounge around and will it to pass. Because she had nothing else to do, she worked on the cycle as if she were composing her secret weapon of escape instead of a pile of toothless bureaucratic trash. Outlining every minute of two hours was grueling in longhand—but she couldn't bear to visit the computer cluster.

Minute One: walk in. Minute Two: put down her bag (she didn't have a bag). Minute Three: look at the kids. Minute Four: say hi to the kids. Minute Five: the kids say hi back. Minute Six: general looking around, observing the furniture, etc. By the time she got to Minute Nine, she was exhausted. But she pressed on, all the way to Minute One Hundred Twenty, which contained her last three steps out the door. The minutes from ten to one hundred nineteen were dedicated to "group songwriting lesson," with no further detail. Her handwriting was such a tight scrawl no one could read it. This would've been easier on the computer cluster, but no—she couldn't. Georgina would hate this plan, but Joan's promise would be fulfilled. Joan would not execute this lesson, or, in fact, any lesson at all.

By the time she dropped her plan in Georgina's office at two thirty in the morning, she hoped she'd never see it again. Breaking out of Georgina's building and into the swampy night, she was still half convinced she was going for a normal walk, didn't admit to herself what she was really doing until she arrived at the computer cluster.

The climate control of the lab sucked the moisture from Joan's mouth. The gray carpet, the drop ceiling, the temporary walls. She'd imagined it frequently, exactly like this, when she was trying to sleep: rows of monitors like haunted eyeballs. There was never any chance she wouldn't end up here.

The gray planes of glass shifted their reflections as she moved between the lonely aisles. She picked a console in the center.

She sat before its dead screen, refusing to wake it. What could it offer but bad news? Though maybe the video, by some miracle, hadn't surfaced. She stared at the screen as though it would tell her without her asking. But then, somehow, by her breath or mere presence, the mouse trembled or the screen responded without it, and suddenly the square of monitor was lit, already logged in, zero credentials required, offering icons for common programs. In pride of place was the gateway to the internet.

Joan scrambled to click anything else: word processing, that masculine blue icon the first her clicker struck.

With the blank document open, scientifically laid out with ruled margins and empty word count, the field of white so flat and inviting, she typed:

Dear Paige

No comma even, no indication to continue. But then:

I think about you all the time. Nothing weird.

Was that rude? Would Paige want something weird? The words poured out, as though her fingers had only been waiting for permission.

I want to sit beside you. I want to walk up and down the beach, collecting the good trash. I want to hold a red plastic cow with three legs and half an udder as you divine her personality, grant her a name. I talk to you out loud when I'm alone.

She didn't, but why not?

I'm not sending this. But I hope you feel it, out there.

She erased the document. Every program on this computer was rife with terror. She should leave. She should go back to the dorm and sleep like a normal person—it was nearly three in the morning. But she couldn't stand up. Her limbs were locked into the chair, her brain hypnotized by blue pixels. She opened the internet, navigated to YouTube, and typed her name.

The shock of the results being exactly like always. This couldn't be real, but there it was, the same old grid: freeze-frames of her rounding corners after performances, hunched under the Martin—sweaty and sheepish like she always was after a show, feeling like she'd mooned the audience—peppered with the few low-budget music videos she'd put together early on with Paige as the actor, lip syncing Joan's songs because Joan never seemed correct on video, too feral, a creature caught in a flashlight beam. Paige was the perfect stand-in, as close to Joan as anyone could hope to get, her full lips and pixie face contrasting deliciously with Joan's rasp. And then, of course, the meat and potatoes of any musician's YouTube offerings: cell phone footage of live shows. She reviewed the familiar stills: her head, singing, in blue, in red, in amber, in shadow, blurry, hair a frizzy mess, blocked by a banner for some showcase, lips warped in song. Her muscles softened. No condemnations, no talking heads, no viral clips popped to number one. The landscape of the search term was just as it should be. Relief washed like water through her.

But then she advanced to the second page, to be certain. And there, at the top of the results, was an image that could've been taken from any of her shows anywhere in the country: Oklahoma City or San Jose or Yuma or Boise. But she didn't recognize it. Her mouth was open too wide, her eyes closed too hard, her hair more swollen than in the other still frames. The heading: *Joan Vole Tuesday LES*. The air thickened, like a blanket drawing tight.

She clicked play. The whirring HVAC of the lab sucked down into the ambient fuzz of Love und Romance: amps and vents and the few lost notes of the Martin, poking their chime through the murk, as Phone Joan tuned the B string down a semitone between songs in the brown blurry landscape of the club, distorted by the internet but so familiar she could smell the beer and dirty scalps. There was the dim Corona mirror, the plastic palm tree, the stocky sound guy weaving through the crowd.

Her throat constricted to a pinhole, her muscles wrenching to pull air up and in. The video was here, and she hadn't heard anything? How many views did it have? Two hundred. Average for a new outtake, as good as if it didn't exist. There were hamster videos with more views, videos of paint drying and water boiling and pimples being lanced. But how was that possible, considering the content? How could two hundred people—or more, because certainly most viewers had given up before the end—have seen her piss on a fan and then gone about their lives without freaking or sharing? Maybe, somehow, the recording stopped before the fan got onstage. Joan wished, for the first time, that she had her phone, that she could bend in and watch the video in her room, alone, without worrying about anyone walking in.

The video was long, the time marker still way over to the left. Phone Joan emerged and disappeared in a soup of bleary haze, the Martin in her arms, taller when shot from below, re-tuning, pacing, strumming, picking. Singing "Rooster, Too." This video had not been edited to spotlight Joan's trespasses. It was a faithful record of the night. Was that why it wasn't viral? But two hundred people had watched to the end. How had two hundred people kept quiet?

As "Rooster, Too" ended—not as energetic a rendition as Joan remembered—Phone Joan abandoned the Martin, blurs separating in the murk. She headed toward the lip of the stage. Phone Joan's face pushed closer—the phone's operator had a view—her bad teeth sharpening into focus in the sight line of the iPhone, sweaty curls cemented to her forehead, stick arms swinging. She bent over the edge of the stage.

Real Joan nudged the screen with her thumb, like she could rewind time, make herself disappear back into the show, the quality of her songs degraded by jealousy and rage but adding up to only one more mediocre concert instead of the night that would ruin her life.

The superfan climbed onstage. In Joan's memory, she'd dragged the fan up from the pit, but she seemed to have found her own way after taking Joan's hand. The fan was so much smaller than Joan remembered, brittle, older. Delicate.

Joan held her breath as Phone Joan approached the super-fan. How was this happening and no one cared? She'd forgotten to check the time of posting—maybe two hundred people had watched it in the three minutes since its upload. But no. The video had been added the morning after Love und Romance, yesterday, and the comments—which she could only manage to blearily take in—were spread evenly over that span of time.

When Joan and the superfan came together, from the distance of the audience, it was like an embrace, the superfan stepping forward to meet Joan. In the dim light of the club, the poor quality of the video, and the additional compression of the internet, the smooshing together was friendly, intimate. How could everyone in the audience, and the two hundred people who'd watched this video, one of whom might well have been Sparrow, all think she'd merely hugged the fan, that their encounter had been one of gentle intimacy? Sweat bled down her spine.

But the pee. Surely the pee would be visible. Phone Joan's elbow jutted out as she unfastened her pants, jostling in a way that was obvious—wasn't it obvious?—what she was doing. But her crotch was blocked by the superfan.

Joan and the superfan separated—yes, when the superfan had told her no. But Joan was still blocked, and the superfan's back was to the camera, so her disgust was hidden, as was Joan's crotch. Certainly the tension in her body would be clear enough, but Joan couldn't read it, even knowing it was there, in the smudgy dark. And Phone Joan did not appear to absorb the superfan's displeasure. In the colored filters of the club she kept a neutral expression—how could she have appeared that normal after humping someone and before pissing all over them? What was wrong with her?

Joan's jaw tensed, teeth grinding, as Phone Joan came together once more with the superfan. Here was where all would be revealed. Piss splashing everywhere, the superfan recoiling. But first, another embrace. A hug like any hug. Time ticked down on the video's counter, a few seconds, maybe a minute, and then Joan separated, and her pants were already up and fastened like the pants of any normal person.

Where was the pee? Whatever stain was on the superfan's skirt blended in. And Joan's crotch, again, had been blocked. Phone Joan was all put together and fine.

Joan stopped the video. Without the ambient noise of the club, her breath was deafening. She had to pause, had to assess. Tendon by tendon, she reentered her body, which was apparently bent over the computer table, the edge pushing into her stomach until it marked her flesh.

She straightened, backed up. Had she and the superfan calmly hugged? Had Joan never exposed herself, never rubbed her pussy on the fan's leg, never pissed all over her? Could Joan have remembered the encounter incorrectly? After all, she'd fled New York in a panic. She hadn't talked to Paige, hadn't even read her texts before throwing out her phone, hadn't spoken to anyone since. She'd been in a frenzy, out of her mind, actually, so it was possible she hadn't remembered the night accurately. Had she simply set her crotch on the superfan's leg without grinding? That seemed possible. And maybe she had removed her pants, but only briefly—she could see for herself, plainly, in the video, that part of the hug had been brief. Seemingly not even enough time to undo her pants and redo them, much less pee. And if she had, it had only been a few drops, not enough for the fan to notice. Her muscles relaxed, melting into the nylon weave of the desk chair. She had an active guilty conscience. That was all. She'd been in a state of self-hatred over getting cut from Paige's album—she must've distorted the night.

She pressed play, watched herself snatch the Martin like a maniac and run offstage so fast she almost toppled headfirst into the crowd. That was the only part of the sequence that was at all awry. Why had she fled like a feral animal if nothing had happened? She stopped the video.

She scrolled through the comments. *Bangers, all* was her favorite. *Decent rendition of Rooster tho heard better.* And: *Short set, what a ripoff!!* The top comment was: *Cute hug=Joan+fan @ 8:16.* That comment had twelve likes and one sub-comment: *Not like JV to be sweet! Lucky fan* ☺.

No one had seen anything. There were other angles from the concert on pages three and four of the search results. These were shorter, blurrier, shot from farther back. Some didn't even capture the hug or stopped in the middle, as though it was so blasé it wasn't worth the memory space on an iPhone. None showed anything like what Joan remembered, as she dashed from one upload to the next, pulling clips up, watching them, clicking away the moment the frame switched to a cartoon of a smiling guitar player as YouTube recommended a children's folk song about saying thank you.

After page four, there were only the old results, freeze-frame after freeze-frame of Joan's eyes closed, her teeth exposed, in navy light, peach light, yellow light. Her figure shrunken and distant, scrawny when viewed over rows of scalps. Her close-up, moonlit face, cigarette long-ashed and caught between lips, her shoulder against a concrete wall—an informal interview, stolen when she was show-drunk. Clammy, shameful cheeks. Joan scrolled all the way to the last page of marginal results—a woman named Joan trapping a backyard vole, a kid showing off her stuffed mole named Joan of Arc, a review of a volume of work by a fiber artist named Joan.

Paige had sent her those freaked-out messages, but maybe only because Joan had run out in a crazy panic and never called her again. Joan sat back, spine pressing against the plastic lip of the chair. So here it was. She'd thrown out her whole life for nothing. She closed YouTube. She stood up. She hadn't hurt anyone. She staggered back to the dorm like a zombie, an itch in the back of her brain like a beetle crawling, and passed out on her rumpled sleeping bag.

10

JOAN AND PAIGE KNEELED ON THE FLOOR OF JOAN'S VINE-gar Hill apartment, snipping construction paper into shapes in the signature Black Tree cutout style, designing their CD covers. A perfect Friday evening in autumn, Bradford pears browning out the window. They were tipsy, the gin Christopher had given Joan standing watch from its glittery crystal like a chaperone. He always gave luxury gifts, then denied he had a trust fund. Three years had passed since Paige and Joan had met at All Time Elodie's. The nineties were over, and, still, Paige hadn't moved out. Joan's rent was so cheap—she had a gift for shocking deals—that she and Paige could survive on part-time work, devote themselves to music. Paige actually cleaned sometimes, and the rats were gone at last, even if the bed was still never made. At first Paige had been dismayed by how many hours Joan worked on music every day, but by now she'd followed suit.

Paige perched on the carpet rolled against the wall. It had been damaged in a sexual encounter, but for months Joan had failed to drag it down to the street. Joan hadn't told Paige this, breathed hardly a word of her sex life, and could barely handle her sitting on it.

"Song list on back," Joan said, tapping Paige's sloppily glued creation.

Paige flipped the paper over and numbered twelve entries. Joan had been right all along: Paige had always had more songs. By now she had even more than could fit on one album. She tapped her pen to her chin.

The other Gonewriters had mentees. Joan never thought she'd enjoy that dynamic, but, living with Paige, they fell into it. First she'd convinced Paige to rope her high school girlfriend into kidnapping and shipping the spooky-sounding Rogue that Paige's parents had bought her long ago when they still loved her. Joan had restrung it and replaced its pickguard, then helped Paige control her strumming, strengthen her arm muscles, anchor her lyrics, urging her to push breath out through her nose to emphasize her squeak—more air, so much more. She had given Paige the space to write whatever she wanted. If Paige wanted to sing about fruit salad, she should sing about fruit salad. Or goats or Tasmania or fancy cakes or whatever trash floated into her brain. She could make any cute detail work. Her sexuality was off-limits, though it could've been the hook. Most of their conversations centered around Paige and music. That was easy because whenever Joan referenced her adventures with men, Paige changed the topic or scurried to the bathroom.

Joan envied Paige for having someone who could correct her the moment she went awry. Joan caught every bum note, every awkward phrase, every floppy rhyme. In the early days her corrections came with patient evaluations of technique, urges toward practice, intervals of training—but by now she could poke Paige with a pencil or kick her shoe, and Paige would know she'd flubbed, would revise the song in real time. Often, as a scrawny twenty-two-year-old, Joan had swapped a lyric back and forth, finessed the placement of a breath or added and subtracted a coda, amended the routing of a tour—wishing someone could confirm whether she was right. That this song was better in direct address, that her picking pattern sounded cleaner when simplified, that yes, the song was done—leave it, she was ruining it. That someone had been around to teach her how to restring a guitar or where to buy the cheapest distortion pedal or how to shake money from a withholding club manager when they settled up at the end of the night. She'd had to scrape her answers from the densest stone; she'd battled a path through the thickest woods, emerged bloodied and furious.

"Which songs where?" Paige asked, raising her pen. "Black Tree always crushes the order. Did you finish listening to *By Twig or By Node*?"

By Twig or By Node was a new sampler of Black Tree artists. "The first half is stronger." Joan had listened a million times, cherishing a different favorite each run through.

"'Last Night' would've been the perfect fucking closer," Paige said. "You were robbed. It would've been so haunting after 'Oh Low Orchid.' And they only included that cheesy Tammy Higgins track because they sank so much into her."

"That's nonsense." But Joan had thought the same, though she would've made "Last Night" the penultimate song, in the dog slot, for the joke of its title, and just to be modest even in fantasy.

"Can you imagine being on there?" Paige grabbed the jewel case of *By Twig or By Node*, which they traded back and forth. "All these people are in the freaking club for life." She touched the back, the handwritten font bold on its pale field.

"No matter what happens." She squeezed the case so hard the plastic creaked. Then she swapped it for her own design, scrutinizing it as though it held equal worth, even as her paper forms pulled off from their backing. The desire in her gaze penetrated this album that would never be.

"This feels, like, almost real." Paige turned to Joan with a gaze that pulled light from the room. "This is dumb, but doesn't this feel, like, kinda real?"

"Totally," Joan said. And it did. As sloppy as Paige's craftsmanship, that gray moon, that yellow sky, the red block letters, Joan had to admit it was a perfect Black Tree cover. "You're killing it."

"Here?" Paige asked, flapping her cover. "Or, like, in the world." She sang the word, as though all the world beyond the walls of this apartment was only a joke.

"Both." Joan had found gigs for Paige in nursing homes and high schools and subway stations, anything so she'd be bulletproof before climbing a real stage, so humiliation hardened her bone deep. She'd even convinced the Gonewriters to accept her into the collective, which they did because they were charmed, though her craft plainly wasn't ready. All the while, Joan's career had shot up. Every day brought some fresh opportunity, even if small, and all that exposure had to accrue into a career eventually. Joan only wanted to maintain, to earn enough to live her cheap-ass life on music alone, which was a big ask. Paige's admiration lent a shine to everything. She adjusted her moon so it sat more crookedly in the sky. "Now you've got that Black Tree look. The right amount unhinged. We should send that in."

"Do you think it will happen for us?" Paige watched Joan steadily. Her face was so young under her weight of curls. "I mean, not Black Tree. Obviously. But something? Or is this all just dumb fantasy?"

"Of course it will." Black Tree was the only label with decent backing still producing indie music, and, despite the dire trajectory of the industry, it thrived. Everyone had said Joan's sound was perfect for their stable. "They're the obvious choice, right? I mean, it's not like we're dreaming of a major."

"I wouldn't want that anyway." Paige cut out a teal oval. "Because it would mean we weren't weird."

"Exactly." Joan stuck a lavender cloud on the orange field of her own cover. She had three albums, though they were all self-released. But she was gaining traction, more than she'd ever expected. It was so cozy sitting with Paige on the floor. Maybe she could share more than she usually hazarded. "Guess what happened with this dude last night." Paige looked down, adjusted her moon. "I literally pulled him off the A train. German tourist."

Paige hunched deeper into her gluing. "Oh."

"He thought I was gay—I had to convince him. I don't know what's wrong with me. He was totally pasty and had no wherewithal." She was talking fast. Why didn't she share this shit with Paige? She'd been planning to for a while. They lived together. They were here on the floor, vulnerable. The awkwardness around sharing was only in Joan's head. "I don't think he even knew where he was going. But I was too horny to wait for his hotel. I took him to the Rambles." Joan had never had anyone to share her sexual adventures with, and she never saw anyone she pissed on again. Saying the words solidified the encounter into reality. Yes, of course, that German tourist had been real, not just a hazy pink memory. "I never pissed on anyone in the Rambles before." She looked up at Paige through her eyelashes, trying to read her. She'd never mentioned her peeing, but Paige knew.

"Cool," Paige said, the word so small Joan could barely hear it.

"I didn't wait to see what he'd do with his jacket."

Paige turned to the window. The night was orange, sherbet haze stuck to the pane. People moved through the mist up and down the sidewalk, restless, the ever-churning blood cells of the city. Joan had thought Paige would be cool with her fetish, or whatever it was, that at least one person in her life wouldn't consider her a freak. But maybe Paige was being normal, and Joan was overreacting. Her hands shook, cutting out another star, so the scissors slipped and snipped her finger. Beads of blood pumped from its tip. She squeezed the knuckle but the blood flowed faster, snaking down her arm in two jeweled lines. What were you supposed to do when you got cut? Who had band-aids if they didn't have kids?

"Oh my god." Paige took Joan's hand. She retrieved a fistful of toilet paper and wrapped it. "Sit on the couch. God. You never relax."

"It's not even a couch," Joan said, but she liked how Paige called it that, even if only to make herself feel better about sleeping on it.

"Whatever." Paige settled beside Joan, their spines resting against the foam. Joan held her finger upright so the paper wouldn't catch and unravel.

Okay. She was okay. Paige cared about her even if she was a pervert.

"Wouldn't it be cool to have a plant or something? Instead of just staring at the dumb wall all the time?" Paige reached out her foot and kicked it, leaving a half-moon in the center. The wall was better with that mark. In all the years Joan had lived here, the yellowish-white paint had always been the same: greasy and lumpy, like it was dirty under the coat.

"There's not enough sunlight for a plant in here. We'd just watch it die."

"What about a cactus?" Paige pushed up against Joan, snuggling. She cuddled in like this sometimes. Joan's family had never snuggled with her, but she found she didn't mind. She inched closer so Paige's head fit on her shoulder. This simple warmth.

"A cactus needs tons of sunlight. No one in a city should have a cactus."

Paige laughed. "That's ridiculous."

Joan leaned more of her weight against Paige.

And then, as abruptly as if she herself hadn't known she'd do it, Paige spun around and grabbed Joan's shoulders. Her grip was so rough that it stung. Paige stayed there, frozen, in that twisted position, an awkward half hug, her torqued spine a swollen line under her T-shirt, so vulnerable. Joan turned her head toward her overpainted New York door, the chain that they never inserted into its fitting dangling. She kept rigid in the embrace, Paige's jagged parts poking all over—elbows and knees and the fingernails she let grow long for picking.

Paige swung her legs around and straddled Joan's lap. Her hips and knees dented Joan's thighs. Joan couldn't speak, her mouth open, tongue drying. Paige tucked her chin to her sternum and let her curls curtain them. She watched Joan, direct and hard, but Joan couldn't read her. And then her lips wrapped Joan's, hot and damp, hands pushing under Joan's shirt and covering her breasts.

Joan arched her back as far as she could without tumbling off the foam. At least with the kiss she didn't have to take in the spiky points of Paige's nose and the cold lumps of her cheekbones, and Joan couldn't be expected to say a word with that mouth ringing hers, chin wet, cheeks flaming. She should say something. She should just say something: *I don't like this. I don't want this. I never thought about you that way, not ever, not once.* The words screamed against the walls of her brain, stamping their mark in the coils. Paige moved so swiftly, so intensely, that she must be enjoying it, out of—what? Desperate horniness? Loneliness? Joan could submit to this one comfort. Paige couldn't be failing at music, abandoned by family, and then rejected, on top of it all, by the one person in her city who truly knew her. Even though Joan's stomach soured thinking of Paige's baby face and dirty hair the first night they met, such a kid.

So when Paige tugged Joan's clothes off, her shirt catching on her nose and ear, her pants sticking around her knees, and Joan was lying belly up, sliding off the blocks of foam, she didn't stop Paige as she ran her mouth—too soft, like jelly—down between Joan's legs in a cold trail, let her kiss her down there, though it was wet and sticky and she wanted to twist free, like she'd spilled sauce on her lap. She sighed after enough time had passed, and Paige pulled herself up. "I've been thinking about that basically every second."

Joan closed her eyes in case disgust shone from them. The dark backs of her eyelids sparked yellow and pink. She closed tighter and the sparks swelled, overtaking the black. Now was the time to admit she saw Paige as a mentee and best friend and little sister. But what if one cruel sentence, deployed for no reason but her own comfort, catapulted Joan back to deep, pre-Paige lonesomeness? Lonesomeness so concentrated she hadn't even identified it until Paige dug her out. "Cool," Joan said, turning to dodge the smell of herself on Paige's breath.

Paige collapsed onto her, a heavier load than Joan would've

imagined, tucking her muzzle into Joan's neck. "Can I tell you a secret?"

Joan froze at the clamminess of Paige's nudity. What if Paige said she was in love with Joan? What the hell could Joan say to that?

"I knew you before All Time Elodie's," Paige said.

"What?" Joan said. "But I'd never seen you."

"I know, I know. But your shows. I'd been to a couple. I loved your work so much, Joan. I was a fan." She scraped her curls back. "Someone told me Mary-Anne Amy Linseed plays All Time Elodie's sometimes. It was my third try."

Joan warmed under Paige. Maybe the weight was nice. "That's why you went somewhere without food." Because that had seemed like a bad oversight for someone as canny as Paige. "You really liked my music?"

"All of it," Paige breathed. "'Last Night,' especially."

"Last Night" was Joan's personal favorite, an ode to the raccoon who'd entered her bedroom while she was losing her virginity: *I see that hunched back bobbing, whiskered face of all my longing.* She'd wanted the guy so bad that she'd wanted the raccoon, too, the bedpost, the molded plastic comb on her dresser, her father, downstairs. She'd wanted to pull the world inside her.

"Thank you," Joan said, the words soft. The foam blocks of the fake couch were easy on her spine, and she drifted to sleep under her friend.

11

THE MORNING AFTER WATCHING THE VIDEO, JOAN WOKE with a scraping voice in the back of her head, like she'd forgotten to feed a dog somewhere, like some soft body was starving because of her.

She stumbled into the kitchen for breakfast olives and found her lesson plan shoved under the suite door, crawling with corrections. She had to hold it to her nose to read it, the words blurring as last night in the lab crystallized. She'd somehow not committed the act she thought she had. She had to keep telling herself that, five times a minute, and still the news was impossible. Georgina's final note, circled and underlined: *But where, Joan, is the INDIVIDUAL WRITING?*

When class time arrived, too late in the afternoon for the sun to still be so brutal, Joan loafed up the hill. All day she'd been trying to feel better, replaying, in her mind, the calm hug in the clip, but a nagging itch scraped the back of her brain. Near the cafeteria, she passed a woman. Maybe a mother, dangling around to ascertain if her kid was adjusting. She was only visible from the back, wearing polyester slacks and a blazer, heels too high for this grass. Her walk had an anxious stutter that indicated helicopter parenting: a mom who'd hollowed herself out for her child. There was a familiarity to the unevenness of her step. Perhaps she was Agnes's mom—she had a similar intensity of motion, a red undertone to her hair. This woman had been trapped indoors with a child for years, training her up to perfection, for nothing. She turned, and Joan caught the slimmest shard of her face, only the edge of her jaw, flesh sagging and tired. Under the blazer she wore a nipple-pink blouse. Her concession, perhaps, to what Agnes had called "the fun side of music."

Joan descended into the classroom, where the kids were lined up against the wall on their precious beanbags. Her anxiety was residual; she didn't have to worry anymore what they'd illegally seen online, whether they'd talked to their parents. No one could threaten her now. She could finish out the summer in leisure, return to New York, make amends with Paige for bailing without notice, reenter her old life six thousand dollars richer. The luck was too blinding to look at directly. She shook out her arms, loosening them.

The kids were slumped on the beanbags. They said, "Hi, Ms. Vole," and stared. Victor wore a quilted gold hoodie, hair in a knot so his pretty face was clear. He wore flip-flops like he was still in Florida, but it was okay; his feet were perfect. Lula, in an army jacket, already had her mouth agape. And Agnes, sitting in front of them all, watching Joan extra thoroughly, the white spot in her bangs a sparkle in the afternoon sun. Joan couldn't bear to meet their scrutiny. She sat at the piano bench and turned away from them, toward the clock.

"Are we doing real class today?" Lula asked, strands of sticky white hair floating toward the ceiling. "Or sitting around like idiots?"

"We can do whatever you want," Joan said. If the kids didn't request to learn, if they didn't want to, she couldn't force them.

"That's valid," Lula said. "Hey everybody, let's be crazy!" Her pitch was needling. She bounced on the beanbag, her army jacket rising and puffing around her at each drop.

Somehow, improbably, the other kids followed, bouncing higher and higher, until Victor, with his ungainly limbs, tipped sideways mid-jump and crashed down on Agnes, crushing her under his puffy sweatshirt. "Ow," Agnes screamed, laughing and fake punching him. Her fists vanished into the gold fabric.

Joan should probably stop them. Probably she was not supposed to let them roughhouse. Once they'd clamored back to their positions on the beanbags, they set themselves up again, watching her with straight backs, hands on knees, like parodies of students.

"What would you teach us if you were going to?" Agnes asked, peeking from under her red bangs.

"Songs without origins," Joan said.

"What's that?" Agnes asked, pulling a patched-up messenger bag onto her lap. The bag was lumpy, as though it contained all her earthly possessions.

"Songs no one owns," said Victor, checking Joan for approval. "Like the royalties disintegrate into nothing instead of making dough." He rubbed his finger and thumb like he was grinding a coin. He had the appearance of a kid who was famous for nothing. A reality TV kid. She shuddered to even look at him.

"That's not the point," Joan said.

Victor lifted his palms. "Sorry, man."

"They're songs whose origins we don't know," Joan said, softening her voice. "Songs without writers." Melodies floated into her head. A cowherd mourning home as wildflowers painted the Great Divide. A woman menaced by unwanted suitors. A child wasting away above a canal while barges slid by. These songs roamed without their owners, wedging into your skull without permission, inviting nostalgia and sorrow and euphoria and despair without the cheese of a celebrity to muddy their credibility as heart songs. They were songs that belonged to the world, that anyone could perform and interpret and modify. They were the orphans Joan sang to herself on nights without men, without Paige.

"That's rad." Victor checked Joan, like they were in cahoots. "Because it's like, if a song is good, who cares who wrote it? Right? Is that right?"

"Sure, bro." Agnes blew air. "So if you wrote a killer song, you wouldn't care if it made one penny?"

Some quality of Agnes's swagger as she pushed her chest out to confront Victor dinged like Paige in the back of Joan's head. Agnes was eerily mature. Maybe from all those years devoted to her guitar. Soon Joan would see her old friend again. Now that the video was benign, she could go home, back to her old life, like nothing had happened. A needle in her scalp—a bug bite. She slapped it.

"I mean, I guess not." Victor sat up straighter, his bun a shiny ball on his skull. "Why would I care? If the song is out there, and people listen, and they laugh and cry and stuff, and it moves them in their core, and they, like, change their life because of it and become a different person and write it on their gravestone or something, I guess that's enough for me."

Agnes rasped a laugh. She sounded like a kid who'd put in the hours. "Glad you're not expecting much."

"I see two ways to create a song of no provenance," Joan said, to cut off their rambling. "Either in the writing—trying to make your song universal or otherwise divorced from you—or by methodology—releasing your song into the world without you." She was getting in too deep. They didn't care about any of this. And explaining would only lead to more work.

"That's the dumbest shit I ever heard," Lula said. "Why would you work so hard and then throw your story out like some piece of garbage?"

"You'd do that," Joan said, "for lots of reasons." She didn't say, *Because you could nearly destroy your whole life over art.* "Because what's important is how a song lives, not how its author does. For example, when you listen to a song, do you care who the author is?"

"Doy, yes," Lula said, twisting in the bubble of her army jacket. "If they're some poser, I don't listen. But if they're hot, I'm like, oh yeah."

"What if you were freed of thinking that?" Joan asked, leaning forward. "And you could concentrate on where the music took you personally?" The students fell quiet. "Whatever," Joan said. This was too intense, all attention on her, expecting an explanation when she didn't know fuck all. "Let's break."

"What?" asked Lula. "But class just started!"

"Go to the bathroom," Joan said. She needed them out of her sight.

Lula and Victor slunk from the room. Agnes checked Joan over her shoulder as she hurried toward the door.

"Agnes," Joan said. "Come here." She tried to mimic a stern yet caring teacher voice, but she sounded all fake.

"What?" Agnes snapped.

"Hey." Joan steadied her breath—why was she nervous about some kid? "I'm going to need you to accept at least the basic premise of this class." Blood flowed hot into her face. Why was she picking on Agnes? All of the kids were a mess.

"Certainly," Agnes said, pushing both hands over her hair,

red bristles between her fingers. "I 'accept' the 'premise' of the 'class.'" She flopped away from Joan. Her knees rose, high and smug, as she marched toward the door.

"What's going on?" Joan said. "This isn't you."

"What are you talking about?" Agnes's face twisted into a knot. "You don't know me."

"I know that no one who makes music the way you did gets away with not giving a shit about anything."

Agnes stared at Joan, narrowing her eyes to slits. But then one eye twitched, and her lips slackened and fell apart, and then tears were falling in actual streams from both eyes, and Agnes was gasping like she was drowning. She crumpled to the floor.

Jesus. Joan had only meant to scare her into good behavior. She hadn't signed up to manage a mental health crisis. How could Agnes act like a mini adult one second and break down the next? Victor and Lula murmured in the hallway. The kid was all heaving and leaky. "Cry it out."

"Fuck you," Agnes said.

There was no way around it. Joan crouched down next to Agnes. Agnes let her. So that was something. "Okay," Joan said. "Now. Tell me."

Her voice all gummy: "There's nothing to tell."

"Crying is more embarrassing than anything you could say."

A growl from the crumpled girl, like a wolf, which would've been alarming if Joan didn't recognize it, somewhere in her body, as the sound of the girl giving up.

"There you go," Joan said. "Show's over."

"Ugh. It's just stupid." She screamed the word, her head still bent at the floor.

"Say it, Agnes."

She raised one arm, swiping at nothing. "I don't know what to do."

"You don't know what to do about what?" Here she was, getting into it. Joan had no choice at this point. The girl was a puddle.

"What to do, like, with time." That hand reaching up again. "All this stupid time."

"You're a kid. You go to school. You come to camp. You can't possibly have much time to manage."

Agnes thrust her head toward Joan. Her face was red and creased into haywire patterns, as though, in the last two minutes, she'd aged in a chaotic and terrifying manner. "The whole world is spare time. That's all there is." She reached one arm up. "Every second is a million years. And there's nothing to do!"

Joan couldn't manage sympathy for the girl. She would've been over the moon to have a parent who cared about her musical development, who devoted time and energy to little Mary-Anne's craft. Think where she'd be now if she'd been offered that. And this girl had taken it for granted so intensely that she'd quit. "So why not pick up the guitar again?"

"Don't you see it's too late? When Victor asked if I would play for you guys, I wanted to die."

"Have you already forgotten how?" Joan could still play in her sleep. Her hands, at rest, clawed into the shape of chords.

"Even if I'm one ounce worse it's a tragedy." Her voice was thick with snot.

"So maybe you shouldn't have quit."

"That's so helpful. Thank you so very much for your oh-so-helpful advice." She stormed out of the room. Down the hall, the rise of indecipherable chats as she linked up with Lula.

And then Joan was alone. Here were the slouching bean-bags, the piano whose keys had been bashed by some blunt tool. Here were notebooks and hoodies slumped like casualties over chairs and dirty carpet, upset water bottles, a plush banana shackled to a key. Now that the kids were gone, their accessories melted Joan. The worn-down stickers on that notebook, the wrinkled button-down with its dirtied grid that must've belonged to someone's father, the water bottle shaped like a gummy bear. She squeezed the banana. With a squeak, it released a sad, sawdust odor, like it had been unearthed from some attic, reclaimed from distant childhood to complete a camp checklist. Without the students, teaching seemed wholly possible. Her arms loosened and dropped to her flanks.

The doorknob jiggled. No—too soon. Leave her one moment of peace, please. Then maybe she could gather strength to push the students toward the light, if such a goal were possible. The door drew open. A middle-aged woman stepped into the room, backlit by a flare of sunshine—the woman from outside, Agnes's mother. Her chin was lifted, her expression cheerful, like she was prepared to greet her daughter. But Agnes was in the hall, chatting with Lula between here and the entrance. The kids hadn't so much as slowed their prattle as this woman passed. A cold wind swept in from the hall, delayed by the woman's body.

The woman stepped into the room, out of the glare. Her head floated closer, clear now without the backlighting—wait, Joan knew this woman, from years ago. That hair, combed back and gelled, was unfamiliar, that sleek blazer woven with fine wool. But those feral blue eyes, that nose effervescent with capillaries, the fine details snapped into some lost corner of Joan's brain. The face itched so far back that this woman must've been a friend from childhood, rinsed out now by the rich lather of money and years.

"Can I help you?" Joan asked, stepping closer, into the orb of the woman's chemical perfume. That was when she caught the extra dimple by the woman's chin, that wart or mole attractively positioned below her nostril. The word flamed like a signal: *superfan*. Joan's hands grabbed for support, but only air surrounded her, a doughnut of nothing.

"Joan Vole," said the superfan, smile high and forced, wonky above her perfect suit.

The fluorescence of the room flipped back to the burgundy haze of Love und Romance. No. But Joan had escaped. She was supposed to be so far away. This was not happening. Joan's every muscle locked. But she couldn't run. The kids were outside.

"Remember me?" The superfan's voice was ruined and dry, like she'd been talking all day. She was real, she was standing there, her heels solid on the rubber tiles, her body casting a dim fluorescent shadow, pooling under her like a dropped scarf. "I'm sorry to catch you off guard. I know this must be a surprise." The superfan laughed, too high, a bad note. "I've been trying to find you, Joan, and I finally did. I got a ride down here from a friend."

Joan was so dumb. Her name must be on the Merry Writers website, where anyone could find it. Her naked groin had grated against this woman's leg. Was the streak still visible on the woman's pants? No, that was impossible. These were different pants; the superfan hadn't even worn pants last time—everything about her was different now, in the sunlight, in these fancy clothes. The kids would return any second—had she told them when to return? "I'm in class." The kids giggled outside. Joan needed her out. But also, the fan had come all this way. Why?

"Don't look so worried," said the superfan, straight and tall in her fancy blazer. "Everything is great. I just need to talk."

"I can't." Joan had to get this woman out. A colleague would see them. Joan's skin rattled like the whole fleshy envelope would shake down to the ground.

"I got your number, but it wasn't going through. So maybe it's odd, but I thought I'd just sorta come down here." The superfan gazed around at the lumpy beanbags, the scattered notebooks, like they were majestic landforms. "It was a real pretty drive."

"You came all this way," Joan said, the words dropping out of her, "just to see me?"

"Yes," the superfan said. "Of course, Joan. It was nothing."

"That isn't nothing." Joan teetered where she stood. "Wait, but that's, like, totally crazy."

"Not really." The superfan's face solidified into crags. "If you could've seen me the last few days, not at all."

"Okay," Joan said, letting the words fall out, heavy, so she could understand this was actually happening. "You're here."

"At last." The superfan's face loosened into bright ease. Her outfit contrasted with the beanbags, like an executive in a kid's clubhouse. "And I feel so much better now that I am."

"Right." Joan kept her jaw firm. The superfan had for some reason felt like she needed to come here, had been freaking out or whatever and needed to see Joan. So let her stand there in her blazer and look at Joan for however long it took. Even if Joan longed to crawl out of her skin, she could give the superfan a few minutes.

The superfan drew a phone from her pocket, screen glittering. Joan stepped back. All phones were spiders. She dodged as the superfan wielded it. "I have this idea, but I need you to be part of it."

The superfan was really here, feet squared, steady, somehow. Her heels had sunk imprints into the carpet. The door was open, where Joan had closed it against the students. She blinked, but the fan remained.

The superfan flashed the freeze-frame of Joan singing from *Joan Vole Tuesday LES*. Her jaw hardened as she touched the screen, moving her finger quickly like she didn't want to linger. A shriek of joy from Lula in the hallway, piercing.

"Have people found it?" Joan's every muscle clenched.

A strip of hair escaped the woman's bun, springy and coiled—that was the hair Joan remembered. "No."

Relief wisped through Joan. "God, thank you." She longed to pull this woman into her arms. This fan rubbing one hand with the other, soothing it like a puppy. How had Joan jumped this woman, rubbed up on her like a post? That moment didn't feel possible in the fluorescent cast of the classroom. This was a regular lady. She was an office worker, maybe even another teacher. Joan's voice emerged a waver: "Listen. Hey. I'm sorry."

The superfan tilted her head. "Sorry for what?"

Joan couldn't manage more than that.

"Joan." The superfan shook her head, slow, incredulous. "What happened with us was an honor. Being onstage with you. Being intimate. Even your—evacuation."

Her voice was emphatic, her words careful. So it had happened. Of course it had happened. How could Joan have thought, even for a second, that she'd invented the incident? That had all been only so much wishful thinking. But look at the superfan—she was happy. How was she happy? "You look tired," Joan said, a wave of concern flooding in. "You've come a long way."

The superfan beamed. "I'm really glad I could come. I just can't wait to tell everyone."

"What?"

The superfan's cheeks wrinkled. "Oh! I'm preparing to

post the video. Along with my story. About how you changed my life. I wanted to tell you in person." The superfan watched her steadily. "I haven't had a sip of alcohol since that night. I haven't gone two days in years." She stood straighter. She was different now, more so than just her nice clothes. "I hope you might share our story, too. Think how many lives we could save, with all your fans."

"No," Joan said, the room going white.

"Really, I haven't. Onstage, I had a kind of clarity." Her focus drifted away, as though vibrant knowledge was packed behind the cinderblocks. "You made me sober. You made me realize I could be special. How could I not share that with the world?"

"Because," Joan said, the word choking out.

The fan tilted her head in curiosity.

With this woman so close, this actual physical body of a real adult human, not some piece of the crowd broken off to alight onstage, but a specific person, solid beside her—dents in the sides of her feet where her shoes had rubbed, thumbnails bitten to the quick, an herby aroma like sage—the murk of Love und Romance, what Joan had done, flooded back. She shuddered so hard she almost dropped to the floor. "Because it was gross. It was dirty. And you should be furious with me."

"You're not gross." The superfan set a hand on Joan. This broad-faced woman, mouth collapsing, had lived a whole life. She'd had a career—real estate, maybe, or dental hygiene— she'd sat in a classroom and opened herself to learn; she'd had hopes and fantasies and struggles with addiction. Somewhere along the way, she'd probably even fallen in love. And Joan had treated her like an object, didn't even know her name, the way all her fans were a mass, a cloud of eyes and ears. She'd harmed this woman, who now was trying to control the story. She stood under the superfan's hand on her, the unique pressure and heat of her palm, like how the superfan had stood in the intimacy of Joan's pee. She absorbed the beige temples of the superfan, her deflated nose. She smelled the fan's breath, stale from travel. She was quiet.

"Okay," Joan whispered. "I believe you."

The superfan embraced her. In the squeeze of those heavy arms, Joan's pulse slowed. Her eyes closed, all the exhaustion pressing down. But no, she couldn't relax. She broke free of the superfan's arms, stepped back. She steadied her voice. "You came to discuss posting the video?"

"Yes, of course, Joan."

"And you agree our decision should be mutual?" The superfan wouldn't have come all this way if she didn't care about Joan's opinion.

The superfan pulled her lip in under her teeth.

Joan squared her shoulders. "Okay, well, I'd like to request you don't post yet."

"There's nothing to worry about. People will understand when I explain."

"But if it's all right with you, I'd like to hold off." Joan filled her lungs. "Just for a little while. So we can plan better. We'll have more impact that way."

The comma appeared again beside the superfan's mouth. But it wasn't a wrinkle; it was a scar. A precise, graceful swoop, like someone had carved it in. "Are you sure?"

"Yes." Joan held her voice steady.

The superfan gave a slow nod. "Maybe, yeah. I guess. If that's what you want."

Air breathed out of Joan in a clear line. "Thank you." All she'd had to do was be patient and kind and ask for what she wanted.

The door slapped open. Lula and Agnes erupted into the room, giggling and falling all over each other. When they clocked the superfan, they froze in a mess of limbs.

"Hello," said the superfan. "I'm a friend of Joan's." In the goofiness of her tone it was clear what kind of mom she'd been, if she'd been one: great with little kids—animated, cloying—but preteens bristling at her corniness. The heartbreak of her children growing up and turning against her, finding her, as the years passed, a graver humiliation.

Agnes grinned, as though here was a surprise guest Joan had invited to play an inspirational jingle.

"Go back to the hall," Joan said, panic pulsing up her torso. She didn't want the kids to even see this woman, had to keep the worlds separate.

Agnes took a step toward the superfan.

"Agnes," Joan warned.

"Oh, hello, Agnes." Relief glittered off the superfan.

Joan hated the girl's name in the superfan's mouth. She wanted to pluck it out, dry it off, return it to Agnes's care. These kids were a species miles from who Joan and Paige had been. Their world was monitored, enclosed. Joan couldn't stand for them to talk to the superfan, to get anywhere near that night at Love und Romance. "Where's Victor?"

"He went to get a guitar," Lula chirped. "So Agnes can play."

"I've followed the career of Joan Vole for twenty-one years," the superfan told the children. "She's my favorite musician in the world." Joan used to think fans watched her with hunger because they wanted to fuck her—and sometimes they did. But usually it was hunger to metabolize her talent. Fan eyes, Paige called it. "I've traveled to see her all over the country. Today I caught a ride all the way from New York."

The superfan was the kind of hard-bitten person who never

left Manhattan: whose feet were unstable on grass and dirt, who'd never driven a car or entered a Walmart or a forest or feasted at a five-dollar buffet or used the bathroom at a gas station. Alarming in the classroom, like a bat crash-landed on a birthday cake.

"That's so cool, Ms. Vole. Someone likes your music." Agnes stepped closer. Joan took her arm and guided her away.

Agnes snatched her arm back, cradled it like Joan had broken it. "Ow."

Joan had to manage this situation systematically. "Listen," she told the fan, gathering her breath. "I'll talk to you for as long as you like. Let's just do it away from the kids."

"We're not kids. What the hell?" said Lula, who still stood in the doorway, arms wrapping her torso.

"Oh, Joan. But that's no good. The students might like to hear what we have to say."

"They do not," Joan said, too loudly.

Agnes and Lula perked up, gazes needling into Joan. "Why not?" Lula asked. Lula's hair was more staticky than ever, white bits floating everywhere, like a shedding cat.

"Go back to the hall." Panic cramped through her. "Can't you do one thing I ask?"

"Don't be like that, Joan," said the superfan. "By the way, have you girls heard 'Rooster, Too'?"

Joan's fists solidified at her hips. "I'm serious." But at least the fan had moved to matters more benign.

"It's Joan's best song."

"Rooster, Too" was a queer rallying cry formulated to retain her "Lakeshore" fanbase. That no one could see how pandering it was made Joan ill. "Let's not do this now." Joan took the superfan by the arm to lead her toward the door. The superfan startled, lips rounding into an O. And Joan was back in the club, that fast. She went dizzy. Her grip loosened.

The superfan spun away, as though they'd been dancing. She opened her throat and sang, "Guys with their eyes rinsed clean of care, guys with their hands on me."

"Stop," Joan whispered. The superfan hesitated, then continued. When Joan performed that song, it was tart and cranky, her bitterness at what she didn't have pulsing through the nighttime misadventure. But the superfan made it a ballad, sad and stretchy with innocent longing, in a way Joan hadn't known it could be, even as longing was always its engine.

"That's sick," Agnes said.

Joan couldn't stop her voice from rising in pleasure when she said, "Not really."

"But it's the story behind the song that made me fall in love," the superfan said, stepping her feet apart.

Fine. Let her tell it. The story all the fans told: Joan, visiting The Cock, yes, but instead of slipping in dressed as Nick Blade's guy, the story had her storming in after a heady day of Pride, rainbows on cheekbones, claiming this male space for lesbians, too, and, in this heartwarming tale of love across subgroups, the men had been willing, that night, the way they never would've been on any real night, to haul the dykes into the mess, and everyone had made love together as one bountiful queer family. The story was even cheeky enough to invent a queer love child, a mascot somewhere out there, seventeen, now—product of some trans encounter or a slipup across ranks. A kid had even come forward to claim the role—a rough little butch from Queens with spiked orange hair, the correct age to the day. Joan leaned against the lacquered piano top. She couldn't have come up with a better launch into queer icon status if she'd tried.

"Joan dressed as a guy one night," said the superfan.

"Wait," Joan said. "That's not the story."

"She snuck into this bar on the Lower East Side. She saw something she wanted but couldn't have."

Joan gulped a hard swallow. How had this woman unearthed her private story, which was not even known to Nick Blade, who was Joan's actual friend and colleague, who'd been beside her that night? No one had been in her thoughts that evening when she'd realized this family was what she'd been missing. If only, as a child, she'd ever caught a glimpse of some wider pee community, some chosen family united around pissing as bodily ecstasy, beyond porn or sex. Any gay child gets a peek at some point, even in a despairing way, through graffiti like *Julius Sucks Dick* or *Fag Heaven*. Or through asking their parents, "Why are those women holding hands?" and being told, "They're sick. They're doomed to hell." At least in those glimpses, there was a sense of a world beyond the child's private perversion. She'd calmed watching those men moving according to whim, twisting like the prettiest girls, pumping their hips like the worst kind of guys, with mustaches and waxed nipples and shaggy bangs, with props oiled specially, with longing and feuds and the zigzagging sparks of electric tension that shoot between members of any subculture.

"What did she want?" asked Agnes, without a glance at Joan, as though they were debating some figure beyond Joan, which, actually, they were.

"Joan knew she wasn't who she thought she was," said the superfan. But according to lore, Joan had been gay long before The Cock, had been gay since childhood.

"What do you mean?" Joan asked.

The superfan leaned in, her cheek brushing Joan's, and whispered in Joan's ear, "Joan Vole is trans."

"What the hell are you talking about?" Joan's neck burned. "That's not true." The icy lacquer of the piano was her only relief. She collapsed against it. The superfan stared, picturing her, like Meredith had, with a little penis dangling in her underwear, or, worse: no penis, and wanting one. She had to calm down. Her thoughts were too loud.

The door banged open, and Victor burst in. A grim drugstore dreadnought dangled from his fist. He almost made its bulbous shape cool with his swagger and shiny bun. "I got it," he said, voice proud but quavering, as though hell-bent on earning credit even as he absorbed the scene. "You okay, Mrs. Vole?"

"Go get more guitars," snapped Lula, as though Victor had interrupted the summer's sole chance for intrigue. She turned to the fan. "Tell us more."

The superfan smiled dreamily. "Joan once did the kindest thing for me that anyone has ever done."

"No," Joan shouted, too loud, like a siren.

Agnes and Lula turned and stared at her.

"Kids, she has nothing to be embarrassed about." The superfan was authoritative in her fancy blazer. "Joan herself might say nothing special happened, but it's not true." Joan's arms shot up. She wanted to pin the superfan to the wall, physically stop her from revealing a word more. But then she'd never respect Joan's wishes about the video. "In the moment I was scared, yes, but I've come to realize that night pulled me out of my rotten life."

"What happened?" Agnes asked.

The superfan swallowed. Joan's gaze went glassy, the rainbow lights of Love und Romance beating across the domes of her eyeballs. "When Joan Vole is ready, she'll tell you herself." The superfan cut her gaze to Joan. "You're lucky you get to spend time with such a brilliant musician."

"Yeah?" asked Lula, perking up.

"Oh yes," said the superfan, hands jumping. "I mean that. Joan Vole is a legend. Her show, just two days ago, it was the best I ever attended. Joan was wild up there, her hair all crazy, screaming the lyrics with her best scratchy voice."

Joan lunged toward the superfan. But before she got there, exhaustion slammed her: the clammy drive, the absorption of so much toxic green, the hundred times a day her fingers twitched for her phone. She could not bring herself to harm this woman again.

"Should I get Georgina?" Victor asked. The guitar drooped, brushing the floor.

Of course. Joan had an administrator specifically employed to back her up. She didn't have to deal with the fan alone, the way she always dealt with everything alone. "Yes."

Victor dumped the dreadnought, which released an ugly chord. He fled. The classroom quieted, relief settling Joan's stomach. Help was coming. When in her life had she ever been able to simply call for help?

The superfan's face sagged, eyes simmering in their soft bags. "But we had an understanding."

Joan cracked her lips. But she couldn't manage to say anything.

The classroom door opened. Georgina loomed in the doorway, Victor behind. Joan went loose. Finally, help.

"What's going on?" asked Georgina.

"This woman interrupted our class." Joan hesitated. "This very nice woman. But she's leaving now."

"I only came to visit Joan," the superfan said. And she did appear normal: blazer still crisp, hair perfect but for one loose thread.

"Campus security will direct you out," Georgina told the fan, her tone low and calm.

The superfan's head dropped as she made her way to the door. Joan tried to catch her eye. Please let her look up once, give Joan any little sign that she'd keep their secret close. But she refused to turn. And then she was gone.

Georgina squared her feet. "Okay, kids." She trained her focus on the students. "I'm sorry your classwork was interrupted by Joan's friend."

"She's not my friend." The superfan had said she'd wait to reveal what had happened. So Joan was okay. She was okay.

"Workshop is over," Georgina snapped. "Kids, return to the dormitory for free time. Joan, a word."

The kids gathered their unused notebooks and pencils, Agnes her drumsticks, Victor his tuba. And then it was just Georgina and Joan.

"What happened?" Georgina's voice was steely, precise.

"She's a stalker," Joan said. The word was wrong, pricking her tongue. "She followed me down here."

Georgina smoothed her navy work dress. "Walk me through, please, Joan. Did you call the police? Or follow any of the Intruder with Intent protocols delineated in your orientation materials?"

Joan's head blazed. "No."

"May I ask why not?" Georgina's cadence jumped.

"Wait, but you're acting like this is my fault."

Georgina crossed her arms. "Let's review the protocol you followed, and then we'll determine fault."

Joan's breath quickened. How was it her fault her classroom had been invaded? "I actually worried she might harm someone."

Georgina set her fists on her temples. "There was a violent individual in your classroom, and you didn't follow protocol? Joan. This is highly concerning."

"I didn't know she was violent—and look, she wasn't. Everything was under control."

"From where I stand, the situation was in no way 'under control.' Victor Ruiz said you yelled at this woman. That she got right up next to Agnes Silverman?"

"I was just annoyed. It wasn't scary." Joan steadied herself with the edge of the piano.

"And you let a student desert your classroom and scamper all over campus? Before this crisis even occurred?"

"I know." She wanted to scream that this wasn't her fault, but it was.

"Help me understand here, Joan. Here you have a malicious stranger invading your classroom. In my eyes, most people would contact an authority. Is this because you don't have a phone?"

"She's not malicious." Her spine wobbled.

Georgina offered an icy stare. "I intend to interview your students, and they may not share your perspective. These are children who've been entrusted to your care. For some, it's the first time they've left home. This is the whole reason for orientation. To ascertain teachers are crystal clear on emergency protocol for situations such as this."

Joan's breath boomed in her ear. Was it this loud for Georgina? "Wait, but this is ridiculous. Why are you blaming me?"

"Look at me, please, Joan. You appeared on campus without notice. You did not complete a Lesson Cycle or your required paperwork. You did not submit your revised plans as promised—and that was already a compromise the likes of which I've never offered to any other teacher. And I have to be honest. Even if it weren't for this ample collection of red flags,

I can't say I'd look kindly on any of my teachers, not even the most trustworthy, hosting a stranger in their classroom. Especially not without permission. And on the first full day, no less, when students are already disoriented."

"I didn't invite her." She roared the words.

Georgina let the growl dissolve. When her voice returned, it was low and calm. "We've invested in you, Joan. So I'll give you one last chance, even as such leniency is beyond my better judgment."

Joan didn't need this woman's scraps. She'd been menaced and insulted. But without this job, she couldn't afford to establish herself somewhere new. She'd be banished to wander the highways, dipping into gigs only until she was inevitably exposed as perverse and toxic. She'd sleep in her car at road stops and circulate around America, fingers twitching to write, terrified to stop driving in case she indulged. A salmon cannery in Alaska. Waitressing in Vegas, running wild after one shift drink. Worse—and most likely—slouching to Coney Island and begging for her lease back, crawling into the burrow of her ruinous old life.

Her feet sank into the carpet. This campus was quiet. She could help these kids, maybe, if she tried harder. She could help Sparrow anticipate the dangers of art, Sparrow who was young and so innocent, who could use guidance. Joan set her shoulders straight. "I regret the invasion." She couldn't bring herself to apologize for what was not her fault.

Georgina raised a hand and closed her eyes. "Just answer me, Joan. You're willing to try?"

Joan hesitated. "Yes."

"I'll start seeking backups today. We have a number of connections up in Charlottesville."

Joan let her breath out. "You won't need them."

12

JOAN HURRIED TO THE COMPUTER CLUSTER, SWEAT STICK-
ing her hair up in mounds. Her hands were slick and clammy,
no matter how fiercely she wiped them. She burst through the
doors, expecting the lab to be adulterated by her previous visit,
but there were the same steady blank screens, waiting, the
same chairs mostly pushed in—except one, still askew from
where she'd leaped from her seat.

She sat in the misfiled chair and called up the first video,
the clearest and longest. She watched it again, half expecting
it to be all new—Joan humping the fan, spraying piss everywhere, the audience gasping and cursing.

She watched it a second time. Could the superfan really
have been fine with what happened? The third time through,
for a fraction of a second, the superfan's head turned to the
side, flashing for one beat. Joan moved the cursor back to the
moment and stopped the video. This was the only time you
could see her face after Joan first embraced her: a blurry smear.
She took a screenshot, opened it, zoomed in.

Her heart stilled. Close up, the superfan's eyes were squeezed shut, her mouth a loop of horror, nose scrunched up as though against a terrible odor. This just in the first embrace. The woman had been harmed. There was no question.

Joan combed through the video, stopping at key moments, slowing it down, examining screenshots. In the second embrace, there, two or three droplets catching the light, projecting from Joan's middle. They only traveled for a second, only when the lights cycled white. They disappeared in the red gel.

In the second embrace, when Joan and the superfan shifted momentarily in opposite directions, Joan's groin was visible, only from 9:29 to 9:31, but it was there, a fleshy flap, and when she zoomed in she found the clear curl of a pubic hair, defined in the pink smear.

How had no one else seen any of these clues? Was she so obscure that no one gave a shit? A pang sliced her. If Paige had committed a crime like that, everyone would've combed the video and seen.

But that was good—what, was she crazy?—that was so good. She was free. Yes, she'd done what she'd thought she'd done, but it didn't matter. The evidence was out there, all these angles, and no one cared. Yes, someone could still find it, but her videos got the most hits in the first hours. The superfan had been upset, yes, initially, but now she was okay.

Joan tried to let the relief take hold, sitting there in the dim basement lab. Let the calm loosen her arms, release her jaw. But she stayed rigid as steel. Like she was preparing for attack, like her skin had shelled over. The superfan's cheer in the classroom only panicked her harder. Stiffly, she stood up. She made her way between the computers and down to the dorm.

*

Back in Community Village, Joan jittered on her plastic mattress. When she closed her eyes, the face in the video sprang up, the pixels etching on her eyelids. That zoomed-in screenshot, the superfan's nose smearing in motion so it was as triangular as a wedge of cheese, her eyeball melting in the corner, the side of her cheek a jagged rush of flesh. But she'd been plainly grimacing, even more terrified than Joan had remembered. And that was even before the piss that now glittered so boldly in the white light that Joan could see it on normal speed. But she had to stop freaking—no one had seen. She was safe. The superfan had said Joan hadn't done anything wrong, and she was the person whose experience mattered. That was how harm worked.

In the hallway, pacing, she nearly knocked into Sparrow. They wore an oversized gray flannel that turned them into a teen boy, hair tawny and ruffled, smear of ink tinting its roots. Joan went breathless at that cherry bow of lips, that unruly mop. They were so pure, so easy.

"Hey," Sparrow said. The word was a round, pretty drop of sound. See—Joan had been spared humiliation so she could have a carefree interaction just such as this. She should live inside it.

"Hi," said Joan, the word too articulated.

"I like your outfit."

Joan looked down, like it could be a surprise. But of course she was still wearing the linen tunic and linen shorts. She wore them every day, like she was institutionalized, never having to worry if she was feminine or fancy enough for New York, not that she'd ever worried much. Sparrow reached out and pinched the tunic at Joan's belly. The material tugged across her nipples. They hardened. Sparrow laughed. "How many of these do you own?"

"Oh god," Joan said, cheeks prickling against the dry, cool air. "One." A grass stain marked her ass where she'd sat down somewhere, the green so rich it soaked into whatever it touched.

"I like it," Sparrow said. "The Joan Vole Uniform of Boredom and Doom." They tugged the bottom hem, flattening the front so it exposed the outline of Joan's torso. Their focus shot up, checking: *Is this okay?* Joan showed her teeth to indicate it was, but she probably snarled.

"Do I pull it off?" Joan asked.

"You could wear a garbage bag and look hot." Sparrow released the linen and returned their hands to their flanks. "Sorry."

"What are you doing now?" Joan couldn't bear to be any more direct than that.

"Drawing." Sparrow smiled shyly. "You sure I can't convince you to model? Just for ten minutes?" They hesitated, picking at their fingernails. "When else will I ever get a chance to draw Joan Vole?"

"Okay," Joan said, the word popping out. Because why not? Why shouldn't she do anything normal and good?

Sparrow's room was a different atmosphere from the rest of the suite: the air crisper, the glow dim and fancy, the shades drawn, and the banker's lamp burning. In Sparrow's fiery face was Joan's old one, laboring away on a song doomed to drown in its own juices. What words would've yanked Joan out of the muck? None, was the sad truth.

Sparrow shoved a calico snake into the crack at the base of the door. So that was why Joan hadn't seen their light from the hall that first night.

Dropping onto the bed, Joan worried it would feel too intimate, queasy. But the blanket was stretched taut across crisp sheets, and the smell that puffed off the fabric was paper.

"This is just a warm-up," Sparrow said, sitting on the edge of their desk chair. "Fast poses."

Joan compressed the head of Sparrow's plastic dog. Its squeak was yearning and alive. The sound the superfan might've made when Joan attacked her, if Joan could've heard anything above the roar of blood.

Sparrow lifted the pink stone. "I do need you to hold still."

Joan willed herself to sink into her body. All she had to do was sit. The easiest job possible. Especially easy in this tidy room, with Sparrow's bottles of ink with crisp white labels, the loose-leaf paper, each sheet so aligned that the stacks formed bricks. Sparrow directed Joan into a series of simple postures: "Look in awe. Look mesmerized. Look like you're watching something closely, no, intently, more intense. Like you're watching a snail climb a man's testicle. Or a sandwich rising from the dirt, its bread inscribed with the story of your future."

Joan raised her chin toward the blue, chilly idea of Norway.

"Like that, yes. You look alive." Joan's neck flamed. Sparrow bowed and scribbled. They squeezed their stone. "Can you look fierce now? Hyper?" Their pencil moved faster, their cheeks flushed. Joan burned to have done that to them. She wanted to stay in this room forever. "How about brutal?"

Paige's baffled face at the door to Love und Romance. Joan's skeleton sagged, muscles giving way to the natural lean of her age.

Sparrow's tongue peeked out, ticking with the slow rhythm of their work. Had Joan even once achieved such holy concentration? She channeled her tension into the poses, cocking her head, mugging sorrow, fine-tuning each muscle toward the assigned emotion. And Sparrow drew. Here Joan was, materially helping. Warmth infused her. She sat higher, craning toward

Sparrow's page. Her arms were longer and stretchier in the blue sketch, her mouth bigger, her eyes holes for tubes of light. "It's nice you don't play music while you work."

"I'm sorry." Sparrow looped their pencil across the white board. "I would—I love music. I mean, obviously. I just can't concentrate while it's playing."

"No, I really mean I like it." The underlayer of silence was rich, edible. No modems whining, no buzz of electricity or water rushing in the walls. Even the scratch of Sparrow's pencil was soothing, like the whimper of waves, if you forgot it signaled the production of art. Joan could almost forget the superfan in the calm of this room.

Sparrow swapped between the blue pencil and the diminished bean of the eraser as Joan relaxed into clay. As Sparrow worked, they mumbled. At first Joan thought they were singing, but there was no tune and the words made no sense, strung from head to tail in waves of quiet nonsense, so soft Joan's muscles melted. Nothing had changed. So why did she feel itchy, like she wanted to scream?

"Softer angles," Sparrow said. They grabbed Joan's elbow and bent it into a gentler curve.

Joan didn't realize she was holding her breath until Sparrow's hand was off her. Were her poses masculine? Was she revealing her gender now the way she had, somehow, to the fan? She'd had a kind of sex with the superfan, after all, so maybe she'd been vulnerable enough for her to see something in Joan that others hadn't. Joan had a flat chest, she was wiry, but those traits were not her choice. She dangled an arm limply, girlishly. Sparrow poked it straight with the tip of their pencil.

"How was Carlotta's visit?" Sparrow asked.

Cold air filled Joan. "What?"

"I heard she visited your class." Class had only been over for an hour. If any teacher ever found the video, this whole place would know in seconds.

"You know her?" The words emerged tight, like Joan was unwinding them from the spool of her brain.

"Of course." Sparrow squinched their forehead, peering at Joan. "I don't think I was ever at a concert Carlotta didn't attend. You know her. Come on, Joan. The only fan you ever hugged."

Joan's tongue dried. "Right."

Sparrow dropped the pencil. "That was sorta adorable. My friend texted me. She was like, can you believe Vole in this video? Fire AF. Her words, not mine." Joan waited for them to explain what that meant, but they didn't. Joan formed her expression into a mold of wise understanding. "I thought it would be one of your tit things, and I was like, whatever. I've followed Joan across the country; I've seen it all. But then it was like, a hug, really? That's the shocking shit."

"Yeah," Joan said. Really what? Really bad? Really intense?

"So sweet. We couldn't believe it." Sparrow rolled their eyes. "I watched it five times."

After five times, surely they would've noticed at least one of the clues Joan had found. Sparrow beamed at Joan like she was a teddy bear. "Thank you?" Joan said.

"Least Vole moment ever. You're getting soft—it's cute." Their smile morphed into a smirk. And did they wink? Did they actually wink? "Now Carlotta coming to visit you? And me, here? The Time of the Fan."

"I guess." She had to steer Sparrow away. She wished she had a phone so she could run to the bathroom and look up Carlotta. "You must have fans too."

They snorted. "There's three people on earth who've read my comics."

"Trust me, you don't want superfans."

Sparrow burst out laughing. "I certainly do not."

Joan leaned back, affronted. "You don't want people to care about your comics?"

"Not to that extent, certainly not." Sparrow evaluated their board. "Anyway, I'm just messing around most of the time. At home I don't have time to think. I'm either drawing before I go to work or when I get home. Whatever happens at school inundates the process."

Sparrow laboring in the black dawn, damp in the armpits, gathering strength to face teens. "So you write about your job?"

They flicked a piece of invisible dust from their desk. "It's a school for troubled boys."

Joan pictured boys from another century, as thick and tubular as men. The softness of Sparrow's arms turned denser, muscled.

Sparrow reached for a stack of boards and fingered a page. Those blocky figures again, careful robots in tidy panels. Their dialogue chunks of perfect text in squared-off speech bubbles. "I had to, like, physically rip this kid's fingers out of his best friend's eyeballs." Sparrow's face blurred in affection, gazing at the board. "He was all wound up, cheeks bleeding, jumping around and talking so fast I could barely understand him. I couldn't send him home—his dad is volatile. So we went for a walk around the border of the school. Just walking and talking for literally hours until he calmed down. We kept circling— playground, basketball court, temporary classrooms, parking lot, again and again. And still I couldn't let him go. This comic is the walk."

In each panel, a tall cardboard snowman strolled beside a short cardboard snowman, ordered text popping from the smaller snowman's head. "You're my favorite teacher even though you're neutered," the small robot said. "You actually look at our faces or whatever. And we can check our phones in class and you don't care! And you have a dumb name. But that's cool. I'm named after my mom's first car. Even though she crashed it like right after she got it, she still remembers it and she was like damn that would be a good name for a boy and it is. Watch out, bro, for that puddle. Ouch, that looks wet! OMG, actually, can we get a doughnut?"

"This is great," Joan said, the words popping out.

Despite the stiff containers of the drawings, somehow Sparrow had brought both characters to life, even Sparrow's own responses, calibrated to calm: "You have a lot of energy today, Saturn. Would you enjoy another lap?" Joan could've read a whole novel about Sparrow and this hyper kid.

"I always use the same ten-panel grid. And everyone's made of boxes. I need to contain. That's the only way it works."

Joan could never hold her songs to any shape. They always wriggled into their own forms.

"What made you hug Carlotta anyway?" Sparrow retrieved their pencil from the carpet. "I thought it was because she was one of your oldest fans. I couldn't believe any geneticist looked like her when we first met. Kinda blew my mind."

Joan had pictured Carlotta a realtor, flapping through open houses, batlike, in a cape, trailing couples as they whispered reservations. Instead she'd hunched over substances Joan could never understand, that she couldn't even picture. Scraps of koala? Transparent tessellated patterns, spread on sanitized epoxy counters. The secrets of the universe, of canaries, of trees, coded into every beveled edge. Carlotta was more brilliant, more knowledgeable about life than Joan ever could be. And Joan had splashed her with her own genetic material, never thinking she could decipher anything from it, treated her like some wild moron. She turned away, pain searing her ribs. She couldn't bear to look at Sparrow, couldn't stand this conversation for one more second.

"I was like, wow, Joan's finally celebrating Carlotta. But turns out you don't even know who she is." Sparrow's eyes lit like they couldn't believe their own cheekiness.

"Something got into me." Joan squirmed, her legs a restless dog caught under her. She couldn't bear to lie to Sparrow. "I went crazy that night."

A giggle erupted from Sparrow. "Yeah, you did." Their face opened, eager, even, maybe, affectionate? Was that possible? They reached out like they might touch Joan. Joan longed for gentle pressure, a palm dragged down her arm, calming, tingly. But as the hand neared, Joan twitched out of its path.

Sparrow raised their eyebrows. "You all right?"

"Yes," she whispered, but her body was as humid and festered as trash. She couldn't bear to sit beside this fresh face any longer. She jumped up and fled.

13

THE NEXT DAY, CLASS TIME SWUNG AROUND AGAIN. JOAN hadn't slept, jerking awake every hour to the smudgy blur of Carlotta's pixelated face. Each time she reminded herself that she had nothing to worry about. But no matter how worn out and sleepless she was, her body a carcass she dragged across the lawn through the heat, every weekday arrived.

Her shoulders tensed as she crossed the sunlit hall to her classroom, scanning every mint-frosted cinderblock, as though Carlotta had tucked herself up in the wall. Just one more class to teach before the weekend.

She stopped at the classroom door. She couldn't force herself forward. She'd come all this way but could manage no farther. The classroom belonged to Carlotta now. Even the light was different, fluorescence mixing poisonously with the day's glare. What was wrong with her? Through the strip of doorway, the kids had collected on a single beanbag, their butts perched precariously on the wiggly sack. Lula was jabbering about a boy in poetry with "cool thighs." Agnes and Victor were punching each other's flanks too hard, competing to sing perfectly in tune.

"You're sharp, dumbass," Agnes said. She wore another home-doctored slip, this one burgundy with yellow lace affixed at random intervals. Had she dressed like this in her prodigy years, like a homeschooled child from Oklahoma? It should've been annoying on a rich girl from Manhattan, but she wore her scraps with charm, swanning around with her noodle arms waving, goth farmgirl chic. Joan liked the idea of Agnes among buttoned-up New York music nerds, rushing onstage in a flap of worn-out lace to thrill the crowds.

"I'll show you sharp." A stinging whistle cut Victor's lips.

Lula bounced with the jostle of the beanbag. At first glance they were a happy bunch, but their eyes were twitchy, their voices ragged. Joan had ruined them already.

Agnes spotted Joan and went still. The other kids turned. Now Joan had to enter. She tried not to step too carefully, like a wobbly horse. "Hello." The word was rounded, false.

She took her place in the middle of the room. Everyone watched her from the beanbag. Darkness settled on their brows. The dreadnought lay on the floor, belly-up where Victor had dumped it. What a goofy shape, what a pathetic trinket, bubbly and cheerful, B string missing, soundboard battered, bridge lifting up. The cheap polyurethane finish had spidered in patches, failing to breathe with the guitar, melting where sun had seared it. The body was swollen, glue failing in the seams, from being abandoned without a case in all this Virginia heat. Maya's guitar had exploded once, in Arizona, lacerating her face. This guitar was right on the edge. Wear and tear might've cheered Joan if they were marks of use, but there was no rhythm to the damage. The scrapes weren't strokes that had escaped the pickguard but gouges on regions of the body that were never touched in song. This instrument had been tossed loose in a truck bed with pickaxes while its owner drove pitted roads. It had been hurled down an aluminum slide every day beside a bony child or fixed to a fishing line and dunked in the ocean, where it bounced over the waves, attempting to attract a musical carp. Joan regarded the dreadnought the way an Olympic runner regards a tread-mill pushed to the back of a closet: belt rippled, keypad sticky with dust. She wanted to bash it to shards.

"Ms. Vole?" Agnes asked. "Is that lady coming back?"

Joan lifted the dreadnought. Its neck blazed in her grip, so intense, so right. She clattered it on the piano bench too hard. The kids jumped. "No." She made her voice slow, calm.

"What was all that stuff at the end?" Agnes's focus twitched between Lula and Victor, as though the three of them had plotted this attack.

"Let's move on." Joan pivoted back to the dreadnought. She reached as if to grab it, but her hand lodged into a claw. Maybe she should tell them what had happened, assuage Agnes's anxieties. Maybe it was her job as teacher to lie down at the altar of student need. They'd perked up when Carlotta referenced the assault, smelling Joan's fear.

"No, she said it was like—the nicest thing you ever did for her, or something." Hunger sharpened Agnes's face, turning it all weaselly. "That lady was going to tell us." Her voice was high and hopeful.

"There's no reason to take anything she said seriously," Joan said.

"That lady's crazy," Victor said. "Just think of her creepy-ass walk."

"You weren't there," Agnes said. "She claimed we're all going to know anyway."

"We could talk to friends from home," Lula said. Handfuls

of dry white hair slumped into her face. "On our Sunday call. We could ask them to look it up."

"No." The word was so loud it couldn't have come from Joan. Agnes shrank back like Joan had slapped her. The kids looked at each other.

"It's okay." Joan stepped toward them. They huddled up like she might beat them. "Don't worry anymore. She's just a fan."

"Is that what fans are like?" Victor asked. "Like they *want* you want you?"

"No." But they were. Or maybe only for Joan. Maybe there was a force in her, a bubbling, uncontrolled substance that magnetized pervs.

Agnes's face twisted in horror, like she was staring down the barrel of a life of slobbering sickos. The sad thing was, at Agnes's age, Joan would've relished the prospect.

"Look," Joan said. She steadied herself before them. Funny how the floor could become a stage like this, by virtue of standing on it, by the kids watching. It was awkward to shift from normal-person mode to teaching mode. "Can we try something?"

"For real?" Lula asked.

Joan handed each kid a piece of paper from a pile on the piano. Lula snatched hers, and they settled into corners of the room: Lula under the ping-pong table, Agnes on the piano, as though asserting her continued dominion over instruments. They spread their sheets in front of them, pencils raised. Joan couldn't believe she'd given instructions that now they were following. Power surged through her. "All right." She paused. The air smelled metallic. "Are you ready?" Pencils twitched. "Write the first line of a song."

"What counts as a line?" Victor fussed his bangs with delicate fingers. "It's just I know people have different definitions?"

"Anything you want. Some people hear the melody in their head." For Joan, the words always came first. "Or follow a story, or an image." Her route was digging into an event, twisting it until it morphed into its own demented narrative, but let them have the chance to write beyond their own petty jealousy or lust.

The kids bent to the task, scribbling away. How easy it was to set them working. Behold their expressions, twitching in concentration. They were trying. Joan was safe, and her students were trying. She was so lightheaded she had to rest on the piano bench. She'd teach them to make music in a healthy way, to appreciate songs without authorship, to construct songs without authorship the way she'd done with "Lakeshore." Relief fizzed through her. These kids had a chance she'd never had to focus on the parts of music that actually mattered.

"Done," Agnes said. The others dropped their pencils.

"Now pass the paper to another student," Joan said. "And continue the song with a second line."

"What? No," cried Lula.

"Just try."

Groans rose from all three monsters. Lula got up and handed over her paper to Victor. He hesitated, then delivered his to Agnes. Agnes clutched hers until Lula tore the sheet from her hands. Lula grumbled as she smoothed it out but then set to work. They were getting it. They were actually getting it.

They wrote and passed. They worked diligently; fists clenched around pencils. Here this was—a workshop of authorless songs, the impossible dream, even if Joan was executing it with the simplest exercise possible. So maybe it wasn't insane she'd run away to this camp, even if she hadn't needed to. Teaching was maybe the only real way to change how creators thought. Her core fuzzed.

"Okay," Joan said. "Victor, pick a song—the one you feel least ownership of—and make up the tune as you sing it."

Victor snatched a sheet. He tonelessly brayed, "A sweating wheel of cheese. Scorpions scramble on a broken rock. I love you, man-lover, so much. The taste of dry, sour cheese crumbling on my tooth. Dust sprays over the plain. I miss my sexy human lover. The cheese grows old and tastes of onion. A desert is so bleak and gorgeous. Will we meet again, my special fleshy lover?"

"Stop," Joan said. "Wait, stop. This is wrong. You each wrote your own song, broken up with other people's lines."

"Isn't that the point?" asked Lula.

"No." Heat crawled up her cheeks. "That is not the point. You're supposed to write one coherent song."

"It is coherent," said Victor. "Cheese is the same color as the desert, and both might smell like sexuality."

Joan sagged back against the piano. But maybe there was still hope. Maybe it was only Victor's delivery that had made the song so singularly awful. Maybe if someone sang the song in tune, with a better melody, they could locate some shred of beauty. Some of the lines about the desert weren't bad. She glanced at the piano. The keys were battered, a strip of wood coming loose at the corner.

"It's broken," said Victor. "Play the guitar."

"I don't know how."

"What?" asked Victor, bouncing on the beanbag. "Yeah, you do. You're, like, a famous singer."

Joan's heart lifted. "How did you know that?"

Victor sank into the beanbag so deeply only his limbs stuck up. "This kid in playwriting has a funny shirt of you."

Joan Vole knows best was the stupid tagline on that shirt. She bit down on her smile. "I don't play these days." She was glad she'd given Paige the Martin. Paige only had that shitty Rogue, which barely stayed in tune two songs running, even in her emerging fame never thought well enough of herself to invest in a halfway-decent instrument, no matter Joan's encouragements.

"It's probably her pedagogy not to play or something," Agnes said.

Who were these kids who applied words like *pedagogy* casually in conversation? Kids at once so much younger and so much older than Paige had been when Joan met her.

The piano wouldn't help that awful song, or a guitar, or an entire orchestra. Joan had failed them already.

"I don't get it," said Agnes, slumping against the beanbag, voice threaded with despair.

"What don't you get?" Joan asked.

"The whole thing." Agnes kneaded a chunk of air. "Like, what's even the point?"

"The point of music?" Joan's jaw locked.

Agnes pushed herself upright on the beanbag, which immediately sucked her back down. "I mean, the point of this kind of music. Like I get what's noble about, like, real skill. Like, when you can see the work. Like a kid goes up there and boom, three notes in you know he didn't practice. The hours matter. That's what they tell you. And you think it's dumb, and you fight it all the way down—like I'm special; I only have to do three hours a day—and one day you realize, watching that kid trying to play the way he's supposed to play, you realize, yes. The hours matter." She was paunchy under the jaw, like an old lady. "But this kind of music, I don't know. How can you write something out of nowhere? Like make it up, and it's nothing, and you just sing it out of your head?" She rattled her fingers.

Joan didn't know the last time she'd played a song out of nowhere. She couldn't have completed her own exercise, writing any decent lyric in minutes.

"Yeah," said Agnes, as though Joan had made any meaningful response. "It's not a piece that was written carefully a hundred years ago and played a thousand times by a thousand geniuses. It's random shit pasted together. And so how are you even supposed to know how to perform it? There's no legacy."

"But that's just this particular exercise," Victor said. "It's meant to be random."

Agnes shook her head, the white spot on her bangs bobbing. "But it always feels like that to me. 'Popular' music. Some muddle of nonsense. What's the point of anything if we're not pushing our bodies to the limit? How can anything valuable come from some random choice?"

Joan stirred in her belly. "If you're steeped in one type of music it might take time to acculturate to other styles." But Joan didn't know if she could do it again either. Whenever she thought of performing now—not that she ever would again, but still—she couldn't stand the idea of talking, singing, moving, words coming out of her in front of all those people. Any misstep could be recorded. Teaching was like that too. Her worst self could betray her any second.

"But songs can be fun," Victor said, pushing energy into his words. "Let's play some of ours. Me and Lula were practicing."

"Yay," said Lula.

"I don't know about that," Joan said. Kids all over campus were singsonging poetry and emoting monologues and breathily confessing nonfiction. Just because she'd failed them on her first attempt didn't mean she had to let them sink into their private indulgences.

160

"Come on," Victor said. "Just to prove a point?"

Agnes frowned into her beanbag. Somewhere in Joan's torso, a twitch. "Fine."

"Hooray." Lula stood. "Me first."

"But remember," Joan said. "These songs aren't yours. At least try to imagine they aren't." She had to insert her lame attempt.

Lula took her position in the center of the room, ominously sans instrument. "I'll sing about my sandwich." She aimed her pale cheeks at Agnes and Victor.

Joan marshaled the energy for a nod.

"My sandwich is pretty, my sandwich is neat. When my sandwich is happy, it's stuffed full of meat." This wasn't singing, more a toneless chant. Somehow, even still, she was off-pitch and strained. Lula grinned at Victor and Agnes. Victor gave a thumbs-up, but there was a sneer on Agnes's lips. "So you may want to know what my sandwich might be. My sandwich is between my legs; it's part of my body."

All three kids exploded in laughter, Agnes and Victor slapping the beanbag.

"Stop," Joan said. "That's it. No more songs." Her breath rose high in her chest. They'd pirated a phone, had researched rumors of Joan's perversion buried on Reddit, in blogs. She set a hand on her lungs, trying to settle them. They'd heard her feistier songs. Or they'd just known. They'd looked at her and known. Even if she hadn't attacked Carlotta, she had this perverted history dragging behind her wherever she went, like a tail.

"Don't be like that, Mrs. Vole," Victor said. "We just want to sing. For Agnes."

"Next time," Joan said, voice clipped. She hated that they'd discovered her true self, after how hard she'd tried to conceal it.

"Please," said Victor. "We practiced."

"So performing will be something to look forward to." Joan willed her voice upbeat, picturing their reports: *Instructor penalized students for her own lack of humor.* "Practice more."

"But we practiced so much already," Victor said, a whine entering his voice, but a whine of confusion. Probably no one had ever declined his performance.

"Yeah?" Joan offered her hands for them to see. Her right nails were grown out by half an inch from the fingertip, longer on the thumb, for picking. They were yellowed and ribbed— most people didn't let a nail grow long enough to age—chipped and battered by strumming. The calluses on her left hand were frosted stones embedded under the surface. Strings had left scars across the backs of her hands. Her fingers routinely froze from tendonitis. She'd known her romance with the "Lakeshore" guy was real when he'd noticed them, the way a sustained lover always did eventually, but instead of recoiling from the mismatched instruments that had handled his sensitive parts, he'd lifted both of her wrists and kissed every knuckle, every joint, every overgrown nail. He'd smeared her hands down his torso, her calluses catching on his nipples.

"Sick," said Lula, gaping. "You have man hands. Are you gay?"

Was that a mean glint in Lula's eye? And how did she think women fucked anyway? With gardening tools? "No," Joan said.

"Mine were worse," said Agnes.

"Not possible," Joan said. "I've been playing since before you were born."

Agnes shrugged, her gaze hard.

Joan had to go somewhere the kids could follow. Maybe Georgina was right about examples. The authorless songs weren't exactly models for what Joan wanted to write. And they didn't even make her want to pee anymore, usually, because she'd worn the best ones out. They swept her to a place far away, where songs shed their writers and became organisms of their own. That thrilling place where art separated from artist. Like a swirl of colorful narrative, unbound from the world. "Let's focus on a particular song," Joan said. "It's called 'Rail Rat Done Wrong Tonight.'"

"Never heard of it," said Lula. "Is it a variation of 'Kumbaya'?"

"No," said Joan. "It's an anonymous Appalachian folk song."

"Oh, shit," said Agnes. "We heard that's bad."

"Excuse me?" Joan said.

"We had this Appropriation Summit," Victor said, wriggling upright. "About, like, the songs that got stolen around here. Like white people stealing the songs of Black people and shit. It's messed."

"Right." Joan had forgotten the kids had any programming outside her class. "That was an insidious practice, and I'm glad you learned about it." She wondered who was behind this summit, if Sparrow had a hand. Joan would never be a good enough person for Sparrow, would never make up for what she'd done to Carlotta. "This is a song whose origins can't be traced to theft. It follows a character called Rail Rat."

"Is he a real rat?" asked Agnes.

"The title just means a man who's no good. But I first heard the song when I was a kid, so I picture him human-sized, with a man's trunk and a rat's head." She'd never discussed a song of no provenance before. Her spongy red insides were on view.

"Ooh," squealed Lula, as though Joan had hit a switch. "I love rodent-human hybrids."

Rail Rat was solid in Joan's mind: rodent head, top-heavy and all nose, leaning forward like his skull might tumble from his shirt collar. One night, when Joan was thirteen, her father had played an album, *Lost Folk Worlds*, a collection of rare ballads resurrected by a Chicago street artist—the album had been pressed on him outside the Washington/Wells L station, and it was one of the few CDs he owned. Certainly it was the first music he'd played around Joan. He was grading trig identity exams on the dining room table while she sat splay-legged on the floor, reading the shaded boxes of Fun Facts in her history textbook.

When the song came on, Joan couldn't believe how one spinning disc transformed her dreary living room into a riot of banjo and fiddle. All these thirteen years, and, with a press of a button, every night could've sounded like this? Regret washed through her for all the songs she'd missed, all the silent nights she'd suffered. Of course she'd heard music, in the shiny chambers of malls and at the lip syncs of grade school talent shows. But never loudly, privately, at home. And better yet, this was music from another time, a flavor unlike any she'd tasted. She was transported to Rail Rat's world: saloons, train tracks, coffee heated in soup cans over open flames. The scrappy mystery and freedom of it all. She'd been so lost in that sepia landscape, so enchanted by that uncaring scamp Rail Rat, that her arousal for the artistry bloomed slowly: if you scraped off the performer's gravelly, imprecise voice, sliding off pitch at every refrain, the tinny ring of his probably rented room, hollow behind his banjo, under all that half-assed production was the genius of the song itself, the nasty charm of the lyrics pushing through, their playful sharpness, the remorseless, brutal way Rail Rat's lover and wife were dispatched in a few words by a train bearing down, and even the mood, those lyrics hovering between giddy and heartbreaking. Here was a wild, bizarre song that made its own life, that had nothing to do with the man who sang it or whoever might've written it in the first place—no known person, as it turned out—that was a whole world unto itself, snipped free of its history of creation. The magical holiness of the song sent a loosening charge through Joan. She wanted to sublimate herself, disappear, become a dog at the feet of the song. She didn't realize she was peeing until her father dragged her up by the elbow.

"Mary-Anne. My carpet."

But she couldn't help it. She longed to roll over, to show her soft belly to the song.

When her father fell asleep that night she snuck down and stole the CD. Thereafter, for weeks, she listened to "Rail Rat Done Wrong Tonight" on her headphones again and again while releasing into the empty bathtub. When the throb of the song dulled and she could listen in public, she marched through school with her finger on her Discman's back button, charged up by this rat man who was so feral and free. Her father never noticed the disc was gone or feared conjuring the night by asking.

"Does the song say he just has a rat head?" Lula asked. "Or is there some chance he has a tail too? Because that would be chill if he had a head and a tail." She twisted on her beanbag like she had her own tail to whip around.

"It sounds kinda cheesy," said Victor. "No offense."

"Cheesy is the last thing it is," Joan said. "It's lively. It's misogynistic. The women in his life die, all but his mother, and he goes on like nothing happened. But the song's so cheeky you don't mind."

"I doubt that," said Agnes.

"It's hard to explain." Joan's own songs had been explained plenty, always nonconsensually, on blogs and in reviews, but also at shows, usually by music nerds, who'd corner her and explain the symbolism of her foggy recordings, her nonstandard modes, the strap imagery in "Rooster, Too" and how it harkened back to folktronica staples, the way the seagull in "Lakeshore" was her conscience, riding her spine as she fucked. The eclairs were the love she'd never have—sticky, oversweet, making her sick— the whale in Lake Michigan was her missed normal life—sure, maybe. But could a song be explained? "It's his personality. It's that we love him, right from the start, so we don't care that he's awful. Or we care, and we like it because we want that freedom too. Freedom from, I don't know. The grief of life? Morality?" The unhinged freedom, the hatefulness was what she'd loved about the song. That anyone could be so unapologetic and get away with it. Later, of course, she'd understand "anyone" meant men, but Joan had already resolved to win that flavor of freedom one day. Sitting on her father's rug that evening, the vinyl odor of textbook pages wafting up, she'd wished she was alone some- where she could soil the carpet and no one would care, where she could enjoy the stinging, cramping pleasure. Making a mess was the ultimate freedom of the moment. You had to so thoroughly inhabit your enjoyment that you forgot the stain and stink of the next minute. She wanted the kids jazzed up, like she'd been. Not necessarily pissing on the carpet, but feeling the way a song could carry them away on its back.

"What's the point of it?" Victor asked, crossing his skinny wrists over his knee and leaning forward. "It's just about some random loser? That's uber depressing."

"The song can take you somewhere else," Joan said.

The kids squinted. "I feel that with songs," Agnes said. "Some songs, sometimes. Like when I first hear them."

"Exactly," Joan said. "You can wear a song out." She was ex- plaining too much. Part of why she loved these songs was that they had different meanings at different moments, changing color like a white wall in the shifting light of day. Sometimes she hated herself for loving Rail Rat, and sometimes she loved hating him. If she explained for a minute more, she'd kill him. And, besides, she owed these kids an ounce of effort, no matter how deeply she hated the idea of playing anything. "Look, I'll just sing it." The idea shot out of her like a fart.

"Cool," chirped Agnes, as though a performance was anything the kids had requested.

"Pass me the dreadnought," Joan said.

The kids stared at her. "Huh?" Lula said. "The heck's that?"

Joan seized the guitar so forcefully that she nearly cracked its neck.

"You call it that?" Agnes asked, but she couldn't suppress a feral grin. "But that's mental. Wait, seriously?"

Let this end as quickly as it started. She wanted to cry having a guitar in her hands. She pressed it into the sweet spot on her chest, warmth rushing in at contact. Even the cartoon shape of a dreadnought was correct over her heart, awkwardly huge as dreadnoughts were, set exactly where she held her Martin, higher than most performers. When Joan didn't plan to strum too hard she loved to play standing up with no strap, foot on the monitor wedge when she couldn't stand the pressure, knee raised to support the Martin, face twisting in delicious discomfort. The muscle memory kicked in now. Her breasts flattened to accommodate the dreadnought, her bicep and forearm overgripping to brace it, her elbow pinning it in place. The position killed her fingers and twisted her wrist, ached her back and neck all the next day, but that was part of the thrill. Maybe that was all the straps in "Rooster, Too" had ever been: Joan's muscles longing for relief.

The kids watched her. That old rush zapped through. What was she doing? She should never have picked up a guitar again.

She lowered the dreadnought. She should smash it to dust. But the kids needed to understand what she'd loved about the song. And playing "Rail Rat" didn't count as performing. Not with this nothing dreadnought. Not with cozy, unclaimed songs. Not for educational purposes.

Joan strummed hard, taming the strings. The action was so high her fingertips stung, the sound pingy and toothy like every rubbish dreadnought everywhere, but not as blaring as most because it was such a junk model. This dreadnought had passed a rough, music-free life, and her job was to jerk it back on course. The kids perked up. The dreadnought's voice slid out of tune, then back in. She'd forgotten how bombastic even a shitty dreadnought was, even with its thin, cheap sound. The kids peered in wonder as her wrist flapped over the strings. Boomy, brassy, awful chords, that grating ping. But despite the quality of the instrument, it was natural playing. Of course it was. Only a couple of days had passed. Joan had played for so many hours—sometimes eight a day—for so many years that her fingers would remember forever.

"Rail Rat came along," she sang in a stuffy voice. "Rail Rat," she added, clearing her throat. The acoustics of the room swallowed the music, like the walls were sponge. "Rail Rat, oh Rail Rat." She was doing this. "Rail Rat set his beans on a flame. Rail Rat spoke to his sweetheart his name. Rail Rat took a whisky in his palms. Rail Rat forgot to call his ma." The lyrics slid out, easy and playful. Her heart drummed her lungs. She was singing again, and it was good, her lips perfectly shaping around the words. "Rail Rat. Oh Rail Rat."

Agnes sat up on the beanbag, biting her nails, watching intently. Victor's eyes were huge and shining, and Lula gripped his knee like she couldn't miss a note. They were only watching like that because Joan was intense, unstable. Her pulse raced.

Her cheeks filled with blood. She'd missed this feeling so much. Her groin pulled for it.

And then, before she got to Rail Rat's journey to the train tracks and his tryst there on the ties, interrupted by his wife, or the shocking roar of the train bearing down on all three figures, unseen in their cloud of blinding emotions, killing the women while knocking Rail Rat to safety, the way he wiped his boots of gore and trotted back to town to pick up his life, floating between saloons, drinking whisky, eating beans and forgetting to call his mother with no apparent guilt, before Joan could squeeze out the next refrain, Carlotta's face bobbed into her mind, smeared in motion. Carlotta horrified—a geneticist, a person. Joan's throat plugged with a rush of acid, and she dropped the guitar.

The roar in her ears was so blaring she didn't even hear the dreadnought strike the ground. She fell to her knees and grabbed her mouth with one hand, shoved the guitar away with the other. Her head rang. She spat on the floor.

"Oh my god," Lula said. "Are you gonna barf?"

Victor scampered from the room.

Joan's torso was scraped raw. And she'd let Victor run loose into the hall again. She should stop him. She reached out one arm, flaccid on the air. She'd had the life she wanted, and she'd used it for harm. Acid thickened on her tongue.

"That was a lot," Agnes said.

Victor rushed in with a mess of paper towels. Joan accepted one, squeezed it into a ball. He used another to blot at the floor, missing where she'd spat.

"It's okay," Joan said. "You don't have to do that."

Victor's arm, still hanging onto the crumpled paper towels, dropped to his hip. "I loved that song."

Joan massaged her neck. "What?"

"I don't know. This is lame." His head tipped toward the ceiling, muscled neck stretched. "But it's like I was there with that rat guy. At the stupid fire."

Agnes and Lula held still, watching him. Like if they moved one finger, Victor would snap back into his normal self.

Victor raised his arm with its cloud of paper towels. "Like, I felt the hot beans. Not the actual beans but, like, the can in his hand. Ribbed aluminum under a loose label." His fingers squeezed the invisible can. "I, like, was there. And not like reading a book. But like it actually happened." His eyes darted around like he was terrified to have been dragged to a fireside decades in the past.

Joan searched him. "You're fucking with me."

"No." Victor squinted at her. "I want to, like, stay there. Like, really bad. Eating beans and shit. Really!"

"Yeah, right," said Lula. "You're too rich for beans."

"For now." Victor squinched up his face. "My parents are splitting." His voice thinned. "It's gross."

"Oh," said Joan, the only word that bubbled out. "I'm sorry, Victor." She should hug him or something, but her arms were stiff and useless.

"Whatever," he said, waving his handful of towels. "It's chill." He bent to scrub the floor, pushing the wad of paper over nothing, missing, every time, the dark blot of Joan's spit, his arm pumping to the silent beat of a lost train.

*

The kids disbanded to the mysteries of free time. As soon as the room cleared, Joan's arms loosened. She hadn't noticed she'd been holding them up, fingers bent into claws, as though fending off attack. The moment she was alone, Carlotta's face mushroomed up, the scouring wool of her skirt, the musk of her fear.

She spun to leave. But there was Agnes in the doorway. Slouching, gaze cast down, face pale and small under the woolly cap of her pixie cut.

"Agnes?" Joan asked, almost expecting this one not to be Agnes but some deflated copy.

Agnes shuffled into the room, head drooped. Joan wanted to laugh, but this was real; the kid was really upset.

Agnes sat on the floor, as close to the dreadnought as she could without touching it. The light slanted a new angle through the basement window as it deepened to amber, washing the room like an old photo.

Agnes leaned forward, so close to the guitar her chin almost touched it. She looked like she wanted to lunge at it and wail away for hours.

"Do you want to talk more?" Joan took a seat across from her. The carpet was scratchy on her ass. "Would that help?"

"No."

"Do you want to tell me why you quit guitar?"

"No."

Maybe Agnes was exhausted from having had to chatter through class like all was normal when the main point of her life had been excised. "That's all right."

"I get it," Agnes said, with shiny eyes. "I wanted to tell you. I totally get what you're going through."

Joan slid her butt back on the floor. But Agnes was still staring. "I don't know what you're talking about."

"Why you freaked in class."

Had this kid somehow figured out the video's clues? But no. Only Joan and Carlotta could decode it, united now forever in their secret knowledge. She forced herself to ask, "What do you mean?"

Agnes's voice was a monotone: "You're freaking out about music too."

Joan's lips went dry. "We're dealing with very different situations." She used her professional voice, swallowing a lump. She'd been in charge of her own grueling hours of practice, had learned the wire recorder by herself, the 4-track, the nuances of ribbon mic placement, had mastered, alone, how to navigate the controlled chaos of low-level touring. On top of it all, she'd studied the fancy shit, amassing her own private background of classical knowledge. She'd had no adult to hold her hand and usher her through. Agnes had nothing to cry about. The girl lowered her head further, like she was about to pass away. There was one high window in the classroom, the size of a shoebox, pressed up under the ceiling, a reminder they were underground. Outside, the sun was high and proud. A long evening stretched ahead, with nothing. "Let's check out this guy."

As Joan moved toward the dreadnought, Agnes backed up, arms shooting behind to catch herself. Joan took the guitar by the neck. The wood scorched her fingers. Every muscle in her urged to thrust it to the floor, but this kid needed it, so she forced herself to set it between them. See? This was okay. She was touching a guitar, and she wasn't dying. "Here," she said. "What can we do?" She chose one of Victor's paper towels and handed it to Agnes.

Agnes held the towel awkwardly by the edges, like it might shatter. Slowly, she brought it down to the soundboard and held it there, as though blotting blood. "What should I do?"

"Whatever you want."

Agnes's wrist loosened. She put pressure on the towel, forcing it against the wood until it flattened, then worked her way around the upper bout and the bridge, peeling off grime and dust and old skin that had worked its way under the fittings. When her towel turned gray and greasy, Joan handed her another. Agnes kept her focus on the dreadnought, as intent as if supervising a child.

"Here." Joan directed Agnes's clean towel to the pickguard. Agnes spat on it and worked the balled paper around the tortoiseshell plastic fitting, rubbing the dreadnought too gingerly, like it would break, her arms stretched to their limit so the instrument was as distant as possible.

Together they wedged the paper towel between each fret to scrub out the grease. Joan wished she had steel wool and fresh inlays to complete the job. Maybe she'd get some for the girl. Agnes worked at every stain on the dreadnought, even marks revealed as impurities in the wood. She washed the dreadnought like its wood was flesh, embedded with nerves and the capacity for pain. There was nothing they could do about the scratches that sank past the finish or the buckle rash or the sticky tuning pegs or the structural glue that would succumb any moment, collapsing the instrument to kindling.

Joan retrieved the baggie that traveled with the dreadnought since it had no case. It contained a few picks in undignified neon hues, a capo with a loose spring, and a fluttering sheet of promotional literature, yellowed and soft, that must've come with the dreadnought's original purchase. At a superstore, probably—this dreadnought had no brand. There was also a set of fresh strings, a feeble attempt, by Georgina, probably, to render the instrument playable.

"Have you changed steel strings before?" Joan asked. Agnes

must've mostly handled plastic. She accepted the packet. Joan shifted on the carpet, leaning in to help, but Agnes hoarded the guitar.

Agnes twisted the pegs until the strings were floppy, then picked out each dead wire with its bridge pin, rapidly unwinding the other side off the pegs and yanking each one off. She held the pins in her mouth like candy while she inserted the fresh strings, threading each down with the pin before pulling on it to secure it with a jerk that would've sliced the flesh of softer palms. She added an extra fret's worth of string at the top of the neck so she didn't get to pitch early, holding each string down with her index finger and inserting the end into its post. She turned each peg around to its tight position, up into tune, lifting her finger free at exactly the right moment, without the aid of a winder. Her fingers moved easily as she calibrated the strings. She didn't even pause as she cut each at its precise spot at the top of the neck. She moved quickly, with careful force, so quickly that sometimes Joan couldn't discern what she was doing. Agnes was a true musician. She wasn't afraid of her instrument. And someone had clearly taught her how to handle it—Joan's father had never bothered to learn, so she'd had to figure it all out herself. Joan kept waiting for Agnes to pause, to build a chord on the neck or strum an open string. But her thumb never disturbed the coils or loosened even the softest vibration.

Agnes's lips were set in a knot, hard and small, squinting so the wrinkles made her old. Her head was incredibly still, set that way, while her hands rattled into a blur.

The last of the sunshine shifted from amber to ocher, falling heavily over them, the only white left in the room the spot on Agnes's bangs. Agnes tuned the guitar perfectly by ear, hardly thumbing each string, so it offered the palest flavor of its note.

As soon as she was done, she raised her hands as though to signal Joan to stop time.

"Okay," Joan said, gently, "let's see what we've got."

Agnes didn't offer the instrument, so Joan slid it off her lap. Agnes had raised this dreadnought up as her child, and now Joan's hands shaped awkwardly around it. She held the instrument by the neck, displaying it as though it was for sale.

For all their work, the dreadnought looked almost exactly how it had when they'd found it, but shinier, the new strings like fresh hubcaps gleaming on an old jalopy.

"What do you think?" Joan asked.

Agnes shrugged, but she couldn't look away from the instrument, turning in the afternoon sun.

*

Back in Community Village, Joan paced across her room. She longed for that battered dreadnought, couldn't forget its smooth wood in her hands, her pussy swelling like the guitar was a guy. If she had it in her arms, she'd play an authorless song, one about a racehorse named Gumball who lost every race but whom the speaker kept betting on, for years: *I know he's a loser, but he's my only one. He never ate oats, just chewed a dog bone. Old Gumball was a goofball; he bit my big toe. Old Gumball was a rough horse with a long way to go.* Joan's knees bent to spring up. She clung to the fibers of the carpet like the room had tipped upside down. She could not play. Even if "Old Gumball" wasn't her song, even if it was no one's song, even if she was honoring or corrupting no artist by singing it, even if, even if, even if.

She kept rooted to the floor, under the spell of that rugged old roan, wonky-eyed, with legs of different lengths, the way his clattering out of the gate at the starting gun rushed the narrator with hope: finally, maybe, one day, this horse will win and it will have all been worth it, for the money, but more, for the story. That insensible blockhead incapable of knowing a man in the crowd cared. Who jumbled his legs across sawdust as better horses whizzed by, who ended last, coat frothing, ears empty of laurels. She couldn't fetch the dreadnought. She'd play until her fingers were lacerated and her old narcissism had foamed back up. She bit her lips till they bled, but in the end, she sang, a murmur, nearly nothing, "If I ever got another chance, though Gumball's long dead, I'd give him my fortune, let him ride in my stead."

14

THE TEACHERS' WALK WAS AT EIGHT THAT EVENING, timed to catch the sunset. Friday Night Treat, Meredith called it. Joan lurked by the window in the hall as the group gathered on the spread of grass in front of Community Village. Willie hustled to join in, rubbing his naked skull and grinning sheepishly. Meredith touched her colleagues on the arms, mouth split in easy joy.

Joan drew her sweater over her naked torso. She wanted to hide inside the damp tunnel of her sleeping bag and will herself into a state of impossible unconsciousness, but she couldn't bear to fester in her room any longer, couldn't blink away Carlotta's expression on the video.

As Joan approached the group, Meredith turned, fresh face floating above a frilly blouse inappropriate for hiking. Sparrow wore a wine-colored hoodie and clutched an apple, all slouchy, more boy than ever. Joan moved toward Sparrow—smelling the laundry soap caught in the cotton of their sweatshirt—but

Meredith stood in her way. "You're coming," she said. "Joan. That's lovely."

"Hill, ho," said Chester, wearing a T-shirt with a glow-in-the-dark rib cage. His hair puffed in the humidity, making him look even thinner than usual. He stood tall, like Joan's personal welcome committee.

They set off, bursting with chatter about their courses. All of them let the students rule the class, as though the teacher were a flesh flap dangling off the body, nonfunctional. Students reciting their own work, pushing paper copies of their own work, providing feedback to other students; students suggesting lessons and points of interest, demanding what they'd like to learn, their own work the foundation text of every course.

"But is their work ready to be examined like that?" Joan asked.

Chester and Meredith looked at her, startled. "Their work is the whole point," Meredith said.

The conversation shifted to updating each other on the year. Sparrow had been single for some time, which Meredith explained was because they needed a break from people pleasing. Willie referenced an accident, years ago, where he'd lost his sister. Chester's partner was a girl, also from Peoria, whom he'd been with since childhood. "But everyone thinks I'm gay," he said cheerfully. "Didn't you, Joan?"

"Yes," she admitted, to his delight. Meredith's boyfriend— hulking, square-headed—was appropriately named Olaf and seemed, by her own description, to be a brainless flesh house. The kind of guy too hometown and guileless for Joan. "Golly," he'd shout as pee flowed toward his face. Joan relaxed into their stories, grateful for a world beyond herself.

As they walked the gentle hills, Joan slowed her pace to fall behind. Meredith dragged a hand across Willie's flank, pushing off from him. Chester held forth about every sub-relevant camp legend: the cows banished for unruliness, the child-ghost who whispered atrocities, the founding father whose footprint was still dented somewhere in the earth. "The footprint goes three feet deep," Chester said. "If you step in it, you'll find certain love." He glanced at Sparrow.

"No thank you," said Sparrow.

"Oh, Sparrow," Meredith said. "Don't be foolish. Everyone wants love."

"Not really." Their pace turned languid. "It's like all the chemicals I used to reserve for that crap, they seeped over the rest of my life instead. I know it's cheesy, but the green out here is a whole different color now, like I'm realizing right now I never even knew what green was before." They shook a hand at the fields of grass, rolling into infinity all around.

Though the afternoon had blazed, the damp evening was chilly. Joan hugged her arms around her Norwegian sweater. So this was Friday night in rural Virginia: off-key cicadas and humidity. Paige would be out with famous musicians in the city, their disarray fine-boned and regal, their conversation, at least whenever Joan tried to join, impossible to penetrate. And Joan was here, with strangers, banished from the kingdom.

Willie turned to Joan, his cheeks round and glowing in the moonlight. If the hair from his beard was on his scalp instead, he'd be an innocent little boy. "We heard you had an intruder."

Joan's limbs stiffened. If only the exchange of information could slow down. "It was nothing."

"It doesn't sound like nothing," Meredith said. "Don't minimize it, Joan. That's scary. With the kids and everything."

"Yeah," said Willie. "I never heard of that happening. Maybe with, like, a famous writer or something in New York City."

"We got through it," Joan said.

"We wondered," Meredith said, turning to Willie. "Why didn't Georgina show up faster? Or the police? It's pretty freaky to think of you stuck so long in a room with a maniac."

Joan drew in her lips. "I didn't call the police."

"But Georgina? I'd think she'd be there in seconds."

"I didn't call her."

Meredith stopped walking. Willie stopped, too, bunching up around her. "Why not?"

Joan wanted to keep walking, wanted to walk right through this line of questioning and into a fresh one. "I don't have a phone."

Meredith's forehead collapsed. "Wait, seriously?"

"I don't need one here." She missed Paige. She twitched, sometimes, longing to monitor the video. But all the texts and phone calls, all the half-attentive internet browsing of the last twenty years, it turned out she didn't need any of it. For better or worse—mostly, now, for worse—every day felt hours longer.

"Huh," Meredith said. She checked Willie.

"Really," Joan said. "It's no big deal." Her voice faded to a wisp.

Meredith hurried ahead, and the group scrambled up the slope. Joan got to walk alone, dodging knots of conversation. She kept behind where Sparrow chatted with Meredith, easy and joyful. Sparrow's chambray shorts allowed for the pleasant bubble of their ass, but their shoes were bad: clattering yellow clogs.

Occasional blips rose from the pad of whispers. Meredith asked Sparrow about a girl they'd dated a while back, and Joan's ears pricked. Sparrow liked women. That was good. But certainly the woman in question was young and queer and cute, not rangy and rough-edged, frightening colleagues with her abject, phone-free life.

The group crested the first ridge of the hill. Campus spread out below. Joan cased for the pink blouse, but that was dumb. Carlotta was long gone, out of her control, all vigilance worthless.

"Hold up," Chester said, halting under the sodium lamp. Strings of hair trembled from his head.

A toad basked in the spotlight, feet folded under his belly. Above him was a cone of light, where a hundred bugs, a thousand—moths and mosquitoes and flies and gnats, a busy society of its own—spiraled up into a vibrating tornado.

Chester beamed at Joan. "When I found her she was just a toad and she's a toad today, she's a toad in her apartment, she's a toad up on the stage, she's a toad at sixteen, toad at thirty, toad at every age."

Chester spoke the lyrics instead of singing them, in his funny voice that was always breaking. But that wasn't why Joan didn't recognize them instantly, though she became wet upon hearing them, as she did at all her songs, even those that shamed her now. Especially, maybe, the ones that shamed her. She shuddered in the chilly humidity. Her own words were so remote she could no longer grasp them. She couldn't stand her overly personal, worst lyrics floating in this group, Sparrow's gaze pricking Joan. "Always the Same to Me" was intended as an honest response to "Lakeshore," meant to explore how she actually felt about Paige: as a friend and artistic companion, someone Joan could cuddle and not burn with desire the way she had with the "Lakeshore" guy, someone who wouldn't cloud her thoughts or ask too much. She'd never known what to call this cocktail of feelings, so she'd picked a random noun to hold them—the Gonewriters had suggested the exercise in workshop. But the song failed because she'd dodged the hardest part, which was actually

digging into the nuance of her feelings for Paige. She'd simplified the complexity and killed it. *A toad when you sing,
a toad when you'll die, a toad when I drive you to corners to
cry.* The toad was wise-eyed, devoted, squishable, waiting at
Joan's feet. Fans thought it was a love song. Even Paige listened with moony eyes, mugging, in a movie star voice, "Joan
Vole. I didn't know you cared."

"My favorite," Chester said, setting a fey hand on his
sternum.

Joan couldn't help her rising pleasure. Even if it was her
worst song, at least it wasn't "Lakeshore." But wait—Chester's
smug line of lip, those eyes twinkling with information waiting to be shared—he was acting like the *Pitchfork* bros, but he
didn't know her work, had been ignorant of it two days before.

"You know Joan's music?" Sparrow asked. They still held
their apple, shiny in the moonlight, hadn't yet taken a bite.

"I looked her up when she got here. Joan Vole is seminal.
We should all know her work."

Joan froze. What had he found?

"'Rooster, Too,' though," he said. "And that epic backstory."

She didn't want to linger on it—surely Sparrow didn't like
the story, especially if they knew it was fake publicity shit.
"That's not my best."

"Or 'Rounding out the Brush.' Take me back to under
the brush, where we spent that night and the whole next day.
Show me the leaves with the print of you. Leave me there for a
thousand years." Even "Rounding out the Brush" was a child's
poem without the caramel stretch of Joan's voice. She couldn't
stand everyone picturing her fucking under a rhododendron.
"I mean, she's under a bush. Come on." He laughed. "Joan Vole
is badass."

He didn't mean badass. He meant promiscuous, unhinged.

The internet said she'd had a hundred girls, a thousand. There were theories that she must've been raped as a teenager, abused as a child. There were fans who'd crafted scenarios online involving car trunks and Dobermans, coils of rats. Trauma must've warped her and made her remote, mysterious, sexual, performative, male.

"That's so cool," Meredith said. "How is she badass?"

Joan drew up, tense. "You like that song?" she asked loudly.

"Are you kidding?" he said. "The brush, the brush, my favorite brush. Let me lie all day. If I'm here at least with you, the scratches fade away."

Such a bald metaphor it made her sick. She stood in the discomfort, her humiliating lyrics hanging, the stares of strangers aimed at her. What a difficult person she'd been: implying she belonged in the queer club, wailing about bushes to prove it. She couldn't handle the teachers picturing her under girls, on girls, in girls. Fans believing such a story was one thing—that lie was ambitious in a way that was justified, hard-edged, male—but these people just wanted to hang out.

"Joan does twisted shit onstage," Chester said.

Joan stumbled on the gravel road, nearly collapsing into the weeds. Moths battered her cheeks. Could she run?

Meredith startled. "Like what?"

"It's worth checking out," Chester said. "Kinda bawdy, goofy stuff. Very playful." Joan cringed. She wanted to say that wasn't true, it was worse, she was horrible, everyone should know.

Meredith frowned. "I guess I'll check it out."

"I have to pee," Sparrow said.

"Me too." Joan braced for some reaction—the group weirded out she wanted to pee with Sparrow, the flare in her voice—but nothing.

"See ya up there," said Willie, his bald head bobbing into the dark as the teachers continued their route.

Joan followed Sparrow off the pavement and into the brush. The silky tips of the grass tickled her nose. The insects were louder in the weeds, so loud she could pretend she was alone. They were in a dense, private forest, padded with pillows of sound, the dark a kindness.

They fell into step in the tall grass. Pushing through the gray nighttime waves of it, sometimes only the pelt of Sparrow's hair was visible, a rodent skating across the tips. Joan's breath slowed with Sparrow beside her. The way Sparrow moved, lumbering and deliberate under that placid, broad head, it was like Joan had been joined by a devoted bear.

"This an okay spot?" Sparrow asked of a clearing.

An old electricity flickered in Joan. Sparrow's golden eyes were alight in the darkness. Joan turned. Electric terror ran through her. But this was okay—it was all okay. She wasn't doing anything perverse, just peeing with a new friend. She unbuttoned her shorts, tamping down the sigh leaking from her lips. "Yes. This is a good spot." Joan used her low, flirty voice. She came alive in a way she hadn't in months, a year, her skin jumping. She unzipped her fly—this was okay, right? This was okay—and yanked down the waistband of her underwear. When the cool air struck her folds, a shiver shot up her spine. She'd never had a charge from showing off for a girl. But Sparrow wasn't a girl. Maybe Joan's starved libido was straining to see their male qualities.

Sparrow checked Joan's crotch, coloring. Did they think Joan couldn't see where their gaze was aimed, with the moon so full? But Sparrow could look as long as they wanted. Their attention was a beautiful heat.

"You can pee too." Joan longed for Sparrow to stay by her

side, but it was funny. She didn't have the urge to grab them and manhandle them into the bush the way she had with the German on the subway or her landlord or her old boss at the restaurant at the slightest prickle of attraction. Sparrow should pee in private if privacy suited them.

In a shadowy corner, arms trembling, Sparrow bent at the waist and yanked their shorts down, folding a hand between their legs and lowering into a squat.

Joan surged at the expanse of exposed thighs, muscled and powerful. Sparrow had stretch marks exactly where Joan had them, on the meat of the hip, a scored history of growth that must've bothered Sparrow for their heralding of womanhood. The marks had bothered Joan back then too, which she'd never really thought about until now. She'd wanted to keep her scrawny child form. Carlotta had said Joan was trans. And Joan had liked being a guy, that time in the club with Nick Blade; it was true. She'd felt bouncy and alive, her truest self. She'd never let herself think that before. What if the fans knew more about her than she knew about herself? Joan's stretch marks had faded white years ago, while Sparrow's were still red. She longed to press her mouth to them, to inhale the heat of flesh.

Sparrow hid their groin from Joan. They might have had lower surgery—Nick Blade's person, Lamar, had. Or maybe they were born with gender difference or hated their standard female parts. Pity washed Joan. How hard life would be if she didn't like what she had. Once she had a dream in which her pussy thanked her for an active, happy life: "I don't fester like the common puss but absorb much sun and meet many people." Joan woke embarrassed but grinning.

"Poor Sparrow." The words slipped out.

"I'm fine," Sparrow said, batting Joan away as they teetered. A few spurts hit the grass, like Sparrow's muscles couldn't release. The strained splats filled Joan with a rush of tenderness. "It's okay I'm here?"

Sparrow's face tilted into shadow. "Yes."

Still standing tall, Joan pulled up her hood and spread her lips and peed, her stream together, never divided, into the grass. The release was strong and satisfying, humid air rushing in to warm her every crevice. Every muscle loosened into gel. This was how the rumor about her body had started. The fact that anyone would think she had a penis made her so angry she couldn't speak. No one could appreciate the tangled power of female junk, not even straight men, which was so crazy and so sad.

The whites of Sparrow's eyes shone. "You pee standing up?"

Heat blushed through Joan. When, ever, had her peeing been admired? At best it had been tolerated en route to fucking. But with those big eyes watching her, absorbing the act, Joan filled with syrup—a kind of peace she hadn't enjoyed since New York.

Her wrists twitched, begging to ease the stream closer to Sparrow. To angle the falling water until it grazed that bulbous clog. But she only peed on men. She held firm to her slippery flesh.

Sparrow watched out the corner of one eye. But of course. Of course Sparrow wanted to pee standing up. This was a gift Joan could offer. "Do you want to learn?"

"Yes," Sparrow whispered across the dark.

Joan could help Sparrow live better between the genders, make a difference so easily. "Do you have any left?"

"I think."

"If you can stop midway, that's promising." Joan already regretted her last drop sliding out, that old sigh of satisfaction and grief blowing through her.

Sparrow stood up bulkily. Their knees pressed together, holding their pee at bay.

"Let me show you." Joan leaned in toward Sparrow. Finally, an excuse to touch them.

Sparrow recoiled. "No," they said. "Just explain."

Joan stood back, but not far. If she couldn't help, at least let Sparrow's body uncramp and reveal itself. She described how Sparrow should plant their feet apart and how to manipulate themself. "It'll feel wrong if you're doing it right. Like, it hurts."

Sparrow rummaged between their legs. Joan set her jaw, willing her pulse to slow.

"Pull your underwear down more."

"No." Sparrow turned away. They fumbled, then released.

The stream was true. Joan could've lifted Sparrow up. Yes. They had it. Sparrow's spine curved back, their head cocked high. They were confident, like they'd unlocked a truer version of themself. They threw their head back, tawny bangs sweeping as their stream arced, a parabola of translucent gold. Joan buzzed with pride and some richer feeling, too, a pocket inside her opening up.

Then the stream split, spraying Sparrow's hoodie, their shorts. They batted around, losing control of their torso. Joan held her ground as spots spattered her shorts and sweater. No one had ever returned the favor, and it was funny, this gentle assault. Warm and delicate. Why had anyone ever minded?

When the spray ended, Sparrow stood there, arms splayed, a constellation spotting their V-neck and shorts. They looked exactly the way they would've looked if Joan had peed on them, dotted and chagrined, confused but red-faced. Old, friendly shame welled in Joan.

"I got some on me." Sparrow's voice was faint, almost inaudible. "I don't think it's bad." "Bad" cracked apart. Joan hadn't been sweetly embarrassed like that in years. She almost missed the feeling, wished she could be that raw again, one more time. Lyrics bloomed: *Little puppy in the grass, ears drag in the dirt.* She shook them out of her head. No writing. This moment was not about her sexual satisfaction or her art. She was only being nice so Sparrow wouldn't turn her in.

She needed to clean Sparrow. That was the decent, obvious job, the job anyone else would've jumped to. But she had no towels, no water. She pulled her sweater off. Hot air wrapped her naked skin, warmer than the sweater. Sparrow's neck jerked up, taking in Joan's bare torso, her tiny breasts that were all brown nipple, then looked Joan square in the face. Joan stood tall so her body caught the moonlight. She squeezed the precious wool into a ball, heavy and fine. She reached out. With the balled sweater, she sponged liquid from Sparrow's limbs, drying their T-shirt and shorts.

Sparrow lifted their arms awkwardly high. "Wait, but your sweater."

Joan fingered the creamy wool, infused with the lonely breath of Bergen, Norway. When the "Lakeshore" guy had given it to her, years ago, she'd been working a double, after which she had a show. Wearing the sweater on the venue's tiny stage, teetering on knees worn ragged from crossing the restaurant, she'd given the fiercest performance of her life: she was worth this fine wool, worth the fingers that had knit it and the miles of ocean the sweater had crossed to reach her. "It's just a rag."

Joan was mindful not to graze Sparrow's breasts or hips. Nick Blade's person had requested Nick Blade avoid these gendered sites during sex. Joan had listened uneasily as Nick Blade discussed the pains he took to describe Lamar's body as Lamar wanted it seen—never say hips, soft, cute, butt—and the compliments he learned to swap in—nice shoulders, fierce, slender. Even secondhand, the intimacy had nauseated her.

Cleaning Sparrow sent a wave of calm through Joan. She applied as little pressure as possible, working her way inward from ankles and wrists, blotting each pinprick of moisture, as carefully as though Sparrow's flesh was tissue paper. She loosened as she pulled off the droplets, the only sound the kiss of wool to skin, Sparrow's mouth a peaceful dash. They were so plush, even their knees were puffy. Getting to touch them, even through the wool, was too much. Joan's pulse quickened. She longed to fall with Sparrow onto the grass.

When Joan blotted Sparrow's armpit, feeling the soft flesh even through their clothes, Sparrow shuddered. Joan stilled the sweater against them, letting the vibrations pulse back through the cloth. Maybe they enjoyed being touched. Touched by Joan, or touched at all? Their eyes were shut. They were easier in themself than Joan had ever seen them. She piloted the sweater around their waist. Goosebumps rose on their arms.

This was too much. She was being a maniac—totally sex-starved. She tucked the sweater under her arm. "There."

Sparrow watched Joan, eyes so big and dark they were all pupil in the moonlight. "Thank you." The words were heavy, shaky. Joan leaned close, feeling their heat.

Sparrow drew up their shorts, tucking and zipping and fastening, patting down bubbles of cloth. Joan wasn't normally shy, but she cheated her hips away.

They were inches apart, a scent rising off Sparrow like Joan's old bed, that aroma of desire and shame. An odor that wound through her life, touching her happiest moments. Joan's torso naked to the humidity. Sparrow was adorable with those startled-deer eyes catching the light. Joan longed to be closer. But no. She was out of her mind. She liked hard jaws, muscles gone to seed, eyelids sagging, rendering them tough and knowing. Joan leaned closer. Her finger rose as though on its own and touched Sparrow's pillowy bottom lip. A tug of old energy moved through her.

Sparrow flinched under her touch. "Are you okay?"

Joan's finger slid off Sparrow's lip. "Of course."

"Did I get some up there?"

"What?"

Sparrow touched their lip. "Did it get all the way up there?"

Joan sagged in relief. "Yes."

"Damn." Sparrow laughed, a crisp note cutting the humidity. A shout from the hillside. Chester maybe, or Willie, impossible to pinpoint in the cushion of black. "Here," Sparrow said, pulling off their hoodie. They wore an undershirt below. Their black binder was visible through it, doing its lumpy, imperfect best.

Joan's tendons itched to pull on her soiled sweater instead, to wear Sparrow's pee all through campus. But second best was this sweatshirt that had been on their back for the whole walk, seasoned with sweat and soaked-in blots of piss. She pulled it on. Below the urine ran a new odor, sour and delicious.

"Want me to walk you back to the dorm?" Joan asked.

"We should find the others. They'll think it's weird."

"Who cares?" Let the two of them enjoy a walk together back home through the night. Joan could draw Sparrow a bath, lean over them, scrub every part.

"Meredith worries about me." Sparrow rolled their eyes. "She'd make the whole group go back and check."

"What a nuisance." Joan's voice faded. They were really giving this moment up.

"It's actually nice. She cares. About the students, mostly. And me."

Joan trudged beside them. As they summited the hill, the wooden fences of the pastures rose into view, trees clipped into lollipops against the navy sky. Joan tucked the sweater behind the fence of the first pasture. A horse watched them, chin hooked over his fence. She approached him, palm offered. The biggest indulgence Joan's father had gifted her was one riding lesson at age eight. She'd ridden around a ring, commanding pounds of muscle, the paper bow on the horse's mane bobbing, so grateful she nearly exploded. Pencil, that was the horse's stupid name, though he was as thick as any pony. Each time she cycled past her father and the gate, she drew up, preparing, on the next circle, to squeeze her thighs and kick, driving Pencil through the opening.

Sparrow came up behind Joan. The heat of their sudden nearness blazed her back like campfire. They held out the apple on the flat of their palm. The horse took it in one bite, crunching it into foamy chunks that he guided down his throat with a long tongue.

"He's our favorite," Sparrow said. "I call him Cobra Face." They stroked the white blaze on the beefy chestnut's forehead, the unfurled hood of a cobra. "His real name is Blueberry or something dumb. Isn't he gorgeous?" Sparrow stole a shy peek at Joan as they stroked his neck. "People say he has a person inside."

This animal had trotted off a battlefield. He swung his neck and his muscles rolled like water. He nosed toward Joan, setting his cheeks in her hands. She lost herself in the jelly domes of his eyes, all that steady darkness. The muscles of his cheeks were like poured chocolate, his veins rinds formed from the pan tilting as the mixture solidified, his lips velvet flaps sheafing his teeth. She stroked that greasy mane. There was so much power in this sturdy animal, these churning muscles, this heat. Sparrow, right beside, radiated their own energy. Joan wanted to slip under Cobra Face and watch him from the grass, stomping with enough power to kill her in one step. His power was the engine of a song about men. Men, yes, men. See? She didn't belong to her fans. Her hips warmed, then tingled, and her groin thawed. The feeling was gradual, then instant. She melted in her underwear as her palms slid down slick hide.

"You're giving Blackberry a boner," Chester said. Joan whipped around. His disembodied rib cage shone in the moonlit half-dark.

Joan dropped the horse's head. He gave a whinny of complaint and shied to the right, his erection dangling like it wasn't quite attached. She'd shifted the heart of a beast, had let herself relax because he was an animal. Cobra Face's body proved she was perverse.

"I'm kidding," Chester said. "Blackberry always has a boner. Something's wrong with him." Willie and Meredith appeared beside Chester. Moonlight bounced through the clouds.

"That's normal for a stallion." Meredith ticked her chin at Joan. "Joan. You're sweating like a dog. Are you all right?" Meredith's blouse somehow wasn't wilted in the least.

"Dogs don't sweat. That's why they pant." Willie stuck out his tongue and pumped it.

"What's wrong with Sparrow?" Meredith asked, fiddling with the collar of her blouse, satin and so tight to her neck it left a mark.

"Nothing," said Sparrow, blushing and beelining to Meredith. Their absence left a hole by Joan. She longed to pull them back. There was no sexual energy between Meredith and Sparrow, so why did it feel, when Sparrow stood beside her, that they were utterly lost to Joan?

Cobra Face kicked and circulated, pushing breath from his nostrils, legs stepping wide. His reaction wasn't Joan's fault.

She surged with relief. She hadn't gotten into his head, couldn't have if she'd tried. He lived in his own animal world. A land of oats and stable blankets and curry brushes scrubbing his neck. But she had done something horrible to another person. That was why she didn't feel better, no matter how she tried to convince herself, even if no one was banging down her door. Her pussy glowing red, then blue, leaking on Carlotta. She squeezed the fence, pregnant with moisture.

Willie's gaze panned toward Sparrow. "Does anyone smell something?"

"That's the barn smell," said Sparrow, too fast. "You must've forgotten it."

"Eliza." Meredith frowned. "I mean, Sparrow. Sparrow! I'm so sorry." She grabbed her mouth with two hands, eyes locked on Sparrow. "Oh my god, I can't believe I messed that up."

"It's okay," Sparrow mumbled.

"It's not. Ugh, it's really not." She shook her head theatrically. Joan shuddered.

"Don't worry about it," Sparrow said into the ground.

"I should worry. I should! But what's going on with you? Something happened. You're pale." Meredith touched Sparrow's hand, furrows shadowing the dome of her forehead.

"Oh," Sparrow said. "No, I'm fine."

"Seriously," said Meredith. "Is she okay?"

"You mean are they okay," said Joan.

"Don't worry about it," Sparrow said, voice hitching into a giggle.

"Oh yeah? Isn't that your hoodie on Joan?" Chester smiled from Sparrow to Joan, raising his eyebrows. "Nothing happened?"

"Nothing," Joan snapped.

Sparrow's face smoothed into a blank, unreadable plane.

"All right, all right," Chester said, pinching a strip of his bowl cut. "Joan Vole knows best."

That stupid stan meme: the candid of Joan playing, hand a blur over the strings, mouth doubled in motion, ears smeared into points, like she was about to bite someone's neck. No one who wore that shirt knew a thing about what she considered best.

"We should all get some sleep," Meredith said. "Long first week." A hollow opened in Joan. The cord of longing, snapped.

The group moved to follow Sparrow. Joan longed to remain in the dark, with the aroused horse, reliving her time with Sparrow, but she followed. They walked in silence, the men ahead with Sparrow, Joan with Meredith. Meredith raised her head, that round, pale face a second moon.

"So," she said, watching Joan carefully. "Settling in okay?"

"Yes."

Meredith ducked her head. "Hey. I hope you don't mind my asking, but I'm curious about your twisted shit."

The words sliced the humidity. "I don't know what you mean."

Meredith flapped a hand, wrist plump and dented by a tennis bracelet. "That's okay if you don't want to talk about it or whatever. I was just curious because Chester said you do 'twisted shit' onstage."

"Oh. Right. It's jokey stuff. Pranks, kind of." Talking about it was odd, after it was all over, like she was in a play about her former self.

"That's cute." Meredith's expression was lively, interested under her blow-dried hair. "What kind of pranks do you get up to?"

Joan was ashamed of how much she'd delighted in the antics. The music was supposed to be the thing. "I guess one night I put dog shit in the venue's ventilation system. But usually it was tricks with my tits. Like playing a show with them out. Or dipping my nipple in someone's drink." Joan didn't care one bit about her breasts when she was offstage. She could take them or leave them in any sexual occasion, always forgot to incorporate them. In clothes, they were so small they didn't show.

Meredith stopped. They were halfway down the hill, shaded from the moon, and Joan couldn't make out her expression, only a gash of shine in her mouth. "You really did that to someone?"

"What?" Joan said.

"Sorry." She cleared her throat, which made Joan jump. "That's a little intense for me."

"It was fine." Her skull rang. "He liked it." That guy had laughed so hard he couldn't sip his drink.

"Maybe he was being a good sport for the crowd?"

"No," Joan said, firmer. "He genuinely liked it. I'm certain." She didn't have to feel guilty about stuffing her tit in a cocktail. Meredith hadn't been there. Joan could read amusement—anyone could.

"Maybe I don't understand the context."

"You couldn't, no," Joan said. "I have to go to bed," She turned on her heels.

"Oh, but Joan," Meredith said. "That's not the way to Community Village."

"Don't worry about it." She kept moving, away from Meredith's irritatingly generous expression.

*

The hot mask of Joan's face cooled. She crashed through horseweed, up the bump of a hill and down onto a fresh path, Sparrow's lingering odor activating with her own sweat.

As soon as the voices of the teachers blew away, new voices replaced them, up ahead, soft in the brush. Whoever it was, Joan didn't want to know. She kept her focus on the halogen glow of Community Village, so small from this distance, tucked between the soft bodies of shrubs. But that was her mind. Her body couldn't help treading softly over the moss, veering off track and toward the bushes. Under the streetlights, the toad's home, two figures embraced.

From a distance, they were as big and old as she was. But when they separated, their dimensions clarified, part by part: the oversized heads, the unnatural slenderness of the limbs, the puppyish flexibility of the skin. And that blond hair, so blond it was blinding, separated strands burning into strings of pure light, the color of no natural adult hair. That bland, wide forehead, hands pulsing with passion. Joan jittered on the grass. Lula's head snapped toward her.

"Ms. Vole?" she said, dropping her arms off her companion, another girl, smaller than Lula, with a pointed face and a ponytail fountaining chocolate hair. A girl—of course. Joan couldn't move, so hard was she concentrating on the scene and its supposed reality. How had Lula been so confidently gripping the elbow of her beloved, like she'd been in love a dozen times before? Her army jacket actually looked cool in the sodium light, her hair brushed back with water. Lula stepped toward her, eyebrows raised, begging. Joan swelled with foaming compassion: here was this dear, strange person, finding love.

But as Lula neared, those cheeks so pale and vulnerable, Joan trembled. The girl's happiness flamed so hot it almost touched Joan. "Go to bed," Joan said, and vanished into the dark.

15

JOAN LEANED HER ELBOWS ON THE STICKY SURFACE OF the Crown Heights bar, pulling up the collar of her charcoal denim jacket. She had fifteen minutes until Paige picked her up. They lived separately now, six years after they'd met, but convened often to walk together all over the city. From across the room, a weather-beaten guy winked at her, stringy gray hair and marionette lines, the kind of individual who couldn't possibly live in New York. "You a dyke?" he asked.

"No, dude," she said, and got up. He got up, too, and she followed him toward the bathroom.

He opened the door to the men's. These decisions were not negotiated. Women sometimes yelled at Joan for being in the women's room anyway, hearing her voice or the rough way she jerked her pants up as she pushed the stall door open.

Here, there was one stall. As soon as a barback finished shitting, they claimed it. "Stand on the toilet," the dude said, as though her boots could betray her gender. She stepped up, loomed over him.

He cut three lines on a cigarette pack. Two for him, as was the wont of a man, but Joan did all three. He snickered. "You rough, girl."

Joan unbuttoned her shorts.

"Yeah, you can't wait?" He pulled out his dick, but it was soft. He jiggled it around as though she couldn't tell it was flaccid if it were in motion.

The coke dripped its acid leak down the back of her throat. The smooth stretch of the high would hit just as she and Paige arrived on the beach. She twitched to be out there already, in the sand, free, with her best friend. Usually she kissed her hookups, squeezed their dicks, for ceremony. But she didn't have the luxury tonight. She had enough time only for an obedient subject. "Can I do this?" She nodded at her groin. If she made the offer upbeat like that, like they were getting a treat, it worked better than the early days when she'd hemmed and hawed, framed the idea like she was dying.

He gave a hoarse chuckle. "Do what you like, girl."

All these years, Joan had managed to keep her pee thing private. She never sang about it, and since she never fucked fans and the Gonewriters were loyal, no one had to know. She never gave her real name to flings. People knew her, but no one had any idea she was in the bathroom of a shitty bar about to explode on some random. "I'm in a mood," she said.

"You look it." He removed his hat and smoothed his bald pate. His mottled scalp matched the hue of his dick.

Her shorts were already down, her worn-out, whatever underwear ringing her ankles. "Just say yes. Please." A whine entered her voice that she hated. Joan never whined. But the pressure pushed her organs aside, making room only for the jackal in her belly.

The dude opened his sinewy arms. Too late for better

than that. Her body couldn't have held out anyway, even if she wasn't meeting Paige. She pushed her pelvis forward and sprayed his flannel shirt. Her torso roared in response, arousal pulsing through her, not an orgasm, not exactly—it never was, quite—but purer, more trembling and looser, like heroin the twice she'd tried it. At least the first minute, at least how she remembered. She could tell herself it was the coke, but really it was her.

Urine splashed into the neck of his shirt, into his eyes, which stayed open in yellow horror. Pee soaked the cigarette pack. Joan's limbs stiffened in pleasure, going still so the waves coursed through. She owned the world. The stall dissolved into a cube of white light.

Panting, finished, she absorbed him below her, cheeks wet like he'd been crying, shirt splattered, dick dripping. She must've aimed in her fugue. The smell that rose off him had a faint chemical tang, not bad. She kept hydrated. "See ya," she said, pulling up her shorts. She was pristine.

"Dirty slut," he said, but his voice was calm, like she'd drugged him, instead of the other way around.

*

Joan dashed out of the bar, shaking drops of piss from her fingers. She hollowed out, always, in the aftermath, shame seeping in like a familiar heat. She let the feelings flow through—she kind of liked them, at least they were part of the deal. She crossed Eastern Parkway and jumped into Christopher's BMW. He'd lent it to Paige last night for a gig out in Bensonhurst and she hadn't returned it yet, so they were driving to Coney.

"You're late," Paige said. As soon as Joan hit the seat, Paige ripped out from where she'd double-parked and shot down the boulevard, the car door flapping until Joan jerked it closed. Paige handled cars like unbroken horses, like she had as a kid on highways in Ohio, no pedestrians in sight. The plastic fox Christopher had hung from the rearview swung so far it struck the plush ceiling.

Joan settled into the cool cab of the car, Paige's cardboard scent collecting around her. She sifted through the CDs from Christopher's console, but it was all demos of his own slutty bullshit and the two albums he'd managed to execute, his headshot taking up the covers of both: that black stubble, that perfect cake of hair, the military jacket he thought was edgy and actually looked kinda cool—Joan could've pulled it off better, though. She sometimes had the peculiar thought that she was a hotter guy than a hot guy. She tossed the CDs back into their divot with a plastic clatter. What maniac listened to his own music in the car? Joan surged with love for him. Paige popped two wheels over the curb to skirt a slowdown.

"I was doing, you know, that thing I do." Eventually Joan had built up to sharing with Paige every adventure she'd had with every last dude, but Paige tensed at the reports, never asked questions. She'd gotten worse since they'd decided to live apart, wouldn't even let Joan get out a full story. But if Joan couldn't share with Paige, then who?

"Oh," said Paige. "Cool." The word was icy. "Should I take Ocean the whole way? Or the Belt Parkway?" She bore down on the accelerator like if she didn't crush it to death, it would bite her feet.

"Ocean." Joan leaned back. "Then we can see shit. It's like extra walking." Paige roared to sixty on Seventh Avenue.

*

Joan and Paige emerged onto the sticky boardwalk, with its seagulls and surf and rowdy Russian restaurants, as the good stretch of the coke hit. Joan's feet sprang, her mind setting fires everywhere it turned as they trekked all the way to Brighton Beach and Manhattan Beach and even across Plumb to Point Breeze, all the way alongside the greasy city sea. Getting their feet off concrete was a gift.

They never paused to observe the flabby men bobbing in the gray waves or the children grinding cheese curls into the sand or the woman singing *Tristan und Isolde* to a boombox from 1980. They absorbed all activities of the beach, but their focus was each other. Joan could talk and walk for a thousand miles, even when she wasn't on drugs. They discussed Paige's childhood and the Gonewriters, Paige's hope for a breakthrough. Mostly, though, Joan coached Paige through the early traumas of a career: door deals withheld, shows canceled for no reason, start times shifted without notice, managers pushing her up against the walls of green rooms, tongues extended to rest in her mouth like dry, dead treats. It was perfect being beside Paige in the city evening, New Jersey blocks of glitter across the water, the sky pink.

New cold infused the sea breeze, blowing in from someplace where it was already autumn. This time of year, Joan remembered the towers falling and how the city had shifted all at once, even though, two years later, that day already was history.

Paige was still working at the job Joan had found her in a friend's bakery, living in an apartment in another friend's building that was renting for cheap. Joan had talked it down even cheaper, bargaining more fiercely than she would've dared for herself. Paige was complaining because she had been invited to perform in a festival but then was disinvited—the booking agent had overestimated the schedule's capacity.

"Is that even a thing?" Paige raked her hair so hard strands pinwheeled to the sand. "Did I do something wrong? Did they look me up? My internet presence is freaking janky."

"No, it's not." It was. But internet stuff was out of Joan's wheelhouse. "I'm sure they're just as disorganized as every other festival. Anyway, festivals aren't your thing." They'd been discussing this festival for a hundred years. Joan's brain longed to jump to the next topic.

"I know." Paige sighed. For years she'd daydreamed to Joan about beautiful, historic venues—the Ryman, Red Rocks, Royal Albert Hall. She hated straining her voice over white men on drugs.

Paige and Joan had already looped back to the stretch of uneventful sand after the party of Brighton and before the campy kid town of Coney when Paige requested they take a seat.

"Seriously?" They never stopped walking once they set out. That was how Joan could tolerate the walks. She'd dissolved her social life after her breakup with the "Lakeshore" guy, couldn't bear to hang with the Gonewriters or attend anyone's show. Every pursuit besides writing her ass off was a waste of time, and she had even limited her release of pressure with randoms—tonight was the first night she'd indulged in weeks. She'd wasted enough of her life in love with the "Lakeshore" guy—visiting Chicago when she didn't even have a show, fuck-ing him and cuddling him and even indulging in activities like going to the movies and sitting in restaurants—and she couldn't squander a second more, had to use every minute to work. At least she needed enough success to feed herself, but of course she wanted more, wanted her work to last. And the only way to get there was writing all the time. If she wasn't writ-ing, she was playing scales or running songs or booking tours, hunched in her apartment not eating or sleeping or calling friends, dirt building on the moldings, no food in the fridge, pounding out song after song, only a fraction of which would ever be usable. But she had to purge the bad ones to dig down to the good.

Walking, at least they were in motion, and it didn't feel like leisure. Still high, especially, the idea of sitting was death. But Paige was pressing her curls behind her ears and nodding that, yes, she did want to sit, she was serious about that request, so Joan followed her to the edge of the surf, where they perched on a heap of sand that was somehow still soft and clean, even as it was churned and battered by merciless shoes.

Joan sat facing Paige so they could continue talking as intensely, but Paige turned the other way, so they sat side by side, facing the sea, which perhaps was normal for beach sitting; Joan never did it. Shoulder to shoulder, they watched the gray city waves, lapping and rolling over each other, taking in sand and offering it back soaked and silky. Joan's legs twitched, ready to spring her free. How long did Paige need to sit before they could return to walking and talking? The sun had been down for hours, and Joan hadn't dressed to sit around. Her bare legs stretched on the damp sand, mottled blue. Still, though, she wished, like she always did on a beach, that she could have her shirt off, her back naked to the last of the sun.

"Joan." Paige's voice trembled. Joan's ass tensed. "I want to say something." The gray sea churned. Paige inhaled a huff like a doe. "You've been remote. For, like, a while now."

"I'll be better," Joan said as fast as she could. Paige sometimes got this way, eyes watery, begging Joan—for what? Joan couldn't tell.

"No, it's just. I don't know." Strands of Paige's hair blew haywire, catching on the ridges of her nose, spiraling into scribbles against the navy sky, the New York night that was never fully dark. "It's been like a year."

A year and three months, actually. Since Joan last saw the "Lakeshore" guy, a lanky high school classmate whose face she'd adored, all craggy and thrilling, whom she'd meet on the Magnificent Mile every time she passed through Chicago on tour.

She'd ended the relationship the moment he raised the idea of moving to New York. When she'd finished the first draft of "Lakeshore," about fucking him in the open air on the edge of Lake Michigan, she'd marveled at how male she sounded: always leaving, making the guy cry, pressing him to fuck her on the dirty beach because she couldn't stand to see his apartment, not ever, not once, couldn't make it real like that. She'd been like a man with him, had topped him hard, ordered him around in her lowest register, tendons standing high in her arms. So she'd switched his pronouns as a joke with herself. "Lakeshore" was truer about a girl, though she'd never felt that way about any girl. But her desire in the song was insane, fierce, on fire. She liked the engine of strumming beneath her words and understanding: This was what it was like to be between a girl's legs and want it, with the stretch of mirrored slate ahead and the glitter of rich-ass buildings behind, burrowing into pussy like she couldn't go deep enough. She was glad to trade her ten or so nights with Paige, her two with Bethany, for the one true night of the song. And she'd played the song, and girls had loved it, and guys had loved it; everyone had found it sharply, meanly sexy in a way it never could've been with the rough-faced, loose-limbed man in his rightful role, and she thought, sometimes while playing it, Fuck yes. She deserved this song.

"I've been distracted." She'd never told Paige about the

"Lakeshore" guy, had been afraid to hurt her, even though that was stupid, even though Paige had boyfriends and girlfriends of her own, disappearing for her own stretches as she wove her way in and out of love.

"Is it because of 'Lakeshore'?" Paige spoke softly. She handled the name of the song like an incantation, like she could destroy it by pronouncing it wrong.

"No." Though "Lakeshore" was the song Joan had awaited for years, forever, the song that was finally on the radio, that people actually knew. That wasn't what preoccupied her. She was making up time after the relationship had ended, rushing to catch up on music.

Joan couldn't stand Paige's fingers trembling as she handled a broken shell. "I'm sorry. I've missed you too."

The muscles in Paige's cheeks dropped loose.

"Hey," Joan said. "It's okay." It was good to say what she really thought for once, to be honest with Paige without fear of hurting her.

"I know I'm being dumb." Paige smeared her eye with the back of her hand. "I know how you feel, Joan. I do."

A flare of relief—she knew. It was okay. But then Paige torqued around and kissed Joan.

Always it happened like this. No buildup. Mistakes on cots in Albuquerque or house show floors in Sisters, the rare night in Brooklyn when Paige was bored or heartbroken. They'd be talking normally and then, out of nowhere, Paige's lips would be on Joan's. And Joan would go along with it to soothe her friend, to keep the peace. But it had been a year—over a year— and Joan had thought they were all good. As Paige's tongue slid into her mouth, as Joan's head inflated, her pulse sped up, beating in her temples, her ears.

Paige drew back. "Are you okay?"

"Yes," Joan said, automatically.

"Is this good?" Her voice shook. She cycled her hands between them in a rickety gesture, signaling, what? Whatever messiness.

Joan's mouth dried to dust. This was her chance. She could say no, this wasn't okay, actually, she'd felt weird all these years. But she couldn't bear to do that to this dear face, couldn't hurt her for one second. Especially high, she could go along with anything and be fine. "It's good," Joan said, and Paige smiled, leaned in, and kissed her again.

"Joan Vole?" Joan ripped free of Paige. A man loomed in sparkly bronze bathing underwear.

The man offered a dripping hand. His chest was clotted with dark curls, but the hair on his head was a blond loaf. He should be chatting up teens in bikinis, not bothering the two of them. "I'm such a fan of 'Lakeshore.'"

Joan was so startled she didn't even shake his hand. Waves vibrated through her. "You are?" Was he fucking with her?

"Favorite song of oh-three. My sister's a lesbo. She told me." The man raised his eyebrows and jiggled them around. Then he aimed a finger at Paige. "Paige, hey. Hold on to this one." He winked, then was gone.

Joan turned to Paige. The beach was as dark as it ever got in the city. "The hell was that?"

Paige was still watching where the man had disappeared around a curve of the shore. "People think your song is about us."

"Seriously?" Joan had to stifle a laugh. Because nothing that happened in the song—not the plein air fucking, not the mission for drugstore eclairs, not the car-sized oval of still water that heralded a whale, not the seagull landing on Joan's back, mistaking her rocking for the waves, not the fingers in each other's pubic hair, shoving their parts closer, not even a shared trip to Chicago—had happened with Paige. Nothing had ever happened with Paige that could drive the urgent heaves of Joan's acoustic. Not even close.

"Oh." Paige's cheeks pinkened. "Yeah. They ship us."

"What?" Who was "they"? Who was "us"?

"Ship us into a relationship. You know, what the kids do." She let out a husky laugh. "It's stupid. Right?" Her chin tipped up, cheekbones flushed.

"They do? Where?" So no one understood the song at all. This song that was her greatest work, that had finally hoisted her up onto the tiniest step stool of fame, even that song people interpreted incorrectly.

"On the internet. Where do you think?" She was stung, though that was crazy. "Just because you don't use it doesn't mean it doesn't exist."

"Wait." Joan set her palm on the beach, bracing herself. "People are talking about us on the internet? And saying we're in a relationship? How do people even know we're friends?" The sand pricked her palm like crushed glass.

"You know the scene. It's small."

"But seriously." Joan turned her head all around, to the little girl in the lime suit, out for a night swim with her grandma, to boys cackling and shaking their mop heads, to the mango vendor. "People are looking at pictures of us together on the internet? Like people are taking pictures of our private walks or something and posting them to the internet and then drawing a bunch of dumbass conclusions?" She felt covered in ants. The idea of some stranger observing them as they walked in private, talking about guys and music and whatever bullshit, nauseated her. She was talking too fast, too forcefully, but what the hell was this? "That doesn't creep you out? People imagining our sex life?" She hadn't even thought to fear that part until she said the words, but that was actually the worst. They knew Joan and Paige had fucked, or had made up a truth that was an actual truth. Joan jumped up and paced the sand. The surf licked her feet.

"It doesn't bother me," Paige said, her voice short. She stood, brushed the sand off her ass. "I actually like it." She raised her nose into the air. "I'm actually proud I know you."

"Jesus, that's not what I'm saying." The sea swelled and advanced, and now Joan was ankle-deep in the brackish water, salt stinging between her toes, leather sandals soaked under the surf. "Of course I'm proud I know you. I just don't want my personal sex life discussed online." But was that the case? Was she really so frightened of a little gossip? If so, why did she piss on so many strangers? Why did she write songs about every passing desire? She didn't use the internet, maybe, getting used to its existence was still an adjustment, maybe, but she wasn't dumb.

"It's fine," Paige said. "Let's head back. I'm getting tired to drive."

Paige was halfway down the length of beach before Joan caught her. No matter what she said, no matter what apologies, she got nothing more out of her that night.

16

THE DAY AFTER THE TEACHERS' WALK WAS FINALLY THE weekend, the first partial week over, Joan's first day in Virginia with nothing. Out in the hills of campus, the humidity was thick on her, but its weight was a comfort. It wasn't the trash-infused breath of a Coney Island summer, heavy with armpit fug and Ferris wheel exhaust—a cocktail Joan could sip all day—but clear and rich, like the sweat from a baby who hadn't yet lived a souring life. The campus was so green it hurt her eyes, so green the hills were lumps of mossy chlorophyll that would sink you into an emerald sponge after one step, so green that, even when the sky exploded into splashy rainbow sunsets, green was still the best color of every day. The students were far enough away, up on the main quad, that, near Community Village, campus was dead still, not even the air moving. Alone, treading the hills, Joan's mind quieted.

She walked all day, trudging the last weeks out of her. When she finally returned to the suite in the evening, miles and miles later, Sparrow was on the couch, soft and homey in an oversized hoodie—a cream one now, though Joan had returned the dirty one. Sparrow's cowlicks stuck out every which way under the lamplight. They raised their eyebrows. "Joan."

"Hey." The feeling of coming home to someone waiting clicked deep in Joan. She had the urge to hug Sparrow. She never hugged anyone. Instead she kneeled down beside the couch, placed a hand on Sparrow's knee, as though that was less awkward. Blood rushed from her hand straight to her head, and she wobbled on her thighs. "I was walking. Were you worried?"

Sparrow's lip hitched up, a tooth gleaming. Their knee scorched Joan's palm. "Yeah, uh—I have to talk to you."

Sparrow stood up and walked down the hall. Joan followed. In their room, they inserted the snake and closed the door, turned to face Joan. That sawdust smell of clean sweat and pencil shavings. They studied Joan as though awaiting some reaction. "You don't know, do you."

"Don't know what?" She kept her voice clipped.

"Seriously?" Sparrow's eyebrows kissed. "If I were you I'd be monitoring this shit so hard."

Joan could barely twist her head far enough to shake it. "Tell me." Throwing out her phone had been dumb. She should be ready at any moment to pull content down, report, red flag, however that worked. She'd forfeited her chance to keep tabs on whatever was out there.

Sparrow took out their phone and activated the screen. Joan felt naked, but worse, like her flesh had been stripped, her bones exposed, yellow, scrawny, insufficient bones, bones that would collapse without the wrapper of muscles and organs.

"It's on Twitter?" Joan asked, as the white interface lit Sparrow's throat. Twitter was the primitive brutal landscape she'd never set foot in. That nasty playground where people burned for the amusement of others.

"Yeah." Sparrow's voice was plain, like there was nothing wrong with Twitter, like it was molded from clouds and candy. They set to typing.

"Wait." Joan's arm shot across the distance between them.

"You don't want to see?" There was a knife's edge to their words. Like, *You did this, and now you can't even look at it? How pathetic, how fearful, are you?*

Joan flapped her hand. She could barely speak. *Go on.*

Sparrow bowed back into their device. They typed a search term and raised the phone. They poked the screen, pixels deforming in a circle like water, then tipped it toward Joan. Her instinct was to shield herself from the digital blaze. Even with just a few days away from screens, the backlighting already seared.

The tweet was authored by an Easter egg named @Lotta_B. Sparrow's breath was hot and close on Joan's arm. The words surged up in a screaming muddle. The text fuzzed, doubled, and clarified into indelible black scratches in the clean white substance of the internet:

ONE I CARE ABOUT INVITED ME INTO HER SECTOR OF GENIUS AND ARTISTIC BRILLIANCE. DRUNK, I ACCEPTED HER CALL TO MEET ON THAT HOT PLANE OF LYRICAL WONDER.

And then, attached by a digital string to the bottom of that tweet:

POSITIVE CHANGES HAVE FOLLOWED FROM THE INCIDENT SUCH AS IT WAS. I CANNOT SLEEP THINKING OF IT.

And then:

I SUBMIT FOR YOU THE "INCIDENT." I LIVED IT AND HAVE VIEWED IT MANY TIMES: THE MOVIE OF MY HEART. BUT STILL I DO NOT GRASP ITS BURIED IMPLICATIONS OR FLAVORS. I ASK, WHAT DO YOU SEE?

The fourth tweet had a link to *Joan Vole Tuesday LES*. When Joan had finished reading, she stared into the phone, as though its radiance could suck her off this planet.

"I was thinking about Carlotta this morning," Sparrow said. "So I looked her up."

"She wrote it this morning." Joan spoke slowly. Those surprising turns of phrase, that blaring text—Carlotta was a real person. This geneticist so brilliant she didn't have to be tidy, with a taste for raw music and an appealing shakiness with language. This mind, working its crooked path through Joan's attack, wrestling with how to communicate what had happened. Joan could see her, hunched in that empty apartment, tapping out the tweet, letter by letter. She'd been ready to wait on the video. But then Joan had to sic Georgina on her.

"Last night." Sparrow tapped the timestamp as though Joan had never used the internet before.

How was Joan here, in this tranquil room, conversing with a colleague, the carpet intact under her feet? She should have evaporated, should've died under the drafting desk. Her trespasses were plain on the internet for anyone to discover.

"Don't freak," Sparrow said. "Georgina doesn't know how to operate Google. She doesn't exist on socials."

"Okay." The word eked out. She hadn't even thought yet to worry about her job, her housing, her finances.

Sparrow clamped their cheek with a claw. "There are some good things. Your name isn't on the tweet. And her account is brand new. Zero followers. Following zero."

Joan clicked the video. It only had a few more views than last time—a normal accrual.

Sparrow lifted the phone from Joan's hand. "I wouldn't have found it if I didn't know Carlotta's name."

"Okay." Joan gulped. "That's good. That's really good." She was breathing again. Maybe Sparrow was right. Maybe really no one would find this obscure tweet. After all, millions of tweets languished out there, unseen. Those brushes in orderly mason jars, the pencils grouped by heat of color. All was okay.

"What did you do to her?" Sparrow's brow knit under their yellow bangs. Their voice was low and soft.

Sparrow didn't know—even still. Only Joan and Carlotta knew what had happened, and now Sparrow would know what Joan wanted them to know, and only that. "Carlotta doesn't mind. She's happy about what happened." The words sounded fake and stiff. "Isn't that what matters?"

"But what did you do?"

Joan could lie. She could say all she did was hug Carlotta, that Carlotta took it too far, that she was unhinged. After all, look at the tweets. But Joan couldn't lie, not to that face. And part of her longed for one more person, at least, to sit with her in full knowledge. "I kinda went crazy." Joan's cheeks flared. She had to spit it out, and then the truth would be out there, between them. Maybe Sparrow would hate Joan forever, but at least Joan would have certainty. At least she wouldn't have to be terrified all the time that Sparrow would find out the truth and turn on her. "I rubbed myself on her." That would be bad enough. "And peed."

Sparrow released a huff like a horse. "You peed on Carlotta? Onstage?"

Joan flinched. She'd never heard it in someone else's words. "But she was okay with it." The words drooped out limply.

"Why?" Sparrow's head tilted. "Joan. What? You're crazy, but you're not cruel."

"I was upset." She'd never thought she'd have the chance to explain. "I was out of my mind."

Sparrow suddenly looked years older. "Like on drugs?"

Joan grabbed her face like she could rip it off, like that would make any difference. "Look, I fucked up. I hate myself for it. And now everyone's going to know." Panic vibrated through her limbs. She couldn't just sit here. "What do I do? What can I even do?"

"Did you think she was into it or something?" Sparrow's cheeks strained, like they were trying to understand. "I know Carlotta's hard to read. She disappears into her head sometimes. But she's one hundred percent straight." They squinted in pain. "And really, actually, pretty shy."

Had Joan thought Carlotta was into it? Only in the sense that she assumed all her fans would be psyched to do whatever she wanted. Which was gross, now that she directly thought the words. It was easier to think of the fans as existing only at shows, their only movement jumping and crying out, their bodies alive only under gel lights. "No. She looked pretty upset."

Sparrow watched her for a long time, focus wandering from Joan's hair, which was frizzing into oblivion, down to her mouth: ajar, cold air entering to dry out her big front teeth. Joan's features crystallized under Sparrow's careful watch. Joan squirmed under their gaze, longing to writhe free. Sparrow bit their lip. "You knew she was upset."

Joan hesitated. Because this was the shittiest part. Carlotta had warned her away, and she'd returned for the second embrace, and worse. Piss, hot and intense between them. She could lie. She could so easily lie. "Yes."

"Fuck." Sparrow's arms dropped, life sagging out of their face. "Well. Fuck. I mean, I guess I have to thank you for being honest."

Joan wouldn't take credit for that. That was basic decency, even if she'd never managed it before.

"But really, Joan." Their voice hitched, ragged, like it was about to disintegrate. They searched Joan's face. "I can't imagine you hurting someone." Moisture gathered in the corners of their eyes. Before Joan could confirm they were crying, Sparrow turned away, ripping the snake from the door.

*

In the computer lab, Joan checked the video a hundred times, as though her vigilance could hold the view count steady. She ravaged the browser with search terms—there had to be a way to stop the information. Dozens of confusing solutions populated her screen. She could dig up the fiberglass internet cable, if she could find it. She could order a deauther and kick all the teachers offline. Just to know the few people around her could never see the video—that was something. Just so Sparrow wouldn't. She skimmed blogs by German hackers. She could order a radio jammer from Europe—it could be here next week—and interrupt the Wi-Fi signal with a radio frequency. She could steal the router, bash it to shards.

Joan collapsed on the keyboard, her nose typing a string of nonsense. She'd drive herself crazy and get nowhere. And even if she stopped the four teachers from checking the internet for the next five weeks, which in itself was impossible, the rest of the world would advance. The plastic keys pushed their squares into her cheek, marking her skin.

17

THE NEXT WORKWEEK PASSED SLOWLY, AND THEN ONE more. Joan kept her head down, doing as little as possible in class to get by, wrangling with the kids to forfeit authorship. In Community Village, she kept to her room. She couldn't bear to see Sparrow or talk to them, couldn't stand their cold gaze. Each time Sparrow fidgeted next door, Joan jumped to attention, as though their shuffling of papers, their bathroom trips, their coughs were coded messages. She couldn't stop herself, now and then, from lingering by Sparrow's room, where the snake was always in place, the brush of sable fur against Bristol board sounding through the hollow-core door. She longed to knock, but it was enough, when she was lonely, to remember now there was someone else who knew, that she no longer had to live alone with her crime. Even if they never spoke again, Joan and Sparrow would always be bound that way. And that was a spiky sort of comfort.

She ate bad dinners that didn't require the stove, waiting until the dorm quieted to snatch fistfuls of ingredients. She was left with muesli and carrots, cold vegetarian hot dogs and pudding, bread thick with spreads that didn't require heat to soften them: cashew butter, coconut oil, mustard. She hand-washed her linen shorts and tunic, lay on her sleeping bag naked until they dried in the sun. She walked to Cobra Face. The stallion's nuzzling skull was the only live thing that touched her, and that was enough, slowing her blood. She avoided people, she taught, she tried to be good. Meredith freaked her out, and she declined Chester's dwindling invitations. With the silence in Joan's room and Sparrow's and only occasional blasts of over-produced pop from Meredith's, the suite was nearly Norway.

She retrieved her sweater from the pasture, hoping to re-christen it as an erotic object. But whenever she pressed the wool to her nose, there was Sparrow squirming as fluid shot through their underwear. If only she could've taught Sparrow properly. The sweater slumped in her closet, releasing a sad toffee odor.

Every day, at least twice, she visited the computer lab to monitor the tweet and video. Every day, nothing. Not a gram more engagement: no like or retweet or bump in views. Every time she confirmed her continued safety, she ordered herself to relax in relief, but every muscle stayed rigid.

She focused on crafting Lesson Cycles, knowing the kids hadn't seen the internet from day to day, assured they were frozen at their original level of ignorance. She accepted Georgina's advice, which Georgina made a show of annoyance at having to hand deliver on real paper, though Joan was pretty sure she liked this ancient method of communication. Joan asked open-ended questions of the students; she asked questions at all. She avoided eye contact with Lula, trying to communicate that she wasn't going to tattle, but whenever she encountered the kid, a calm heat flashed through her. Love was happening at this camp. In this world, somewhere, even with a cranky, annoying child, love was possible, and that was almost too intense a fact to keep, rolling around like a coal in her brain. She built lessons with different modules for different learning styles: lectures, activities, private work time. She endeavored, for at least a little while every class, to encourage the students to write songs together, to write songs on tissue paper and melt them in water, to record songs and leave cassettes anonymously around campus, to assemble found songs from words on trash, and while they humored her, eventually she always caught them writing in corners, on personal projects, alone.

Occasionally she shared a song without origin, but only the lyrics now, and only provided a volunteer read. The kids mocked the barge song, rumored to have been written by a child dying of cancer. They called the girl "emo," which was so wrong—but when Victor read the lyrics, in his high, pre-cracked voice, Lula touched her eye with a tissue, and Joan couldn't stop herself from seeing him, skinny back hunched around a suitcase, shuttled between the homes of his parents.

The kids begged to play their own work, and she caved. She curled into herself through their songs. Victor endeavored to turn the tuba sexy and experimental, tossing his head around as he blasted off-key snorts of boy breath from the wide brass mouth. Joan had hoped his "Rail Rat" breakthrough would improve his work, but he was worse now. On harmonica he alternated between corny trills and passages of spoken word: "A man is walking down the street, he wishes he had food to eat." (Harmonica) "He doesn't have a single cent, he spent his dollars all on rent." (Harmonica) "His clothes are rags, his face is gray, his odor is quite bad today." (Harmonica) "If you see him walking by, won't you help him not to die?" (Extra emphatic harmonica) "But for one fact, he's same as us, he lost his savings on a bus." (Bow.)

She kept her teeth together as she provided neutered commentary on Victor's smug parables and Lula's bawdy puns chanted over slugs of tuba, redirecting them to abdicate ownership in any little way. Victor nodded and took notes, but every time he presented a song, it was just as humiliating. Lula didn't seem to care if she improved, just brought in new songs, again and again, and performed them with relentless pleasure. She did not betray having been caught out late at night, still stubbornly sang of men, a proud glitter when she caught Joan's gaze. Joan felt guilty every time she talked to Lula, though it was Lula who stood to lose for her transgression—kids had been sent home for less, and Joan could almost convince herself it was out of generosity and not the silly pang of jealousy that she failed to turn the girl in. At least now it was clear that Lula's rhymes about banging men had nothing to do with Joan.

And Agnes. Ever since they'd cleaned the dreadnought, Joan was skittish around her, jumping if Agnes called her name, cutting her gaze away when she got close.

So Joan had to steel herself when she went in to teach that Friday of the third week. Two more hours, and then she'd have the whole weekend not to worry about the kids.

Entering the classroom that afternoon, the students bounced upright in their beanbags, stiff and tall, at the ready. Over the last week, Joan had devoted a handful of daily minutes to building a communal song. Her attempts at block-long processes consistently failed; the students grew restless, longing for the fleshy familiarity of their own work. So she'd sprinkled in a complex process between other modules, overthinking the next step each night in her room, never explaining the point of any of the lead-up, letting the kids think she was filling cracks of time with busywork.

The first day of the weeklong process had been devoted to image gathering. She'd dumped magazines on the floor, purchased from a convenience store off Route 29 that it had taken her all evening to walk to and from because she'd been afraid that if she got in her car, she'd never stop driving. The students were puzzled by the order to cut up magazines, though Joan had assumed collage was a hated tradition of all childhoods.

"But aren't magazines super expensive?" Victor asked, like he'd forgotten he'd shown them pictures of his family's beach mansion.

They gamely grabbed the scissors, hands slipping over glossy pages. At first they were distracted by the news they'd missed without their phones—a celebrity had purchased bread, a bigger iPad was available, hogs had escaped a truck in Dallas and now enjoyed the free life. Once she managed to divert them into clipping and collecting, they were incompetent slicers. Magazine shards floated in the dim basement, and their unicorns and sexy men and banks of heather were surrounded by halos of white paper. She discouraged them from selecting images they personally favored, but a heap of healthy-toothed men soon accumulated by Lula's side, the gayest thing Joan had ever seen.

The next day, Tuesday, Joan served them back the images, which they didn't remember twenty-four hours later. She instructed them to turn their piles upside down so only chunks of texts and quartered, unchosen images were exposed and then fish out random sets of three. When each student had ten or so such rows, Joan had them write one sentence per row. She nixed their first attempts, which were too descriptive. A lion, a yellow tomato, and a tiny hottie could not be "A lion, a yellow tomato, and a tiny hottie." Instead the sentence must blend these images in all possible ways: "Brad Heritage lacks the courage to attend an Italian dinner of blond cougars." The kids whined but set to rewriting. That day's process had nearly sapped their patience and consumed half the class, but Joan harvested three sets of sentences at the end of it all and, reviewing them in her bedroom later, found them nearly inspiring: "Chocolate falls over a lake of shoes," "Pigs are evil according to hot men," "Jumping Lukes cry perfume in Arizona."

On Wednesday, she redistributed the sentences, which she'd freed individually from their sheets and passed by the handful to each student. She was startled that, at each stage in the process, the students seemed to remember not at all their previous work. "That was a hundred years ago," Lula said of Monday.

The students snipped the sentences apart and stapled them into patchwork paragraphs. Each student ended with one meaty paragraph, scattering rejected words like confetti at their feet. The paragraphs migrated one student to the left. On Thursday, the students were pressed to draw an illustration encompassing every detail in their paragraph, which also honored the climate of the paragraph at large.

"What?" Victor squeaked. "But I can't draw."

"If I'd wanted to draw, I would've signed up for dumbass comics," said Lula.

Their protests were feeble and good-natured. By now they were invested, and, even more mysteriously, they seemed to be enjoying Joan.

"Don't worry," Joan said. "The worse the drawing, the better."

Joan hadn't looked at the drawings after class yesterday, snapping them immediately into a folder. She'd let them settle overnight in the privacy of their manila home.

Now, on Friday, Joan opened the hand-me-down folder,

an old student's name carefully lettered on the tab: "Mason, Bo." She removed the first drawing. The kids inched forward into a close curve. She set the drawing delicately on the floor, smoothing down a corner that had accordioned. The page was filled edge to edge with a network of machinery, thick with buttons and panels and vents and marched upon by men with gape-mouthed smirks. The pencil work was dense and muddled, thick glimmering wires and pipes intersecting in grids of graphite. Some figures walked on four feet; some had tails of a single eyelash. Cubes dropped or hovered between the levels of the machinery the figures trod upon. The page was all foggy silver. The students crawled closer.

The next drawing was so lightly rendered that its swoops and curves were barely affixed to the page, as if a look could dislodge them. This artist had more skill—the tufted ears of a borzoi were silky—but less confidence. Some shapes were wispy and complicated: human forms lobed and sprinkled with fingers down the spine and dangling from the groin, curlicues swaying from ears, pine needles embedded in a human hip.

The final drawing boasted a plainspoken technique, letting the content rise up as yet more distressingly peculiar. A long-nosed bird pushed through the anus of a gorilla. A group of men took matching steps on a band of grass suspended in the sky, only to topple over its edge and continue their march upside down on the band's underbelly. Ice cream melted into a puddle that children drowned in and the gorilla drank. Iguanas battled a helicopter. A handsome man was penciled in under it all, winking, as though all the activity took place in his perverse mind.

The students had crept so close that Joan smelled their pleasantly sour breath. They hushed, studying the panels.

"Okay," Joan said. "This is how it works." Three heads

tipped up reverently, as if she knew what she was doing. And Agnes, leaning forward, willowy frame bent over the drawings—what was she thinking? Would any music she ever made be enough again? No life lay after genius. "You first." Agnes's whole face lit, as though she'd been singled out for some great honor. "Begin here." Joan tapped the machinery. She had no idea how the students had extracted these masterpieces from her chaotic process, but she knew exactly whose was whose. The machinery was Lula's: all that blocky, weighty logic, all those men formed with a straight edge but off in every proportion. Each drawing was a cross-section of the child's mind. Agnes could hardly stick her wisps down on the page, feared her own talent. Even as she made her marks, they floated away. And Victor's drawing was clogged with suppressed energy. "Sing as you go. Make up the tune, but don't worry over it. Let it flow out. Let it control itself."

"What do I sing?" Agnes whispered, as though the stakes were monumental. As though, if she sang the wrong note, she'd decimate their entire chain of work.

"Sing the images. But don't worry too much. If you depart from what you see, all the better."

"How long do I go?"

"A verse, however you define that." Joan hadn't planned any of this. "When the song starts to fade or slip from reach, tap Lula. Lula, you sing the third picture; Victor, the second." Though it didn't really matter who sang what. The students regarded the pictures like they'd fluttered, fully formed, from the sky. "Then circle back to Agnes. Extract refrains and motifs as you wish. When the song tells you it's done, make this gesture." Joan swept her hands together and ripped them apart. The students lurched back as though she'd demonstrated magic.

They nodded, calculations whirring behind their faces, like

they were memorizing every word. Joan would've been horrified to improvise a song before the Gonewriters, would've feared their derision, their laughter, but, most of all, their praise: all commentary humiliating and vulnerable.

The students readied their bodies over the panels, steadying themselves into crouches, closing their eyes.

"In the dense, in the dense, in the dense deep world." Agnes's voice was shaky but clear, with a creamy tone. "There's a dog, in the dense, there's a man, in the dense, in the dense gray deepest fog."

Joan opened her mouth to correct the repetition, to ask her to retry, starting stronger. But she crushed her tongue down with her teeth. Agnes tapped Lula, whose cheeks pinched. "The dog of the fog is a monster's great log, this fog I lost myself in."

Victor slapped the floor in time. "And the man has a plan for the animals tonight, the animals of the dense, dense fog. His plan is sick and wily, but for me it makes me smile. I like his very sickness in the dense gray fog."

The words were simple enough and affixed, in their way, to the images. The tune was an elegiac march, its delicate, lullaby stomp perfect tether for the maniacal lyrics. Maybe Victor was only able to create art when he was one of a group, like his true place was as support system, helping other artists achieve their dreams.

Joan turned the drawings upside down. The kids startled, like she'd snipped their seat belts. "Now let the song speak to itself," she whispered. Electricity webbed the back of her skull.

"In the fog, in the fog, in the dense, gray fog," Agnes sang, louder. "My man has his plan, a scary, hairy plan. He's up ahead, he hears me, and as he moves, he nears me, and he tells me twenty stories of his all-time favorite dog."

"The dog," Lula sang, in her oversized army jacket, hands

buried in the sleeves, white hair awry, perhaps from another late night, "isn't present in the fog. The dog is deep beneath the moss, this dog whose silky body's lost. The dog who died years before, five or ten or even more, from a hidden poison spore."

Their voices were lovely and untrained, not pushing beyond their capacity like usual, projecting to impress, but badly tuned and uncertain. Like a CD Joan used to have: a school performance of pop songs sung by children in the 1970s, directed by a forgotten music teacher, that somehow, despite its poor recording and the institutional echo of the school hall, became a cult hit. The anonymity of the voices did it, the vulnerability, the soloists' note holds so fragile and trembling.

Her students reddened at their silly lyrics, the creaks and limits of their voices. But the song would've died in the maw of a polished singer. The man's perverse plan involved digging up the carcass of his dead borzoi, who'd been so elegant that he'd had to poison it to maintain his own dignity: "So distinguished, thus relinquished, a much too perfect friend." He and the speaker—the man's new, human love—gazed upon the corpse—tawny and majestic, immaculately preserved after years of interment. The fog closed in as they dragged the dog's corpse down into a sooty mine, full of mechanical miners laboring away at every level, and lay down together as three perfect loves in the bowels of the dead bottom of the mine, to sleep forever.

As the students fumbled their way through the doomed march of the story, their voices shifted to meet in the middle: a single tenuous, feathery voice, a whisper-sing. They swapped turns without signal, seamlessly, like one being unspooling the song from its depths. Joan couldn't believe they were managing this: a perfect song of no provenance, sung out of nowhere from a chaos chain of decisions made of whimsy and joy. A song beyond what any of them could ever hope to conjure on their own, a song that was more than any one of them, more than Joan, more than this room. She'd led them partway, and they'd taken the rest of the path on their own. This was teaching, not the one-on-one ego trip of mentoring. This work was genuine. Her brain floated over her torso.

When the song concluded, Lula executed Joan's gesture, perfectly sweeping, with a level of grace she'd never yet commanded. And they were done.

Three heads rose to Joan from the blank pages they'd sung to, beaming.

"That was magic," Joan breathed. "I can't believe you guys." She set her hand to her neck. Blood pulsed under her skin.

Clapping from the threshold. All four heads whipped around to find Georgina leaning against the doorway. Joan startled.

"Bravo," Georgina said.

"Did you watch that whole thing?" Joan's voice emerged an anxious thread. The song was full of dog corpses and proud lovers and suicide pacts and an undercurrent of perverted menace.

"You all were so absorbed I couldn't bear to interrupt. But don't worry. I'll leave now." She bowed and mouthed to Joan, *Talk later.*

And then she was gone. But before Joan could say anything, Victor interjected, "Don't make fun of the song, Agnes," he said, his voice a rushing force. "Even if it's random shit pasted together."

"I would never," Agnes said, the words pushing out of her with emotion.

"I loved the dead dog." Lula clasped her hands. "That was seriously chill. Who made that up?"

"I don't know," said Victor.

"I didn't," said Agnes.

"You all did," Joan said, her voice shooting out. The most perfect song of no provenance she'd ever heard. And she hadn't needed to sublimate herself to it. She'd simply listened.

"Did you record it?" asked Agnes, turning to Joan. "You did, right?"

"I did not."

"What?" Agnes groaned, wheeling around to her friends. "One of you did, though, right?"

"No devices," Victor said.

"But we can do it again, right?" Agnes said, bouncing on her feet, bangs flapping. "We just sang it, so we should be able to sing it again. Hold up. 'In the fog, in the fog, where the moon don't ever shine.'"

"No," Victor said. "That's a different song." He must have had a cool father, nodding his scruffy chin to Lead Belly as he mulled over his divorce.

"Didn't it start with the dog?" Lula asked.

"No," said Agnes. "No! Someone else made that part up. I started. Right?"

"What even was that tune, though?" Victor thumped his head as though he could shake it free.

Agnes sang frantically, emitting sounds that were badly off: waltzes, dirges, but mostly tunes too sped up, like she couldn't relax enough to sink back into the rhythm of the song.

But that was good. That was what Joan wanted. "You sang the song, and now it's over."

"But no," Agnes said, jostling the beanbag. "We wrote it one second ago! We can get it back." A strain rose her voice.

"You can't," Joan said. "And listen. That's a good thing."

"How is that good?" Agnes's voice was ragged with panic. "We worked on that song for a whole week."

"It existed," Victor said, the words wisping out. "And now it doesn't." A plain smile, like satisfaction had relaxed the muscles of his face.

"You guys did it." Bubbles filled Joan. Even if they didn't understand yet, that was okay. They were on the road.

*

The students packed up and left, a float in their step. They were quiet with each other in a way they never had been, reverently sorting their supplies and filing out.

"Joan," Georgina said from the threshold. "I caught you." She stepped into the room.

Joan froze. "Is everything okay?"

"Yes. Why? Is it not?" Georgina depressed middle C on the piano, didn't react when it came up silent. She turned to Joan, her hair a perfect gray soft serve. "I want to share how impressed I've been."

"Are you kidding?"

"Of course not." Georgina ruffled her feathers and scowled. "Your students are happy and engaged. They bound around this place like it's theirs."

"Oh." That meant nothing. All the kids bounded around. The place was a playground. This was summer camp, after all. They were probably trading hand jobs behind the oaks.

"But more to the point, I'm glad you're settling in. You seem content." Had Georgina not once observed Meredith grimacing as Joan approached? Had she never noticed Joan lingering behind Sparrow, hoping for them to turn and glimpse her? Had she not seen Joan tucked up alone in her room, willing the others away, all the while secretly hoping they'd knock?

"I love it here," Joan said, the words springing out, embarrassingly eager. But it was true. And today had been nice. The one positive act of her life was mentoring Paige. Crouched on filthy floors, urging her to run through a picking pattern again, one more time, slow the anchor rhythm, skip a beat, drop the third finger in that refrain, there, you have it, perfect, there. All that patience and micro-progress was so lovely, Paige gaining confidence, building her style.

"Oh, Joan." Georgina's cheeks lit. "I'm proud of your arc with us."

"Thanks." Joan stepped backward, joining her hands behind her spine. She had to hold herself together with every ounce of strength.

"I must admit I was cross with you for your classroom invader. The students were frightened. But today—I don't know what to say. Complete turnaround."

Joan could drift up to the basement ceiling and stick.

"My point person in Charlottesville ran some numbers for me," Georgina said. "I already have a writer on hand to teach fiction through the academic year. But I'd love to add songwriting, if you're willing. It would be full-time after-school teaching." She paused, watching Joan expectantly, but Joan couldn't catch enough air to respond. Georgina was joking—she must be. "I know you have a life up there in New York. But might you consider the role?"

A whole year of peace and kids watching her with expectant faces. "Me?"

Georgina laughed, bracelets jangling. "Yes, of course you."

She cupped her soft muzzle. "I admire your ferocity. And change—that's meaningful to me."

Remaining here among the emerald vines, in an actual town, where Joan could be accountable professionally. Where she could lead young songwriters onto the right track. Maybe this was better than Norway. Maybe she'd go wild again if she was isolated, if no one was there to supervise. Georgina had seen Joan feral, and she'd seen her now. She'd understand a relapse but also wouldn't tolerate it. So long as the tweet stayed buried, Joan could be all right. Her voice, when she managed it, was small: "I'd love that."

Georgina's cheeks shaded a soft pink. "That's wonderful news. Let's see how the rest of the session goes. We'll talk details later."

Georgina left Joan in a daze.

*

Halfway across campus, in the rich afternoon sun, high-stepping with her news, Joan came upon Agnes perched on a knoll with a ukulele in her lap. She was strumming and humming like any kid hobbyist, head tipped back, like she was filling herself with the syrup of music. Joan stopped in her footsteps.

How could this kid sit so loosely in the grass, legs relaxed and open, arm pumping to play? This kid who'd shown up at camp a mess, grieving her old career. And now she could sit here, noodling away, like she'd suffered no sour history. Joan's legs ached to run. Let her get to her room so she could dream of the real job and easier kids of the future.

Joan crept along the path, trying not to bend the grass too

loudly. She could slip by unnoticed. But as she drew even with the girl, Agnes's eyes snapped open.

"Ms. Vole," she cried, covering the uke as though she'd been caught naked. "I'm not doing anything."

The ukulele was printed like a watermelon, so lightweight the wind could've carried it off. It was plastic and shiny, not even fabricated from the cheapest wood, the neck tight on the body, the colors so bold you could spot it from an airplane. It was a $29.99 toy, dragging all the manic sweeties of YouTube, the whiff of its four-stringed low bar to entry. "You can do whatever you want," Joan said slowly, trying to make herself believe the words, suppressing her urge to shatter the instrument on the concrete path.

Agnes's cheeks reddened. "Okay, I admit it. I took up this stupid thing." She raised the uke. The way Agnes handled the instrument was unsettling, too dear. She loved her little toy. She'd turned, overnight, into a kid content with basics. "It's super simple. I think it took ten minutes to figure out."

"Hm." Agnes wanted Joan to be impressed, but the instrument lay miles below the kid's capability.

"Actually." Agnes hesitated. The magenta flank of the uke caught the sunshine, too brilliant. An instrument should never be neon. Instruments should be quietly beautiful, like the Martin, leaving the sound the star. "Can I play what I'm working on?"

No rang in Joan's mind. *No, no, no.* If she had to listen to Victor or Lula's ditties, that was one thing. But she couldn't bear the defeat of genius. "I should be going." The sun slanted lower now, golden. "It's getting late."

Agnes's eyelashes dropped on her cheeks. "That's okay. I get it."

"If it's quick, I guess." Joan clenched against the words, but now it was too late. She'd said them.

Agnes stationed the uke on her knee. Her fingers found their positions blindly, her wrist angled elegantly over the sound hole, the knuckles of her left hand precisely aligned with the neck. All that overcautious positioning out of place on the watermelon. Her discipline had filtered down, even with this inferior instrument, even with her own fledgling material and not the work of dead masters.

She flew through a set of fingerpicked measures, detailed and rapid. Jangly, but when was any uke not? Her fingers crossed the frets speedily, her picking fussy, her rhythm too straight: overly precise hangovers from embodied training. But she was accurate. Unassailable, if rote. Sort of heartbreaking, after Villa-Lobos's Étude No. 7.

And then she began to sing, in tune, but so faintly Joan had to lean in to make out the lyrics. Partly because they had none of the rhythm and pattern of song, no logic to the words.

"Your new best friend, your new best friend, a beautiful selection." She was basically speaking, the intricacies of her picking pattern all that made the song a song. "You are lucky to have found here your new best friend. Polish off the body of your new best friend. Clean the neck when you finish with your new best friend. Do not scratch your new best friend with any length of steel. Your friend was made with all the best of all material." She took a breath with an animal squeak so loud Joan startled, as though she'd forgotten an actual human was making this song, she'd been so borne along by it. "With proper care, you'll always have your new best friend." Agnes hesitated, as though this was the first time she was reaching the end, as though she didn't know yet how to wrap it up. Her fingers dawdled on the strings, dangling awkwardly. Had her fingers ever stuttered before? Joan had to turn away. But then Agnes found her footing. "With proper care, you'll have a friend for all these lonely years."

A single spare chord dangled off the song's edge. Agnes checked Joan. The song was still sinking in. The Martin. Joan had left it out on the street. Her guitar who'd made her who she was, who she'd serviced for years and taken ultimate care of, the only possession she would've moved from apartment to apartment if she could only take one, and she'd left it on the street without even waiting for Paige to grab it. The Martin might've been kicked into a gutter or filled with raw sewage. It could've been battered by children or resold or smashed for fun. Her Martin that had only ever been patient and lived selflessly for her. Probably it was wood chips now, stripped of its fittings. She blinked a dozen times, pushing back hot gel. No. She would not cry in front of this girl. "We just had a lesson," Joan said, dropping her voice an octave so it wouldn't break. "On divorcing ego from writing. We wrote a song that belongs to no one. And this is what you write?"

"I didn't write it." Agnes's voice flattened. She gazed, dead-eyed, past Joan.

"Didn't you?" Her eyes stung.

Agnes drew a piece of paper from her pocket. The scrap of promotional material from the dreadnought's baggie. Agnes had eliminated some sections, elided others. But it was all there. She'd made a song without any spontaneity at all, had created while protecting herself. The very idea caved a hole in Joan's skull.

"You just copied this?" Joan rattled the page. Her hand shook.

"Um, yeah."

If all she'd done was steal language, how had she animated the song, which, plain as it was, sort of came to life, simply by changing the word "guitar" to "best friend"? It was what Joan knew of her history, maybe. So that was unfair, the context of the performer activating the song.

"You said we could use found texts, that was one way to divorce ourselves."

"Right." A guitar, waiting in its case, if it was lucky enough to have one, which the dreadnought did not. Hoping it would be lifted out with clean hands, treated with care. Which it hadn't been. Joan's torso softened to rubber. "I have to go."

"Wait," said Agnes. "But what do you think of the song?"

"Good," Joan said, too quickly. She turned and hastened down her path.

18

JOAN HURRIED HOME AS FAST AS SHE COULD, AS THOUGH Agnes might chase her across campus. She'd done well with the kids today—the last five minutes didn't negate that. And now she had a job prospect, unimaginable two weeks ago. She'd be employed in Virginia for a whole year. A bubble puffed up inside her.

The sun was swollen and orange at the horizon, shadows stretched long under the trees. At every step, her bladder bumped her G-spot. She had to pee so bad she could barely walk. She hadn't let herself get to this state since she'd arrived in Virginia—she'd been professional, utilizing the bathroom at regular intervals, drinking normal quantities of water. She tried the doors of a couple of stately buildings en route to Community Village, but they were locked due to the hour or the season.

Wrestling her keycard into the slot at the dorm, her genitals urgent and angry, the stored pee radiating heat, she hesitated. Why not go in the yard? Evening had fallen, and the lamps were on in every unit. No one looking out from inside would see her. And she deserved it, hadn't given into her own satisfaction even one time in Virginia. She deserved one small pleasure, a celebration of her news, a treat after the stress of the last three weeks. Maybe she could be a better teacher, a better person, if she released a little tension.

She went around back of the building. Now that she had a plan, the urge was manageable, a sexy weight pressing her, and she strolled more slowly. She could've waited even longer, sipped an iced tea and tortured herself. Pushed a finger under her belly button, a whole hand.

She found a dogwood and pulled down her pants. She hovered her naked vulva over the earth, sinking so low the grass tickled. She shuddered against the gentle brush. No one had touched her for a thousand years.

The sweetest delight was the minute between when her brain commanded release and her body agreed: her favorite. That moment when she longed so desperately to let go but wasn't yet able, whatever man below her knowing what she wanted, free to escape but unwilling. That pause, her quivering lips, impotency escalating her pleasure, desire delayed by her old training to be a good girl, to hold it.

She trembled, swelling, heating, and then, release. That stick of liquid connecting her to earth, searing her folds like a swimming pool jet. That first rush of pressure so intense she couldn't suppress a moan. Air breathed from her in a clear line.

When the pee was done, she let her folds sit out, drying in the evening breeze. As she pulled her pants up, satisfied and free, the perfect end to the best day she'd had in forever, she caught Meredith's eye—Meredith, who was seated at the battered picnic table, still as a deer, spine straight in a silk top, a plate of hot dogs before her. Joan hadn't seen her, hadn't checked because no one sat at that table, not ever. The teachers lived inside the AC like it was the only breathable air.

Meredith watched Joan, hand twisting in a billowing sleeve. Shame surged from Joan's groin up to her scalp, holding her in its claws. She rushed with it, like she was performing again. The shame was nearly as concentrated as her ego, back when she'd written a perfect song, or played one. In fact, it was the exact feeling. Delicately, Meredith rose from the table and hurried inside.

Joan remained a statue in the yard, pants half down, ass burning in the open air. She was okay, she was so okay. She'd felt shame before—she could handle it. She hadn't done anything wrong this time.

Carefully, formally, as though Meredith were still watching—which maybe she was—Joan dabbed herself with a leaf, trying not to throb at the pleasure of the contact, pulled up her underwear, and buttoned her pants, stilling the quiver of the aftershock in her knees. She smoothed down the fabric of her crotch as though she was heading into a job interview. She stepped across the field and opened the sliding glass door, tensing her muscles so she wouldn't wobble, one foot stepping forward to claim the earth and then the other, walking like a totally normal person.

Meredith and Sparrow were whispering on the couch. When Joan entered, Meredith's forehead flushed, and she dropped her gaze into her lap. Joan hesitated on the threshold, her ass still stuck in the humidity, her face a mask of dry AC.

"How was your day?" Sparrow asked. Joan relaxed, grateful for even these easy words—she'd barely spoken to Sparrow since the tweet.

"Great, actually." Joan pushed out the words, trying to sound normal. She'd had a great day, that was true, nothing had changed that. So she'd peed outside. Everyone did now and then. Maybe Sparrow had been in the bathroom and Joan had an emergency—people did that, right? Children, at least? She forced her mouth into a grin. "Can I sit here?" Her knees swayed. If she didn't sit soon, her body would sit for her.

"Sure," Sparrow said, voice too shrill.

Joan lowered herself into the armchair. Meredith tensed as she settled, shrinking in all that coral silk. "My class was good." Joan forced her voice into a cheerful register, but it emerged ragged. "It really worked, actually. For the first time." And after, bonus, Agnes had written a decent song at last, had worked the words over until they sang with a sorrow beyond herself.

A flicker across Meredith's gaze: a flare blazing and dying out. "Right."

"Did a kid write something brilliant?" asked Sparrow. "That's always so much better than when I do it myself."

"Yes." Joan felt that exact way but hadn't put it together because never in her life had she expected to find any thrill equal to one of her own songs gelling. "It feels more impossible somehow because you weren't there for the work." Joan willed herself to forget Meredith lumped on the couch, pink face buried between silk and waves of blown-out hair. Joan tunnel-visioned on Sparrow the way she had to in certain concerts: focusing on a glittering blue bottle in the back of the bar because her fans were too hungry for her to handle.

And Sparrow was so easy to look at, their features soft at the edges, hair and flesh and eyes all tawny. Joan had stood with this person half naked on a hillside. She'd watched them try to pee the way they'd probably always wanted to pee, cleaned that soft arm, that mound of thigh. And they seemed genuinely interested in talking about Joan's kids. So fuck Meredith. Joan erased her from the room.

"The first two weeks they totally fought my plans." Joan

forced herself to override Meredith's intense focus on her, the space between them hardening to steel. "I couldn't help them at all." An audience slipping away for the first time in her life. "But today it shifted. I can finally be a good teacher."

Meredith jumped up.

"What?" Sparrow asked, head snapping toward her. "Meredith, chill, okay?" A hard, cold vein in Sparrow's tone.

"I have to go." Meredith's voice shot out. She fled the room.

Joan's skin roasted from the back of her neck around to her cheeks and forehead and the tip of her nose. She turned her face into her shoulder to hide whatever ugly color she'd turned. "I'm sorry," she mumbled.

"Why?" Sparrow's voice was cautious, like they already knew and were only asking out of politeness. They shifted inside their baggy hoodie. They seemed to own a rainbow of hoodies. This one was mustard with mint stitching.

"She saw me pee," Joan said. She was being honest. That was what she was doing here. Last time she'd been honest and it had been okay.

Sparrow tilted their head. "Like, she opened the door on you?"

"No."

"That's not your fault. Everyone forgets to lock the door sometimes. Come on."

Joan relaxed into the palm of the armchair, as though that was what had happened and Sparrow could provide accurate comfort. "So you don't think she's angry with me?"

"Oh, she definitely is angry with you."

Joan stiffened. "Okay."

Sparrow pinched their brow with two fingers. Finally, they said, "She hasn't found the tweet. None of them have."

"Oh." The word breathed out. Crisp and easy. If the tweet

was still hidden, if Sparrow hadn't shared it in some giddy, late-night moment, all was well. And look, Sparrow, relaxed in rumples of mustard cotton, was speaking to Joan like she was a decent person. "That's good."

Sparrow squinted. "Right."

"Seriously. Thank you." She couldn't even find the words. But talking to someone who knew what she'd done, one of only three people in the world who knew, and being treated like a reasonable human, filled her with warm steam.

Sparrow grunted and shuffled themself up on the couch. Darkness was spreading now from the corners of the room, oozing in toward the last of the golden sunshine coming through the glass door.

"Sparrow." Joan's voice was shaky. Did she want to know? She'd been so alive five minutes ago, pissing in the grass, body squirming under her brain. "What happened?"

Sparrow's shoulder rose to block their face, that slow, steady shoulder, that rock of calm. "Nothing's changed. I mean, with your situation. With the facts or whatever."

"But you're acting weird." She didn't want to know. But she had to know.

Sparrow winced. "Sorry."

Air left Joan at the confirmation. For this whole conversation, there'd been a flatness she'd tried to ignore. She gripped the puffy arms of the chair. "Just tell me."

"I don't know." Sparrow hugged themself. They shrank, only taking up half the couch. "I guess after our walk, Meredith was pretty weirded out. She looked up your antics and was surprised you're working at a kids' camp." Their words extruded: "I guess your, whatever, tit stuff has escalated since I was a fan?"

As her career had started to slide, maybe—just maybe—Joan

had flashed the audience more, humped the Martin, exchanged the word "you" with "dick" in every song for an entire set. Her heart flapped in her throat. "But that crap is harmless."

"I work in a high school. So yeah, I just found it silly." Their voice trailed off as their golden head turned in the lamplight.

"But Meredith didn't."

"Meredith's protective of the students." Sparrow squished into the corner of the couch. The sun was setting now. Their body was ringed in electric tangerine. "She loves this place, and she's decided you're a threat. I've spent all afternoon putting her off talking to Georgina." They pulled their hood up.

Ice trembled up Joan's spine. "She wants to talk to Georgina." The yearlong job. Joan had barely had time for it to settle into reality and already it was lost. "But I love it here."

Sparrow rubbed their cheek. "I think I convinced her. I think you're okay." They adjusted their legs on the couch, the cushion squeaking and squelching as though it longed to be left alone.

"But that's good, right?" Joan wanted to let the subject go right here. "You still look upset."

"It's just—I don't know." Sparrow chewed their lip. "I'm sorry." The words were like thorns from that soft mouth. "It's just." They sighed. "I guess I kind of agree?" The words out, they grimaced.

"Okay." Joan had to keep her voice steady. This was fair. This was only fair. She'd decided to be honest with this person. She could not let her mind rush ahead to Sparrow cutting her out.

Sparrow filled their lungs. "I was nervous to, like, I don't know, say that to you." They squirmed, the couch squeaking.

"No, I'm glad you did." There was a pleasant kind of release in responding to someone else, in paying attention, dumb as that sounded.

"It's just—I do sorta agree with Meredith." They hesitated, examining Joan. "Because I know what all those—activities or whatever—led to."

"Right." Joan wanted to slide off her chair and through a hole in the floor.

"I don't want to think badly of you." They held Joan's gaze, then darted their focus away. Their lips trembled into a smirk. "Ugh. It's intense looking at you. Like I can't get used to you so close."

Joan jolted with an illegal pang. "That's nice."

Sparrow sat back so far they disappeared in shadow. "I'm being too forward. I'm sorry." They checked the ceiling, which caught the last of the daylight: a rich, red square. "I'm not usually like this."

"What do you mean?" She tried to keep her voice light.

"I never said what I thought at all when I was a girl. Or, I mean, like, living as a girl."

"Yeah?" Joan spoke softly so she'd seem like a safe person again, like maybe how Sparrow had thought of her before the tweet: a harmless, scrawny tit-dunker.

"I've felt like a different person since I transitioned. That's stupid to say, being that's kind of the whole point." Trapezoids of golden light divided their chest, their thigh, as they wriggled in and out of the last of the orange sunshine. "I knew I'd be different in all the physical ways, obviously." Joan often forgot Sparrow had breasts, so intense was whatever support they employed. "But I didn't budget for the confidence." They leaned forward with an awkward laugh. Their breath warmed the rim of Joan's jaw. It was hard to tell in the dim light, but their cheeks seemed to have changed color. "Like, that I'm sitting here talking to you about this shit. It's wild. I would've gone to bed when Meredith did, even a year ago, run so fast from us alone. But here we are."

Joan longed to draw Sparrow out, but she had to be tactful. She couldn't play the lumbering cis fool, the way she had with Lamar, blurting shit that seemed fine until it was out of her mouth and she understood, by Lamar's expression, it was offensive as hell. "Thank you."

Sparrow's shoulders bounced. "It's nothing."

"What about, like, hormones? Or have you arrived at a good place, gender-wise? I mean, I think you have. Not that I think you shouldn't do more. I mean, obviously that's not my choice—sorry." Joan should shut up. "Tell me if I'm being gross?"

Sparrow released a breath of laughter. "You're fine."

"Ugh, I'm not." Joan covered her face. "I'm an idiot."

Sparrow sat up on their knees. "I mean, obviously I hate when people are like, what does your junk look like?" Their voice was relaxed now. "But usually it's the opposite problem. Like all my friends are so afraid of being bad allies that they ask me nothing and just pretend I'm the same as two years ago, which is awkward. But anyway, no. No HRT." They slid a hand between cushions. "Maybe it's because I never got to be one, but I still kind of feel like a boy."

Joan wouldn't mind it herself, going all the way back to childhood to reset. But she could never shake off the interim shit. She'd lived a thousand years, and every person she'd fucked and every show she'd played and every song that had failed her was gumming up her brain, blocking paths to newness.

Sparrow squirmed to the other end of the couch, which was now lit in a butterscotch post-sun haze. They were like a puppy who couldn't stay still. "I'd feel awful looking like a cis man. Even though, if you gave me the option back in the day, I would've thrown a parade for male puberty. I would've grabbed male puberty by the hips and kissed its lips." Their shoulders bobbed. "You get it. But it's too late now. I'm this mix. Like the things I went through as a girl, no man has ever felt. And, yeah, sure, I could be, like, this special, new kind of man. But I'm not that cool." Their hair had shifted into a feminine wave. They shook it out. That was why they were always fussing their hair—it was clear, in the evening light, how quickly it could deform their entire countenance. They pushed it back into its mushroomy center part.

Sparrow's experience vibrated somewhere lost in Joan. "That makes sense."

"Really? Other trans people get offended at that kind of shit."

"No. I feel that way too. Like—halfway." Joan felt she could follow, actually, like the room had yawned a gap for her. "I have this thing."

Sparrow cocked their head. They were really listening. "Yeah?"

This was Joan's chance. To be honest with someone in an ultimate way. And not just about transgressions that had already appeared online. To give them the opportunity to know the whole her, or whatever. Her arms trembled. She held them down. "Like, a pee obsession?"

"Wait," Sparrow said, a funny sort-of smile jiggling their lips. "Really? You're not messing with me?"

Joan filled her lungs. The gamey reek of Meredith's sausages: familiar, warm. This was easier in the fading light. The amber sun muddied Sparrow's features, blurring their expression. "It's, like, a kink thing, I guess. I mean, obviously." Joan tipped her head up to the drop ceiling. "But if I'm being honest, it's always felt like more than that. Like sorta attached to music. Whatever it is, it's like I can't separate it from myself."

Color rose into Sparrow's cheeks. "That's cool." They scanned Joan.

"Listen," Joan said, her voice tinny. Now that the words were out, she could float to the ceiling, stick to the dome of the light fixture. "I don't tell anyone this stuff."

"Why not?" Sparrow squinted.

"Really?" Joan asked. "You can't guess?"

They laughed, and the air rushed back into the room.

"You're such a freak," Sparrow said. "I like you for it—like, kind of a lot."

All Joan could eke out was: "Really?"

"But I feel like—I don't know." They dropped their arms so hard against their hips that they shuddered. "Walking around in the wrong body, feeling the way everyone looks at you is wrong, the way your mass turns around a lamppost is wrong, the way you appear in the mirror, wrong, the way someone touches you while you're fucking—it's all wrong. You can't really compare that to anything else. I mean, I don't want to assume, but—were you comparing it?" Their voice spiked.

"I didn't mean to compare," Joan said, though she had. But of course their experiences weren't the same. No two pebbles on earth were the same. But whenever Sparrow talked, there was this chime way in the back of Joan's mind. They weren't the same, but some thread connected them.

"Okay," said Sparrow, ribs moving. "Sorry. It's just—I always thought you were gay. Like, your songs are pretty explicitly gay." They shifted. Then tried again, careful this time: "I don't want to think this about you. But were you doing that on purpose? To get fans or something? A little?"

How often had Joan been terrified her fans would discover she was straight, that all this time she'd been deceiving them? Once she'd had an audience, she'd worked her ass off to keep it. She would've done the same with any audience of any flavor. She hadn't picked lesbians because they were vulnerable or because there was a vacuum of queer role models or for any reason at all—they'd found her. Couldn't adults choose on their own what music spoke to them? But Sparrow's expression was dense, protected. She'd have to try to tell the truth. "Sometimes a song becomes its own creature, like, uncoiling without you. And then it has teeth. Chicken legs, scales, whatever. And it's ready to defend itself if you mess with it."

Sparrow's chin ticked up and down. "So that happened with the gay ones?"

"Only 'Lakeshore.'" She'd had an agenda with later songs. She'd had a twinge about focusing her approach, though there was a kind of queerness about her—she didn't look much like a "woman," had never had relationships or intimacy except once, she was a cast-off—and there were so many worse cases of appropriation. "I did make some gay on purpose." She'd never admitted this before to anyone. Her lungs stiffened, stopped working.

Sparrow picked foam out of a hole in the couch. "When I was a kid and listening to you—I was like twelve, probably—I had this phase where I searched out any picture I could find of you. There weren't that many back then." They looked straight at Joan, as though remembering they could lift their head and just see her now, any time they wanted. They softened. "There was one of you kinda turning away, mouth open, after a show—like some fan snapped it for their personal website or whatever." Back in those years Joan had tried to keep every image of herself off the web besides the single one she'd sanctioned: her face in shadow, the steely Hudson behind her, the clouds dry and heavy, resting on the frizz of her hair. She'd wanted to be mysterious, didn't want anyone seeing her bad teeth or skinny arms whose tendons made her prematurely haggard.

Whenever another picture popped up, she reported it, hassled the poster under fake names, but the pictures occasionally endured despite her efforts. The one Sparrow mentioned in particular rankled her because she was so ugly, caught off guard in the stark blare of a building's safety light. She could tell even if no one else could that she was aroused from the set: her eyelids low, her lips falling apart, her bladder, beneath her moth-eaten sweater, full to the brim. She'd been on the prowl when the fan's flash caught her, and even when she contacted him under her real email, begging him to take it down, he'd stonewalled her.

Sparrow shaded their eyes. "I consulted that picture all the time. Like multiple times a day. Your jaw was so butch, the bone, like, bursting through the skin. Your hair was brushed back in such a way that it was like a guy's. And I'd look at it and be like, damn." Their voice thickened. "That could be me. I could follow this cursed fucking path I already know I'm on, that scares the shit out of me every time I take off my clothes, and I could end up, at the end of the road, as cool as this freak." Sparrow pulled a cheesy hunk of yellow from the cushion, let it land on the floor. They looked up at Joan and shook their head.

Joan twisted away, mouth screwing up into a knot. Her legs pulled toward the door, straining to get out, to run from this steady, direct person. But her bottom half would have to go without her. She forced all the muscles in her neck to pan back to Sparrow. She made herself gaze directly into Sparrow's face, absorbing the floppy downturn of their lips, the disappointed softening of their chin. "I'm sorry."

Sparrow set their jaw. "I'm sure you had reasons."

"They don't matter."

"Tell me anyway." Sparrow lifted their chin.

Joan steadied her voice. "There are a few." Shame hot all over. She twitched in the armchair, trying to feel its solidity. "I wanted my career to work out at any cost." But other reasons nagged at the back of her head, more intimate reasons, reasons she'd never said out loud. She opened her mouth to say them. But she couldn't. "Also, I guess, stuff didn't feel so heavy back then. In my world, you could do whatever with gender." Christopher was straight and cis but played shows in dresses, especially back in the nineties. Nick Blade wore eyeshadow and a crystal brooch long before Lamar transitioned and his relationship turned queer. "It's kind of wonderful, if you can take it all as play."

"It's not a joke for me," Sparrow said. "Which I get sounds pretty lame to a rockstar."

"It's not lame," Joan said, voice pulling with feeling. "But maybe it's good if the world is open to fucking around. Then there are paths for those who take longer." Joan rushed on, so she could get this out. "Like my friend Nick. He played around with girls' clothes for years before finding his queer side. If we'd shut him down, who knows what would've happened." Maybe Nick Blade would've rejected Lamar when they came out as trans. Maybe he would've lost that love, transcendent and stronger than any Joan had witnessed, spanning two decades now and three genders.

"That's real. I'm not mad. I kinda was at first—back when you said you were straight. But that's my own bullshit."

"I'm sorry." With Sparrow's gaze drooping like that, their vulnerable words, Joan wanted to say more, but her voice stuck. "It feels good talking to you anyway." Even this lame sentence was barely a whisper.

"I had to say something." Warm pink spread over Sparrow's cheeks.

"I want you to say everything you ever want." Joan's words rang in her torso.

"Tell me, then," Sparrow said, leaning forward to the edge of the couch. "About your pee thing."

Joan pressed her hands together, tried to feel the solidity of her palms. "I guess, ever since I was little, I've loved to pee. Like an offering to whatever awes me." The words floated into the dark room.

Sparrow set their hands on their thighs. "So when you're in love, you piss on that person?"

A knot hardened in Joan's stomach. "I don't really know. I've only been in love once, and it was like fifteen years ago."

"What?" Sparrow cried. "How is that possible? You're famous."

All Joan could do was lift a hand, palm up. There was a reason. Though it had never gelled until now. Her voice gummed up.

Sparrow placed their hand over their mouth. "But that's so sad." They watched Joan with true, open-hearted pity, like they wanted to carry her off. All that loss of love that could've stabilized Joan through the fluctuations of her career. Everything could've been different if she'd only opened herself.

"It's okay," Joan said. "I have music." The words clattered out. Because she didn't anymore.

"I'm jealous of that." Sparrow had melted into shadow. Joan should switch on a lamp.

"You are?" Their voices were soft, their faces close. Joan sat on the edge of the chair, Sparrow on the edge of the couch, leaning forward, toward each other. Joan could've talked all night.

Sparrow glanced back toward their room. "Sometimes what I do feels pointless. Since no one sees it."

"No." Joan pushed her ass forward so far she almost slid to the floor. "That's beautiful. That's, like, the beautiful way." The two of them could find their own Norway, some tiny, cold village: the Upper Peninsula of Michigan; Door County, Wisconsin; a Canadian border town in Montana or the North Country—all the highway exits Joan had blown by on tour, exits every musician would blow by forever on any tour, leaving Joan and Sparrow to their quiet. And maybe together they could one day enjoy art the way Sparrow did: Sparrow at their table, Joan plinking away at wordless ditties that never had to be finished.

Sparrow leaned closer, then stopped. "There's something you aren't saying."

The word pushed out: "What?"

"I don't know. I can just tell." Sparrow's eyes were all over Joan, those eyes that had watched her for over a decade, seeking clues in every stray wrinkle or escaped curl, knowing all.

"I guess—it's gender stuff." Joan's voice was too quick. "Like, something. In that realm."

"I knew it," Sparrow whispered.

"It's my own separate thing. I'm not comparing." She didn't know enough about what she even was to compare. She sucked two hard lines of air up her nose. "But I feel like a guy when I do it. Like, when I pee on people." She opened her fist and closed it again. Her hand was a fleshy machine in the darkness. "And other times. Kinda a lot of other times. Not exactly like a guy. But definitely not like a girl. Never like a girl." Feelings of wrong and right in her skin rose and fell like waves throughout the day, unconnected to any narrative she could trace, or even always to gender, precisely. "Like a jackal or a monster, but a lovely one?" That was a stupid way to put it. Some loose, multigendered thing. Or nongendered. She couldn't even tell.

"I can see it," Sparrow said, their voice a hiss. And the way they watched Joan, scrutinizing every part, Joan believed them.

"I never told anyone that." She'd practically never even thought it before. "I'm in deep confusion. That's all I can say."

"That's cool," Sparrow said, the words so clear and easy they worked all the way through Joan, breaking up her muscles and relaxing them to goo. "There's always more to figure out."

That tender face floating in the shadowy room, understanding. Joan's body went heavy and strong, melting into its natural form for the first time in her life. She'd never felt like someone she was close to, physically like this, intimacy or whatever you called it, had actually seen her strong arms and buckteeth and the frizz on her head for how Joan herself saw it, as not sad, aging woman but a whole different category of beast. She leaned closer. Sparrow's scent was bread: fine and golden. And then Sparrow was leaning in, bulky and flexible, like a lion cub, all sparkly, homey notes rising from their mouth.

Joan throbbed for those lips to catch hers. She longed, in her animal heart, to disappear with Sparrow in the tangle of each other's bodies, for the warmth of foreign organs pulsing against her, the primordial heartbeat of *all is okay*. Her fingertips grazed the inside of Sparrow's naked wrist, blood pushing under the hot bag of her skin.

She pulled back. Not yet. She should leave this in a good place. The conversation had been more than enough for tonight. She shouldn't reveal her maniacal side. She could crawl into her sleeping bag for once at peace. Sparrow would be here tomorrow. And that was the best gift Joan could hope for. She extricated herself from the circle of warmth. Sparrow's brow furrowed as Joan backed up, beating a question between them so hard the air vibrated. Joan nodded, acknowledging it. She said good night.

19

ONE DAY, OUT OF NOWHERE, PAIGE INVITED JOAN TO her apartment with a formal text she went so far as to sign: *Love, Paige,* though by 2014 they were way too far into the era of cell phones for anyone to be signing texts. For the seventeen years since they'd met, excluding their first three years living together, they'd spent precious little time in each other's apartments. Their relationship took place wandering the city and in the dirty backs of venues, listening to their friends or each other or bands they'd heard were sick. Joan had never consciously considered why this was, but, as she took the stairs out of the subway at Newkirk Plaza and crossed Ditmas, she understood that, of course, of course, all those plans made for nearly a decade in their roaming wanders must've been her subconscious limiting opportunities for Paige to suddenly be kissing her, sweeping Joan off to a land she never would have chosen to visit. Thankfully Paige had only made moves on her sporadically through the years. The occasional blips had been a small price to pay, a reupping of intimacy, every bit worth suffering for the maintenance of friendship.

Joan had only once seen this newest apartment, though Paige had lived there a year. Paige didn't move as often as Joan, but she'd relocated four or five times since Vinegar Hill, always upgrading by one step along some axis—a safer neighborhood, a south-facing window. She was patient, incremental, never jumping rashly on a friend moving out or a hot tip, while Joan deserted her leases early because a neighbor hassled her about playing at midnight or a friend or venue could be closer, or simply because she couldn't stay put. She'd find herself someplace dirtier and tinier, a shower in the living room, cockroaches in the oven, and it was, Oh, fuck. Here I am again.

Paige lived in a brutalist chunk of concrete on Flatbush above a children's clothing shop. It was just like her to consider the giggles and baby powder that would float up from such an establishment. In apartments past, Joan had lived above a butcher shop and an opera school. Her current building housed a methadone clinic, kitty-corner to an eighteen-plus club. Paige had lettered her full name beside the button for her unit, while her neighbors had been satisfied with scribbles or nothing. Joan hovered her finger over the bell. Wisps of pencil trailed from the letters where Paige had attempted to erase them under the pen, the dot of the *i* a perfect circle, the *P* with a cursive loop decorating a stem that was too stiff for elegance.

Upstairs, Paige opened the door wide. Her face was bright, and she wore a high-necked ivory sweater she'd bought at a thrift store for two dollars. At the time Joan hadn't understood why she chose it off the rack, but she'd been wrong: the contrast with her dark hair and eyes was striking. Paige grabbed Joan's hand and dragged her in. "You're four minutes late," she said. "I almost started without you."

Behind Paige was a small but tidy room, walls white and empty, moldings pristine. A window with bars looked out over Flatbush. Even with the window shut, the scrape of tires and blare of horns rattled the room. Paige had set up a rug, shell pink with paler pink stripes, that she'd found on one of their walks. Joan had laughed at her for yanking the dingy thing from between piles of trash bags. Someone had thrown spaghetti on it, and it had stunk up Paige's arms the whole walk home, dripping noodles as passersby turned to gape. But now the rug was clean, its pile combed, and even the sun-bleached quarter of it seemed intentional, like a subtle modern design. The built-in bookshelves were mostly empty—Paige didn't read and toured too frequently to keep plants—except for a photo of Joan, unframed and curling, propped against the plaster. Joan didn't remember the occasion of the photo, but she might've been on some ferry, the ocean a blur of gray behind. She leaned against a railing, hair whipping into curlicues, obscuring her nose and mouth but leaving naked one shining eye of mischief.

Against the wall stood the Rogue, set up on a rack like a worthy guitar, beside a table and stool, chaotic with papers and headphones and capos and picks, the sole sloppy sector of the unit, this window into Paige's art, shoved into the corner. When they'd lived together, in the early years, Joan could always tell when Paige was writing a song. A churchy silence cloaked the apartment, thick and golden, Paige bent over a composition book like a schoolchild, murmuring lyrics to some natal tune. The quiet had made Joan restless. She attacked her own new songs with brutal chords and her rawest voice.

On the red and chrome square of the dining table flickered candles between plain white plates carefully aligned, mismatched wine glasses, and silverware on beds of folded paper towels.

"What is this?" Joan asked. "We're having dinner?" When had they ever once had dinner? Bites along the way, sure: a dollar slice, gummy bears, night coffee, crepes rolled around melted cheese. But they never felt the need to sit down and formally consume.

"Did you already eat?" Paige looked down at the plate of sliced supermarket bread in her hands.

Joan had hoped that after "Lakeshore," she'd finally get to stop worrying about money, that having a song on the radio, a song people actually knew, would naturally translate to an accrual of funds. Just so she could survive the next chunk of life. But she still had no paid tour, no record deal, still had to skip half her meals, still was scrawny and fucked. "No."

Paige grabbed her temples. "What did you think we'd do? It's seven o'clock. A more classic dinner time doesn't exist."

"Walk or go to a show. I don't know. Isn't Christopher playing Gem League?"

Paige scrunched up her face with that little-kid annoyance that always made Joan want to laugh. "Wouldn't I have said if that was what we were doing? And you really want to see him play?" Joan notoriously found Christopher's music tedious: endless chronological verses about fucking then fucking over a sea of women, learning nothing, ever, through endless chains of entanglement.

"Sorry," Joan said. "I didn't think we'd want to sit in some apartment all night."

Paige's lips fell apart. She turned away. "Leave anytime." She scurried into the galley kitchen, which was recessed in a nook. Somehow she managed to fold herself inside its upright coffin.

Joan dangled in the clean, small living room, full of Paige's body smell, which was always, somehow, pine. She felt wrong being there alone, cast her gaze into the carpet so as not to glimpse anything private. She sat down in a plastic chair, which was too small even for her scrawny ass, like a chair from an elementary school classroom. What was wrong with Paige? The room was five or six steps in any direction. Couldn't they go back out into the world? What was this bullshit about staying inside? Who wanted to sit together in a tiny room, which, clean as it might be, smelled like person because the window was never open? Even if that person was Paige, it was still gross.

Paige brought out bowls of bean soup, which she ate every day—her punishment food, her food for eating alone. Her version of Joan's not eating. Maybe it was all she knew how to prepare. But here it was in white plastic bowls, sprinkled with cilantro and drizzled in oil.

Joan accepted her portion, and they ate together, along with a salad of wet lettuce. Joan always forgot how good a hot and actually nutritious meal was, sliding down her throat and heating her insides, chiming some forgotten need, not cold lumps of whatever choked down in a panic, too foul to be finished. She usually feared the comfort of food, but that night she let herself succumb. Paige kept looking up at Joan and grinning, like she was surprised Joan was still here, like they didn't see each other all the time, like they didn't talk constantly, like Joan's presence was anything special.

The moment Joan pushed her last bite of soup between her lips, Paige thrust down her spoon. "I can't wait any longer."

"What are you waiting for?" Muscles tightened in Joan's ass. "You don't have to wait for anything, for whatever. I mean, what?"

"I have to tell you something." Paige jostled on her seat, pushing herself up and down like she was cantering. "Joan, I've been dying of it." She savored the word like dying was only the richest pleasure.

"Then tell me." Since when did they wait even five minutes to tell each other shit?

"I don't know—it's weird." She quivered so hard her mouth blurred. "I just did—I don't know."

"Paige." Joan reached across the table and anchored her wrist. "Calm down and tell me what you want to tell me." Was the girl dying? Did she have cancer? Joan swelled with responsibility. Whatever it was, she'd be there for the kid, 100 percent.

"Black Tree," Paige said. The words were separated by such a vast gap that Joan didn't understand at first. Paige opened her hands and spread them out. "Just—Black Tree. Joan. Can you believe it?"

The room swelled into a cavern. Joan's torso hardened the way it did when she opened an email from a venue after she'd requested to do a show or received a letter from a label where she'd sent a demo, even just finishing the last note of a song and waiting for the audience response. Paige couldn't open her mouth fast enough to reveal what the hell she meant. How did she have information about Joan's status with Black Tree? Had she heard a rumor that Joan was about to be signed? "What about Black Tree?" Joan's words echoed against the walls. She had the queasy feeling of teetering on the edge of a canyon, her whole life about to drop.

"I got signed." Paige jiggled on her chair. "I got fucking signed." She spoke the words like they weren't any language she understood. "Can you believe that?"

"Who got signed?" The words extruded in a paste.

"Me." Paige jumped off the chair, her elbow unseating the forks in the lettuce and scattering leaves over the rug. "Me, Joan. Literally me!"

"For an album?" Paige had self-released her first album to light reception. She'd asked Joan about every step of the way, even about the dumb stuff, like the shade of white for the liner notes. And now she'd gone and submitted a whole new album without asking Joan for a scrap of advice?

"Yes." Paige circled the room, back and forth and every which way, crossing the rug and back on the bridge of its stripes. "My own album. I mean, this is, like, real. Right? They can't take it away, right, once you sign? They don't do that, do they? I know I have one already, but this is a real album. I never thought it would be real."

"Right." Joan hollowed into a stone cave. Almost all her albums were self-released. The two that weren't were on a label so minuscule that they basically were. How could she offer Paige help now? Paige would need nothing from Joan ever again.

Paige jumped around like a child. Like she couldn't contain herself. She slapped her hands on a shelf in the built-in bookcase. "I'll put my first copy here. Beside your picture."

Joan went still, concentrating on the streaks of bean juice ringing her bowl. They spiraled. Paige had been welcomed onto the next step up without Joan. Soon enough she'd have new friends three levels above Joan, four. A dozen hot hipsters more knowledgeable to help with every detail, to expose how much of a scrappy amateur Joan had been. For years Joan had told herself she'd been annoyed by Paige's questions. But she couldn't stand the idea that they'd disappear. Her brain was a tangle of bright nerves.

"Joan?" Paige turned. "What do you think?"

"How did it happen?" Joan's words emerged flatter than she intended, hard.

Paige at last stopped bouncing. She cocked her head. "Why did I get signed?"

"Yeah." The word was small.

"Um." Paige stared at Joan. "Because I have a record they believe in?" The last word broke off, a bitten shard. "Because the execs like me? Why does anyone get signed? And why would it be any different for me? What, you think I'm some loser? You think I fucked my way in?"

"I obviously don't think you're a loser." She should've gone further. Caring words about Paige and her music clogged her throat. This was her chance to rave about what a talent Paige was, how powerfully she deserved the success that was coming to her, how there was no one else Joan would've more fervently hoped could achieve a deal with the best—really the only—label for the kind of work they did. And she believed all of it, with her whole being. But she couldn't say a word. Couldn't get past the certainty that this was how she'd lose Paige. "This is great."

Paige's lip trembled. She bit down to hold it in place.

"Seriously. I just didn't realize you had a whole album yet." That was the only explanation she could offer for her weird-ass reaction, even as it made no sense.

"Are you kidding? What do you think I've been doing all these years?" She waved at her particleboard desk. The last time Joan had seen it, in Paige's Inwood apartment, it had been coated in wood-patterned stickers. Paige had painted it a creamy mint, but the seams of the laminate showed. "You know I write all the freaking time."

Joan couldn't help it. A snort, out the side of her mouth.

Paige leaned back, eyes flinging open. They stared at each other for a hundred years. But, come on. Joan didn't eat, didn't sleep, didn't wash herself or clean her apartment, didn't indulge in romance. All she did was write fucking songs. Paige had time to scrub moldings and rehab rugs. She had time to shift from apartment to apartment in a thoughtful manner until she achieved the best apartment she could afford. Joan would've slept at the bottom of a sewer if it gave her more time to write. She would've held in her shit and taken a pill to relieve her hunger for the rest of her life.

"You're not happy for me," Paige whispered.

"Don't be dumb." The words were too harsh. The floor shifted under her. Of course a label wasn't everything these days—not like it used to be. Just financial backing, and they didn't put the resources into everyone. But still.

"Isn't this what you wanted?" Paige stepped back toward the door, like she'd flee her own home to escape Joan. "What was the point of our work together if you were just going to be mad when everything worked out?"

Joan stilled her brain to answer. The only response had to be that she'd never expected the plan to work. Had never expected Paige to rise out of her league and beyond. That all Joan's work would lead to losing Paige. "I'm sorry."

"Sure," Paige said, tone flat. "I'm heading out."

"Wait." Joan's voice beat in her ears, way too loud. Paige couldn't just walk out. Ants crawled up and down Joan's neck. Walking out was too sad, too permanent. She stepped toward Paige at the door. Paige shrank back against it like Joan would hurt her. Joan's arms shot up, palms out, innocent. She'd never hurt Paige, not in a million years. Slowly, predictably, like approaching a feral cat, she reached out a hand and set it on Paige's elbow. Maybe their problem was that Joan wasn't forceful enough with her feelings, so Paige always had to doubt them. Just because Joan didn't want to have sex didn't mean Paige wasn't the most important person in her life. She drew Paige toward her so her mouth was against Paige's ear. And then she said, "I love you."

Paige watched her. That elegant whippet's face, a face Joan could never believe was actually attracted to hers, which was craggy and weather-worn, chiseled inexpertly from bad rock. And then Joan was leaning down toward her, and their lips were moving against each other, Paige's eager against Joan's, Joan overwhelmed by her intensity, as though Paige was experiencing a different physical sensation.

But Joan should get into it; she should be there for Paige, be present in this moment for once, actually invested. So she kissed harder, matching Paige's force, gripping Paige more firmly, kissing like she was hungry, like she wanted Paige more than anything, like she needed to be naked with her that instant.

She walked Paige backward across the room until she'd maneuvered her through the door to the bedroom.

She'd never been in Paige's bedroom before. It was smaller than Joan's old one in Vinegar Hill, also only big enough for a bed, but only a twin. A quilt that Paige had owned since her childhood in Ohio was tucked in neatly at the corners, a faded lavender design such that Paige would never select now. The hem of the quilt was ragged with wear, gray from where Paige had sucked on it as a child, trying to sleep in a hostile household all those years. A tiny hopeful nightstand was pushed against the bed, featuring a plastic lamp with a curvy torso, meant to be elegant but really just cheap. Joan had never pictured Paige in bed, but here was where she went, every night, tucking herself under this old quilt and sipping this stale water, alone by the glow of this red lamp.

With jelly arms, Joan laid Paige down on the quilt and kissed her neck, kept looking back to remind herself Paige was attractive, she was gorgeous. There were people all over the world who would've given anything to fuck a girl this hot, who wouldn't have believed their luck. But Paige's face cooled Joan's limbs. This face was that of a little sister, a best friend. But Joan owed her. She closed her eyes and kissed harder, tasted the salt of skin and reminded herself skin was skin, and that she could've been kissing a sexy man.

In all their times fucking, Joan had never gone down on Paige, was always able to get her off with fingers. But this time she pulled off the white thrifted sweater, still clinging to the musty aroma of the grim store they'd found it in, and yanked down her jeans. Paige gasped when Joan trailed her lip all the way down her sternum and belly and hooked it over her vulva. Joan had never gone down on a woman before. She concentrated her full attention on not feeling it. This wasn't happening. The slickness, the moisture kept building and rolling out, but she focused on the buried ball of Paige's clit and worked at it until Paige's skin went limp and easy, hot where it met Joan's palms. Joan froze. Paige grabbed her and pulled her up. There was that old familiar face, relaxed and calm, settled on its bed of dark curls, regarding Joan with startled bliss and eyes that took in every light.

20

AFTER TALKING TO SPARROW, JOAN WENT TO BED EARLY and slept in the crumple of her mildewed sleeping bag under a spongy darkness so thick she could've bitten off a hunk, dreaming of leaning in toward Sparrow, their almost-kiss. She had a future, finally, doing actually helpful work. She woke in the same position she fell asleep in, arm thrown over her head, mouth wide, mind pulling up deliciously from heady soup. The sun was already thick through the windows, so hot it threatened to boil the crisp, climate-controlled air. She surged up—lesson plans, preparations, how she could design a period dynamic enough to follow the graveyard dog spore—but no. It was Saturday. Her third weekend at camp. She couldn't believe so short a time had passed—sometimes it felt like she'd been here for years. She wilted back against the pillow. Yesterday had been perfect. The kids and their spooky march. Sparrow's face, soft and understanding, still as vivid as though it lay beside her on the pillow.

But then she registered what had woken her—outside her

bedroom was a festive clatter: footfalls, bodies bumping
through the hall, loads dumping on the carpet and vibrating
her particleboard bed frame. The suite was astir, as though
Meredith and Sparrow were being evicted.

Still in the oversized venue T-shirt she'd been given in Little
Rock in lieu of a dinner buyout—*Jam Hound* in Gothic script,
with a jowly bulldog strumming a guitar made of bones—she
ventured the hallway.

Teachers scurried through the unit, shuttling boxes and
bags and armloads of bedding. Joan made her way down the
hall, her big, soft T-shirt flapping around her skeleton. Willie
was stationed at the counter. His scalp reddened as she passed,
and he bowed to squirt mustard on rows of sliced bread. Meredith peeled leaves off a head of lettuce and set each in its own
yellow pool. She worked carefully, twisting the leaves into the
mustard, her tongue poking out of the corner of her mouth, lin-
ing up the ruffled edges of the lettuce so they overlapped evenly
with the bread, so each teacher's sandwich was a work of art.

Willie set a hand on Meredith's as she completed a sandwich. She beamed back at him. They were fucking. No. They
only wanted to. Joan was so dumb to have never noticed before.
But here it came, uninvited: the entire dragging tail of Meredith and Willie's history, similar to no affair of Joan's, though
theirs was the common route. They'd flirted publicly for years,
Willie retreating each July to the lush hills of Pocahontas
County—hills Joan had crossed on tour—curling on his futon,
attempting to conjure Meredith's oversized head and chocolate
hair. The way he'd tugged on himself but it didn't work; Meredith didn't exist in West Virginia, not even in his mind. The
way Meredith thought of Willie not at all as she led her ordered
life in Montana, then remembered him again each June. *I can't
believe it's been a year.* She fell anew for his curling lashes, the

rigid explosion of his beard, his bumbling prettiness. The way they called each other beautiful like they were kidding, the teachers' whispered theories. And despite all that, after a night of word games and drunken gossip, when the group had long since dispersed, one of those rare late-night moments alone, thigh to thigh on the plastic couch, Meredith stung with guilt over the idea of her partner back home, Willie worried his breath stank. Meredith leaking blood from her crotch, Willie depleted from acting smart, making up with strained servitude for being the least wealthy and least educated and least published among them. He didn't have it in him to kiss her gracefully, to touch her cheek without snatching, to select words that weren't flat-footed and rough, to reveal he'd liked her for years, but not creepily. One time only, circumstances aligned. Last summer. The last night. Delighted shudders, flesh jellied together. And here they were now, worried the rush could bear them away again. Joan couldn't believe she'd missed the clues.

Chester breezed through with an armload of firewood. Joan perked up. The one person who still asked her, sometimes, to hang. Joan should ask him about his job, his LA social circle. She pictured him with a terrier and a garden of yuccas and ornamental orange trees, his freckled cheeks blistering under the blaze of endless clear skies. "What are you up to?"

He watched her, startled, like he hadn't remembered she lived here. "Getting ready."

"Getting ready for what?"

"Uh, camping."

"I love camping." She'd never been.

"Well. You probably don't want to come at the last second."

"I do, actually." The words popped out without permission, three hopeful bubbles.

"That's okay," Chester said, face scrunching as the words

extruded out of him. "I think we only have one site. Sparrow says it'll be pretty crammed already with four." His voice broke twice on "crammed." "And they said you probably want to rest this weekend anyway."

"Since when was this the plan?" Their quarters were small. Surely she would've heard talk of logistics, witnessed a shopping trip, an exchange of tents, something.

"Sparrow got the idea last night, and we got up early to get ready. We're almost out of here." He bounced the firewood, grimacing.

Joan swallowed a golf ball as he shouldered past. He hadn't made sense. Joan had only gone to bed too early, before she'd had a chance to be invited.

Willie followed Meredith all over the suite, ferrying dirty dishes and utensils just as the "Lakeshore" guy had followed Joan, one eye on her, hand raised to clamp her thigh, guide her by the elbow. For years Joan had half hoped the "Lakeshore" guy would surprise her at a concert, clear the barriers and hop the stage, or write her a note, admit he'd seen himself in a song, anything. But he'd pushed her aside the same way she had him. In Joan's last nineteen years, stalking men at parties and bars and spraying all over them—filling with power in the moment and then, in the wake of their reactions, washing in delicious shame—she'd forgotten the sweetness of relationships. Chester was on supplies, but Sparrow was nowhere. Joan checked every corner of the suite, shrinking from the hard gaze of the teachers as she passed through and through again.

Finally, she checked outside, that godforsaken picnic table that no one had ever used before last night. There was Sparrow, whittling marshmallow sticks with a steak knife. At their tawny form, hunched over the table, Joan loosened, her arms pushing out from her sides, stance widening.

They looked up, fumbling the knife and notching their stick. "Joan."

Meredith burst through the glass door. "Do you have all the sticks?" She brushed past Joan like she wasn't there.

Sparrow pointed out a pile. Meredith collected some sticks and stepped back to the door, but she hovered, watching, her slacks fastened high so her belly puffed out. Sparrow's hand never slowed, running the knife over the stick again and again as though the implement would need to kill a bear. Wood chips built at their feet as the stick narrowed to a thinner, paler point.

"You're going camping without me," Joan said.

"Yes." Sparrow infused the word with intensity. But Joan couldn't judge the flavor. They didn't sound exactly angry, at least.

"Why?"

"Don't question it." They spoke softly, but Meredith was watching. Sparrow swept up the remaining marshmallow sticks, their fist bristling with twigs, enough for every student in the program, should they be invited along.

"I thought things were good with us," Joan whispered. After she went to bed, Meredith must've told Sparrow about Joan peeing. That must have been it. She'd made Joan out to be a pervert. Joan wanted to push her nails into her arm again, pop the blood. "Just tell me what's going on."

"I can't." The words were so soft Joan could barely hear. Sparrow turned, spikes pricking out, like they were daring Joan to hug them. They absorbed back into the unit.

*

From the dignity of her bedroom, Joan overheard enough scraps to understand the group was destined for the Blue

Ridge Mountains. She'd passed signs for Shenandoah on her way down, the most poetic name for any place on earth, those four trilling syllables a mini song in itself, cameoing in several of her favorite songs of no provenance. A misty place, maybe, clouds pierced by navy mountains, where a rogue could wander before setting the correct course of her life. No place she'd ever thought she'd get to see. She'd played every major city in America, but wilderness had no use for her, so it remained unexplored.

As Meredith and Willie and Chester coordinated about peanut butter, firewood, pen knives, and white gas, a longing pulled in Joan's gut. She wanted so badly to be beside Sparrow, but Sparrow had been told all about Joan's perverted public peeing. Joan had even moaned—she'd forgotten. She must've looked fucked, eyes closed, feeling herself. Of course Sparrow hated her. They'd never bother with Joan again, would never sit and talk with her into the night. Joan wilted into her musty sleeping bag.

The sounds of glee concentrated in the hallway and then the living room and faded as the group passed through the front door, tuning down to nothing as they bounded up the stairs to the parking lot. Joan watched them through the window, moving close together, as though if they left a foot of space between them their alliance would shatter. And then their car started— which of them had a car? Joan didn't even know—and wended its way out of earshot.

The silence that followed was unbearable. Turned out, the building had never once been actually quiet—always the squeaky compression of a floorboard, the snap of a light switch, the crumple of a tissue. And now, nothing. Nothing but Joan's own breath, deafening between her ears.

The day was endless, a hot fluid drip of sun scrambling her

brain in the frozen air. Without Sparrow shuffling through the walls to electrify the drudgery, the air in the tiny room died. Joan longed to walk with Paige down the beach, picking out Breezy Point across the bay, stepping over babies lolling in the sand, warped subway passes, the footprints of the lonely and furious. Even an hour with her old friend would revive her, would help her get through the rest of summer. Because how could she keep living here, with everyone hating her? And they didn't even hate her for the right reason but because of some prudishness, some dumb purity crap. She could manage, maybe, if Sparrow still liked her. But Sparrow's cold gaze, marshmallow sticks prickling, was too much.

Joan tried to write lesson plans at her desk, hand-washed her clothes, even boiled some pasta. Through all her activities, every decibel of silence from Sparrow's room was a reproach. That steely face, unwilling to even explain why they'd turned— its afterimage throbbed the quiet as she flapped out her damp linen and laid it over the back of her chair.

As evening fell, it occurred to Joan that Sparrow had said Meredith had threatened to go to Georgina. Any minute she'd be fired. Why else would the teachers be so rude? They'd known she'd be gone upon their return, fired in shame for peeing in public, that they'd never see her again, so they'd treated her like garbage, like she was already gone. Or worse—Joan couldn't bear to think this—Sparrow had told them about Love und Romance. Joan couldn't stand the idea of Georgina's face crumbling at Joan's trespasses after she'd taken a risk on Joan. She'd rather vanish.

She thrust her shoes into her duffel bag, her clothes, her toothbrush that she wasn't even trusting enough to store in the bathroom. In minutes her scant items were packed, and her room was like she'd never stepped into it, a pile of lint in one corner, the corpse shape of Joan's duffel still dented into the rug.

She crossed the parking lot with her bag in the purpling evening, filled her car, and shot through campus and down the darkening Virginia highway.

She drove for miles, her Corolla a knife slicing the cake of dim humidity. A hundred miles north, the forests surrendered to temporary churches, cars on blocks, billboards with fetuses menaced by scalpels, a fleet of used cars caught under a cobweb of rubber flags. The hills were gray in the middle distance, blunt-tipped and soft, the mountains soft, too, but blue, way over on the edge of the sky, houses pressed against the highway, a hound caught sprinting in her headlights, stretching his speckled body along the shoulder, proving his grace.

Fingers of wind pushed through her hair, breaking up the humid lump. The wind beat so hard into the car she couldn't think, but the farther she sped from campus, pounding between brake and accelerator, the shallower her breath. She couldn't stand the idea of never seeing Sparrow again, grew restless with every mile she put between herself and Community Village. But it was worse, right, to wait to be banished? She was doing the right thing, taking her fate into her own hands. This way she could keep some dignity. This way Sparrow would see she was sorry for what she'd done. But Sparrow—every time Joan pictured that golden face, her belly bottomed out.

She'd felt that way from the moment she'd glimpsed them through the glass, drawing. Sparrow, who labored with perfect concentration, without a care for where their work ended up. Sparrow, who made art for art's sake and never in a million years would succumb to toxic jealousy or assault a fan. And who'd even gone so far as to appreciate the good in someone like Joan.

But the way Sparrow had watched her this morning—it was over. A fall in esteem so sudden it must be permanent. Joan pressed the gas and shot through more towns. When her head cleared, she'd decide where she was going, but she'd rather have no destination—just far. She'd stop when she almost passed out, pull over and sleep on the median, cars ripping by all night, close enough to tear off her mirror.

She took a break outside Mount Jackson, at an ice cream stand in a field, composed of tarps supported by ropes staked to the earth. The stand claimed it was open, though by now it was very late. The sign must be a mistake, but through the tent's window she found a teenager, red wasted eyes and feet propped on tubs of product. As it happened they didn't sell ice cream—Joan had invented that promise from the blue font with snow stuck in the serifs—but flavored ice, which was better anyway, a red-and-yellow scoop of it in a paper cone all Joan needed. The syrup spread cool through her.

As she lingered in the dark, eating her cone, the teenager watched her, arms drooping from the cutout in the canvas wall, steady, bored, as though she were his responsibility. As though the moment she returned to the highway, he'd forget her, but for as long as she was here, he'd make certain she was okay.

She deflated at the live triangles of his shoulder blades, his cheeks puckered by a history of acne. This kid—out in some random Virginia town, with his own life full of garage band gigs and siphoned gasoline, friends from down the block who still loved him, hopes for a different city, faraway—was worrying about her, even fleetingly. She sat on one of the chairs, its plastic gone gray with mildew, and lazily licked her ice. Somehow it seemed possible that if she sucked out the color slowly enough, her world would right itself before the dessert was through.

She didn't notice that the boy had emerged from his tent until he was scrubbing down the table closest to her, rubbing a jumbo sponge over a rainbow of sugar discs adhering to the surface. He was only half attentive, his wrist loose, his focus out at the mountains, which were dark against darker sky.

"You closing up?" Joan asked. After all her years in food service, she hadn't once sat through a cleaning, even if that meant scramming before her food was done.

"We never close," said the boy.

"Really?"

He laughed. "Really, lady." He lifted his sponge, stained purple and orange. He squinted at her. "Why do you care? You a waiter or something?"

It must've been her ranginess, her ropy arms, her slouch, the hour. "Teacher." The word slid out nicely. Less hopeful than "musician." The word evoked all the people you could help.

"I don't miss school," he said. There was a pull of sorrow in his tone. Like he'd hoped to miss it.

"I hated it too," she said, softening her voice. "It's different when you're in charge."

He floated the sponge to his nose as though sniffing the fruity ice long dead. "You give your kids a break sometimes?"

Lula with her pale poker face and secret amorous night life, Victor beaming under his bangs. And Agnes, with her watermelon uke. They'd tried for her. That ridiculous exercise, with the magazines. Joan hadn't been any genius to think it up, hadn't unlocked brilliance in the kids with her random-ass improvising and busywork. No. Agnes hadn't written a decent song because Joan had floated the idea of found materials. The lessons had worked because they'd decided to try for her, because they cared. Her bones loosened. Her eyes stung. She was dumb. And they were perfect. "Actually, I really love them."

He pushed the sponge over the armrest of her chair, knocking her elbow off. This close, sour notes rose from his tank top, like he'd played basketball in the sun before work. He'd come over because he wanted to talk to her. His walk was bouncy, like her dour specter had sort of made his night.

"I hope you sell a lot of ice," she said, because it was the only stupid comment she could think up.

He snorted. He pushed his sponge over a blue puddle so viscous that it stuck, laughing at himself trying to shake it free.

Agnes with her funny perfect song. A song with no melody and no chorus, no verse, no bridge, no refrain, a song that hadn't been written and wasn't really sung, a song sprung from a scrap of corporate copywriting that nonetheless had moved Joan so intensely that she couldn't even sit with it.

Her kids cared. And they awaited class on Monday. If she didn't show, they'd be disappointed, even if fleetingly. She shouldn't leave before she had to. That was cowardly, which was fine, but it hurt other people, which was not. If she was allowed to stay, all next year she'd have a paycheck, a quiet place to live, a boss who'd glimpsed her savage history. More students cycling through, maybe even as good as her darling weirdos, clear-eyed, ready to learn. She could teach them all she knew so they might enjoy an easier path through music.

She let the boy do his job until she finished her ice. When he tucked himself back into the booth, she returned to her car, turned around, and drove home.

21

THE NEXT EVENING, THE OTHER TEACHERS RETURNED. A frenzy in the hall and out front—the guys and Meredith jovial, giggling, slumping bags down. Joan hid in her room. She'd researched the hikes: Bear Fence Mountain, Dark Hallow Falls, Old Rag Trail. Each its own baleful tune. The idea of going somewhere not for any gig but just for fun was unreal. She hadn't felt the urge for tourless travel in ages, but now the idea was pure, clear freedom. Joan's goblin hand could grab Sparrow's soft one as Sparrow slipped at the edge of some cliff and reel them back to safety. They'd embrace in the sunset, gazing at blue mountains.

Joan strained, but she couldn't catch Sparrow's voice in the mix. A chill ran up her spine. Sparrow dead in the woods, a broken ankle in a local hospital—but of course not. Of course the group wouldn't be jubilant in that case. She tried to relax, but the longer she didn't hear Sparrow, the closer to the edge of her bed she slipped.

A knock on the door startled her. She opened it. Sparrow: grubby T-shirt, soiled shorts, ashen face. Their hair was dull, cowlicks flat.

"You're invited tonight," they said.

"But didn't you just get back?" There was a way, then, maybe, to do the last days over: Joan and Sparrow in one sleeping bag, stars burning through the tent's mesh.

"Night of Sharing. Remember?" Sparrow bounced on one foot, glancing at everything in the room but Joan: the crumpled pillow, the remnants of a dinner of raw broccoli, the pee sweater balled in the corner, unwashed.

"No."

"We're all sharing work. On the guys' porch. Didn't Chester invite you?"

"When is it?"

"Now."

Chairs scraped above Joan's head. The teachers had waited until the last second to ask her.

*

The porch sported fairy lights wound around the banister, a kerosene lantern flickering on a stool in the center of a circle of chairs. The porch was a private, illuminated square, the humid night banished beyond. All the chairs were occupied, none reserved for Joan.

"You came," Chester said, hand shaking on a manuscript. His hair had inflated in the humidity of the mountains, a bubble now around his face.

"I can stand." Joan leaned against the railing, too hard. It groaned behind her. So they were still upset with her. Meredith must've told them about seeing Joan pee, spent the weekend turning them against her. Sparrow hadn't said anything—no. There was no way.

Willie and Meredith had dragged their chairs in close, probably hoping no one noticed how their hips touched. Sparrow sat on the other side of the porch with the slab of laptop in their arms. Joan's skin buzzed. Now that she was here, with everyone staring at her in wonder and shock, she needed out. Her only comfort left was that Georgina had chosen her for the special job. Maybe none of them would've wanted that dumb job anyhow, but still. Every time she thought of it, she glowed.

"All right." Chester sat up in his chair. His voice was grave and steady. This must have been how he presided over his classroom. Joan's attention gathered to him. "I guess we'll start?"

Meredith butterflied a galley of her book, whose cover featured a sad-eyed pony. "The work of this book tunnels through the life of a horse into the life of a little girl." Her words were too modulated, like she'd practiced.

"That's wonderful," Sparrow said. Everyone else supplied tepid "woos," their focus wandering to the moon.

Meredith read. Joan was grateful to relax into the words. This was an easy way of socializing—listening, like a child at bedtime. She didn't have to talk, didn't have to fear offending.

"My horse," Meredith read, adjusting her cowl neck so it slumped to the side, "was named Lifetime of Fear. A palomino thoroughbred, large for a kid but not for his breed. A retired racehorse. A champion. I never gave him a nickname. And when it was time, I shot him between the eyes."

She described how Lifetime of Fear was her only friend as a child, how whenever her parents fought about money or whether to resettle in the Main Line of Philadelphia, Meredith sat on a tuffet of hay beside Lifetime of Fear and confessed her flaws.

"I was sassy. I was making my parents fight. I didn't brush

Lifetime of Fear enough, and when I did, I used the body brush before the currycomb." Meredith's voice was a leaf falling, delicate and shaky. Joan softened toward her. "I was curvy for a twelve-year-old. I gave too many blow jobs. My problems absorbed into the coat of Lifetime of Fear. Once I left the stable, I forgot about its dim cave. I went right back to sassing my parents and sucking dick." Joan pulled for this kid, hunched in shame on the hay.

Over the course of the reading it became clear, despite Meredith's attempts to obscure the truth, that her parents were New England WASPs who'd moved to Montana to retire at forty and dabble in gentleman farming, at which point Meredith, age eleven, had taken it upon herself to identify as salt of the earth. She'd never been a dusty toddler riding sheep in the rodeo. Meredith must've felt like a phony. That was why she tried so hard.

Meredith described her high school boyfriend with the micropenis: "His dick was a button of flesh, but there was something about him I couldn't forget."

"I mean, that's pretty memorable," said Chester.

Meredith set her chin high. "I'm not joking." She turned back to the text. "He talked to me like I was a real person." Her voice squeaked. "And maybe it was just his affliction, maybe it was that he took months to find the right angle and hated that I'd seen him twisting above me, but he actually asked me when he wanted to fuck. He actually bought me Twizzlers. And I wasn't an easy kid, if you can believe it."

Joan longed for Meredith to keep going, to spill all her secret sorrows. She could've stayed in that cozy, private barn all night. Willie giggled.

"Really." Her eyes dampened. She turned from Willie to the moon. Even Meredith's crush thought she was sort of lame.

Joan had the impulse to say, "Hey, you're okay." But Meredith continued without her, describing going off on Lifetime of Fear when he paused to shit during a show, twisting his head around like he wanted to watch himself. "All these Montana ladies staring at me, these fancy ranch ladies, waiting for me to freak. I hated giving them their show, but I couldn't stop myself." Her voice broke.

She closed the book and jiggled it. "Seventeen ninety-nine. A steal for my soul."

Joan fidgeted in her chair, but everyone else chuckled half-heartedly, like they hadn't been listening.

"I can't say more than this, but I recently met an intern at a certain famous book club." She winked.

"Huh." Joan couldn't help it; the word hiccupped out. The teachers glanced at her, then quickly away. Now that they'd been turned against her, of course they'd assume the worst of her response. They'd never believe she was genuinely worried for Meredith. But Joan herself had suffered so many close calls. She'd met the CEO of Island Records at a bar, flirted with a man in a grocery store who ran the biggest distro company for indie records in America, helped change the tire of a woman on I-95 who was revealed to be a Danish princess and promised to act as Joan's patron for years to come. Moments when powerful people flash-flooded with gratitude—for Joan's help, for simply being attractive and peculiar and talking to them—and then promised more than they could give, more than they'd want to give the next day or the next week when they returned to the rolling grind of professions, needy children, listless spouses. If anyone consulted a photograph of Joan later, after meeting—scrawny and frizzy with gapped teeth—they'd forget her indescribable mystique. In photographs she was an orphan clinging to the bulb of her

Martin. Joan was forever on the next step down from fame, about to lift her foot and place it on that topmost, gleaming stair, and so many times, her foot slid free. The step below, which had once been miles high, was lowlier each time she dropped back onto it. In Meredith lay a version of Joan: the gambler who bet it all on two cherries. Joan wanted to wrestle her off the highway of desire.

After Meredith came Chester, who read seventeen parts of an experimental play set in a breadbasket, interrupting himself to provide lengthy historical context concerning minor American presidents and the French Revolution.

"The roll, the roll," he recited. "Has pumpernickel seen the lofty roll?" He rotated his face with slow drama.

Despite the subject matter, the play was engaging, the various breads charming. What mind had conjured this madness? A roll and a loaf fought for who boasted the saddest personal history—the loaf had lost its starter yeast to suicide. Chester must've been a little boy with a wild mind, endearing himself to his parents at every turn. They'd listened to him and delighted in his ramblings, appreciated his every whim as a new missive of wonky genius. The idea warmed Joan's chest. But when Chester moved to discussing how a theater in Des Moines had shown interest in producing the play, at his personal expense, Joan willed the insect buzz rising from the lawn to blanket his voice. She should shake Meredith and Chester, warn them that Meredith's book would come out, that Chester's play might be produced, and still they wouldn't find the fulfillment they sought, not next year—and she could tell they believed their happiness lay that close—and probably not ever. Unless they had Paige's capacity to achieve startling success while maintaining mental health, but the Paiges of the world were few. In all Joan's touring, all her time at clubs and the

Gonewriters' Collective and encountering hundreds of musicians, she'd only met one.

"Good luck," she said, unconvincingly.

Chester squinched as though she'd tossed boiling oil on him. Meredith wrenched her head away, like seeing Joan would solidify her into marble.

Willie read poems that were fragmented jumbles of spiky imagery, each with winding, intellectual titles like "To Icarus on the Occasion of My First Informal Education." He wove his fingers through his beard as he recited, gaze unfocused. To listen was to rock-climb a wall of brilliant jewels—the colors were rich but blinding, and there was no place on all the slippery beauty to fit her hands. But she fell into the stanzas like they were music. How was he so bumbling and plain on the outside, his beard a jagged fury, when inside him were birds made of concrete, skies raining chips of luminous plastic, men with bubble noses? He must've been through so much: the accident, the loss of his sister, and maybe further back, hard, knife-sharp spikes of trauma piercing his childhood, that he could only half remember and couldn't completely understand. There was no peer left to explain to him what had happened. All he had had was poetry.

When he finished, Meredith turned to Joan. "Don't say anything about his poems."

"What?" Joan said. "I didn't." She'd enjoyed the discombobulating experience of being awash in color and light.

"Good," Meredith said, placing a protective hand on Willie's knee.

"Listen." Joan tried to speak gently. "I've been on this road a bit longer than you."

Sparrow jumped up. "I'll go next." The words darted out. They fumbled to establish a projector on the stool, leashing it with cords to their laptop. As they fussed with their equipment, Joan's legs squirmed under her. Sparrow was shaky, barely upright, like they didn't want to share. Panic swelled in Joan. She couldn't bear for Sparrow to bomb.

"You know." Joan reached out for Sparrow's arm. Her fingers brushed the soft edge of their flesh. "You don't have to share."

"Of course they'll share," said Meredith. "We're all sharing."

"If Sparrow's nervous, they don't have to."

"I'm fine," Sparrow said. A yellow square of illumination popped onto the plastic siding, a cozy window spied at night.

"Ooh." Meredith sprang higher in her seat. "Is this one about your kids?"

The square trembled as Sparrow rooted around on the computer, clicking a mouse pad, striking keys. What if, after all the effort toward organizing the brushes and ink, all the funds invested in all that fine-toothed Bristol board, the work was terrible? Or merely serviceable? Either Sparrow had no chance and thought they did, or they had some chance and they'd suffer even more years, shoved forward on waves of half-meant praise, before reaching the shore that marked the edge of their talent. An image filled the light.

The projected panel was inky and dense, the figures outlined with generous, rubbery brushstrokes, restless marks that broke their outlines, slashing around in choppy halos. The characters were human, undeniably so, but hailing from some other world. Their eyes were ink black and soulful, their hair fuzzy streaks of dry brush or densely packed worms. There was more black on the page than white, and every mark had been applied feverishly, joyfully, building a live density.

Sparrow read, "The crowd bitched and twitched and waited."

And it was a crowd. That was why the panel was so packed.

There were women and funny, slim-faced men with earrings, stuffed into a trough cheek to cheek. The title, *Beep Beep*, was lettered in careful gothic script, a drawing in its own right, white font popping from the rich black field. As Sparrow clicked to the next panel, and the one after that, the figures revealed themselves to all be women. Even the characters with mustaches or thick jaws had breasts, at least flat ones, or that uniboob Joan had tired of among her fans. She always wanted to tell them to splurge and have two.

The images scrolled by, the ten-panel grid abandoned, every cell its own shape and size, following the story of a butch lesbian named Duck with spiky hair and a bead of metal driven into the flesh below her nose. Duck chatted with members of the crowd, who'd gathered to enjoy the work of a performance artist named Jelly Who-Who.

This was good work. This was solidly amazing work. Joan didn't even like comics, but she would've read an entire book about these funny square heads, textured clouds of hair, and unsettlingly live eyes. The characters were bubbly and slick, like that random sketch of a horde of children Sparrow had drawn. The hands, grabbing bottles of beer, sported four big toes instead of fingers. Duck's mouth evolved from a dash to full, shouting lips, creases included, depending on how much she liked her chat partner. The work was never silly, even as it borrowed a cartoon language. Joan hadn't experienced actual good work in years. Not even Paige's songs had ever reached the level of truly great—they were unique, her style infectious, her outfits elegantly sexy, her face that of a trusting child. She had the cocktail but not the depth of genius. Joan wanted to peel the square off the side of the dorm and eat it. She was thrilled for Sparrow that by some crazy alchemy, they'd built the velvet density of this world.

Jelly Who-Who was a slender, short woman, hair a cloud

of scribbles, teeth of a beaver, eyes of a hawk. She was radiant, such that you could tell, even from her mini inked figure, that she was magnetic, gorgeous, proud. She took the stage with feet spread wide, acoustic dangling from her neck. But Joan didn't grasp the big picture until Jelly Who-Who started playing and lyrics sprang from her in bubbles: "And the city is behind me, the black brightened city, the lake is before me, the flat colored lake."

Those were the only lines Sparrow had dared to include. Maybe they feared copyright infringement. Because how cheeky, to steal from the one song everyone knew.

But not everyone knew it, as it happened. Only Chester turned to Joan, though he did it so performatively, hands open and stretched out, that he might as well have screamed that the song was hers.

Joan kept her focus glued on the projection. Because maybe, despite the inky fluff on Jelly Who-Who's head, despite the teeth, she wasn't Joan. Jelly Who-Who was lovelier than Joan, after all, a child-sized supermodel in cartoon form.

Jelly Who-Who played a few more songs, none of them belonging to Joan. A stadium's worth of lesbians jumped and hooted and beamed gelatinous hearts from their eyes. Lesbians cheered like that at Joan's shows, maybe, but Joan blocked them out for survival.

"Jelly Who-Who is wild," said a lesbian. "She's a wolf."

Jelly Who-Who became a wolf, with rumpled fur and buck-teeth, wormy dick dangling from the tufts between her thighs. She circled the stage, still singing, dick dragging in the dust, nostrils flared for the hunt. Joan grabbed the porch railing. The wolf looked like Joan—exactly like her—frizzy fur, rangy legs, bucktooth fangs, soft dick.

"No," said Duck. "Jelly Who-Who just does what we all want to do."

Jelly Who-Who shifted into a hamburger, three breasts squished between the buns instead of meat.

"Duh, what?" said the lesbian talking to Duck. The buns squeezed together, and the nipples shot streams of milk.

"Like someone asks a shit question—an interviewer or whatever—and Jelly Who-Who says, 'That's a shit question.' She's not wilder than us. Everyone agrees it's a shit question. But Jelly Who-Who actually says."

"Bitch, you're too deep for this shit."

The bun crumpled, revealing, in scattering crumbs, the slender, naked figure of Jelly Who-Who: no breasts at all now, chest flat and nipple-free, vulva a tangle of flaps and shiny, inviting nubs. Here was perfect cartoon Joan. That glazed confusion was exactly how she pictured her pussy: lobes shifting to bend to whatever new desire. As Jelly Who-Who sang more intensely, she morphed into a leaky tree, a bonfire shooting testicles to the sky, a badger with no head and two asses, a lollipop, a rabid deer, a pool of limpid vomit. In between she flickered back to herself, always morphed from the original: eyes glassy, sweat erupting into pimples on her great square forehead, pants-free with a dozen models of genitalia, drowning in the fuzzy suit of a bear. Her mouth shrank into a fleshy hole. Her feet pushed apart on the boards. And then she was a woman again, and her tongue unfurled, bulbous, with a window of shine at the tip, like a cartoon apple. The heat of a song jagging out of her in burps, her body a conduit for the electric melody. Joan's bones vibrated as the comic flashed by. The breast burger, the long-dicked wolf—this was exactly how performing was, how she herself was: a grizzly animal-thing, thrashing and hitching to an invisible beam of energy. She missed it. She missed it so fucking much.

"Come onstage," Jelly Who-Who cried. "Whoever wants!"

Duck elbowed dykes all around, bumping tattoos and nose rings and couples affixed by the mouth. When she reached the stage, she frog-legged her arms and pushed up: our hero, first to arrive.

Duck and Jelly Who-Who watched each other from across the guitar. The guitar was a mashup of dreadnought and parlor, as though Sparrow had tried to master the shape of the instrument, like they almost knew. Duck and Jelly Who-Who advanced toward each other. They kissed.

Sparrow lingered on the kiss for three panels, four, five panels of close-framed open mouths shifting position only subtly. So many panels of what was probably two seconds in life had the effect of jerking Joan down into the sewer of that kiss, but with whom? Joan was crouched inside both mouths, tongues darting through the slit between lips. The kiss was so inky, so cartoonishly sensual, that Joan's underwear soaked through.

The perspective zoomed out to waist level. Jelly Who-Who's hands were buried in the spikes of Duck's hair, with Duck's hands low on Jelly Who-Who's spine. Jelly Who-Who curled her back to make room for the guitar, lashed to her spine the way it would never be lashed to Joan's. But even with the guitar between them, there was a choreographed chaos to the kiss, a sloppy sweet push and pull that made you root hard for even so unlikely and sudden a union.

Over the course of ten panels, Jelly Who-Who's hand drifted from Duck's cheek to her neck to her collarbone, back along her jawline, then dropped to her shoulder. Duck's eyes bugged out, watching the hand. At last the hand settled like a starfish on Duck's breast. Duck froze. The kiss stopped. The hand stayed. A pin-thin line of saliva connected their lips as they parted. And then Jelly Who-Who squeezed Duck's breast.

A sound extruded from the nipple. Spelled out in that fine gothic lettering: *beep beep.* The words lingered for two panels, three, fading, a slow dissolve, into black. Duck's face, frowning in surprise. The audience froze. And then, all at once, exploded. Jelly Who-Who and Duck stared at each other, noses touching, mouths straight lines, eyes hooded and questioning, What did we do? Duck dove into the clot of lesbians, expression shifting between shades of unwell. Lesbians received her, queasy-faced and shaking their wrists like they'd handled shit. The last panel was a solid black screen, so rich a darkness that Sparrow must've inked it with hundreds of loaded strokes.

The teachers clapped. A cloud abandoned the moon, and the porch washed in light. Sparrow pinkened through the blur of clapping hands, sneaking a glance at Joan. How were they smiling right now?

"Jesus, Sparrow," Meredith said, smashing her hands together. "You made that? Did you really make that?"

Sparrow blushed. "I mean, yeah, I guess."

"How did you do that?" Chester asked. "That was, like, a thousand times better than those freaking box men. No offense—but holy god."

Joan stiffened to a stick, like she could slip through the banister and disappear. Sparrow had committed her worst moment to the page—watered down, yes, sure, but they had—and shared it with colleagues. For what? A couple of jeers and smirks. Ditching Joan to go camping was grade school shit. This was ruinous. "What the fuck." Joan's voice scraped her throat.

"Joan?" Sparrow's voice was alive with fear.

"Why did you do that?" Joan's bones quivered, ready to

fling free of their flesh. Sparrow had used Joan's experience. That was wrong. That was totally wrong.

Sparrow's face was doughy and perfect-soft, too innocent to have stolen the worst night of Joan's life. They bleated, "You didn't like it?"

"I don't understand." Joan's voice shook its way free. She couldn't articulate her anger without revealing the secret of Love und Romance. Sparrow had put her in the worst position—and why? Joan had done nothing to this person, had felt only admiration. Heat accumulated in her, blazing, like she'd swallowed lava. "But you act like such a good person."

Sparrow clutched a cable. Their fingers burned white.

"Don't talk to them like that," Meredith said. But her voice was a husk, like she suddenly feared Joan.

Joan's brain was an electric coil. She couldn't untangle it, so she spewed: "No artist ever existed who's morally superior but personally cowardly. That's politician shit." Air sliced up her throat. But the teachers were blasé, like they hadn't put together what Joan had done from the comic—and how could they? The reality of Love und Romance was more horrific than any comic strip.

Sparrow's eyelashes lowered. Their cheeks were wet. "I'm sorry. It was a dumb idea."

Meredith rubbed their back. "Don't listen to her."

"No. Joan's right. It was fucked up." Sparrow scraped their forehead. "I was trying—never mind."

Joan was vindicated. She turned from Sparrow's crumpled face. If the teachers knew the true story, they'd see that what Sparrow had done was wrong, that Joan's reaction was paltry compared to the offense at hand. But it didn't matter. Fine. Let them think Joan was an asshole. Joan stepped toward the stairs down to the lawn. She'd go to bed, forget all this.

"Joan's just mad about her own shit," Willie mumbled.

Sparrow's shoulder hiked up. "Willie."

Joan peered at Willie, lit softly under the fairy lights across the porch. His eyes were eager and guileless under the shiny dome of his skull. "I don't have shit," she said slowly. Why should she care about some dumb camping trip? Since when in her old life had she ever once longed to sit under a canvas flap in dank, buggy woods? Back in Brooklyn, she would've laughed off the very notion.

"Paige was your friend, right?" Chester said. "So it's kinda fucked."

Joan stumbled backward. She seized the porch railing, but it wasn't firmly affixed. The hollow plastic lifted in her fist.

"Wait, you don't know?" Chester said, slapping the balcony.

Joan's spine dug into the railing, the plastic cratering against her. She could hardly bear to ask, "What don't I know?"

Chester's mouth caverned. "But how did you miss it?"

"She doesn't have a phone," Meredith said.

Chester shifted as though he were sitting on snakes. "Ah."

"Just say it," Joan breathed. She hadn't checked the tweet since Friday, had been too preoccupied with moping and running away.

Chester's bangs settled along their perfect line over his forehead. "Too bad it wasn't one of her modest shows. Which she still does, bless her. You might've been okay. This was a doozy—I'm sure you know her schedule—the Fillmore in Detroit. Friday night. She outed you."

Paige had dreamed for years of the Fillmore. "She outed me." Paige, standing on that historic stage, before thousands of people, announcing Joan was straight? The idea was uncomfortable but also sort of a relief. Joan had no investment left in pretending.

"Your crazy concert. You know." His trunk twisted in the soft glow of the fairy lights. "Want to see?" He already had his phone in hand, stepping into the circle.

Protests clogged in Joan—she wanted nothing less—but Chester already had his finger on play, the screen illuminating his chin, and there Paige was, tiny inside the phone, somewhere far away, on a stage strewn with shattered rainbows, clad in a white wool tunic and plaid leggings, hair elevated and untamed, the way it always inflated by the end of a set. Shadows cut dramatic shards into the planes of her face. Her guitar was slung on her back. She gazed into the mists of the audience. Her vision was askew—that was obvious immediately. She couldn't hold her focus stable.

Her only movement was a subtle swing in her hips. The stage was lit a hot white, every nook and cranny beyond was dark. Paige grabbed the mic with both fists as though it could anchor her. Her knees buckled, too elastic—she was drunk. Joan had so rarely seen her drunk. Only the night they'd met and at a few of her first shows, when she was all nerves. Very occasionally, early on, the nights she'd hit on Joan.

"Apologies for the cancellations." Paige leaned out of range of the mic, lips moving soundlessly, shuffling her feet to stabilize. She pulled the guitar around to her front, slapped the strings with an open palm. The Martin. The chord sounded, ringing into the belly of the hall, vibrating in Joan. The video was in soft focus, the audio tinny, but she'd know that velvet tone anywhere. So Paige had rescued it from the street—relief bloated between Joan's ribs. And she was using it. Another chord followed, then picking: "Cloud Land." Paige sounded great on the Martin—its richer tone lent the song depth and a vein of sorrow. As the song gathered steam, Paige opened her mouth as though to kick-start the lyrics but then announced, over the picking, "I know you guys are worried." She removed her hand from the neck and picked open strings. "I see the posts. Thank you for that—uh." She shook her head. Her hair rattled, wisps spewing.

She spun around, back to the audience, cool blue light on her spine. Her picking died—off-rhythm, too slow, then trickling to nothing. Her hands flopped to her flanks. The curve of the Martin framed her. Although Paige weighed more than Joan, the Martin was bigger on her, the heft of its perfect mahogany overtaking her. She leaned back into the mic. "So sorry. Like, sorry."

Joan's throat contracted to a pinhole. Paige had been skipping shows, drinking onstage. Joan hated not knowing what random strangers knew about her best friend. Paige turned back to the audience. Her eyelids were half-mast, head drooping, like she'd crumple to the floor at any second. Joan had the urge to drop into the phone and ferry her offstage before she overdosed, but of course, the video was two days old. Paige hadn't died. She noodled around, but she was too drunk; she couldn't coordinate the rhythm. Full seconds passed between messy grabs at the strings.

"Why?" came a shout from the audience, followed by a spurt of cheer.

Paige sighed into the mic, too close, breath sizzling. "I won't say." Paige never spoke in public about her personal life, disliked the whining of artists, the definition of self against trauma. "Because I don't fucking know." She tossed her head like a horse. "Blargh. What am I thinking? Like in this exact stupid minute?"

"Yes," from the audience. The same voice—steady, male, young.

"I don't fucking know." She spoke as though she and this

audience man were alone in a room. "I ran to New York when I was a kid. I don't know why I'm thinking about that so much lately." She held a finger to her temple like she was picking down into her brain. "I wanted the whole glittery chaos. I was a fool. Obviously." She spun the flesh at her temple. The video was eerily crisp, zoomed in with some phone that was higher tech than its own good, and even from this distance Joan felt the looseness of Paige's skin—too slack. "And that kinda shit happens to every idiot teenager who thinks someone wants to mentor her. Right?" She shook her hair like she wanted it off her head. "Right?" No one answered, nowhere in the masses of the Fillmore. She pulled the sleeve of her tunic. When it sprang back, it was brutally creased. "I'm not saying more." She rattled her head too hard. "I won't pretend I wasn't young and cute. But I was a crap singer. I had no skill. I couldn't play my piece of shit Rogue—I was useless. With her. In every way that matters." Joan held still. On screen, Paige lifted a hand to her neck. Her fingers vibrated, skeletal in the blinding wash of light. "It's just—sorry, Carlotta." A murmur swelled in the audience, muted, like animals in the grass. Paige raised her head. Her face was blank and startled, like she'd imagined she was alone. Joan's legs twitched to push her free.

Paige wheeled around, slammed out a chord. The audience cheered. The video cut out.

Silence fell over the porch. None of the teachers spoke. Their gaze itched Joan. "She didn't say my name," Joan said, her voice creaking out. But she knew what had happened. They wouldn't be having this conversation otherwise.

Chester typed her name into the search bar, and there was the old video, now the number-one hit: *Joan Vole Tuesday LES*. And there, its view count, in plain typeface: almost three million.

"No. That's not right." She touched the screen like she could scrape off the digits. How could that number have anything to do with her? "That's fake." Her words emerged flat, like she was acting. But the humidity was sticky on her arms. The night was hot. This was real.

"Paige has reach, man," said Chester.

He'd already darkened the screen. Paige hadn't done that to her. How could Paige have done that? Joan's vision swam, dots filling the porch, pocking Chester and Sparrow and Willie and Meredith. "Someone must've faked that video. Paige's one." Could that have been an actor, out there, in Paige's clothes? Copying Paige's sway, her cute raspy drunk voice? Condemning Joan the way the real Paige never would?

"It's one of a dozen angles posted," Chester said. "But does it matter? You have three million views on your video either way. Which is pretty badass, actually."

Joan grabbed his phone. With a greasy finger that couldn't get purchase, she scrolled through the comments. All the old ones had been buried by timestamps and catalogs of evidence. Randoms on YouTube had found all the clues she had—the pee splatter, Carlotta's distressed expression, Joan's pubic hair— and more: the frightened stutter of Carlotta's step, a stain on her skirt visible in three frames, a dark dot on Joan's pants visible in one. Joan's zipper three teeth higher before the hugs than after, a puddle onstage, visible for fourteen seconds in two installments—how had Joan missed it? Another commenter linked to Carlotta's tweet, which had exploded with likes and retweets. Several commenters noted how you could see Carlotta, at the end of the video, after Joan was gone, chased down by a figure who some held was Paige Serratt. Joan had never watched to the end of the video, so humiliated she always stopped it the moment she ran out. Commenters argued vehemently that the woman in the crowd could not be Paige, but Joan skipped to that part, and, of course, it was. So that was how she'd known.

Last night Joan was out in the hot summer night, eating ice, with zero notion that her world had disintegrated. How could she have sat out there, with the cicadas and the sleepy teen, sucking out food coloring, oblivious, anonymous? How was she allowed to have a sugared tongue on a quiet summer night, thinking fond thoughts of her students? The job in Charlottesville, gone. How lucky she'd been—three weeks without anyone knowing what the video meant, almost two weeks with the tweet personally condemning her. But worse—she slumped against the railing, rattling it—Paige.

"Are you okay?" Sparrow's voice rang clear in the dark. "Joan?"

"She doesn't realize." Meredith's voice was a wisp.

"I know I fucked up, okay?" Joan wanted to cover her ears. She didn't need anyone to say more. This was it. Her life was over. But Paige hadn't meant this result—she must not have.

"It gets worse, I'm sorry to say." Chester brought up a website on his phone. Joan recognized the white-and-red motif: *Real Men*, a podcast championing the canceled that had grown insanely popular in the last years. Alfred Honey had been featured in a minor story, as had more prominent canceled men: a politician with a fourteen-year-old girlfriend, a director who abused sex workers, a rapist comedian. Occasional women were spotlighted, but only the really nasty ones. Like a middle-aged prepper in Kentucky who burned hoodies on her lawn. Joan gaped at the slashing graphics, focus blurring. Chester hit play on the top video.

"Joan Vole: grungy nobody to modern-day saint," growled the host of *Real Men* over his own headshot: a bearded dweeb

with sweet eyes. "This is real rock and roll. A badass girlie bust-
ing sensitive snowflakes and flashing her tits, pissing on dykes
without a care for the wrath of pansy feminazis."

"Stop," Joan said. Chester did. "I can't." Her organs were
about to fall out. She wanted to die in a puddle of liquid meat.
Real Men had an international platform.

"Damn," Willie said. "Sorry, Joan." He rubbed his beard
like he'd already moved on to the next thought, like any next
thought existed after this.

Joan peered between them, trying to catch Sparrow's eye.
Sparrow turned, flashing the back of their tawny head.

"At least Georgina won't see," Chester said. "The whole
world could know and Georgina would be the last."

"Obviously Joan has to tell her." Meredith fluffed her cowl
neck so it rose to her cheeks. "You have to go before class tomorrow, Joan. You know that's the right thing for everyone."

If Joan didn't tell Georgina, Meredith obviously would. Or
some student's parent would catch on. The Gen Xers might
miss a viral video, but *Real Men* wormed its way into every
feed, riding the backs of rage posts into the algorithms of the
most progressive. She stood up on unsteady legs. She teetered
toward the stairs, gripping the banister as hard as she could.
No one called out or tried to stop her.

Navigating down the stairs and into the suite took a thousand years, but finally she was safe on the chemical-scented
carpet, watched over by hulking institutional furniture. Now
that she was closed up in the suite alone, away from the attention above, every drop of life drained from her. She swayed
where she stood, so weak she couldn't hold herself up. She
crashed into the armchair.

The plastic adhered to her as though the chair longed to
join them together into one beast. She should wrench herself

out, should escape to the privacy of her own room. But one more second. Just one second of rest. Paige had canceled concerts. She was in a bad place. She never would've told on Joan, not the Paige she knew. She must not have anticipated the fallout. But either way, their friendship was ruined. Joan had no one now—no job here, no best friend to return to. She closed her eyes.

22

HOURS MIGHT'VE ELAPSED BEFORE A HAND TAPPED JOAN'S arm and Sparrow's voice wriggled in: "Are you okay?"

Joan opened her eyes. The armchair plastic had melted into the substance of her cheek, her bare arms. Sparrow loomed in the lamplight, peaceful and round. What, did Sparrow want her to leave already? Let her rest a minute, then she'd go, forever. None of the teachers would ever have to see her again.

"Hey," Sparrow said. "Let's talk."

"I get it," Joan said, squeaking into the rubber cushions. "Everything's fucked. Sorry, okay?" She pushed herself out of the chair, skin ungluing with a pop.

Sparrow reached a hand to Joan's sternum. "That's not what I wanted to say. Can we go to my room? Please?" Sparrow pointed to the ceiling. "They're still upstairs, but they won't be forever."

The idea of Meredith thundering downstairs pitched Joan into the maw of the hallway. She wobbled toward her room. In seconds she'd be locked away. She could have one night of peace—shuttered in a room with no eyes on her—before she banished herself to nowhere. Her airless future darkened her vision.

She slammed into her door with two hands, trying to force it open.

"Joan," Sparrow said. "Stop."

Some fragment of Joan longed to hesitate, to listen, could've rested her head on a few soft words, but no—no. Joan was fucked up, but she never would've made a friend's misery into art. Not in a million years. "That was messed up," she muttered, hands still on the door, which, somehow, wouldn't open. "What you did."

Sparrow grabbed their temples. "I was trying something. I was like—I don't know." Their arms slapped their sides. There was a rigidity in their expression that Joan hadn't seen before, an urgency. "Just come to my room. Please. I'll explain."

"No." Joan pushed her way into her room. She was pitching toward the bed, releasing herself into a free fall, when hands circled her waist.

Joan's skin under those soft palms sparkled. When was the last time anyone had held her by the hips? Men were afraid to touch her, just lay back, hairy bellies up, letting her do what she was going to do, cowed and horrified and dominated and pleased. So the last time must've been Paige, whose touch she didn't even register.

Joan went limp, allowing herself to be dragged across the hall. She let Sparrow lead her to the center of the room, where they replaced the door snake, blocking all light and bad feelings from the hall. The room held her, cool and crisp and quiet; Norway. The pages of *Beep Beep* were spread out on Sparrow's desk. Joan wandered to them. The top page was the kiss. The ink was so dense that Joan wanted to drop down into it, wanted to live in that cartoon world where she'd done nothing too severely wrong. "You're a genius, you realize."

"That's nonsense."

"It's true." Those plastic faces were so melancholy, the uncanniness of Jelly Who-Who's world, caught in that unsettling landscape between cartoon and reality. Joan touched the edge of a field of ink. Now that she was here, safe in this quiet room, the tragedy of the night was no longer Joan's shit raked up for scrutiny but Sparrow, robbed of praise.

Sparrow turned the kiss over, exposing the back of the board, patchy and dark where the marks bled through. "It was a stupid idea. I was trying to square you."

Joan was exhausted. And what was the point of any of this? She shouldn't have come in here. She should be locked in a black, merciful sleep. She wanted to fall on Sparrow's bed and dissolve into oblivion.

"I liked you so much," Sparrow said. "And you'd done this awful thing. I don't know." Their hands splashed around. "I was trying to, like, investigate. To figure out how it happened."

"Okay." The idea of Sparrow working through Joan's sins was cozy and close. In a sick way. "But you didn't have to show everyone."

"It didn't matter." Air hissed out of Sparrow. "They knew already."

Sour pushed into Joan's mouth from some dark pocket. "Because you told them?"

"Of course not." Sparrow rolled their eyes. "I found out about Paige's, you know, announcement or whatever after you went to bed Friday. It was up the instant it happened. And it took the internet about five seconds to put it all together."

Joan swayed on the carpet. She couldn't stand hearing Paige's name. Even if she hadn't called Joan out on purpose.

Joan had only ever been mad at her once before. That evening in Love und Romance, that once, that was it. And that hadn't been fair.

Sparrow stepped closer to Joan. That smell of warm sawdust. "So I got the teachers out of there. It wasn't such a weird idea—we usually go camping once or twice a summer anyway, and it's always last minute." They looked out the window, which was a flat, black field, like the final slide of their comic. "I thought maybe up in the mountains, with spotty service, they wouldn't find out. Or at least I'd buy you time. They found out immediately, of course. But then I thought I could convince them you're not so bad, far away where you didn't have to see them process. And when that failed—when they were pretty much dicks about you all weekend—I thought, well, maybe they could get there the way I did." They nodded at their pages. "Failed every time."

Joan's skull lightened. "I thought Meredith turned you against me." Joan swayed. She needed to sit.

Sparrow leaned their head back and huffed out a puff. "Fuck no. Are you kidding?"

"But you guys are close."

"Sort of, but we share about one opinion on life."

Joan didn't realize what was happening—her lungs convulsing. Laughter. Kind of unpleasant when you thought about it. But what a relief to see Sparrow's face loose.

"Look, I'm sorry," Sparrow said.

"You're sorry? I'm the shit one."

"No, me too," Sparrow begged, like shittiness was some golden honor. "I should have told you why I was going camping. I didn't think you'd trust me to, like, take care of it. And I shouldn't have drawn that comic." They scraped their forehead with their thumb. "I thought it was, like, a tribute. Like the best beautiful version of what happened. But I'm dumb."

"I was a dick to you." How had she snapped at this perfect person? Her legs wobbled. How was she still standing? "And out in the field, when I made you go to the bathroom." Joan shuddered. Sparrow's discomfort, the mess. It was too horrible.

Sparrow shook their head so hard their cowlicks reorganized. "Are you kidding? I loved that lesson."

"You were humiliated." How awful, even just the memory of Sparrow's cheeks darkening as they crunched up out of view, guarding their groin.

"I've practiced. I can do it now." Sparrow stood up straighter, chest out. They were sweetly proud, so grateful. In the last forty-eight hours they'd done so much for Joan, and Joan hadn't even known it. This bear cub against the crushing churn of the internet. "I'd show you, but I'm shy. I'm not like you."

"Thank god."

Sparrow bowed their head. Even their neck blushed. "I wish I was. I'm a pussy."

Maybe the art didn't always have to come first. Maybe it didn't matter if the song was better with the "Lakeshore" guy as a girl—maybe there were higher-order concerns, like the feelings of live people. Maybe if Joan ever made music again she could figure that out. If only she could start fresh, she could be Sparrow, just a little, maybe, making art for only the purest reasons. And the way Sparrow watched her, with unadulterated affection. They'd said they really liked Joan, even after they learned about Love und Romance.

Hesitantly, Joan stepped forward to close the distance between them. She set her hand on Sparrow's soft cheek. "You're so dear."

Sparrow lowered their eyelashes, blood rising into their cheeks. "Ugh. Don't say that."

"You are." Joan turned Sparrow's head to the right, then the left. Boy from the front, girl from the side. Their skin just as clear up close. Pleasure rumbled through her. "Look at you."

Sparrow peeled Joan's hand off their face, held it under the lamplight. Joan's overgrown nails gleamed like claws, her calluses lozenges sunk into the flesh. They refused to soften, even after nearly three weeks without the Martin. "You're a monster." But they said so with love.

A chime sounded in Joan. She was a monster, yes—when she played, free and inhuman. She was sexless and brutal, her body a conduit for the song. And that was beautiful. That was rare. And Sparrow had seen it in a way no one ever had—not even Paige. Sparrow had made that chaotic, spiritual state into art, when Joan herself had forgotten its good.

Joan kissed Sparrow. Their lips were springy and damp, and wet heat poured through her. Sparrow didn't taste like men, saucy and complex, or like Paige, always, considerately, like mint or nothing. They tasted of damp, powerful heat. They had one of those rare faces that was as attractive close up: their forehead smooth, their cheeks, their features organized enough to absorb at close range. Joan set her hands on Sparrow's ribs and pulled them to the bed, dropping them, spine down, under her. Sparrow lit in surprise, eyelids luxuriously closing.

Joan straddled them, kissing their neck, their jaw, their sturdy brow, all the parts of their face that belonged to the boy they almost were. Her pussy grazed Sparrow's belly, heating through the linen. She was crazy; she was comfortable—what was this? When her hands strayed to Sparrow's chest, bound with some cruel garment, she retracted. "Is that okay?"

"Don't ask," Sparrow breathed, their gaze alight and fierce in a way Joan had never seen it.

And then they were naked. Joan was unusually natural when nude: tawny and slim without startling bulges, besides some sorry sags in dark corners, easier in the world than when clothed, like she became her true self, like she could fall to all fours and run through the woods, screaming and jumping on the spines of elk. But she'd only ever felt that way alone. She felt it now with Sparrow, though, natural and easy. She climbed on Sparrow, who'd even removed their binder, the tissue flattening into their chest. All their body was as smooth and soft as their face—softer, even—their belly chubbier than it appeared in clothes, their hair pale tufts caught in their armpits and groin. Joan heated as her coarse flesh pressed against Sparrow's curves, though she was careful with their female parts, in case. Their hands brushed between each other's legs, testing the moisture, but never pressing, never entering. Joan longed to be touched; waiting ached. But she moved slow. Checked that every step was okay.

"Are you doing this because you want to be queer for real?" Sparrow asked.

"Of course not." Jelly Who-Who had been so much hotter than Joan, so much less creepy and aggressive and remote. Kissing Sparrow, Joan could believe that was who she was, at least to Sparrow, at least so far.

Riding Sparrow's belly, Joan pushed them down into the mattress. She'd fucked the "Lakeshore" guy like this, riding him until his dick chafed. A network of pleasure webbed up, so paralyzing she nearly collapsed. She wanted to stay up here in this magic cloud for an hour, a day, would've died of it. Sparrow's focus strained, their tongue out, their concentration on their own pleasure unbelievably hot—how was this sexy person watching Joan with those lazy eyes and that heartthrob hair? They were real. They were so real. And then, from her torso, all at once, the feeling grew and turned unbearable. That force of golden pressure, like she'd explode from within, her walls shattering as she incinerated into a flash of pure radiance. Normally the warning was many minutes long, the buildup half the joy. But here Joan was, already at the edge, belly bursting, too late to stop.

"I'm gonna let go," she said, her voice soft, as though tenderness could make the words less true.

"What?" A dazed expression loosened Sparrow's face.

"Sparrow," Joan said, leaning back. "I'm sorry. I'm going to pee on you." She squeezed her legs together as a spoonful escaped.

"Anything you want," Sparrow said, their eyes rounded, glinting with—Joan was certain—arousal. "Please."

Permission released the valve. Had Joan ever received sincere permission? Only grudging consent from horny guys. Joan released, washing that clear skin, those chubby handfuls of tit, liquid pooling in Sparrow's collarbone even as more flowed out, joy rattling through her with the release. Joan had long ago learned to maintain control of the top of her body while the rest went wild, so she kept her back arched, her shoulders high, could've even spoken, but couldn't bear to, couldn't check Sparrow and risk absorbing disgust. She felt again like herself as a child, peeing to "Rail Rat." This magical release, like her bottom was dropping out, that she'd never experienced with another person, this letting go, this complete submission. She loved Sparrow for it.

Her lungs seized. She was insane, her poison bubbling up like she was pissing all over a man she hated, like her father was about to snatch her by the elbow. She couldn't look down, couldn't bear to watch Sparrow in her spray, realizing, at last, finally, that Joan was a vile mongrel, a piss witch.

Perhaps other expressions had crossed Sparrow's face before Joan finished and chanced checking, but by the time she did, the expression that had settled was lips apart, head tipped back so far it sank into the bed. Sparrow was smiling, with pee on their cheeks. A shudder coursed through Joan bone-deep so her stream lost course, striking the mattress. Before the trickle slowed to nothing, Joan sprang off the bed.

She trembled in the center of the room, droplets tickling her thigh. She'd never felt bad for the guys, for the cat, for the kid at the base of the slide. But her arms were leaden now. She wanted to scrub Sparrow, outfit them in fresh clothes, bed them down somewhere dry.

Sparrow sat up, their expression dazed, like they'd just awoken. "Why'd you stop?"

"I'm sorry." Joan held her mouth like her mouth was her pussy and it was two minutes ago. The pleasure of her first sensual pee in decades rang through her. "God, Sparrow. I'm so sorry."

"Why are you sorry?" Sparrow gave a slow, easy smile. "That was amazing."

"You don't have to lie."

"I'm not lying. That was hot. Your face." Sparrow leaned back against the wall. "Jesus."

"You like it too?" Joan was being a prude, but her torso was spongy and vulnerable, and she couldn't quite say the words.

"Not, like, specifically." They laughed, like they couldn't believe Joan's innocence. "Anything that turns you on turns me on."

"Right." Such a simple maxim.

Sparrow grabbed their T-shirt and dried their torso. "I thought you were fucking with me the other day."

"Do you still think that?"

Sparrow giggled. They balled up the shirt and tossed it to the corner of the room. "Uh, no. I do not."

Joan had to bite back a stupid grin. She wanted to sit on Sparrow, disappear into them.

"Do you wish you had a dick? Is that what this is about?"

"No." Joan wished her pussy could be treated like a dick: worshiped, sexualized, built into monuments and skyscrapers, but that wasn't the same. "Wait. You do."

Sparrow's head reared back. "God, no."

"Oh." Joan was so simpleminded. Lamar would've laughed in her face. "Is it okay how I touched you?"

Sparrow laughed, gentle and easy, as though Joan had asked the dumbest question in the world. "You're a fucking maniac."

Joan leaned forward. She yearned only to be on Sparrow, above them, all over them, molding into them. "Can I touch you anywhere?"

"Please."

Joan let her hand cup Sparrow's flank. Sparrow's eyelashes raised. Joan's hand slid down to their hip, brushing off moisture as she went. There was muscle under the fat, sturdy, steely. Joan held them firmly, as though if she released, Sparrow would float away. She let her other hand slide to Sparrow's breast. That was firm, too, the nipple sharp. "You're strong," Joan whispered.

"I like when you touch me there. I've never liked that before." They squirmed shyly.

"Come here."

Joan pulled Sparrow in by the waist and straddled them, and this time their fingers were inside each other, this time

Sparrow told Joan exactly what to do, where to touch and how—they wanted fierce pressure, speed and pain in such a way as Joan had never imagined, they liked their vulva slapped and their eyeball licked—and this time Sparrow peeped like an owl, and Joan might've, too—for the first time in her life, she couldn't untangle the sounds, all of her body was her pussy, incinerating her mind—and then they were coming together, Sparrow's face cramped and cinched while their focus was lost to another world that Joan wished she could see too—and then they slumped beside each other, the mattress crinkling to receive Joan, reminding her it was built to protect, that no spill would linger. They slept in their mess, the nutty aroma of Sparrow's breath so new and intimate it cut the ammonia.

23

THE NEXT DAY, JOAN WALKED TO CLASS IN THE HAZE OF last night, a stupid smile stretched over her face, yearning to reboard that plastic mattress. Nearly a month into Merry Writers, her life was through, but Sparrow was still caught below her, soft and given over, watching Joan release. Sparrow's hands on Joan's face, teeth clicking hers, pleasure networking in such concentration it hurt. Love bloomed like mushrooms in Joan's throat, her torso, her back. She hadn't felt this way in almost two decades, the mushrooms growing into her nerves and charging them so intensely she stumbled.

In the circle of grass in front of the classroom, in the late-afternoon sun, she overtook Lula, who was skittering to beat her. Joan's heart swelled at the skinny girl rushing across the grass, her white hair flagging. She called out.

Lula turned, steps stuttering back, away from Joan.

"Hey," Joan said. "Lula." She caught up with the girl. Walking next to her, the kid was so petite. This was their fourth week together. Joan was easy, finally, beside this kid in tube socks and the crumpled slouch of her olive jacket, even in this heat. She wore a mustache of sweat that shined as her head bobbed in the sunlight. "I'm sorry I didn't talk to you. About the other night."

"Ew," Lula said, tugging down the sleeves of her jacket so her hands disappeared. "Seriously, don't."

"I won't report you. But is everything okay?"

A grin cracked her face. "I mean, yeah. Doy. Totally okay."

Joan hustled the girl ahead. Lula, even Lula, had found someone. She hadn't even had to perfect her art first. Nowhere near close. The idea sent a pink warmth through Joan.

In the classroom, the kids were giddy, energized from the weekend. Victor bounced on the beanbag while Agnes cheerfully cried, "Cut it out, Victor. No, stop, seriously."

Victor grabbed the dreadnought and dragged it to the corner like he was going to put it out of its misery. Agnes and Lula jabbered happily on the beanbags, not even noticing he was gone. Ensconced in the darkest corner of the basement, on the carpet and under the popcorn ceiling, Victor leaned over the guitar and jammed out a tune. Joan bent toward him. He sang, "Woe is me, woe is me, I'm a man, give sympathy," with a plain, serious expression. A pressure, straight to Joan's core. She couldn't bear to listen. After all her hard work.

He flipped his hair back and kept singing. His sunny cheeks, his bobbing chin. The way his lips parted around the blunt hammer of his words. How his body went all loose and easy, his spine elastic, his mouth open in cheer. She hadn't seen him act like this the whole time she'd known him. She hadn't realized how much he must've thought about his parents splitting and all that was ahead for him, whatever that meant—nasty fights, separate apartments, financial restrictions, Victor forgotten in the swirl of new anxieties—until she saw him throw off the worry and just sing. Her torso loosened.

When Victor finished his song, Joan lifted the dreadnought by its cheap, cheesy neck, so light it could float away. The kids stared at her, giggling, even Agnes, slapping each other's knees, like somehow they knew.

"What's up with you little freaks?" Joan asked.

"Ms. Vole's in trouble," sang Lula.

Joan's mouth cracked to receive the dry, cool air. She twisted away from them.

"We got an eval," Lula sang. If only she could sing so tunefully when performing. "None of the other genres did. Not even that nonfiction lady, and she, like, yells at her kids. That means you're in trouble." Relief coursed through Joan. She was okay for one more second.

"You're not supposed to tell her," Agnes said.

"Whatever," said Victor. "She'll find out."

The kids grinned like they'd screwed her, or like they'd filled the evaluations with jokes. "You have to take those seriously," Joan said.

"Too late," Lula chirped.

Joan's hands closed into fists. She'd come back for the kids. She was ready to be good, no matter how screwed she was, and they'd betrayed her? "You already handed them in?"

"Yup," said Lula.

"Ms. Vole." Agnes was smiling. "Don't freak."

"'Joan Vole is her own person,'" Victor recited. "'The kind of person HR might not love, to put it bluntly.'" Joan's hands cemented to the guitar. The video was the ruin of her old life. This time in the classroom was supposed to be the last good work she'd ever perform. "'But for us creative summer students, Joan Vole is the best teacher we've ever had.'"

They erupted into nervous giggles, watching her. "We all said stuff like that," Agnes said. "Don't flip out. Sorry."

"Why would I flip out?" Joan's voice echoed as though her mouth was a chamber. Were they being serious? They were so giddy she couldn't tell. Her mind was still fuzzy from rounds of pleasure, from sleeping, even if briefly, beside someone who'd made her come.

"Guys, look, she's happy," Agnes said.

Joan turned away, pretending to focus on balancing the dreadnought against the piano bench. She could barely steady the instrument. They really liked her? The students studied their notebooks, ignoring the emotion that must've splashed her face. "Agnes," Joan said, the idea dawning as she spoke the words. "Would you play your song for us?"

Agnes tipped her head back. "Wait, really?"

"Yes," Joan said, glowing for this little girl—because that was what she was, so wide-eyed, unsure, even now, about her own talent, even after years of winning competitions and collecting praise. "We'd love to hear it."

Victor clapped, his mouth open in silent wonder. Agnes freed the watermelon from her bag and placed it on her knees. Her hand trembled as she set up the first chord. And then she played.

Her voice was clearer this time, the cloud of shyness gone. Sounding even younger than she was. When she sang that her friend was made of the best materials, her voice snapped, like the friend was gone now, like all was over. There was sorrow in Agnes's soft voice that hadn't been there last time, a dampness sagging the tribute, and it struck Joan for the first time how lonely it was to sing a song to someone who couldn't sing one back, and how that was the case with any song—you sang and you received no song. Didn't even expect it, wrote new songs, again and again, without hope of reciprocity. All your decades writing songs, and no song ever came back. Her eyes stung. She swallowed.

When Agnes finished, nodding the way she must've when

she crushed a recital, Joan and the kids cheered, frothing up the energy of an audience much bigger than three. Agnes sat back.

"Agnes," Joan said. She would speak plainly. Just say the truth. "Your song works."

"No." Agnes leaned away from the compliment like it was a slap. Joan hadn't been kind enough.

"I'm serious." Joan tried to smooth her voice, make it syrupy and nice. "You've taken this material that's meant to sell a consumer on his purchase and invested it with emotion. I never thought of that kind of turn. It's actually genius."

Agnes hid her face in her shoulder. Victor leaned over and hugged her, his forelock tumbling over his eyes. Even Lula was relaxed for the first time. And then, Georgina's voice, murmuring in the hall.

A perfect time for a visit. Joan's best moment. Georgina pushed open the door. Joan could at least prove herself before the axe fell so she wouldn't be remembered as a total monster.

But there, beside Georgina, in a pool of calm elegance, stood Paige. That face. Perennially fresh and curious, even after all that had happened, shiny eyes tracking Joan. Paige was here.

She wore a turtleneck and sage houndstooth slacks—classic Paige: a touch eccentric, yet glamorous, expensive. There was natural grace in her burgundy turtleneck, her eyes and mole and hair so dark that her head was like a charcoal drawing. That hair gathered in a loopy bundle, that slim nose, that elastic mouth: the hallmarks of Joan's old life. Her friend. A muscle sprang loose. Paige was here. In Virginia. And, confusingly, she was beaming at Joan.

"Oh, hello," Georgina said, gliding in with Paige behind. "I'm sorry if we disturbed you. I would've warned you, Joan, but your phone. I was just giving Ms. Serratt a tour." That voice full of apology—air eased out of Joan. "Hello, kids. We have a guest on site. Ms. Serratt was touring nearby and offered to stop over. She heard about our good work." Georgina patted Paige. "She asked to look around in case she might support the program down the road."

A chirp popped from Joan, too loud. Georgina glanced at her over the heads of the kids, brow crinkling.

"Hi, Joan," Paige said, voice reedy. The teens looked at Joan, cheeks tightening in attention.

"Oh!" said Georgina. "You know each other."

"Of course," Paige said. "We're colleagues."

Paige wasn't surprised Joan was here—but of course this was no accident. The smell of pine filled the room, crisp needles, like Paige had slept in a forest.

"Thank you, Georgina. Joan." Paige's voice was high and solicitous. "It's great to be here."

"I love your work," Victor breathed.

"Thank you." Paige secured her lips over her small, even teeth. She hated compliments, or any fan engagement. This was her grimace saved for empty venues, breakups weathered with obscene grace, and, once, the removal of a cyst—that translucent lump so ungainly it must've flown onto her shoulder from some uglier soul.

"All right now," Georgina said, backing toward the door. "Ms. Serratt had better be on her way. We can't wear out her generosity."

Paige hesitated, checking Joan, and then turned to exit. As her body spun away, her mouth disappeared behind her turtleneck, her expression turning unknowable. As she slipped out, she raised one eye to Joan, glinting. Joan's feet twitched as they held her, somehow, to the floor.

The door closed. Joan grabbed the dreadnought. Holding it was all that kept her from falling into a shuddering mess. In a few minutes, maybe, please, Paige would be out on Route 29, far enough away that Joan could relax, this surreal, fucked moment finally over. Joan blinked at the afterimage of Paige's features, her mole, emblazoned.

"I wanted her to stay," Victor said. Joan cramped through with a pang. She teetered. She wanted that, too, if only for a minute. Just to gaze longer at her old friend, to exchange a few mundane words.

"Why weren't you happy to see her or whatever?" asked Lula. "Victor said you're friends."

"Not exactly." Joan slumped on the piano stool. She had to distract them, had to collect herself. "Listen, everyone. We never properly discussed 'Rail Rat.'"

The kids cuddled on the beanbags, tipping their chins toward her like funny little satellites. "We don't know who wrote that song or why. It could've been written by anyone for any reason." She caught her breath. "Maybe a woman wrote it as a critique of songs where women are disposable. Or maybe it was written by some dick who hates that no one loves him. I went back through possible origins on message boards and blogs."

"Like what?" asked Agnes.

"Some say there's a giant rat living along the tracks between Clemson and Toccoa. That he comes out for the air horn. There's a photo, but it's blurry."

"Sick," breathed Victor.

Joan's voice loosened. Soon she'd finish class, and could find Sparrow, jump back on that plastic mattress, and melt down into another session, forget everything. "People say they saw a man from the train who resembled a rat because of the fluff on his arms. Or some say there was a stand of dead buckeyes on the side of a peak in Tennessee, shaped like a rat. A man in a Cessna spotted it. It shook its tail at night."

"Which is the song, do you think?" asked Agnes. There was a new quality to her voice, a pull.

A sigh escaped Joan. The perfect question. "All of them are the song."

"It can't be all of them." Lula said. "A man and a rat and a dumb bunch of plants?"

"Listen to what you're saying. Rail Rat is a man and a rat. You picture him that way, Lula. And me too." Lula on her bed at home, conjuring a man with a hamster's soft head, a guinea pig's voice, a mole's sea star nose.

"I guess." A smile muscled up those pasty lips.

"The song was born because all those ideas were out there, spinning in the communal imagination. And the threads tangled together on their own, without human interference." She could almost convince herself that was how the song had happened.

Agnes's neck grew straight and tall. "I can see the appeal. To write a song no one wrote."

"Idiot," Lula said. "That's not the point."

"It is, though," Agnes said, her voice hushed and thrilled. A tingle raced up Joan's spine. "It's the only way to forget who made it."

"Exactly," breathed Joan.

Agnes was vivid-eyed, fiery bangs standing up, like she might scream, or bite.

*

The students gone, Joan remained, dangling, in the room. She punched dust from the beanbags, gathered Lula's gummy worms, their tricolors faded. She made the room as tidy as possible in its musty, mildewed slouch, but once it sparkled, she continued tidying and adjusting. She set the dreadnought carefully on the piano bench, like she was putting it to bed—Paige must've noticed it, since she expressed an annoying affection for even the most useless guitar. Joan's limbs twinged at the idea of leaving the room. As long as she was between walls and under the compressing force of a roof, she was okay.

Finally, she left. Stepping into the afternoon, the air was too open, the sky infinite—how did people walk around under all this atmosphere, their bodies fragile sticks, without getting sucked up into the void? She hadn't made it halfway across the quad when she clocked, way down the field, Paige and Chester in conversation. She halted in the damp grass.

From this distance, she couldn't hear them, and they hadn't noticed her yet. Chester leaned into Paige, his back hunched. Joan was cut with the urge to run between them, remind Chester it was Joan's music he'd only recently admired. But that was dumb. Paige's hands moved too quickly, like she was brushing away a cloud of flies. Joan kept her feet firmly in the grass as though she was at all safe here, in the middle of the field, spotlighted by golden hour.

Paige gestured Joan over. Pulled across the lawn by her old life, Joan found herself ensconced in the threesome, the eager heat of Chester's breath on her cheeks, so turned on was he by discourse with a celebrity. Though that was mean, probably; that was simpleminded. Maybe they had a true connection, though Paige wore her most guarded, professional face. The expression that, if ever turned on Joan, would kill her.

"I'd better talk to Joan," Paige said.

"Glad you two made up." Chester tipped his chin. Joan returned a blank stare, and he slunk off.

As soon as he turned away, Paige thrust her arms around Joan's neck. Joan stumbled back as she braced herself to bear the sudden weight. "Joan," Paige said, wiry arms like steel around Joan's throat, strangling. "Jesus, you're here. I was wasted. You know I was wasted, right?"

Joan forced a hand between her neck and Paige's arm. Her throat opened, and she caught a breath. "Hey." In Paige's arms, Joan stiffened.

Paige squeezed so hard she eked the last stale breath from Joan's lungs. "Your smell. Your fucking smell." She sighed. "It's too much."

"Yes, thanks." Joan squirmed out of the embrace and stepped back. Paige's face cast such a light. Joan squinted and squirmed under it. "What's happening with you?" She had to know every minute of the last three weeks. For twenty years she'd known every detail of Paige's life, and she rushed with sorrow not to know anymore. The cool green light of afternoon fell across Paige's cheeks. Joan had never seen such fresh light on her friend.

"I found you." Paige's voice broke, eyes showing veins in a pretty red web. "I can't believe you're here." She shook her head at the vines hanging into the path, this wet tangled landscape that was alien to both of them. "In Virginia?"

"I've been here the whole time." Joan felt she'd been here months, years.

"I didn't know." Paige rubbed her forehead so hard she left a mark. "I went to your apartment that night. I thought. Well— never mind."

A rock in the face. The knowledge, slamming Joan and knocking free her teeth. Of course, when Joan disappeared, that was what Paige had thought. The Martin, abandoned. Her belongings in the trash. The garlic cloves huddled by the stove-top, scraps of peels blowing from end to end of the kitchen floor. Her knife on the cutting board. Joan had forgotten she'd given Paige a key. Paige had never used it in the two years Joan had lived in Coney Island.

And why hadn't Joan killed herself? Plenty of people did for less. Was she so selfish that the idea had never crossed her mind? But leaving New York was enough like dying, rolling over the Verrazano and into the branching highway choices, knowing she'd never see the city again, not Paige, not anyone she'd known there. She'd left the beach and her towering slab apartment building and her landlord's surprisingly patient caresses and the Gonewriters' Collective and her venues and the Martin and sex and music. She'd left forever once before, already knew a city and a life, a collection of friends and family, could vanish after one drive. She'd never again see the beachfront aquarium or the webbed tower of the Parachute Jump or the clot of pigeons eddying on the corner of Ocean Parkway. She'd never again sing at the Bulkhead Café or Deep Under or Fame Hound Music Hall. She'd never cross Brighton Beach at sunrise or the Lower East Side at dusk, pushing past shimmering button-downs, gnawing a crepe.

"Why are you here?" She didn't know how to stand before Paige—steadied to run, exposed and vulnerable? Should she have indulged the hug? That mole, those eyes, so vivid she wanted to scream.

Paige's focus skidded over the hills, where the sun lowered to meet them. Never in their lives had they stood together anywhere so spacious and remote. Buildings had packed them in, kept them insulated, the pulse of other people softening the noise of their singular connection. Joan had never noticed how bony Paige's shoulders were, pushing the wool of the turtleneck, or maybe that was new. A divot had formed at the corner of her mouth: worry, maybe, or malnourishment.

"I had to see you," Paige said. "I've been dying since Friday.

This was my first day off tour." She bounced in her strappy sandals. "I need to talk to you."

Joan's chest opened—she'd missed Paige terribly. "You want to get married?"

Paige laughed, too high-pitched, too long.

This was deranged. Paige was giving her nothing. Joan teetered on her legs. "Are you messing with me? You hate me now."

"What?" That face, all innocence, strained around the jaw. "I could never hate you."

Joan hugged herself. "Then why did you talk about me at the Fillmore?"

Paige flapped her hands like it was nothing. But they flapped too long and too erratically, tendons standing out like cords in her forearms. "Forget that. That was bullshit. It was a misunderstanding. Please. Just let me talk to you."

The sun lowered one click as the shadow of Paige's nose stretched across her cheek, a dark arrow to her ear.

"Fine." Joan scanned the campus behind Paige. Paige's color was wan against the raging green, the way Joan looked when recording an album, abusing her voice all day, not sleeping, sacrificing social activity so she wouldn't go hoarse. Where could Joan take her? She couldn't bear Paige and Sparrow under one roof.

The cafeteria. The kids had already been dismissed, and the offerings were left out a little while in case the faculty wanted to buy dinner, which they never did. "Here. Let's get food."

Joan started up the hill, moving them away from Community Village. Paige fell in beside her, their footsteps quiet on the grass. Joan couldn't believe she was inches from the person who'd ruined her life—this slender, soft arm had ruined her life, this wool-clad shoulder, these crow's feet, this scrawny ass—but this was Paige. Her dear, lost friend.

They moved through lush waves of buttonweed and clover

and up the brick steps into the tall glass-enclosed cafeteria. Joan paid the old cashier—just five dollars each, cash. A lady aged and angry, left alone by busy children, commuting to the school from a trailer somewhere in the hills to perch on this stool and offer industrial meals. Joan and Paige hovered over the steam table—three different forms of potatoes, lumps of meat bathing in its own juices. Joan couldn't believe there'd been hot food steps away the entire time she'd been shuttered in Community Village like it was the last structure on earth. Back in New York she could rarely afford restaurants, so this was the most food she'd seen together in ages.

"Looks brown," Paige said.

"We have to be quick." When Joan failed to return from class, Sparrow would assume she'd freaked, which was exactly what Joan would've normally done—she might've even quit the camp and run if the night with Sparrow had occurred a few weeks ago. She hadn't experienced such attraction for years, not since the "Lakeshore" guy, hadn't been in any real danger of love all this time.

As Paige scooped scalloped potatoes and french fries and tater tots onto her plate, Joan studied her luminous skin, the soft set of her mouth. Perhaps Paige hadn't known the internet would piece together what she'd said onstage. She'd been drunk, after all, sleepless and obtuse. When Joan was onstage she entered another world, forgetting anyone she knew could hear, much less that handheld electronic eyes were recording.

An occasional random crossed through the cafeteria— stray students, workers at the college. Joan shuddered at each intrusion. Any of these people could be one of the millions who now knew.

She chose a table in the corner and sat with her back to the room. Green was the only color Joan could stomach anymore.

The brown of potatoes, the white of flatware, the peach of the cashier's cheeks were all too much, those muted tones a jangling rainbow compared to the roaring emerald beyond the glass. She pushed a fork into the soft body of a potato. She was a bear crawled out of hibernation, the rim of her vision fuzzy, jumping at any noise.

Paige handed Joan a plastic cup of water like Joan was a child. Joan gratefully clasped it, raising it to block out the room.

"How's your apartment?" Joan asked, hands on the greasy table. Even if one of Paige's yellow abstract paintings had been relocated to a different wall, any of her log-like modern cushions dented by the ass of a visitor, Joan had to know. "Have you seen the Gonewriters? Did anyone have a show? Has tour been intense?" However long it took to detail every event of the past three weeks, Joan was here for it.

Paige cocked her head back. "Why are you Ms. Nosy now? You never ask me shit."

"Yes, I do," Joan said. The smell of food was too rich, like a barnyard. "Of course I do." But maybe, actually, she didn't. Maybe she'd always just known. She flinched as someone blustered by within inches of her spine.

"How are you? That's the real question," Paige asked, concern sharpening her face.

"Me?" When was the last time anyone had asked her that? The answer spread like warm glue down the back of her skull. "I'm happy." The word glittered through her. It was true.

"Okay," Paige said, her voice strained. She set her hands on the vinyl tabletop. "We need to find a way out for you."

"With the verse?" Did Joan have to officially undo herself from the rights of the album? Sign some nondisclosure agreement?

"What?" Paige asked.

"The verse. That I was going to sing."

Paige shook her head, dazed. She didn't remember. "What? I came to apologize. And to get you out of this insane mess."

Was Paige really here, sitting over potatoes, in Virginia? Joan pushed her plate away. The potatoes were pale and soupy, like they'd been mixed with cream.

"*Real Men*." Paige thumped the table. "Joan. Did you not see?"

"I saw." Joan couldn't bear to think about the racist troll who loved her. "But why would you want to help me anyway? You think I'm a bad person."

Paige huffed a sigh like a teenager. "I told you, that was a misunderstanding. I didn't know what I was talking about." She fidgeted so high in her seat that her forehead bumped the light fixture. "Ow. Look. This is a disaster. It's a fucking travesty."

Joan missed her potatoes now, all the way across the table. At least before she'd had something to stab and mutilate. "Yeah."

"So why aren't you freaking out? You need to be freaking out. I raced down the second I could." Paige's cheeks were red, sunken.

"There's nothing to do." No one had asked Joan's permission to feature her. No one would indulge her request to remove herself. That was how the internet worked. It took what it wanted in its digital arms and sprinted off.

"There's always something to be done."

Joan's lips twisted. "You feel guilty."

"Yeah. I do. I fucking do." Moisture built in Paige's eyes. Joan should assure her it was all right, but it wasn't. "I've been planning, like, nonstop. And I think I've got it."

Even the words exhausted Joan. "Okay."

Paige slapped both hands on the table and leaned over the

sea of starch. "I bring you back to New York tonight, and you go on the show."

"What show?"

"*Real Men*, Joan. What do you think? They'll have you on in a heartbeat—they're just dying to have you on, I'm sure. Come back with me to New York tonight. We'll get you on next week. You explain your side to Chad Tolbert."

Joan had forgotten the troll's name. She hated to hear it, wanted to block her ears from ever receiving those syllables again. "Paige."

"No—listen. Listen. Don't freak out." She spread her arms and knocked her plate aside. "You explain your side. You're amazing, Joan. You're a renegade dream! There's no way he could twist your words. Even if you just tell him fuck you and piss on his microphone—it could work."

Joan could already see how *Real Men* would edit the encounter to make Joan into even more of a conservative shitbag. And even if the plan did work, just no. "I'd rather die."

"But here's the thing." Paige's voice rose. The sleepy cashier lifted her head, bleary, like she'd forgotten she was at work. "Even if it goes bad, at least you can milk it, right?"

The flavor of bile. "What?"

"I mean, at least you can gain some new audience, right? Squeeze some money out of it all, maybe get big in the wrong way first, but then you can pivot later, when people realize Tolbert's a dumbass, which, obviously?"

Cramps waved through her. "No fucking way."

"But Joan, ugh." Paige flapped her hands hopelessly, a bird unable to take off. "What will you do otherwise? You have no money. Let's be real. You're just hanging on. Right? I mean, how are you even still employed?"

A shudder ran through Joan. She was trying to forget how

much danger she was in. "You mean because you hinted to the world that I did something fucked?"

Paige's neck went red, blood crawling up her cheeks. "No. Forget that. I told you. I didn't—forget it. They'll fire you here any second. And who'll hire you after that? How will you make music?"

"I'm not exactly making music right now." The words clunked out like stones.

"What? Why? Because of all this shit?"

"No." Her voice scraped dry. "I just can't."

Paige leaned back, as though the condition could be contagious. "Do you have tendonitis or something? Or nodes?" She clasped her throat in sympathy.

"No." Joan felt the phantom pain of both afflictions. Any musician could. "Music is toxic for me."

Paige laughed, that rattling, old laugh that pained Joan. Couldn't they be back on the Coney Island beach, walking and talking for no reason, instead of holed up in this stinky cafeteria, not eating potatoes? "Shut up."

"I'm serious. I had to stop." The fluorescent tubes cast Paige's potatoes a sickly yellow.

"You're joking." She leaned back so far her chair tipped. "Joan, Jesus. How many people in the world have anything they'd be happy doing twelve hours a day? No one even fucks that much."

Joan picked at her arm. "Yeah, but it messed me up." But even as she said the words, they were so lame. What if she was simply an asshole? And would've been as a secretary, a lawyer, a deep-sea diver?

Paige's eye sockets pooled shadows. "That's the dumbest shit I've ever heard. This place made you crazy."

"No," Joan said softly. A wave of beef aroma drifted by.

Paige flattened her hands. "But in any case, you can't stay.

That's what I'm saying. And getting another job will be hard—right? Even, I'm sorry, impossible? We can agree on that?"

"Because of you." The heat of lava built in Joan's torso. Paige had fucked her. She'd totally fucked her. Drunk or not, on purpose or not, underestimating the capacity for the detail-orientation of internet trolls or not, Joan's life was over. And yeah, it was her own fault she'd hurt Carlotta, yeah, there'd been a close call with the tweet, but the fact remained: no one had found her out until Paige. She backed up, chair squeaking on the tiles.

Paige waved a hand at Joan, almost clipping her nose. "I'm trying to help here. You get a little exposure, you collect a chunk of cash. Enough to last a year or two—and that's huge, Joan. That would mean survival for you. In a year or two, the world will look different. People forget."

The bleakest possibility stormed behind Paige's face. Joan's throat coated in sour gunk. She couldn't swallow through it. She'd known how bad her situation was—of course she'd known. But seeing Paige watch her this way, eyes wet, mouth open, turned the knowledge heavy and real, cutting through muscle and fat as it dropped through her. "You don't think I'll survive this."

"Not really." Paige's voice was tiny.

"You're guilty, and this is how you'll set your mind at ease."

Paige closed her eyes, then opened them. She was suddenly as young as the night they'd met, in the dim orange of All Time Elodie's: that springy step, that dirty hair. "It's my fault. And now you've got to think practically."

Joan jumped up from the table. "No." A conservative racist incel audience was worse than death. All she wanted was to play music—that was it. The idea rattled through her, a perfect vibration. Just make her music again, divorced from this shit. Paige was right—who had anything they liked this much? "I'm never fucking doing that." She stormed out of the cafeteria.

24

JOAN BURST INTO THE NIGHTTIME HUMIDITY, WHOSE density never failed to startle. Paige was right behind. Joan slowed. She could never run from her friend.

They walked out into the campus, not saying a word. Every so often Paige swallowed a lungful of air, as though she only remembered to breathe at the last second before passing out. "But how will you live?" Paige murmured as they left the quad, her voice thin.

"That's my business." Joan would figure it out. She'd hang on here a little longer if she was lucky, if Meredith didn't march up to Georgina first chance she got, and after that, how would she make money? Three million views. What did that mean, in practical terms? How much of a slice of America was that? Tiny, percentage-wise, yet huge. A large city. Chicago, actually. And then there was *Real Men*, but since she didn't have statistics for that one, she could pretend her episode was the first ever not to go viral. Could she be a waitress on the Upper Peninsula anymore? Could she work in a gift shop in Norway? How would she even reach Norway if her job here was cut short? She was paid at the end in a lump sum.

Paige followed Joan on the most obscure route possible, through a second, scrubbier quad with kudzu reaching up the backs of buildings and jumping powerlines, dumpsters yawning, some student's Diet Coke planted upside down under a chokeberry bush. The whole campus was empty, but this forgotten quad was another level, like it was empty on move-in day, at graduation, like you'd happen upon it on your fiftieth reunion and wonder that you'd never seen it.

Once they broke through the shabby quad and into dimmer, more remote wilderness, Joan's lungs relaxed. The kids were in bed, these saturated fields empty of gawkers. And then, there, waving its arms over campus, was the tree Joan had spied on walks, but only from a distance. The tree was a towering mess on the clean-cropped lawn, as though whoever managed the grounds feared touching it. Muscled, tangled bark peeked through meaty leaves. But as they approached the canopy, stillness radiated.

"Can we go inside?" Paige asked, in such a soft voice Joan couldn't bear to deny her.

They peeled apart a cascade of waxy leaves and entered the open circle under the branches. Scabs of moonlight scattered over the soft floor.

"It's like nature church," Paige murmured, crunching into the circle.

Joan dropped down with her back against the trunk. The tent of leaves insulated them from the world outside. Paige sat facing her, cross-legged. Under the canopy, calm settled between them. The walk and the evening had tamed them. For the first time all night, Joan could forget the three million. Not even their past could seep through the leaves.

Paige's chin lowered, a hank of hair slipping from her elastic, slicing her face in half. They should talk. They were here, in this quiet at last, under the few stars visible through the thicket. Paige should apologize. Joan should apologize. They should leave everything perfect before Paige went home and their lives unfurled without each other.

And then Paige was sliding closer over the dead leaves, as though she'd read Joan's mind, getting cozy for what she had to say. She leaned in toward Joan, as though to speak, as though even in this most private and protected place they required yet more intimacy. When she got close enough, she tucked her muzzle into Joan's neck. And then she was kissing Joan's collarbone, small, soft kisses, like moths fluttering.

"What are you doing?" Joan's arms stiffened. Her waist tightened, her breasts brushing Paige's. What if Paige loved her? She got those shiny eyes, sometimes, after sex, in the moments of their intimacy that Joan preferred, when they talked, naked, not even touching. "Paige." The kisses climbed Joan's neck. The ants followed, tiny feet tickling all over, her flesh shuddering. "Come on." Joan's head went heavy. She'd never once managed to say no to fucking someone she didn't feel like fucking. Maybe, as a performer, she'd clung to the belief, evident and unquestioned, that her body had to be available to anyone always. "You said I took advantage of you."

"That was a thousand years ago." Paige's voice muffled into Joan's skin. "And I don't know. What I'm doing."

"Don't kiss me," Joan whispered. "I'm a dick."

"I know," breathed Paige.

And then the kisses were on Joan's throat and up the turn of her cheek. One popped, deafening, on her ear. Joan normally took pains not to cringe at Paige's ear kisses, but she couldn't help herself. The moment their lips met, Joan slackened. The kiss, as ever, was like eating apricots—never as flavorful as you hoped, the texture spongy and dry or else yielding too easily.

"Hey," Joan said, as gently as she could. "Paige."

Paige leaned back, watching Joan. "What? You don't like me anymore?"

Joan hesitated. She couldn't scare Paige away. The very idea fluttered panic into her. She hadn't given in all those times as a kindness to Paige. She'd given in to keep a depth of intimacy Paige wouldn't have offered otherwise. "I don't want this."

Darkness rushed in between them, cold and liquid, taking Joan's breath. Paige frowned. "Why not?"

"Really? You just spoke against me before thousands of people."

Paige's face crunched into a fist. "No, I didn't."

The wind rattled their tree tent, leaves clicking. "Paige."

"Whatever I said was stupid. Forget it, okay?" Her eyes shone. "Be here with me now." She set a hand on Joan's cheek. Her palm was so cold Joan had to force herself not to twitch out from under it. If only Joan could fall into Paige, sensory explosions detonating, transporting each other to another plane the way she had last night with Sparrow. If only they could've been taking care of each other that way for years. Or if there had never been the expectation at all. If Joan had even once been honest. Paige's hand drifted down Joan's cheek, catching on her jaw.

Joan seized Paige and shook her so Paige's hand fell off her cheek and Paige had to look her in the face. "Talk to me."

Paige's lip lifted to show her gums. So here came the apology. Paige was sorry; she'd been drunk onstage; she hadn't meant what she'd said. Their relationship had been murky, sure; they'd helped each other and fucked each other along the way. But who didn't? Especially in indie music at the end of the millennium. Their relationship hadn't been clouded in any vicious way, in any dark or exploitative way. It was only muddy in a human way, in an understandable, forgivable way. Paige raised the silver triangle of her chin. Her lips trembled as they parted. "I was nineteen."

No. Paige had been sixteen when they met. But—right. She'd been nineteen the first time they'd slept together. Joan had lost her virginity at fifteen to a middle-aged maintenance worker at school. She'd considered herself mature enough at the time, and still did. At nineteen she would've laughed at anyone who implied she was young, much less a child. "Paige," Joan said gently. "I'm not so much older than you."

"Six years is forever at that age." Paige breathed out her nose. "I'm not saying you fucked with me. I've just been thinking." She rubbed her forehead. "The Carlotta thing. It, like, made me think back to when we first got involved. I know it's not the same. And I know I was technically an adult and everything. But you were, like, my hero. You were killing it in music."

By twenty-two Joan had played a handful of storefront bars. "That's absurd."

Paige's eyes glittered. "You were living the life, Joan. Waitressing and playing and eating ramen and sleeping around, not coming home for days if you didn't feel like it. You were this free creature. You were perfect."

"Not exactly." She'd been hungry, panicked, desperately ambitious.

"You can't imagine how it felt learning a life like yours even existed." Paige's chest rose with a breath. "I worshipped you."

But Paige hadn't been a child, and Joan wasn't her teacher. Agnes, Victor, Lula lined up on their beanbags, waiting to learn. There was no comparison. "So you weren't just drunk that night."

Paige punched the ground. Leaves shattered under her fist. But her eyes were moist.

"You meant to tell on me," Joan said, realizing it was true as she spoke the words.

Paige reached across the broken leaves and clasped Joan's hands. Joan should not get mad. Talking about an experience was anyone's right. And Paige had protected Joan—she had. She could've named Joan, could've mentioned Love und Romance, or the fact that they'd fucked. Paige had every right to tell whoever she wanted whatever had happened to her, even if who she wanted to tell was three thousand people in Michigan. Joan swallowed a lump.

And now there was Sparrow, big-eyed heir apparent, with their puffy cheeks and fumbling at the pee lesson. Twenty years younger than Joan this time instead of six. And they'd even said they wanted to be a boy, wanted to redo their childhood. How stupid could Joan be? She was replaying the same fucked dynamic.

And then Paige was pushing against Joan with her pointy breasts, those breasts that hadn't seemed done growing when they'd met in the nineties but were. Those cones poking Joan were so familiar, safe and platonic, the opposite of Sparrow. Joan worried, as the skinny arms wrapped her, that Paige might try for sex. But this was just a hug, just a dry, sweet, platonic hug, and they lingered in it for a long time.

When they parted, Joan said, "I scared you." The magnitude of Joan's New York exit washed over her: Paige running all over Brooklyn, Joan's shit gone, the Martin.

Fatigue showed in Paige's wrinkles. She didn't even have to nod.

Leaving without explanation was the worst thing Joan had done. Almost as bad as what she'd done to Carlotta. She squeezed Paige's hands. She squinted, pulsing apologies with her palms. Apologies for the Martin on the street, the surest sign of death she could've offered, her empty apartment, the garlic, the weeks of silence. One day she might be able to make it up to Paige, but probably not. And she'd have to live with that.

25

JOAN LED PAIGE BACK THROUGH CAMPUS TOWARD HER CAR,
over the hill with the horses, between paddocks. The night was
dense, forcing its humidity against them. Joan wished it would
push harder, a wet gust, that their steps would slow to nothing,
that the walk would take a thousand years, forever. The hum of
cicadas muddled her mind, and she scraped it for a shred of logic.
What would a rational, calm, sane person do? Probably Paige
was right. If Joan went on *Real Men*, she could disappear after.
She could make it to Norway and live for years on her profits
while she ferreted out a new life. She'd suffer a couple of months
in the worst of spotlights before the coziness of anonymity forever. And there was comfort in someone else deciding the plan:
good, relaxing, like Joan could let Paige carry the remainder of
her life forward. But she couldn't stand the idea of the show and
couldn't bear leaving here, even if staying only meant angering
Georgina and scaring children. The sun was down, but the sky
remained a navy velvet. Voices sounded low on the hillside.

Approaching the pastures, they found Chester leaning

against a fence, the rest of the teachers murmuring in a stand of trees like fretting birds. Joan froze. Every time these people looked at her or talked to her from now on, they'd see a monster.

"Joan," called Chester. "Your friend's still here."

Joan's heart skidded as the group stepped into the light, all watching Paige. Except Sparrow, who turned when Joan emerged. "Joan," they cried, their voice bright and clear. Paige turned to Joan, head tipped.

Sparrow rushed up to grab Joan's elbow. The nerves in Joan's arm rioted, like the touch was a move, like they'd fuck right here. Sparrow whispered, "I've been working on them."

Chester opened his arms to Paige. "I hope you've enjoyed our little paradise. Willie is such a fan."

Paige wrenched her gaze away from Joan to turn to Sparrow. Sparrow released Joan and melted back into the group.

"I love the new single from *Guileless Storm*," Willie said. "And, obviously, every track on *Pink Haven*." He walked with swagger, watching Paige with intense scrutiny, like he could pin her with his gaze. Joan spiked with jealousy. His beard, his tattoos, his woman's eyelashes. He should've been her fan. The thought flashed, hot and mean. She shook it away.

"Yes," said Joan. "Paige is a phenomenon."

Paige stood straight-backed and easy through the assessment, in a cone of moonlight.

"The chick from 'Lakeshore,'" said Chester, as though they needed context, as though they hadn't all just watched the Fillmore video.

"What's 'Lakeshore'?" asked Meredith, fidgeting with her fingers.

"Joan's most famous song. Doy," said Sparrow, voice pinging up from the recesses of the group.

"Play it for us, Joan," said Chester.

Joan stepped toward the woods. "We should head back to the dorms. Paige has a long drive." Joan could see her off, then find Sparrow. Now that they were so close, Joan pulled toward them. In an hour they could be in bed again. Her nerves lit and jangled.

"Yes, play it," Sparrow said. "Joan, you owe us. From the Night of Sharing."

"Another time," said Joan, meaning never.

"Please," Sparrow said.

Meredith turned to Paige. She said, her voice easy, "We all shared work. Every one of us but Joan."

"Is that right?" Paige raised her eyebrows to match Meredith's. "Every last one of them but you, Joan?"

The teachers stared at Paige from across the dark lawn, this motley group Joan had spent weeks with, staring at her best friend. That Paige was standing here, on this dark hillside that Joan had wandered for hours alone, made Joan itch.

"Maybe it would be good for you to play." Paige bounced on her toes. "You need to get back in practice."

"But it's time to go," Joan said. At the dorms, she'd admit she was remaining in Virginia, that she'd never go on *Real Men*.

"We have time for one song, I guess," Paige said, peering off over the trees as though judging the distance back to Brooklyn. "And withholding isn't very fair, now, is it?"

Joan's feet sank into the earth. Because she hadn't shared. Maybe somewhere, subconsciously, she'd thought standing back was a kindness, that if the other teachers heard her sing, they'd despair at the gap in talent. Damp grass squeaked underfoot.

"I don't have my guitar." She'd never perform a cappella. Her voice alone couldn't carry a song.

Paige vanished into the furry dark.

"Don't," Joan called, but the woods returned nothing.

The teachers stared at Joan, awaiting her next move. She backed out of their gaze and retreated to the pasture. The moment their attention was off her, she washed in relief. She leaned against the fence, splinters scraping her forearms.

Cobra Face trotted over, and she stroked his chocolate neck, her hand gliding down its ridge. His pulse was a mouse loose under his skin.

Sparrow appeared beside her, their hands on the other side of Cobra Face's neck. "I missed you," they whispered.

The fuzzy edge of their voice ran straight through Joan to her groin. "Me too." Their breath mixed. Joan could almost see it: the hazy heat pulsing up from their centers.

That sweet face in darkness, across the hide of that muscled neck. Joan longed to kiss them, to grab them by the waist, but as she reached out, a murmur rose from the teachers.

Paige crested the hill with a guitar upright before her. Joan deserted Cobra Face, not turning to see if Sparrow followed. But when Paige handed over the neck of the instrument, it was the Martin, glossy chestnut brown, slim like Joan, her old friend, suspended between them, like an ex wearing a coat of shiny unknowability at the edge of a party. She was shocked Paige had brought it all the way to Virginia, angry at Joan as she was. Paige presented it like a feast. She, too, loved parlors. Joan had instilled that taste in her, at least. Joan should've offered it to her years ago.

Joan buzzed as she accepted the guitar, fingers heating as they met lacquer. Here were the bone nuts and saddle, the marked, old wood. She was onstage again, heat coiling between bladder and throat, no matter if there were two hundred people watching or five. Sparrow settled before her, chin tipped up.

Joan considered protesting as her fingers met the cool wood of the soundboard. She could claim she'd lost her voice, which was raspy on a good day—early cigarettes had marinated her perfectly, as her caramel tone would've been insipid without its smoke. But maybe she should see if she could even play anymore. Maybe she could overwrite the bullshit these people knew about her. And, besides, the Martin was in her hands. Her Martin, which she hadn't played in weeks, magnitudes longer than she'd ever gone without urging songs from it.

The other teachers sank into the grass. Joan was flooded with that preshow sense of having arrived for a position no one else could fill. Even if the world mocked her publicly for her antics, privately for her pissing, they'd shut up and listen when she played. So that made her their clown? So what.

She set her foot on a rock. The hip of her old friend jigsawed neatly onto her thigh, the wood solid and old, the nitrocellulose still tight, alive and breathing as the Martin breathed. She stroked the checking on the body and her torso relaxed. She often marveled at how solid guitars were for being flaps of wood bent and pasted together. The chill of night had thrown the strings out of tune. She turned the pegs and adjusted each note. Her Martin obeyed.

She snapped her wrist down over the strings. Sound filled the forest, that old, daily twang. Playing unplugged was nice for a change, that precise, direct ring of aged wood, so different from the voice of any other instrument on earth. Her child. How she'd missed it.

The group leaned forward, their heads lined up in a circle under her. Standing above them made a kind of stage. Heat knifed Joan's core.

"'Lakeshore,'" Sparrow whispered, because they could read the song from just that chord. And why not a song that was fifteen years old, that was not about the woman sitting before her, though the world thought it was? Why not walk directly into the stickiest, most painful performance the group could solicit? They'd forced her to play, so let her play.

"And the city is behind me, the black brightened city, the lake is before me, the flat colored lake." She sang the raspy chant that opened the song, the icing on the cake of fast, complicated chord grabs and hammer-ons. Everyone said Joan's music was stripped down, but every note of every chord was exactly how she wanted it for her messy, fierce sound. The parlor was a relief after the dreadnought, so much more focused, the mellow of the mahogany, its range such a better complement to human vocals. She turned tender to sing again, especially her best, most urgent song. "And my girl's stepping toward me, her feet in the sand. My girl's getting close but I don't turn my head. I'm caught here already between lake and skyscrapers, I'm caught here on Lakeshore, I'm waiting for her." *Waiting* broke into three strained notes, opening her up, like a boy's voice cracking for the first time. Joan had missed this song with her whole body. Maybe if she'd played it at Love und Romance the last weeks would've been different. If only she'd had one final session of glory and talent lurching out of her, one five-minute chunk where she was fierce and perfect, which she could've nursed like a dwindling mint on her cruel bed in Community Village these last weeks.

The moon had gathered clouds, its globe shimmering through the haze like a lamp in a scarf. Sparrow rested back on their arms, watching Joan with eyes lidded and smoky, their stare so pointed that half the teachers watched Sparrow instead of Joan. Paige glanced at Sparrow, fidgeting and frowning.

The song ran out of Joan in a surge, issuing from somewhere remote, her body the arrival station. "Before she can reach me I spin around slowly, I spin around quickly and grab at her feet. She looks at me sweetly, she looks at me frightened, she looks with a legion of love in her eyes. Then we're in the sand rolling, our bodies together, writhing like fish that fell dry from the lake." Joan's fingertips were raw, like they'd been sliced by the buzzing coils, as though her calluses could have atrophied in so short a time. She lived inside her elastic, emphatic growl, the voice of a mean teenager singing for that lost Chicago guy and the girl she'd made him, and not only for him but for the Joan who'd believed, with at least one chunk of her heart, that she could fit love into her life. That she could dash to the Midwest and snatch it in gulps without torpedoing her career, that love wouldn't spread like ink through everything, that she wouldn't have to pause songwriting every five minutes to lie in bed and picture his bony vulture face, that her lyrics wouldn't turn cheesy and in the clouds, that he'd never request more of her time. Below her was Sparrow's face, as wide and hungry as the guy's, in the shadows, with that set to their jaw they'd worn since Paige's arrival.

She sang about the seagull landing on her back, how he buried his legs in her skin and pecked through her hair, how she didn't feel him because of the pleasure building in her gut, so taut it ached. She sang about how her girl didn't know Joan was coming with the seagull on her back, how Joan bit down on her scream, not because she cared if a stranger surprised them—in fact, she longed for salvation from the unbearable flame in her, needed it snuffed—but because she couldn't stand for the girl to stop. Not until she'd ridden her hard for hours, left them bruised and ragged. Her voice dipped out of singing and into the speaking whisper that made the song because her cadence trafficked directly to the listener's groin. "And just as the claws on my shoulders slip deeper, and just as the girl underneath me cries out, I know that I'll leave her, but for now it won't matter, with my girl's face below breaking open with joy, with the sand on my knees and my mouth and my teeth, when the gull flies away his feet stay in my back."

She strummed a wordless round, and then, with the hard stroke of the last chord, let the Martin spring from her hands and fall on the cushion of wet Virginia grass.

The Martin lay still, its ivory pickguard pooling moonlight, Joan wet and vibrating from the notes still ringing through her. She was tired in a good way, in a beautiful way, like she'd swum for miles in a cold gray sea. The group broke into applause, the sound so loud her shoes slid back in the grass. Willie reddened as he banged his paws together. Only the whites of Chester's eyes showed, as though the song had jerked him off. He slung his head back, smug and proprietary. Sparrow shook their head, mouth agape. "Joan," they said. "Jesus." Joan bowed her head, hiding the color in her cheeks.

"That's your song?" Meredith asked Paige. People rarely addressed Joan directly about her music, as though she was an idiot savant. "I want a song like that."

"You can't have mine," Paige said.

"You can have a book about horses that you wrote yourself," Joan offered.

Meredith snorted, but her cheeks had high color. She was galvanized. They all were. Steam rose off the teachers, a manic energy. The song had won them over—not Joan, not weeks of Joan. Her music was better than she was. Her muscles flexed like she could spring into the sky. She could do this. She could still do this.

"So." Sparrow's voice pushed over Chester's chatter. "That song's about Paige?"

"That's what everyone says." Paige glanced at Joan. At least the song had made Paige happy. What else mattered? "Joan never talks about her music."

There was an edge of warning in Paige's voice. Besides, the statement was false. All Joan and Paige talked about was music. "I talk about my music."

"Not the inspirations," Paige said.

"No one asked me."

"You did everything in that song?" Sparrow pushed the wedge of hair off their forehead. It sprang back like blond cake. They spoke to Paige but watched Joan. "You were with Joan, like, romantically? Like by Lake Michigan? In public?"

"Not exactly." Paige squinted at Sparrow, as though she could squint them out of existence.

"Did you live in Chicago?" Sparrow asked, voice strained. "Like the girl in the song? Were you and Joan in a long-distance relationship?"

Paige straightened her neck, head stacked high like a prize. "Joan is a figurative writer."

"How is the song figurative?" asked Sparrow.

"Some of it's figurative," Joan said. "Like the eclairs."

"Yes, the eclairs," shouted Chester. "Such woeful chocolate icing. Such anemic filling." He'd thought carefully about Joan's random image, even if he'd never known Joan's work before. She softened.

"I don't know," Paige said, her voice small. Even the cicadas hushed, the wind dying to a cloying swish. Dark curls interrupted the white length of her neck as she searched the sky for an answer. Paige flummoxed was such an unreal phenomenon that Joan went still all over. "I guess, if I have to explain it, Chicago is, I don't know. The city of the heart. Cold and huge and glamorous." Paige pushed up the twigs of her fingers. "But homey, sort of. Not real like New York is real. Everyone knows someone in Chicago, but no one actually lives there. And the distance is the psychic distance in a relationship. That exists no matter how close you ever get to another person."

Paige had done so many backflips to make sense of how the song could be about her. Joan went queasy at the thought of her listening to it, studying the Reddit thread, running this pretty speech over in her head, twisting the meaning into a shape for herself.

"Joan doesn't write about what she exactly means." Paige's mole flashed like a secret. "She gives us the song, seagulls and all. And it's ours to make sense of."

"And the sense you make," Sparrow said, rising on their heels, "is that Joan Vole is secretly in love with you, though she doesn't even want to date you."

"Damn, Sparrow," Willie whispered.

"Sparrow," Joan said, the word hoarse. She'd never heard this crisp tone in Sparrow's voice before, that slim, possessive blade. She liked it.

"It's more complicated than that."

Paige withered on the grass. Joan would've thought defeat impossible with all her beauty and fame, all the ferociousness of her teen years, but look at her shoulders, sunken, her gaze, diffused. Joan's presence had crushed her.

Paige had acted correctly at the Fillmore. Joan never would've seen the darkness between them if Paige hadn't taken extreme action. The thought left a greasy sheen on her tongue. If she'd slept with Paige, again and again for years, because she was afraid to say no, that was pathetic. But worse was that she'd done so while Paige was younger and weaker. Joan hadn't only wanted affirmation, but affirmation without challenge, from a kid who considered any scrappy music career the coolest life on earth, who couldn't differentiate between a dive bar and Carnegie Hall, the sale of a few hand-pressed records and actual fame, not even when, years later, it stampeded toward her.

"Ooh." Chester's focus bounced between Sparrow and Paige.

"Shut up, Chester," Meredith said, setting a protective hand on Sparrow's knee.

It was clear from Sparrow's bland, steady expression that they'd never heard Paige's songs, not even by accident, that lions and rainfalls had never looped in their head in bouncy, plastic tones, that they were immune to Paige's charm.

"Let's go," said Joan. The cicadas' song rose from the bushes. "It's late." She got up, collected the Martin, and stepped toward the road. No one budged. Meredith whispered to Sparrow in low tones, but the blandishments, whatever they were, failed to loosen Sparrow's posture.

"You should know," Paige told Sparrow, her voice low. "I'm taking Joan back to New York. She's had a wonderful time here, I'm sure."

"You're leaving?" Sparrow turned to Joan, tendons high in their neck. "Wait. Joan?"

"I'll talk to you later, Sparrow." Joan placed her hand on Paige's back. Her spine was frozen under her turtleneck, like she'd died. Joan's hand urged to pull away, but she forced herself to hold it steady. She owed Paige a conversation. As deeply as the idea shuddered through her bones, this was right. "I'm going to speak to Paige for a minute."

Sparrow's eyes locked on Joan's—some hot feeling, simmering. They ripped their focus off and hurried out into the dark field. Joan locked her feet to the earth to keep from chasing.

*

Joan led Paige away into the wilds of English ivy and clover, bats thrusting themselves at the sky like frenzied scraps of paper. She held the Martin to her chest like someone might rip it from her. She didn't know where she was going. Not until she'd herded Paige down the hill, past the ghosts of horses under starlight, did she remember the benchless gazebo by Community Village, its hexagonal walls higher than most, shadowed and private. Its silhouette a thumb at the foot of the hill. No one would find them there, in the most forgotten leisure structure on the planet. She ducked into the doorway.

Paige leaned against the wall opposite Joan. Her long body clarified as Joan adjusted to the thick, interior dark. Joan would be gentle, keep tonight an easy memory, filling this slatted structure with good feelings: a place to visit when they missed each other. She leaned the Martin beside Paige, giving it back.

"It's uncanny." Paige's cheeks caught the moonlight through the slats.

"What?" Joan asked, a dark syrup seeping through her.

"How much she looks like Benjy."

By repressing the name of the "Lakeshore" guy, Joan had trained herself to melt on hearing it. "How do you know about Benjy?"

"Joan, come on. You were so obvious."

"I wasn't." Her cheeks scorched. "Anyway, they don't at all. Look like him."

"Only in the face. Benjy was much taller, obviously. And skinnier."

Benjy and Sparrow looked nothing alike, not as a whole and not piecemeal, each feature exactly opposite: Sparrow's eyes bigger, their nose blunter, their eyelashes longer, their color ruddier, their skin clearer, their hair fair instead of black. The way they moved: Benjy like a vulture, Sparrow like a puppy.

The way they talked: Benjy languorous and pleasured, Sparrow so careful. The way they touched Joan: Benjy like he was starving, Sparrow tentatively, then melting into Joan as they moved as one. Benjy had watched over Joan with protective fear. Sparrow hardly glanced at her. Joan forced her voice quieter. The wooden structure had a churchy reverence. "You're provoking me."

A sad lift to Paige's lips. "If I were, you'd deserve it."

"Fair." If only Joan wanted to go back to New York with Paige. She could have the sunrise over Coney Island, her old apartment, probably, if she offered enough blow jobs. And the friendship. The money that might come—that would come—from going on *Real Men*. No matter how devastating it would be to offer herself to a troll, urging her toward lewd acts, at least she'd know exactly what everyone listening thought about her. And there'd be true freedom in its wake. "But you know they look nothing alike."

"It's you," Paige said, gaze steady on Joan. "You make them alike. It's the same energy."

Yes. Electric and terrified, burned to the ground by every touch.

Paige dragged her sleeves down over her hands. "Do you also talk to her all the time about wanting to piss on other people?" A wet catch in her voice.

"What?" But Joan didn't do that to Paige. She protected her. Years ago, she'd stopped sharing details.

Paige watched her hard, like she could see through her skull. "No matter where things were with us, you couldn't stop." She grabbed her arm and squeezed. Her fingers dug trenches in the flesh. "So you do that with Sparrow, too, right?" A lift at the end of the name, like she had to force herself to say it.

"No," Joan said.

Paige snorted. "I doubt that."

"I don't. I stopped doing that shit with guys anyway." And it wasn't because she was stuck out here. She hadn't longed for a random dude once, not in weeks.

"Why? Do you pee on her?"

If Joan had anticipated the question, maybe she could've braced herself. The heat rushed up her neck and into her cheeks before she could stop it. But she could never have stopped it. The answer was all over her face.

"Jesus." Paige stepped back into the dark recesses of the gazebo. "Is that what you wanted? Like, with me?"

Joan couldn't answer. Maybe, if she'd been an entirely different person, many years ago, she could've expressed her real feelings to Paige and received all she wanted, every need contained in one person. Though probably she never could've willed herself to fall in love. "I was afraid you'd think I was disgusting."

"Never," Paige whispered. "It's not even that weird."

The moment she said it, Joan wished she'd never asked. She couldn't consider the possibility of having been open enough to Paige to let her be everything, to have learned attraction somehow. Some other parallel life of joy and fulfillment, showing its face years too late. She bit her lip until the tension popped, iron heating her mouth. "I'm older than you. I should've been honest about what I needed."

"What do you need?" Paige's voice was so light it floated into darkness.

"To be your friend." The words were dumb. They clanked out of her like links on a rusty chain. "Plain friends." Maybe it sounded like rejection, but here was Paige, still, years after everyone else had fallen off. "I want that still."

Paige's expression knotted. "So you never wanted this?" An anemic gesture, a flap of the hand, at herself.

Joan ached to release the air between them. To tell Paige that yes, yes, of course, she was all Joan had ever wanted. "I'm sorry. I should've been clear with you." Joan had the power, the years.

For forever, Paige said nothing. She stared at Joan, eyes blazing, the darkest hue in the dim cylinder of the gazebo. So much swirling behind those eyes, and then a settling in them, an understanding. This was Joan's harm. The years of dishonesty. Paige hadn't been able to earmark, exactly, what had been off because Joan had hoarded the information. "Don't do that to this new girl." Paige's words were metal, clattering to the floor. "Or I'll kill you."

Light spread through Joan. Because she wouldn't. She'd already shown Sparrow sides of herself that she feared the most. She only had to keep being honest, all the way through. "Sparrow isn't a girl."

Paige's mouth slotted open, then shut. The whistle of a sigh, like old air, released. "I see."

Joan stepped toward Paige. She'd hug her, and they'd be friends. Exactly how it should've always been. She held out her arms.

Paige shrank back. Her voice wavered. "You're bleeding."

Joan touched her lip. The cut, hot under her fingertip. Paige spun around and was gone.

Joan hurried to the door cutout, calling after her. Paige's silhouette, on the crest of that dark hill, was slim and perfectly cut against the last light still stuck to the surface of the sky. She'd left the Martin. Joan was certain, already, that they'd never speak again.

26

JOAN LINGERED IN THE GAZEBO, ACROSS FROM THE shadow of the Martin. The moon sank, and the platform darkened. An hour passed, or two, and a gray mass of teachers crossed outside, a few feet away on the path, without noticing her, in a murmuring, close bundle. They shut themselves up in Community Village, the night extra silent now that the whole outdoors was empty.

Joan leaned back against the creaky wood. When she emerged from the gazebo, she'd have to find Paige's rental gone. She brushed the Martin with her hip. She wanted to stay up all night with it, remind herself of its curves and its voice. That she'd almost lost it, even to Paige, cramped her so hard she bent in half.

She deserted the wooden enclosure, passed by the parking lot, empty of the only car that mattered, the lamp in Sparrow's window off for the night. She couldn't stand to go back inside. To sit in the silence of a building full of people who knew what she'd done, who waited for others to find out so they could

joyfully condemn her. And Sparrow, all the more tragic for for-
giving Joan.

She climbed the hillside, carrying the Martin. The night
was pale with a mysterious glow. A mumble shook the sky, a
fizz. The clouds were full and puffy, afternoon clouds. A perfect
day's panorama with the colors tuned down to their dimmest.
A bright line, the scrawl of a highlighter, raced through a low
cloud and disappeared. Lightning, trapped in cotton islands.

In the pasture, the stallion trod the fence, from one end
to the other, restless, kicking earth. Joan settled on the grass
to watch his dark body push through the night. Head twitching back, stirring up a rich odor with his hooves. She leaned
her skull against the soft wood, and there, across the field, the
smudge of someone.

Sparrow was alone, cross-legged, edges clearing as Joan's
vision adjusted to the dark. "You're here," Joan called, stepping
closer.

"I figured you'd be back." The cicadas roared. Sparrow's
head bent.

Joan longed to curl with them on the grass, to feel their
belly against hers. But she had to be clear first. This time, she
would be perfectly clear. She sat down across from Sparrow. "I
have to be honest."

Sparrow turned their head, flashing their soft cheek.

Joan scooted closer, leaving a respectable distance between
them. Deciding was easier than following through. She looked
at Sparrow directly. "Paige and I aren't together. But we have a
history."

"I gathered." Sparrow drew a finger through the grass,
sounding the softest xylophone.

"We used to sleep together."

Sparrow nodded. See, this wasn't so bad. Joan had told the

348

truth, and so far it hadn't made Sparrow erupt in rage or sorrow or accuse Joan of being a predator.

"I'm not going back to New York." Joan filled with relief the moment the words were out, as though, even with Paige gone, she could still be wrenched away.

Sparrow's shoulders sank. "Okay."

"That's the good news." The words were syrup, stuck in her throat. "But also, I'm worried about this thing with you."

A gauzy cloud was dismissed, and the moonlight intensified. The taut shine of Sparrow's cheeks, the hard edge of their jaw. "Why?"

"You're so much younger." The wind pushed a clump of Joan's hair into her face. "It's a rough dynamic."

"Joan. What? I'm not a child."

There was Paige nineteen and there was Joan nineteen, a rabbit and a wolf. "You said you wanted to be a kid. Like, a little boy."

Sparrow's expression was blank. "What are you talking about?" They ripped out a handful of grass so hard they left a hole in the field.

"Remember?" Had they not said that? "When we were in the living room? And you were talking about your, like, transition?"

"What? Joan. I want a trans adolescence, not a real one. That's completely different."

Joan steadied her voice. "It's not your fault. This is a pattern for me." Ignoring the dynamics was what had gotten her in trouble. Lightning skittered above, cloud to cloud, so high it was silent. "I draw someone into an involvement that doesn't serve them. I let them believe what they want to believe, misuse my power and treat them like a prop." Probably it had all started with the fans. But here she was, doing the right thing at last. So she was old. So what? "So I want to be clear. If we do this, I have to be very careful."

Sparrow's head pushed back on their neck. "Your power?"

"Maybe how you acted when we had sex had something to do with that." Because it wasn't any coincidence in the end that Sparrow so happened to be the one person on earth who liked Joan's peeing. It was so much more logical that they'd gone along because they thought they had to, because they weren't a man, entitled to disgust. "I coerced you into going along with my shit." Here was what a person did, what Joan had never learned to do. A person spoke a hard-won truth, giving up what they wanted in sacrifice to a better self. A person didn't have to be an amoral, pleasure-seeking hound.

"You didn't coerce me into anything." Sparrow wiggled up-right. "I'm insanely stubborn. What turns you on turns me on. It was fun. This is fucking stupid." A blip of lightning lit Sparrow's jaw, that soft set. "Do you really feel, when you're actually talking with me, that I'm that much younger?"

Sparrow's head was soft, a cozy moon. Joan relaxed her brain and studied it. "No, actually."

"Did you really feel, when we fucked, that I didn't want it?"

At the word, Joan's nerves lit. "Never."

"There you go."

Joan lightened, like she could float up to the sky. "So you want this? Genuinely?"

Sparrow stared hard at Joan. "Of course I want this."

Wind in the grass, bugs, a deafening fuzz. "Because I come from this stupid world, where people don't really grow up. So it's hard for me to know what's healthy."

Sparrow snorted. "And I'm just some simpleminded school-teacher who could never understand a complex, deep-hearted musician?" But they were smiling.

"More like a dumb baby musician."

"I get it," Sparrow said. "Don't worry so much."

Joan had been obsessed with the worst in herself, which was only, really, the deepest flavor of narcissism. Maybe the scarier, better job was having a real relationship, making things good from the inside, the hard way.

She leaned forward and took Sparrow's shoulders in her hands. They were soft and sturdy, life pulsing through them, complicated processes tangling below the surface. Those cheeks, clear-edged and glowing against the night sky. She set her face on one, letting heat leave her and flow into Sparrow. She rushed through with the sense that all was right at last.

27

FOREVER HAD SEEMED TO PASS SINCE PAIGE HAD AP-
peared in Joan's classroom, but it hadn't even been twenty-
four hours. Impossible—a trick of squishy time. Joan arrived
to class with her Martin, having traded her linen outfit for a
T-shirt and worn-out denim shorts, nodded at the students,
perched and alert. They jumped from their seats to greet her,
chattering new ideas for songs. They were writing one together,
blindfolded, the words twisting down the page.

"That's perfect," Joan said, touching the paper that so many
hands had warped and creased with sweat.

She stationed herself on the piano bench, the Martin on her
knee. When she'd left New York, she could've gone anywhere.
She could've taken a job at a bar or a clam shack. But she'd
come to Virginia to teach songwriting. Even when she thought
she'd let go of music, she never really had.

And here were her kids. No matter what had happened last
night, they were here, scrunched against the wall, eyes on her
wherever she went. Lula, white folds of hair framing whiter

cheeks, concealing her secret assignations with goofy ditties about men. Victor, when motionless, just like a girl, all his dreams impossible, but somehow that was beautiful, the purity of hope crystallized in this pretty boy. And Agnes, uke strapped over her back. For the first time, with three eager heads lined up before her, Joan wanted to know everything: where they'd be living when she died, which lovers would desert them, what neighborhood trees they'd come to love. They were almost as old as Paige was when Joan first met her, which seemed impossible. They were so young, so easy to mold and fool and ruin. Paige must have once been as blank and eager, as willing at Joan's feet. A wave slapped through Joan, a cold shock.

"I'll open class with a song." Joan sat on the piano bench, facing the kids. She'd stayed up all night cycling through picking patterns—brutish, ornate, lifted—lyrics that were bald and cheesy, lyrics that were too cool to chance emotion, lyrics that weren't songs. She'd tried to make a song of Carlotta's tweet, taking a page from Agnes's book, but it had come out robotic astral goth shit ("plane of lyrical wonder"), had tried to recreate the graveyard spore dog song, had made songs from her lesson plans and the comments on her video ("Joan Vole Tuesday LES" had rhythm at least), but it had all flatlined. Finally she'd approached the one subject on earth she could logically hope to write about. The song was raw and stupid, but here she was, and if she wanted to sing something personal to the kids, she could only use the scraps she had.

Strumming the Martin vibrated her muscles and made her want to puke. The way, every time she walked onstage, she walked in step with the chance of failure, and that was the only way she manufactured enough adrenaline to try. This time she knew she was going to fail, and still, her fingers worked the strings.

The chords followed a simple progression: A, D, E, bridge hanging on B minor. Nothing off-key and haunting like "Lakeshore." No minor scales, no finger picking, no capo. Just a bright, simple folk song.

"Green weeks, green days, it's all I have to give you, babe, here in this place so far from anything I've known." The best song Joan had ever written she'd written for love, when her head was in just this place: steamy and frizzy and floating free. So, yes, she'd slacked off on practicing when she was with the "Lakeshore" guy. Yes, her calluses had softened, and emails from venues had gone unanswered. But she'd written the song that had made her career. The best song she'd ever write. "When I see your soft face, like a moon in this green place, I almost weep, it cuts too deep. I want to bathe you as you rest, splash my water on your chest, I almost weep, as you're next to me asleep." She strummed harder, her wrist sore. She was Jelly Who-Who, morphing into a sandwich and a fox. This was what she'd missed, this heart of her life. The snap of cold coils on her fingers, hand tight on the Martin's neck. She made up the lyrics as she went: "Long days, green haze, I miss you in a thousand ways, even from my crumbled fall, even while we share a wall." Her cheeks heated, her mouth stretching into mad patterns. Her knees drifted apart, shoulders softening and falling back. Her head, when she sang, became the head of the soft-dicked wolf, opening to a million teeth and a petal-pink tongue. The kids watched, mouths ajar, but she didn't care if the song was raw or cringey; she was throwing herself all the way into it, spine bending like rubber, voice breaking into her favorite scratchy register, like she'd been singing all night, which she had. "This is dumb, I hate to say, though I'm broken, torn and frayed, no matter what is wrong with me, no matter what our lives may be, that I love your every way."

She set the Martin down and faced the kids, who sat forward over their knees, tracking her every motion. She surged with the wild hope that they would find a life in music, a feeling like this one, right now, each kid in their own right. Lula in a neo-vaudeville revival; Victor, self-appointed moral messenger; and for Agnes, a true career, if that was what she wanted: deserved credit for songless songs. Songs that were song-free in a way Joan had never imagined. That they would each lose their love somewhere down the line, that music would fuck them, and then, at the last second, they'd push out a song and grab hold again, and then, even for one set, for one song, like now, they'd really sing. As a shadow crossed the threshold and Georgina lay her hand on Joan's wrist, nodding at her to stand, Joan hoped for their stardom with all the energy in her sinewy chest.

Acknowledgments

Thank you first and always to my faithful and brilliant agent, Samantha Shea, for editing this book for years and believing in an unusual project. Thank you to Kendall Storey, dream editor, for seeing the potential in this book and improving it dramatically with your ambitious and insightful edits. You opened up what it could be. To Kaiya Shang, my UK editor, for believing in me and giving amazing notes, for staying in touch and cheerleading for years. The book wouldn't be what it is without the three of you. I'm so lucky and so grateful. Thank you so much to Andrea Córdova, Rachel Fershleiser, Megan Fishmann, AJ Hendrickson, Laura Berry, Elizabeth Pankova, and Wah-Ming Chang. Thank you to Farjana Yasmin for the dream book cover. And to Julia Connolly and Sandra Casado for the dream U.K. cover. Lots of thanks to Susie Merry. Thanks also to Valerie Borchardt and Pauline Cochran. And to the entire teams at Catapult and Chatto & Windus and Georges Borchardt.

To the real-life music stars I'm so lucky to know, who tolerated my questions and were patient and illuminating (all mistakes are my own). For reading the entire book through a music lens and providing sage advice on the music layer, as well as craft: first, Anna Vogelzang, for such a careful, detailed read, and for teaching me so much. And for being the first to bring Joan's songs to life—such an eerie and beautiful experience. Second music reader, Josh Arnoudse, for brilliant insights into the music and story levels and for lending me your knowledge and talking me through every detail even while a man spilled his sandwich on us. To Raky Sastri, for the final music read, a blast of crucial knowledge at the finish line, and for so much consultation along the way. You play more instruments than anyone I know, to the chagrin of your dog but to my amazement.

For talking me through my musical queries, my friends Olivia Verdugo, Adam Brock, and Elisabeth Halliday-Quan. And those I got to meet along the way who were so generous to speak to a random person and share their knowledge: Paul Herzman, Jordan Perry, George Lam, Ruby Fulton, Robert Maril, Travis Thatcher, Leigh Isaac, and especially Cameron Knowler. Thank you to John Shakespear and Caitlin Watkins for interpreting Joan's songs, and to those who may in the future.

Thank you to my talented student Carson Oliver, master of slang, for advising on portions of this book. Thanks to Andrew Shield, Ib Tunby Gulbrandsen and Henning Johnsen for Norwegian knowledge. Thanks for help on internet blocking tech: Grant and Stefan Kremser (aka Spacehuhn). Thank you to Marion Belcher, horse consultant. Thank you to Margaret Ross, poet-genius, for talking to me about songs through the lens of poetry.

To the following heroes who read this book twice, very different drafts, and provided indispensable feedback: Sterling HolyWhiteMountain, Kate Folk, Brendan Bowles, Fatima

Kola, and Matthew Denton-Edmundson. To those who read full drafts and provided amazing advice: Adam Schorin, Josie Sigler, Ali Shapiro, Janice Shapiro, Mindy Chaffin, Taylor Grenfell, Mat Johnson, Jamel Brinkley, Devyn Defoe, Gothataone Moeng, Neha Chaudhary-Kamdar, Asiya Gaildon, Jamil Kochai, Evgeniya Dame, Nicole Caplain Kelly, Georgina Beaty, and Kirstin Valdez Quade. Thank you so much to John Conklin for reading so carefully for the last details. Thank you extra much to Kate Folk who continued to brainstorm with me at various junctures of despair and confusion through the years, gifting me again and again with her unreal memory, brilliant problem-solving, emotional acuity, and visionary thinking. And Brendan Bowles who did the same, through international texts and on a memorable sunny Potrero Hill walk. To Fatima Kola who was always down to read, who is ever a genius, and who speaks of Joan like a friend. And thank you so much to Elizabeth Tallent, who read as rough a draft as anyone, and who made the journey ahead sound thrilling and adventurous, while still communicating all the work to be done.

To the gems who gifted me precious advice during this process (on book and life): Melissa Febos, always, always, the best advice, even when I'm not ready to hear it! Claire Vaye Watkins, Young Jean Lee, Becca Albee, Braden Marks, LuLing Osofsky, Julie Rossman, Michelle Chun, Lorrie Moore, Julie Buntin, Matt Wood, Katie Kitamura, Sam Chang, Caroline Cirone, Leigh Newman, Lydia Peelle, Justin Quarry, Nancy Reisman, Major Jackson, Jane Hamilton, Steph Mahnke, Sarah LaBrie, Kirsty Clark, Gwen Tulin, Duncan Riddell, Shoshana Adler, Candice Amich, Sarah Wang, Maud Streep, Miranda Featherstone, Francesca Mari, Aisha Sabatini Sloan, Jaquira Diaz, Barrak Alzaid, Reese Kwon, Jennifer Fay, and Karan Mahajan.

To the beautiful people who let me borrow their homes during the writing of this book: Emily Bielagus, Shoshana Adler, Anne Detzner, Gabriella Levine, Miranda Featherstone, Gabriel Rocha, Nicole Salazar, Claire Pritchett, and Tulip.

To the residencies that supported me throughout the writing of this book: VCCA, where I started this book, and Djerassi, where I finished it. MacDowell, StoryKnife, Yaddo, the Sitka Center, Willapa Bay AIR, and Ragdale.

To the fellowships that supported me throughout the writing of this book: the Fulbright, the Stegner Fellowship, the Rona Jaffe Foundation Writers' Award, and two fellowships from Vanderbilt University.

Thank you so much to my colleagues and students at the University of Michigan, Stanford University, and especially Vanderbilt University, for which I include an extra shout-out to my dream colleagues, brilliant MFA students, and amazing undergrads. I'm so lucky to have been inspired by you alongside writing this novel.

To the real beauties of Virginia, nothing at all like the people in this book: Greg Brown, Sarah McColl, Serena Chopra, Diane Cluck, Zac Fulton, Henry Hoke, Sallie Merkel, Derrick Weston Brown, Margo Figgins, Jeff Martin, Laura Eve Engel, and all my other colleagues and students who shared that beautiful place.

And thank you as always to my nuclear fam: Sarah, John, Chris, and Gillian Conklin and Annie Adamsky. Plus the young ones: Sage, Remy, Jacob, Cole, and Eden. Love you.

Final thank you to my magical friends for keeping me steady and happy enough to perform the sometimes fun and always rewarding but often difficult and painful work of writing this novel.